THE
THIEF
AND THE
NIGHTINGALE

A NOVEL OF MEDIEVAL SPAIN

K.M. BUTLER

For my wife and daughters,
who are more precious than all the music,
culture, and wine in this and every world

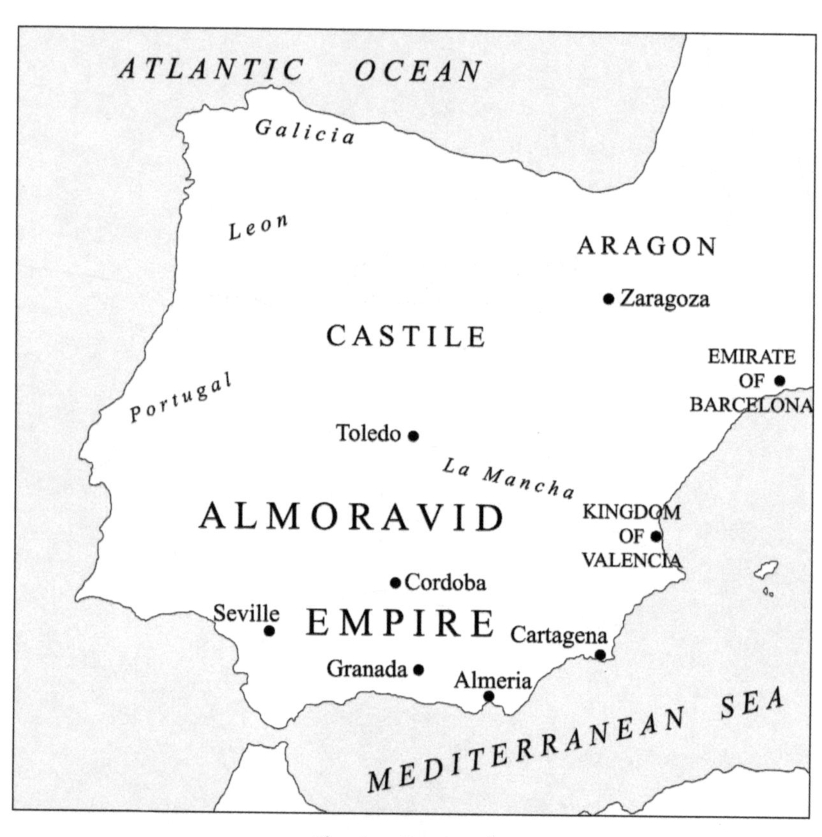

Iberian Peninsula
AD 1091

The
Thief
and the
Nightingale

I

ALMERIA

October 1, AD 1091

CHAPTER ONE

YASIN

THE CALL OF the *muezzin* summoning the faithful from the Great Mosque reassured Yasin ibn Faraj about his decision to leave Almeria. While he had witnessed crowds flocking toward the melodic vibrations of an oud's strings or the ribald warbling of a poet's recitation, never before had daily prayers drawn such crowds. For the past three days, though, his fellow citizens had seemed determined to make a spectacle of their daily supplications. The false piety would have made him laugh, in different circumstances.

He could hardly laugh now, though, with veiled desert fanatics controlling his city.

Yasin adjusted the lay of the brown cotton satchel slung over his shoulder and pressed himself deeper into the shadow of the nearby *hamam* to shelter from the fading crimson of the setting sun. Perfumed steam billowed from the bathhouse's entrance and drifted past the alley, obscuring the thinning crowds as they rushed toward evening prayer.

What was keeping his brother and sister?

Above the tops of the *tapia*, rammed-earth buildings, a column of gray blended with the hazy heat covering the neighborhood. Somewhere hidden in that smoke, the emir's palace still burned, like so much of his city. Yasin sighed at the thought of the ruined taverns, gardens, brothels, and the other delightfully decadent refuges within these walls. Everything that made Almeria the jewel of al-Andalus was gone.

The choking taste of ash clung to the back of Yasin's throat no matter how often he swallowed.

His gaze darted up and down the street. Every moment risked discovery, and it wasn't like his siblings to be this late.

Several long moments after the *muezzin* fell silent, the long two-toned blast of a goat horn startled Yasin. Not until the distant trumpeter added three shorter blasts did he remember that tonight marked the end of Yom Kippur. He admired the Jews' defiance of their new rulers. That shrill horn signaled pride and courage.

He tightened his grip on the strap. His fellow Christians sounded no bells now. He doubted they ever would again. They understood what this conquest meant. The tolerance of the past eighty years was over. Mozarabs like himself who valued their faith would have to leave. Too many had already begun converting to Islam to curry the favor of these desert fanatics.

He clenched his jaw until his muscles hurt. These Almoravids had trampled over everything Almerian, only to be rewarded with meek submission. It was an outrage.

Perhaps two dozen strides further up the avenue, a pair of indigo-veiled Berbers marched through the migrating crowd.

Yasin retreated another foot span into the alley and sucked in a breath. His heart hammered, surely loudly enough for them to hear. He pressed his free hand to his chest, vainly trying to flatten the bulge beneath his coat. They'd notice his boots and satchel and would search him. When they discovered the leatherworking tools and pouch of silver coins beneath his long, blue *jubba* coat, they'd execute him. The Almoravids were still permitting Peoples of the Book to depart, but not with their wealth or the means to earn more.

Yet, he had to risk punishment. He'd need these tools to earn his way in Christian Toledo.

Close enough that Yasin could hit them with a thrown apple, the veiled conquerors stopped beside a musician who was gathering his possessions to join the crowd. A few indistinct words led to shoving. At the musician's protest, one of the veiled guards seized his stringed oud. While his companion restrained the protesting man, the Almoravid raised it up above the heads of the crowd and brought it down in a sharp motion. Moving bodies concealed the impact but not the sounds of splintering wood and snapping horsehair strings.

That scene had played out many times over the previous three days. So many magnificent instruments would never play another note, lest they produce an objectionable song. So many street corners would remain forever silenced by the terrible indigo wind from the desert.

Yasin exhaled a long breath when the veiled ones departed toward the great square. Only once he could no longer distinguish them from the crowd did he risk peeking out to search for his siblings.

He saw no sign of them. Something was wrong.

By now, only a few figures hurried down the wide avenue. The scraping of their shuffling feet against the cobblestones blended with the few Islamic prayers that seeped out the windows of the stone houses on either side. Deep shadows invaded the street as the sun dipped lower.

"They're not coming."

Yasin stilled. His Adam's apple grated along the cartilage of his throat. He knew that voice well, had heard every possible variation in pitch and volume. Last night, he had become very familiar with its shrill hectoring and thunderous shouts.

Yasin turned to face hazel eyes glaring like torches in a forest of sandalwood skin, framed by a canopy of umber hair. That face differed from his own only by the depth of its creases. "What have you done, Father?"

His father, Faraj, raised his chin. "I reminded my children this foolish flight to Toledo would ruin their family and buy only hardship."

Yasin could imagine that argument working on his brother. His father could twist lies to the silhouette of truth. But his sister, Amira, had suggested this escape.

"I'd like to hear that from their lips."

"Do you respect me so little that you think I would lie?" The corners of Faraj's lips twisted into the well-practiced frown he used when haggling with customers.

The feigned offense roused Yasin's anger from last night's argument. "I put little past a man who would command his children to trade their faith for wealth."

Faraj straightened. "The Almoravids tripled the *jizya* on non-believers. We all have to convert or we'll be ruined. Your siblings understood that."

Yasin wished his father was lying, but neither Amira nor Salim was here now. After all their careful plans, their eager confederacy in preferring exile to capitulation to these rough desert invaders, they had abandoned him. First his city, then his father, and now, finally, his siblings.

A hollow loneliness replaced his apprehension. "You exploited their affection for you."

Faraj snorted. "And you carry no affection for me?"

Yasin flexed his neck muscles to still their sudden twitching. "Less so than before you swore to disown me if I disobeyed."

"What of your sister? Your mother? What happens to them if you refuse to convert?"

If his sister decided to stay, she would suffer the consequences for it. But Yasin pictured his mother's face, torn in anguish when Yasin had refused his father's commands. If he could spare her more pain, he had to try one last time.

"How can you submit to desert fanatics who burned our city?"

"Our people lit those fires, not the Almoravids," Faraj countered.

"The imams and scholars led those riots. Thank Allah they threw open the gates to the Almoravids first, else nothing might have survived."

Yasin scowled at the new deity in his father's vocabulary. "Your new faith sits on you surprisingly easily. So easily that you now force me to convert as they forced you."

"You blame them for too much," Faraj insisted. "No one forced me; I chose so we might all benefit."

He was wrong, of course. The veiled ones knew that raising the tax on non-believers would force conversions. The Quran forbade executing protected *dhimmis*, but disposing of disobedient converts was another matter entirely.

"Yet you rob me of that same choice. You have no right to command this, and certainly not for your benefit."

"For *our* benefit," Faraj corrected. "Our fellow Muslims will hire us now. We'll be more successful than before."

He spoke as if the distinction mattered. "Look what the Almoravids did to their fellow Muslims." Yasin had watched in horror as the fanatics had cast out the women and children of the royal household, ransacked the palace, and dragged the emir away in chains. He could still hear their whimpers. "They'll come for us eventually."

"Only if you run to Toledo. If you flee, they'll suspect us all of false conversion. Don't you care about your family?" Faraj stepped forward, extending his hands. "I love you, Yasin. I only want what's best for you. For you and all our family."

Yasin might have believed that of a man who hadn't abandoned his God and all hope of Heaven. "You ask what I cannot give." His whispered words echoed off the sides of the *hamam*. "What do I have if not my faith?"

"But…" Faraj shook his head as if gasping for the words. "How can you claim faith now? The women, the gambling, the quarrelling… You sin all the time."

Yasin's lips curled as he recalled the silversmith's daughter from the previous night. Had he known what he would return home to, he'd have probably stayed and risked being caught. "But not the one unforgivable sin."

"How can you be so selfish?" Faraj's voice hardened. "I've given you all my knowledge and skill with leather. And this is how you repay me? By endangering our future?" Faraj's cheeks reddened, and the vein at his neck pulsed. "Ishmael or Isaac, we would worship the same god. I ask such a little thing."

"Such a little thing?" Had he imagined the words? "Almeria was the jewel of al-Andalus, where Christian, Jew, and Muslim could live together, and the Almoravids ruined it. Now, you command me to abandon the truth of existence to please your new masters." Breath spent, he spoke his final few words in a deflated hiss. "You demand everything."

"You scorn all I've sacrificed for you." Faraj growled and spat on the ground between them. "You are no son of mine."

Eyes locked on his father's, Yasin noticed the change in them, the hardening around the eyelids, the strain around the muscles. No longer did he confront the father who had shared biblical stories around the hearth at night, who had patiently taught him how to shave designs into leather. Those eyes had occasionally regarded him with affection, sometimes with admiration, and frequently with irritation. But now, they were the eyes of a stranger.

So, this was how a man disinherited his son.

Yasin drew a long breath. The Almoravids had done more than shatter the jewel of Almerian sophistication, learning, poetry, and culture. They had turned his father—forbidding and commanding those closest to him—into one of them.

Toledo. Though it had fallen to the Christians six years earlier, merchants in the market claimed much of its culture remained. And the Castilians who governed there might preserve it against these Almoravids.

Yasin turned to the avenue. The journey would take weeks, and he had no reason to delay if his brother and sister weren't coming.

"Goodbye, Father. I pray your prosperity outlives the sacrifice of your faith."

"Then go!" Faraj's words stabbed the hollow void of the alley and echoed off the walls. "Run to Toledo with the other Mozarab scum who abandoned their homeland. You're no son of mine!"

Yasin stepped into the alley and marched toward the gates. If he'd converted as his father wished, he'd have ceased to be the man he was. He may not be his father's son in Almeria, but he would remain Yasin ibn Faraj in Toledo.

II

TOLEDO

AD 1094

THREE YEARS LATER

CHAPTER TWO

YASIN

"Would it help if I didn't know she was your sister?"

The three men blocking the only door out of the bedroom hesitated and shifted their gazes to the complicated indigo cotton folds of the *tagelmust* veil concealing most of Yasin's face.

Whether the question surprised them or they needed a moment to translate it from Arabic, the delay bought Yasin enough time to plan his escape. He blinked once, clearing his eyes of the incense rising from a censor smoldering on the table beside the bed. Out the window beyond the haze, twilight faded. He had to move soon, or the concealing crowds would thin too much.

He pounced on the room's only other occupant, a young woman, and drew her against him with an arm around her midsection, close enough to nuzzle her neck. Her muscles drew tight, and her stomach pressed against his wrist with each quickened breath.

The two youngest men started forward, rage burning in their eyes. Their elder, raven-haired like the young woman, threw his arms out. "Stop, you fools." He clenched their tunics tightly enough for his fingers to turn white. "He might harm your sister."

"They still care for you," he murmured into her ear. "A good sign." Yasin spread his fingers out to caress her belly. On impulse, he glanced down her loose off-white linen shift that utterly failed to conceal the slope of her breasts. His linen *qamisa* tunic, baggy black *sirwal* pants, the indigo cloak that matched his veil, her shift… Too many layers separated them. Her soft brown skin stirred delicious visions of writhing passion.

He certainly had good taste.

"Father," one of the younger men hissed. "How can you endure this?"

Soon, this young woman's father would realize he couldn't. Yasin had accomplished all he could here and had little opportunity for additional mischief.

Into her ear, he whispered loudly enough for her relatives to overhear, "My love, I will forever cherish our nights wrapped in pleasure. Think of me from time to time, for I will forever stir at the thought of you."

He pushed her toward her relatives with a satisfying slap on her backside.

He started for the window before she reached them, closing the distance in three great strides. He dared not waste time looking backward, for their surprised cries had already given way to shuffling feet.

In the moment before he leapt through, Yasin wondered if perhaps the wind had blown the rope aside. September in Toledo could be unpredictable. The fall was only one story, but this damned Almoravid veil would probably tangle in the breeze on the way down, and he couldn't land safely if he couldn't see.

He twisted as his head breached the window into the cool dusk air, searching for it.

There it was!

His hands closed around the knotted rope dangling from the roof as his momentum carried his body through the window. His shoulders screamed from the strain of bearing his full weight, and the rope burned his fingers when they slipped a little. He released a cry of pain, but his grip held. Bringing his feet together on one of the knots, he hauled himself up one at a time.

A hand clamped down on his ankle and tugged. His shoulders screamed again, but his grip held.

One of the young woman's brothers hung out the window, glaring at Yasin with eyes like fishhooks.

The poor man was looking in the wrong direction. He should have been looking down.

Yasin jerked sharply to free his leg. The unbalanced brother spilled out the window and fell, landing with a painful grunt that made Yasin cringe. Pride and honor certainly exacted a heavy toll.

He had nearly reached the roof when two more heads poked out of the window, first to survey the fallen man struggling to stand below, then turning to glare at Yasin. "Desert filth!" the younger brother cried as he reached for the rope.

Hauling himself onto the roof, Yasin drew a thin ring knife from a slit in his belt and whistled down at his pursuer. The man snapped his head up.

Yasin held the knife against the rope. "You might want to grab something."

Eyes widening, his pursuer began to retreat. Yasin waited until he reached the window before slicing the rope. As it fell, it struck the brother who had already fallen on the shoulder and knocked him to the ground again.

Yasin couldn't help himself. He barked out a laugh. What a delightful night!

The shouts were growing, though. With a few rushed steps, he leapt across the narrow alley separating the next building. It was taller, so he clutched the edge and hauled himself up. Flakes of the crumbling brickwork dug into his fingers and agitated the burns from the rope.

"Have you seen a veiled Muslim?" cried someone below.

Rapidly moving torchlight reflected off the walls of the nearby buildings. They were fanning out to search for him, and from the chatter, more than a few neighbors had joined in. He had to move fast.

After crossing two more roofs, Yasin found another alley. Though it twisted like the rest of this city's streets, its snaking path led to the cloth market some distance away. Satisfied, he slipped over the edge and dangled by his fingers until he gauged the distance. He dropped down and, with a hop-step, saved himself from falling into the filthy water pooling along cracks in the stone beneath him.

A glance up and down the alley satisfied him that no one lurked nearby. With a shrug, he discarded the indigo Almoravid cloak to the muddy ground.

Looking down, he scoffed and rubbed his hands over his usual clothes. That accursed cloak had ravaged his tan, knee-length linen *qamisa* tunic. Removing these wrinkles would take hours. Grumbling, he reached up to unwind the layers of the complicated *tagelmust* veil, exposing more of his face and head with each rotation. Holding the long folds of indigo in one hand, he straightened his kinky umber hair as best as he could with the other. If he knew he'd endure this level of dishevelment, he might not have left his room this evening.

Bending down, he carefully laid the long strip of indigo in the deepest pool of wastewater he could find, grinning at the slapping sound as he dipped it again and again, saturating it in filth. Rising, he hooked the discarded cloak with his boot and dragged it to another puddle. A muddy stain spread across the surface, turning the indigo into a dusty gray. For a few moments, he savored the defilement of the Almoravid garment.

Shouts of outrage from the market penetrated the bends of the alley. In this neighborhood, no one would notice another abandoned strip of cloth, and he doubted anyone would realize its color in the darkness. Still, he couldn't take any chances. He needed to distance himself from it, no matter how much he enjoyed ruining it. He rushed down the alley.

The sparsely populated cloth market, a paved expanse fifteen horse-strides wide, separated rows of *tapia* buildings housing work-shops. Long shadows blanketed the avenue. Most of those shops were closed, but some traders who ran the free-standing stalls that filled much of the open space hadn't quite finished packing up their wares for the evening.

Most had turned, tight-lipped, to study the mob of angry Tole-dans rapidly approaching. Yasin's father had looked much the same when he'd feared the Almoravids would ransack his workshop upon entering Almeria three years earlier. Every merchant worried about looters and rioters.

Leading this mob were the charming young lady's father and brother. Yasin hoped the other brother wasn't too seriously injured from his fall. He hadn't meant to harm anyone.

A grin tugged at his lips as Yasin recalled the rope falling on him, but he suppressed the urge to laugh. Now wasn't the time.

The square was relatively empty, and the young lady's father was approaching rapidly. Yasin forced himself to calm in case he needed to make a quick escape.

"Did you see an Almoravid run past?" the man rumbled in Castilian.

"An Almoravid?" Yasin repeated, using the momentary delay to swallow his relief. Those angry men were searching for a Muslim desert fanatic, and Christians rarely saw past the indigo veil. He had chosen his disguise well. He narrowed his eyes to prevent himself from smiling. "Jesus protect us…" He fumbled for the silver cross beneath his tunic and kissed it.

"Yes or no?"

"No," Yasin stammered. "What has he done?"

The man's eyes widened. "That isn't your concern." With a grunt, he strode off to interrogate the next bystander.

Few forgave or forgot walking in on a Christian daughter and her Muslim lover, and all that anger would fall on the Almoravids. Yasin still had far to go to balance the scales for Almeria, but it was a start. Even if the purpose of tonight's exploits failed, he'd at least accomplished that much.

A good day's work.

YASIN

Yasin spent the next two hours in the local church, praying that God would forgive the sin of impersonating a heathen. Such a prayer normally required only a few minutes, but he lingered both because of the depth of his taint and to give the mob time to disperse.

After donating his customary tithe, Yasin worked his way back to the young woman's home. Keeping to the shadows of the alley, he eyed the windows and doorways for hidden watchmen until the final candlelight faded from within her building. Satisfied, he lowered another rope from the roof and entered her window again.

"I was wondering if you'd return tonight," a woman's voice whispered.

Yasin shifted to let more moonlight through the window but kept a firm grip on the rope. The corners of the room came into perspective as his eyes adjusted. The girl from earlier stood alone beside her bed with arms crossed. Though she wore a cotton dress over her shift, he could still discern the curves that had delighted him.

He coiled his foot around the rope and leaned against the wall by the window. "We have unfinished business."

"I suppose we do." She padded over to a chest in the corner. The latch squeaked as she raised it, and she froze, craning her neck toward her door. After a moment, she eased the lid open and withdrew a worn leather pouch with a rich patina.

Yasin rubbed his hands together as she approached and presented it. The weight felt right as it settled into his hand. His fingertips tingled with a rush of delight. Leaning into the light, he opened the drawstring and peered inside.

Silver coins always reflected the light in the most beautiful way.

"It's all there," she insisted.

He tightened the drawstring again. The house was quiet; he could afford a few moments of conversation. "How did things go?"

"They believed it." Her hand snapped to her mouth, and she continued more softly, "If only they'd listened when I told them I'd never marry that man."

Yasin smirked, recalling her description of her intended husband. "Why should parents let us live our lives when they can live them for us?"

"It would have saved them this embarrassment."

"And a fair bit of coin." Yasin raised the pouch, which she'd probably stolen from her father.

"I pay it gladly to break my betrothal. They think I've sullied myself with a Muslim."

"If you like, we could give truth to that lie." Lowering his chin, he grinned. "Seems a shame to deny yourself the pleasure of a sin you've already been condemned for."

She scoffed loudly enough to hurt his feelings. "I spoke truth when I said I preferred the nunnery. My faith is genuine. I could never do such a thing."

"A pity." A woman who could conceive of a false seduction to wiggle out of a betrothal would make a fiery lover. Faith was fine nourishment for the soul, but nothing soothed the body like wild, thrashing lovemaking.

Some people simply didn't know how to enjoy life. But who was he to object to the way she conducted her affairs? If she sought a convent instead of marriage, he'd happily feign a torrid affair to help her achieve it.

Without another word, he pressed his fingers first to his lips, then his forehead in a final salute before ducking through the window and into the night.

YASIN

Despite his late night, Yasin dragged himself out of bed early to straighten his wrinkled *qamisa* before he began his day's work. Exhaustion was no excuse for a shabby appearance.

His landlord's wife was already heating a griddle in the hearth downstairs. She hovered nearby while Yasin pressed his tunic, and he suspected her chores were designed to give her an optimal view of his bare chest beneath his *jubba*. Hard coin and smuggled Almerian wine had overcome his Castilian landlord's reluctance to rent to a Mozarab, but no bribe would help if he suspected Yasin had slept with his wife. Yasin rushed the sleeves to finish before the woman decided to do more than appreciate from a distance. Doffing his cloak just long enough to don his tunic, he slipped out the door.

Already, traffic filled the winding avenue, and Yasin felt every eye judging his rushed appearance. Mortified, he turned his back to the crowd and adjusted the lay of his clothes.

As he did, he felt a familiar tug on his waist. With a quick snap, he seized a tiny wrist that had managed to slip past his cloak to touch the pouch hanging from his belt.

Its owner, a wild-haired boy of no more than ten, twisted in Yasin's grip. When that failed, he kicked at his captor's shin in outrage. Yasin moved his leg aside, and the boy missed and lost his balance.

Now, the wide eyes rose.

"Poorly timed." Yasin curled his lip. "You should have bumped into me when I turned to leave." Still, the young pickpocket had promise. Yasin released the little wrist to fish a copper piece from his pouch.

Freed, the boy darted into a seam in the crowd and disappeared.

Shrugging, Yasin rolled the coin over his fingers before slipping it back into his pouch. Hopefully, the advice would at least keep the lad out of a Castilian prison. He'd heard they were filthy.

Clenching his pouch defensively, Yasin shouldered his way

through the morning crowds of the leatherworking district with growing irritation. Customers haggled with peddlers selling their wares from temporary stands that filled too much of the street. The crowd shifted and a man in a grimy brown tunic bumped into him, wrinkling Yasin's clothing again. He shoved the man aside with a grunt. Why did the city permit all these itinerant traders? It certainly wasn't for the taxes. He'd seen higher quality leather in the gutter last night than for sale here under the morning sun. All the trade was in copper—not silver—and too few customers were entering the masters' shops for the highest-quality pieces.

Work like his own.

A young woman balancing a portable wooden oven on her shoulder called to the crowd. The rye bread inside, beside the coals warming it, had banished his hunger more than once when he'd been running late. The leatherworkers all knew she was generous with the fig chunks.

Among other things. His lips curved into a smile.

Hesitating, he pressed his fingers against his full pouch. A quick meal would only send him to his labors sooner, and he refused to give his employer one more drop of sweat than necessary. He could afford a proper meal after last night's exertions, and he had the time.

He shouldered his way to a set of benches in front of an open shop. Juniper poles held linen awnings that shaded the area from the sun at midday, though the angle of sunlight this early rendered them useless. Inside, mutton and chicken roasted over an open fire, and several boxes of fruit sat atop a table near the back. Three young girls in high-waisted Castilian dresses fluttered back and forth, distributing food.

The gray-streaked and grizzled woman who oversaw it all marched toward Yasin wielding a wooden spoon. "Get out!" Her voice sounded like a poorly tuned oud. "I'll not ruin my morning with your twisted words. Go!"

Eyes widening with mock hurt, he cast his hands before him. "Do you treat all your customers with such discourtesy?"

She grunted. "Only those who steal my food."

Despite his best effort at control, his lip quivered. "Surely, you wouldn't turn away an appreciative patron."

"Patrons pay. I've yet to see a coin from you." She gestured roughly toward the crowd. "Off you go."

"You haven't?" He ducked his hand beneath his *jubba*. When he raised it again, he held silver coins between two pairs of fingers.

The woman snorted. "That might cover your last two meals." She extended her hand and snapped her fingers. "Give 'em here, and I won't call the city guards."

With two flicks of his thumb, he spun the coins a quarter-turn, revealing they were actually two stacks of two, pressed together. "For whatever hot food you have and a large goblet of your strongest ale."

The woman rubbed her hands on her apron. She executed a bow out of place amid the bustling street. When she rose, her hostility had faded. "Have a seat, sir." She snatched the coins from his hand.

Yasin settled on a bench beneath a pale red linen awning while the owner barked orders to her employees. One of them, a young woman in a stained tan dress, kept appraising Yasin during her labors. A lock of light brown hair escaped the ribbon constraining it. As she brushed it aside, her sleeve fell, revealing an iron band around her wrist.

He flipped a silver piece over his fingers while pretending not to notice her swaying hips as she refilled customer goblets. She was working hard. Perhaps a night of pleasure might help her relax after the long day.

The gray-streaked owner returned bearing a carved wooden goblet in one hand and a wooden board with sliced peaches, a bowl of soup that smelled of beef, and a chunk of oat bread in the other.

His gaze darted to the serving girl before returning to his hostess. "You served me yourself. I feel honored."

"You shouldn't." She planted the board before him with a thud that nearly spilled the soup. "I don't want you distracting my slaves like last time."

She withdrew, leaving him alone with his food. He reached for the goblet first and stared into the amber liquid. The previous night, he had been pressed against a young woman in a shift. Now, he was enjoying this intoxicating delight. If he'd stayed in Almeria, he wouldn't have done either since the day the desert rabble had swept through and forbade everything worth enjoying.

Smiling, Yasin raised the goblet. *May you rot in hell, you veiled fanatics.* He took a long swig.

He was enjoying one of the peach slices when a shadow fell over him. A bearded man, a few years older than him, loomed with arms crossed over a thickly woven wool tunic poorly mended in several places.

Esteban.

Yasin stuffed the remaining peaches in his mouth too quickly to savor the taste. He very much doubted he'd be allowed to finish his meal in peace, and he'd rather hurry the delicacies than waste them.

"How can a filthy Mozarab afford such fine food?" The proud tilt of Esteban's chin let him look down his Castilian nose at Yasin. Despite his uneven ears and the sagging skin beneath his chin, the angle of his cheekbones suggested some foreign blood in the not-too-distant past.

A step behind him stood two other leatherworkers who split their attention between him and the shifting crowds surrounding them. They often followed Esteban, quarrelling with everyone yet dressing as though they never profited from it. How inefficient.

"Who did you rob to afford it?" Esteban scowled. "You didn't earn it with apprentice's wages."

Yasin knew he should probably ignore him, but he couldn't pass on the opening. "Certainly not with what you earn." He gestured down the street. "I saw some street peddlers selling your work. Some of it's almost suitable for carrying goat urine to the tanners."

The muscle along the left side of Esteban's neck tensed, pulling his flabby skin tight. "Shouldn't you be on your knees right now, praying like the other Muslims?" His voice carried over the local conversation, drawing the attention of a few other diners.

Judgment and condemnation swirled in their narrowed eyes. Not everyone agreed with King Alfonso's promises of protection for the city's Muslims. Being mistaken for one was dangerous.

Popping a piece of bread into his mouth, Yasin forced himself to remain relaxed. He pitched his voice higher to carry over the noise. "Esteban, how many times have I told you I'm a Christian?"

"So you claim." Esteban eyed the crowd. "But you dress far too much like an Arab."

A pithy response was wasted on such a man, but perhaps not the crowd. "I can understand your confusion, as you clearly know nothing about fine clothing." A few chuckles sprinkled around him and relieved the tension in his muscles.

"I'll never understand why Master Sanchez hired you."

"For the same reason he didn't hire you. He has an eye for talent and quality."

Cupping the bowl in both hands, he took a sip of his soup. Perhaps this was an entertaining way to start his day, after all.

Esteban knocked the bowl from Yasin's grasp, sending droplets of soup flying. Jumping back, Yasin pulled his *jubba* out of the way, but the hot liquid burned as it struck his freshly pressed *qamisa*.

He'd tasted just enough soup to whet his appetite, and now the rest lay in muddy rivulets on the ground. He'd worked hard for those silver coins, and now they were wasted. He should have bought some fig bread from that roaming peddler instead.

Esteban's lips twisted into a wicked grin. "Now you look like the trash you are."

Clenching his hands into fists, he rounded on the other apprentice so quickly that Esteban fell backward into his friends. A pouch dangled from the man's belt by a leather strip that frayed like the rest of Esteban's handiwork.

Yasin's rage melted into wicked satisfaction at a blossoming idea.

"It's a wonder you can smell anything over your stink." He sniffed in Esteban's direction and grimaced. "I'm sure your friends appreciate

locating you by scent. Perhaps it's good that you're such a poor craftsman you can't afford to visit the *hamam*."

Esteban scowled. "Filthy Mozarabic scum." He was close enough
for Yasin to smell ale on his breath, probably from the night before.
"You should have stayed with the Almoravids where you belong."

Yasin lowered his shoulder and charged into Esteban's chest,
knocking the other man back. Fists came down on his back, but Yasin
paid them no attention. With a flash, he drew the ring knife from his
belt and slashed once before slipping his hands back beneath his *jubba*.

The others interposed themselves and yanked the combatants
apart. "Esteban, stop!" one of them cried. "Master Iustez will put you
out if he hears you're quarrelling outside his workshop." He shook
Esteban by the arms. "Think, man!"

Esteban scowled and shouted past them. "This isn't over,
Arab-lover!"

Yasin saluted as the others dragged Esteban away. Once they'd
disappeared into the crowd, he withdrew Esteban's coin pouch from
within his *jubba*. The severed strap still dangled from when Yasin had
sliced it in the scrum. "You're in for a surprise later today."

Popping the final sliced peach into his mouth, he headed toward
his employer's workshop.

CHAPTER THREE

SARAH

THE GEOMETRIC MOSAIC that had adorned the façade of the Great Mosque since before the Castilians had rechristened it as a cathedral bore unsightly gaps. Fragments of tile and flakes of cracked stucco piled up on the paved square near the base of the wall. A whole section of the mosaic at eye-level had fallen off, leaving a divot where weathering had begun to eat away the *tapia* wall beneath.

Enough tiles remained for Sarah al-Bayda to imagine the beauty of the original mosaic wrapping around the high, carved doors and extending up all three stories. Yet the decaying ruin of arches in bold, contrasting colors left a hollow pit in her soul. While the Christians hadn't deliberately destroyed this testament to the glory of Allah, nor had they bothered to preserve it. Like everything else in this city, the outward structure remained, but the holiness had vanished like a snuffed flame on a windy day. Toledo was a pale shadow of its former splendor.

Several dozen of the faithful knelt, aligned east, in the square this morning. Their imam's voice echoed off the prison, the courthouse, and the other buildings housing the city's administration. Sarah envied the serenity on their faces as they performed *salat*. When she offered her prayers, she could rarely take her time and was often interrupted. But these men ignored the passing hordes of scowling Christians and armed guards ringing the square.

Sarah's feet itched within her patched leather turnshoes. She longed to celebrate with them, to declare her faith for all to hear. Instead, she pulled her moss-colored wool shawl tighter around her tawny face for the same reason this congregation had dwindled over the previous five years. Rumors of beaten Muslims and looted shops, despite the Christian king's assurances of protection, discouraged displays of piety.

Scratching her forehead where her shawl rubbed against it disturbed a lock of her dark golden-brown hair, and she tucked it back inside. As she lowered her hand, a burr on the iron bracelet around her wrist snagged the fabric with a terrifying rip. Freeing the threads, she sighed. She'd have to stitch it again. This shawl, too, was wearing thin, like everything else in this city.

Inhaling a steadying breath, she backed away from the square. She had little enough free time to waste it on regret.

Amid the thickening crowd, someone collided with her. Averting her green eyes, she retreated down the edge of the crowd toward the markets without waiting for an apology that would never come. This wasn't Muslim Granada. She couldn't expect the same decorum here among barbarians.

The crowd thickened further as Sarah reached the market stalls flanking the city's central avenue. Unlike Toledo's other streets, this main avenue ran straight, free of the awkward kinks separating one district from another. In the far distance, past the haze of countless cooking fires and heat reflected off the *tapia* buildings, was the blurry silhouette of the main gate.

Her ears untangled the linguistic soup of four languages and seven dialects. A peddler and customer haggled in Hebrew over the price of a set of silver scales on her right. A priest shouting his condemnation of avarice atop a barrel also proclaimed his low birth through his country-inflected Castilian. In Arabic, a pair of officials instructed the city guards to close down a stall that had arrayed its goods too far into the street. Though unintelligible, a few rolling French phrases punctuated the intermittent slapping of sword blades on mail chausses as the crowd parted before a pair of knights. Fragments of Berber, Leonese, and Portuguese accents slid in and out of the shifting crowd.

Rows of wooden stalls lined both sides of the street as far as she could see. Closest to her were the silversmiths and goldsmiths whose wares glittered in the morning sun. Jewelry boxes and gilded hand mirrors sat beside meticulously woven gold necklaces and gem-encrusted rings. Catching her reflection in a silver bowl polished to a mirror shine, Sarah fussed with her shawl.

As usual in the mornings, a crowd had gathered around the fresh fruit piled atop the tables of a dozen adjoining stalls. Though she easily slid past the ripe dates and firm pomegranates, she halted before the pile of peaches. The deep hues of amber, maroon, and orange called for her to draw forth its sweetness with a squeeze. She could imagine the sticky juice on her fingers and the succulent taste. For a moment, she considered whether she might snatch one without being seen. The crowd was thick. Surely, the peddler was too distracted filling customer requests to notice—

With a flurry of movement, the peddler whirled and slapped a tiny wrist advancing on one of the dates. A ragged boy squirmed and evaded the grasp of a nearby customer.

"Curse you, filthy thief!" the peddler shouted as the tiny figure ducked into the crowd.

Sarah swallowed with a dry throat and shuffled past the next several stalls. Her heart hammered in her chest. That might have been her. And while she could move with grace, she lacked the speed of that little urchin.

By the time she'd restored her poise and banished the terror of foolishness narrowly avoided, she'd already reached the cloth sellers. Though they had their own district to the west, a few of the most skilled weavers displayed some of their ruder work. Linen so light that it fluttered in the wind. Monogrammed *tiraz* silk kerchiefs and tunics. Intricate lace sewn into dizzying patterns resembling birds and flowers. Gauzy cotton so fine that while most imams would still consider it a veil, it concealed nothing.

She turned her back on the tantalizing fabrics and pushed aside the delightful memory of it flowing over her skin. Given her circumstances now, she was lucky to have even this itchy, light brown woolen dress and turnshoes that kept the mud out.

The library complex loomed behind a nearby weathered, two-story *tapia* house. Beneath that view sat her favorite stall in the markets.

Disappointment forgotten, she skipped toward the small juniper stand. The weather was neither too humid nor dusty to cause damage, so beneath a thick leather awning sat the finest musical instruments in the city. Here, in this unadorned stall, were the true treasures of Toledo. Clay drums with perfectly matched hide tops, angled zithers, and both bone and wooden flutes sat along either end of a simple wooden table. In the center, three stringed ouds lay on their sides, braced by the right angle of their necks. All had five identical black horse-hair strings and looked to be made from fine maple, though the wood of each bore different stains and patterns. In the back sat the long shafts of two stringed rebabs, their ball-like drums and grounding spikes obscured by wares before them.

A portly, olive-skinned Mozarab with a thinning pate of gray hair smiled and extended his arms. "Sarah the Fair, I wondered if I'd see you!"

Covering the bottom half of her face with her shawl, Sarah lowered her eyes to acknowledge his translation of her name. "An honor, Master Suarez."

Sweeping a hand over the crowd, he asked her, "Have time for a performance?"

The sun hadn't yet crested the cathedral. "A quick one. Perhaps the rebab today?"

He retrieved the instrument and its curved bow while Sarah settled on a nearby stool. After she had arrayed the folds of her dress and shawl carefully out of the way, he handed her the precious instrument. She leaned the rebab against the outside of her thigh and positioned her fingers.

Drawing the bow over the three strings, Sarah released a quick sequence of introductory notes before beginning a tune she'd heard in the streets of Baghdad many years earlier. With each stroke of the bow, the whining cry of the rebab rose above the noise of the market in aching emulation of two separated lovers.

The closest ranks of the crowd turned at her first notes. By the end of the first verse, several had gathered to listen. By the end of the second, she had attracted a respectable crowd. Though her teachers would be outraged, she allowed herself a faint smile of swelling pride.

Nearly two dozen men and women were watching her with the usual mix of wide-eyed reverence and relaxed satisfaction by the time her song came to an end. She held the final, weeping note longer than usual to bask in their attention for even a few more moments. But eventually, the bow reached the end of the string and the rebab fell silent.

Though she smiled her gratitude for the chance to play, the craftsman was attending to a customer and did not see. She ran her fingers over the taut strings one last time before rising and returning the rebab and its bow to their spot behind the table.

Thoughts lingering on the entranced crowd, she adjusted her shawl and glided the rest of the way to the library. Her fingers still itched with the vibration of those strings, and her ears echoed with the soaring notes. In these moments, when her deliveries aligned with weather fine enough to display the instruments, she had the chance to use her education as a *qiyan*. Music warmed her spirit as nothing else could.

The city library was a sprawling complex of several buildings that occupied its own block a street off the market avenue. The heavy oak doors bore carved scrollwork and geometric designs, a pictorial representation of Allah blessing man with wisdom. She sighed. It was yet another relic of the *taifa* of Toledo that came to a whimpering end nine years earlier.

The guards had changed since she'd departed this morning. A black-bearded man Sarah didn't recognize straightened his yellow tunic as she approached. His lecherous gaze dwelled on all the usual parts of her figure.

She tightened her shawl and suppressed a shudder of disgust.

"Here comes a fine lovely." He nudged his partner.

Sarah recognized the other guard, a well-muscled youth who had never let his lust show so obviously. He merely glanced at her and grunted. "She's a library slave." He pointed to the iron bracelets peeking out from beneath the sleeves of her dress.

She fidgeted and brushed the bracelets up her arms, out of view.

"Then she's bound to serve," the bearded one purred. "Come, slave. Let's put you to good use."

Breath tightening, Sarah stumbled backward, clenching a fold of her shawl with a shaking hand. From her first moments in chains, she had dreaded this moment. But to be shamed and humiliated in public...

"You want a girl to satisfy your needs, buy one." The younger guard jutted his chin toward her. "She's the king's property. I won't lose my head because you can't control your urges." Grimacing, he opened the doors and waved her forward.

Sarah shuffled into the library, but only at the thud of the door closing did she release a shaking breath and press her hands to her stomach to still her shivering. New guards were always trouble until they learned the consequences of abusing the library staff. Every time, the fear of what they might do before learning that lesson terrified her.

Yet, so long as she did her job, she was safe from ruin. She was a slave, but she had clothes on her back, a cot to rest her head upon, and protection from lusty depredation.

Inhaling a steadying breath, Sarah recalled the Prophet's admonishment against vanity. Evoking men's desire was dangerous, and simply covering her hair evidently wasn't enough. She'd need to be even more careful in the future.

A shuffling priest entered through a side corridor and grunted. "Slave, did you deliver that edict?" His voice sounded like a bleating goat after the soothing tones of the *rebab*.

She lowered her gaze to his blistered feet and worn leather sandals. "I did, sir." Any further response would only prolong his scrutiny.

"Took you long enough." Though he gave her a withering glare, he merely muttered, "The workroom needs sweeping. Get to it."

She watched him go with relief. Interactions with priests were almost endurable when she feigned deference and kept her mouth shut.

After retrieving the most serviceable broom she could find, she entered a large room illuminated by shafts of light from the narrow windows. On either side of a central aisle were rows of tables with large benches.

Too early for the priests to have finished their prayers, it was mostly empty. Only one pair of scribes sat together, murmuring. The first, a Jew wearing a gray kippah cap, read from a crinkling codex bound in dark leather. He spoke about cosmology in Castilian so softly that Sarah had to crane her neck to hear his words. The priest beside him dipped his quill in an inkpot and wrote short passages on a nearby scroll every few moments.

Translation. It was the finest, most sophisticated work a scholar could do. A translator needed not only fluency in multiple languages but also a working knowledge of the subject matter to correctly choose the right intention of the original text.

They needed her training. But five years in this library had taught her the priests would never allow a Muslim slave to conduct such fine work, let alone a woman.

Gripping the broom tighter, she eyed the bits of shaved quill, piles of dirt, and scraps of discarded paper scattered across the floor. She wouldn't be allowed supper until she finished, and only cold stew would remain if she took too long.

The brushing of her straw broom over the floor and her scraping footsteps echoed off the high-vaulted ceiling, making a kind of music. The mumbling men at the worktable faded away. She found herself adjusting the rhythm of her motions to make a more pleasing cadence as she cleared two of the corners, slowly working across the room.

"Sarah?"

Shaken from her reverie, Sarah at first thought she'd imagined the whispered word, but the priest at the worktable gestured her over with wide-eyed urgency.

She approached, concealing the bottom half of her face with her shawl as she'd been taught in Baghdad. The scroll the Jew had been reading in Castilian was written in flowing Arabic, and the wooden core bore the title, *Almagest*, Ptolemy's great astronomical work. Corresponding Latin filled the scroll beside the priest, who had a good, clean hand for writing. The last line ended mid-sentence.

The priest glanced toward the doors on either end of the room before pointing to a section of the text. "Sarah, what's this word?"

Excitement bubbled within her chest. Ever since she'd been caught reading a codex left open in this workroom a couple years earlier, rumors had spread about her *qiyan* training. The servants jealously gossiped about her knowing heathen sexual techniques, but the scribes ignored those lies. On occasion, one would ask for help with a difficult translation. Unlike their peers, Sarah was no rival to their ambitions.

Shifting her grip on the broom, she leaned in for a closer look. The ink had bled for much of this section, rendering the text illegible. Yet Sarah had studied the *Almagest* extensively, and between her recollections and the remaining ink, she pieced together the context.

"I believe it's *Thoth*, a month in the ancient Egyptian calendar named for one of their gods."

The Jew leaned over the text. After a moment, he shrugged and nodded. "Water has ruined the rest."

"Only a third of it's readable." The priest grunted. "We need a better copy."

She folded her hands at her waist. "Will there be anything else?"

Fishing a finger into a money pouch, the priest tossed her a copper coin. She fumbled her grip on her broom to catch it. Before she could inhale to thank them, the men stood and gathered their supplies.

She clutched the coin as they departed. It wasn't much, but these occasional coins let her afford a fine linen shift and a little perfumed oil, women's niceties the priests weren't likely to notice. This one would go to a new shawl.

Sarah finished her chores quickly and departed through a much narrower, dimly lit corridor. Several doors down, she lifted the latch and pushed open a scratched and worn pine door that fit imprecisely into the opening. In the corner of the small chamber sat a linen and wood-framed cot with a thick wool blanket. Leaning against a weathered chest beside the cot was a mahogany oud whose black stain had worn away at the back of the bend and several places along the neck.

Home. Or, at least, what served as home these past five years. Sarah closed the door and positioned the latch. Unwinding her shawl, she tossed it on the chest.

Lying on the cot, she dreamed of a future without sweeping, scholars, or lecherous guards.

YASIN

Shortly after noon, the perfumed servant of a count arrived at Master Sanchez's workshop with a sack of leather footwear to be mended by the end of the day. Though the master leatherworker initially resisted the unreasonable request, the silken lackey's suggestion that the count might revoke his patronage changed his attitude. Yasin and the other apprentices suddenly faced a much busier day that threatened to spill into the night.

Yet, Yasin had spent years learning techniques from his father that these Christians scorned. By the time the church bells rang six hours past noon, he presented his work to his disbelieving employer.

Though Master Sanchez scrutinized each piece, he found no fault and released his finest apprentice for the night. As he left, Yasin gave his glaring peers a coy wave.

The final echo of sunlight was receding below the horizon. Already, the crowds had thinned. The city guards would start harassing pedestrians to head indoors soon, so Yasin kept close to the buildings. He had encountered enough of them over the years that he didn't want to risk stumbling upon one who recognized him.

Pickpockets and thieves typically didn't prowl the craft districts. Apprentices earned too little to be worth waylaying and the master craftsmen either kept to the main streets or traveled with protection. Still, as Yasin weaved through the alleys, he kept an ear open for the scrape of a blade over a leather sheath or boots grating over cobbles. Yet, he heard only fragments of conversation seeping out from the tall buildings flanking the alley.

He stepped out into the square abutting his landlord's building. With the crowds having departed, so too had the peddlers from this morning. A few men loitered near the entrance of the two-story tenement next to Yasin's own building, and a craftsman was straightening a crooked shutter outside of his shop.

The day that had begun with a fat coin pouch and a satisfying argument with Esteban would end with a good meal and a long sleep. He couldn't ask for a better one. This city bent to his will like a generous lover. In the past three years, he had proven he could get away with anything, from smuggling and fraud to theft and burglary.

A shuffling from behind drew his attention. A shadowy figure emerged from the alley he had just left and lumbered into the square. This man was coming straight for him without bothering to conceal his intentions.

Yasin swallowed a surge of anxiety.

Quickening his pace, he lowered his hand to the knife concealed in his belt, but his shaking fingers struggled to find the ring handle. His last real fight had been with his brother over the last candied apricot, fifteen years earlier. And if he recalled correctly, he'd endured both a black eye and watching his brother consume the spoils of victory.

He had to reach home before that man caught him.

Turning forward again, Yasin gasped. The loitering men had abandoned their spot and were fanning out to surround him. They had already cut him off from both his door and the alley he'd always intended to use if guards ever showed up looking for him.

He was trapped. He'd walked into an ambush, set right outside his home.

His pulse hammered in his neck as he offered a silent prayer to God to preserve him for the next few moments. Four men wouldn't gather to inflict something as mild as a black eye.

Behind him, the dragging footsteps scraping along the cobbles grew louder. Yasin anchored his feet, preparing to spring backward to catch his pursuer by surprise. He stood a better chance against one man than three. He might even reach the shadowed alley leading back to Master Sanchez's workshop.

His chest pressed against the leatherworking tools beneath his *jubba* with every rapid breath. Some of those tools had points. They might help in a brawl, but retrieving them would take too much time.

He crouched a fraction, preparing to spring up.

"You kept us waiting, pickpocket," came a familiar voice from behind.

Yasin whirled to confront a smug Esteban, who had halted and was grinning in triumph. Yasin longed to wipe that gloating expression off his face.

The three men were still approaching from the other direction. Now, he recognized two as Esteban's friends, along with a bearded man in a heavy wool cloak. Concealing a club, perhaps? Surely not a sword; no one who could afford that luxury would associate with an apprentice leatherworker.

Time. He needed time to think. "So, you've tired of insults and moved on to false accusations?"

Esteban barked a sudden laugh that unsettled Yasin more than the approaching men did. He clenched his teeth to contain his unease.

"Money pouches don't just fall off a belt."

"I've seen your work," Yasin countered. "I wouldn't be so certain."

Anger flared, but Esteban's smile remained undiminished. "You think you're better than me."

That was his way out. "Care to test your skill against mine?" He arched an eyebrow and formed just enough of a smirk to incite a reaction. "We can head to my master's shop right now and craft any item you choose. Best work wins?"

Esteban merely shook his head. "I doubt you'll ever touch leather again."

The certainty of his tone sent a shiver down Yasin's back.

The three men had halted a few steps away.

"What's it to be, then, a beating in the street?" The argument that had worked that morning might serve him still. "I doubt your master will look kindly on you brawling with another apprentice."

"You think you can talk yourself out of anything," Esteban growled. "But you forget something."

"What's that?" Yasin arched an eyebrow, genuinely interested in this pearl of wisdom.

"This city belongs to my people, not yours." Esteban waved two fingers at the man Yasin didn't recognize. "I don't need to beat you when I can simply have you arrested."

The bearded man threw off his cloak to reveal the sash of a city guard over his yellow tunic.

Yasin scoffed. "You called the guards?" Apprentices quarreled with each other all the time, yet none would dare to call down the guards on another of their kind, let alone one of their own craft. "On what charge?" He glared at Esteban. "Outwitting an idiot?"

"You stole my coin pouch," Esteban said.

"Where's your proof?"

"My own word and two witnesses." He pointed to his companions behind Yasin.

Now Esteban insulted his skill! Yasin had cut that pouch flawlessly. No one had witnessed anything.

"Your friends, you mean?" He raised his hands to the city guard, who was approaching with a rope in his hands. "This man and his friends would say anything to smear my good name. He's jealous of my skill and covets my position."

Yasin had intended to accuse Esteban of one of his many crimes. He may not have gotten to this guard first, but he could weave a tale better than most, and surely better than Esteban.

The guard raised an eyebrow. "Why should I trust a Mozarab tainted by heathens over three Castilians?"

Mouth suddenly dry, Yasin froze. No words would change the Islamic style of his clothing, his hair cut short in the fashion of the *taifa* courts, or even the balanced poise of his bearing. They all marked him as something not quite Christian to these hard men of the north.

Esteban's smirk of triumph grew as the guard bound Yasin's wrists. "You should have listened when I told you to go live among the heathens." Esteban's foul breath suggested he was well on his way to getting drunk.

"I'll have this straightened out by tomorrow," Yasin's voice quavered with far too much uncertainty.

Esteban's, on the other hand, did not. "By then, Master Sanchez will have turned you out, and no one in Toledo will hire a thief."

Despite the very real possibility that Esteban was right, Yasin's ears echoed not with this man's taunts but with his father's words. Faraj had feared these men of the north more than the strange desert nomads who had desecrated the lively chatter, the tinkling music, and the swaying hips of his Almeria. Yasin had thought him mad. The possibility that his father had been right gnawed at him.

Esteban leaned forward and whispered in Yasin's ear. "I've endured watching you strut through my city for far too long."

This morning, Yasin had given in to his urge to embarrass this arrogant Castilian with a penchant for artless insults. Now, God had punished his sin. A single mistake would ruin everything he'd built these past three years.

This time, he couldn't blame the Almoravids, only himself.

SARAH

Her wooden comb caught on another knot as Sarah pulled it through her damp hair. Clenching her jaw, she tugged hard. A moment of tension led to a sickening crack as one of the teeth snapped off.

"Ugh."

Withdrawing the comb, she studied the damage. Several teeth were already missing, so it took a moment to identify the latest casualty near the center. Sighing, she picked through the knot with her fingers. A little oil would make her hair less prone to tangling, but that indulgence seemed even more impossible now that she had to buy a new comb. She already doubted her shawl would survive another tear, and she couldn't do without one. The library might provide a cloak for winter, but those men didn't understand the importance of modestly covering her hair during her deliveries. The few coins she earned from occasional translations wouldn't pay for it all.

Most knots untangled and her patience exhausted, Sarah settled on the edge of the bed. Her shawl and light brown dress hung from hooks along the wall, still dripping from their weekly scrubbing. The wooden bucket that had served as both her wash basin and bath sat in the corner. She'd need to return it before the maids noticed its absence, but that would have to wait until she was dry. She couldn't walk the hallways of the library in only a wet shift. While the scribes and priests should all be gone, she dared not risk them seeing her half naked.

She retrieved the oud leaning against the wall. Resting the stringed instrument on her lap, she coiled her fingers around the short, bent neck. An experimental pluck of the center string induced a delightful shiver as the vibration echoed off the walls.

Though small, her chamber was acoustically pleasing. She began to play a celebratory song written by Ziryab over two hundred years earlier. Each note lived two lives, first as itself and again as an echo married to the note that followed. The rhythm rolled across the chamber and carried away her frustrations. The waves of chords set her ears tingling with delight.

Strumming the strings, Sarah thought back to the first time she'd played the oud in the gardens of Baghdad. At the time, her cheeks had burned beneath the outraged glare of her eunuch teacher as she plucked all the wrong notes. The memory provoked a faint smile.

Eyes closed, Sarah clung to the last note. She had never played in Granada, her home, but at least music still rang in the halls of this library, one of the grandest in al-Andalus. While she played, she could almost imagine that the sorrows of the past decade hadn't happened.

"You play beautifully."

Her eyes snapped open. A Castilian in a long black, belted tunic of fine cotton smiled and leaned against the frame of the open door.

She bolted upright and backed away. What sort of man entered a woman's room without asking? She could feel every spot where her shift, still wet from the same basin she'd used to rinse herself, clung to her hips and breasts and thighs. She must be revealing a shocking amount of her figure.

Her visitor was no lecherous priest or scribe, though. His confident posture, free of tension, spoke of high birth. Her eyes kept focusing on his long sandy hair, swept back from his forehead. Most of the scholars and priests in the library wore caps. What hair they had adorned their chins as thick beards. Yet this man had no such beard, nor did he evidence the tidy styling of the Muslim south so common among the Castilian court.

Recovering, she spared a glance for her dress, hanging on the wall peg. "I apologize if my playing disturbed you, my lord. I thought everyone had gone home."

"You need never apologize for beautiful playing."

She lowered her head to conceal a blush. While the crowd of listeners in the market had delighted her, this intimate acknowledgement filled her with profound satisfaction.

"I am Gonzalo Martinez, son of Count Martin Garciez."

Neither name meant anything to her, but he referred only to his father as a count, not himself. She studied him again, and a more careful inspection revealed fraying along the edge of his tunic and a mended tear on the inside thigh of his cotton pants. He had noble birth but no title.

"Where did you learn to play?"

Excitement flared. Rarely did any Toledan express interest in her background. To most, she was merely a slave. "The Emir of Granada sent me to Baghdad to study *adab*." *Adab* encapsulated all noble and virtuous characteristics worthy of emulation and celebration. Pursuing it was the finest possible course of study, excepting only the study of Allah and the Prophet, of course.

Gonzalo drew an excited breath. "You're a *qiyan*?"

Not for many years had anyone so favorably reacted to learning that she was one of those esteemed performers of Muslim courts, famed for their knowledge of poetry, history, and music despite their official status as slaves.

The admiration in his voice planted the seeds of a new idea. Except for a few slaves, they were alone in this wing. She had enticed him with her playing and intrigued him with her training. Like all *qiyans*, she had planned to elevate her status through a strong marriage; she'd just expected to marry a Muslim. But her present circumstances didn't allow her to quibble. After five years of meaningless labor, this was her way to freedom.

She pursed her lips into a seductive pout. A few words murmured with a purring voice would draw him to her. If she was lucky, he would take her right here. She was at the right part of her cycle to avoid pregnancy. Her training hadn't included carnal techniques, contrary to common belief, but it had taught her how to cultivate interest. She drew in a slow breath, preparing herself. She'd have only one chance.

"I am." The purr of her voice sounded strange to her ears.

Breathing faster, he licked his lips. "Is it true you're taught to… entertain?"

If she did this and anyone found out, they would believe all *qiyans* were whores. She didn't care. Other *qiyans* could safeguard their own reputations. If she could ensnare him, this lord could lift her out of this life and end her constant fear of a lusty guard acting on his base hungers.

Hips rocking as she advanced, Sarah rested a hand on his chest. Perching on her tiptoes, she kissed him. "Allow me to show you."

SARAH

Lord Gonzalo's gasps of surprise and satisfaction suggested that her dedication to variety—undoubtedly greater than that of a chaste Christian—pleased him.

A son of a count was a lower rank than she'd aspired to attract while training in Baghdad, but away at his estate, she could keep accounts for his holding and he could provide her with the poems and treatises this library had denied her. She could fill her days with all the instruments available in al-Andalus and the Spains and read poetry late into the evening. And paper… He could give her fresh paper to compose new poems and songs, which she could perform for the wives of the other lords. She would raise his reputation as he raised her out of slavery.

Yes, he was a Christian, but she was better off as a heathen's wife than a slave. She would no longer endure the complaints and commands of these priests nor fear of what ills might befall her in a dark corner of the city. She would be safe, sheltered from the world's dangers and uncertainties.

After he had finished, Gonzalo was breathing rapidly, but not enough to suggest poor physical condition. His fingers grazed the inside of her knee before he stood and dressed.

Shift still bunched at her waist, she angled her legs to the side, offering him a view of her bare legs all the way to her hips. When he hadn't glanced over by the time he'd tied his belt, she said, "Perhaps next time, we could become better acquainted."

His eyes gleamed. "We're fairly well-acquainted now."

"I'd like to know more about you," she continued. "Perhaps I could play for you at your estate?"

"That's not possible."

Every muscle in her body tightened. "Did you not take pleasure from our time together?"

He shrugged. "As much as can be had from a slave, but not enough to endanger my prospects by being seen publicly with one, particularly a Muslim."

The cold words shattered her visions of a tolerable future like the snapping of an oud's strings. Having finally drawn the attention of a man of class, she'd assumed her skills would win him over. Who could resist a trained *qiyan*? Her music had attracted his interest, her appearance had stoked his desire, and her body had delighted his senses.

But none of that could overcome the iron bands around her wrists or her devotion to the Prophet. Hope gave way to shame at her swirling failure. She pulled her dress back down to cover her legs.

But her failure wasn't limited to this one man. The casual certainty of his voice heralded a similar failure with anyone who might liberate her. She had assumed these Christians thought as Muslims, seeking to improve their status by marrying a woman who could recite and sing and adorn his household with accomplishment. *But not enough to endanger my prospects.* Why should any Christian nobleman—or even a wealthy merchant—differ in that judgment? Anyone in this city with the means to secure her future would never endanger those means by associating with a Muslim slave.

His view of her body severed, Gonzalo pressed his hand to his chest and bowed his head. "God keep you." He turned on his heel and ducked through the door, leaving her with the receding echo of his footsteps down the hall.

This wasn't Granada or the *taifas*, where men respected the status of a *qiyan*. In the eyes of these Christians, she had no value worth cherishing. The precious training that should have led her out of poverty and desperation would not avail her here.

Her hopes had been in vain. She'd been used but not appreciated, enjoyed by not savored. Sinking to the cot, Sarah curled up within her shawl and wept with the agony of a wasted life, her soft sobs echoing in the silence.

CHAPTER FOUR

YASIN

THE SQUEAL OF the latch releasing startled Yasin to his feet. He suddenly felt woefully naked in his wrinkled linen *qamisa* and black pants. The guards had confiscated his *jubba* and belt when they found his ring knife and leatherworking toolkit, and he longed for its comforting weight now.

The sturdy oak door to his jail cell slowly swung inward. Anything could be waiting beyond, from an order for his release to an executioner. Of all his crimes, pickpocketing carried the mildest sentence, but who knew what lies Esteban had told? He had spent too long in Muslim lands; they could think he was a servant of the Almoravids, seeking ways to reclaim Toledo. Nor could he appeal to a Muslim or Jewish judge. He was a Christian, even if his brethren didn't quite believe it.

Yasin swallowed a rush of panic when the swinging door exposed a glaring man wearing a brown, belted tunic instead of the traditional yellow of the city guards. Who was he? He had used a key to open the door, yet his motions lacked the urgency of a jailbreak. This man didn't care if anyone saw him, which suggested authority.

Of more immediate concern was the sword dangling from his belt and the confident stance that suggested familiarity with its use.

"Are you Yasin ibn Faraj?" the man demanded in mountain-accented Castilian. His jaw rocked back and forth, making a scar along his chin dance.

In another place, Yasin might have made a snide comment. Three days of isolation had drained his humor.

"I am."

The visitor stepped aside and bowed as a second man in a black patched but finely woven cotton tunic stepped into the room with his arms clasped behind him. The supple leather of his belt was an expensive indulgence that hinted at nobility. While his boots were made from similarly high-quality leather, they bore scratches along the seams that indicated frequent mending.

The visitor's eerie, black-ringed grey eyes surveyed the room. "So, this is a prison cell," he said in a surprisingly pleasant voice.

"One tends to find them in prisons." Glancing at the swordsman standing outside the door, Yasin regretted his reply. He had to control his tongue, at least until he understood this man's position. "Though, I welcome the opportunity for conversation."

Arching an eyebrow, the visitor nodded to the man waiting outside. The door swung shut. Yasin twitched at the echo of the lock snapping into place.

The visitor settled his weight on his back foot, at apparent ease while locked in the small cell with a suspected criminal. Did he care nothing for his safety?

"My name is Gonzalo Martinez." It was a Castilian patronymic, following the same structure as Yasin's name.

"Are you my host?"

The black-ringed eyes widened. "I am no jailer," came the haughty reply. "I am a courtier and scholar working for His Majesty, Alfonso VI, king of all the Spains."

That explained how he managed to bring an armed man into a royal prison. His leather and black cotton suggested he was one of the lower nobility, but his mended boots made Yasin doubt he was a count, and certainly not a *senor* of a local town. If they had crossed paths on the street, Yasin might have risked lifting his pouch.

"What circumstances cause a courtier to visit a prison?" Yasin asked.

"I understand you're a smuggler and a thief."

This man must think him a fool to admit such things openly. "I'm a simple leatherworker apprenticed to Master Sanchez."

"Your landlord tells my men otherwise," Gonzalo said. "He mentioned smuggled wine."

Anger flared at the ingratitude. Curse that landlord! That wine might have secured a nicer room, but Yasin was a fool to have believed it'd purchase silence.

"Smuggled?" Yasin widened his eyes to feign surprise. "I had no idea."

"I didn't realize leatherworking was such a risky trade," Gonzalo continued. "When my men arrived to your room, they discovered someone had already ransacked it."

Esteban. Lips tightening, Yasin mentally weighed the damage he could have caused. His landlord owned the furniture, so that probably survived relatively unscathed. But had he discovered the pouch of silver beneath the false floorboard by his bed? Yasin hoped not.

He inhaled a fortifying breath. He could start over if he had to, provided he could free himself from this prison.

"You've been charged with pickpocketing, smuggling, theft, and assault."

"I never assaulted anyone!" The scars on his hands had come from hard work, not fisticuffs. Even the thin one from when his lockpick had slipped and sliced into his index finger occurred during a particularly complicated job. "Those are the lies of a jealous man."

"When my men asked around," Gonzalo continued, "they heard your name associated with a range of schemes." The man's smirk made Yasin wonder how many of his contacts those men had threatened. He'd have to smooth things over with each of them. His recklessness with Esteban was ruining both his trades.

Yasin offered one of his most charming smiles. "Rumors are so often unreliable."

"Leatherworking requires deft hands, does it not?"

Yasin narrowed his eyes. This nobleman kept coming back to that topic. Why?

He wasn't about to be tricked into an admission, though. "Along with a firm sense of practicality. Many of my craft have come to harm by taking too many risks."

"So I see." Grinning, Gonzalo crossed to the wall and pressed his hand against it. He moved casually, as if content to remain here all day. "How do you enjoy your prison?"

"I'd heard rumors about filthy, rat-filled cells, jagged walls that dug into one's back, and uneven floors that made for restless nights." Those tales had unsettled him enough during his first attempt at smuggling two years earlier that a passing guard had frightened him into abandoning a satchel of bead necklaces. But this cell had a smooth stone floor and walls that admitted neither rats nor rancid water. A wooden cot even spared him from the cold stone. "This cell is a welcome surprise."

Gonzalo met his gaze. "Then I suppose you're in no hurry to leave."

Yasin swallowed. The charges Gonzalo reported were far more serious than a lifted money pouch. Esteban had clearly told quite the tale. "I wouldn't say that."

Gonzalo lowered his voice. "What if I could get you out?"

Yasin pressed his hands against his *qamisa* to still their shaking. Three days was all he cared to spend in this stone hole, but nobles did nothing out of kindness. "I'd be curious to know the cost."

"I want you to steal something for me."

A laugh at the irony bubbled forth before he could stop himself. Once the first sound began to echo, he gave up trying to restrain it. These stone walls probably heard far too little laughter.

No wonder this man kept asking about his criminal experience!

"I'd be delighted." He wiped nascent tears from his eyes. He'd steal from the king himself if it meant making Esteban's list of lies—well, not exactly lies, but Yasin had been careful not to leave evidence—disappear. "How can I help?"

Gonzalo's gaze had hardened during the fit of laughter but softened again as Yasin spoke. "When His Majesty captured this city, he acquired the emir's library. Those thousands of texts contain both Muslim and ancient secrets. Since then, his school of translation has been working to unlock that knowledge."

Yasin considered the priests preaching against the infidel in the marketplace and the fine examples of common Castilians like Esteban. "I'm surprised the king values Muslim writings that most Christians would burn."

"Yes, well…" Gonzalo fidgeted, unsettled for the first time. "The burnings in those first chaotic days cost us some important texts."

Yasin snapped his fingers. "You need replacements."

Gonzalo nodded slowly. "The most important one was written by Ibn Sina the Persian, called *The Book of Healing*."

"Happy to help." Paper was valuable, but used paper wasn't. It'd be kept somewhere dry but likely not locked up. Stealing such an object was fairly easy. The only difficulty would be reaching it. "Where can I find it?"

"The royal library in Valencia."

The mirth drained from Yasin's face. "You want me to steal from El Cid?"

"Rodrigo Diaz, yes." Gonzalo's lip twisted at the name. "Muslims call him El Cid, *the lord*, but we call him El Campeador." The teacher of the battlefield.

Regardless of his sobriquet, the ruler of Valencia was legendary, even in Almeria. He alone had resisted the Almoravid wave that had flooded al-Andalus; of all the *taifa* kingdoms, only Valencia remained independent. Despite being outnumbered, Diaz had once captured the ruler of Barcelona and his entire command staff. Yasin still dreamed about the wagons of ransom he must have received for releasing him.

Lord Gonzalo offered not only the chance to leave this prison, but to see some of that treasure first-hand. Yasin's fingers itched with anticipation. "You're certain he has a copy?" He'd hate to travel across Iberia for nothing.

"Valencia had one before Diaz conquered the city, and he has a great appreciation for knowledge. He wouldn't have allowed it to be destroyed." The final words carried a grudging respect.

"You're certain there isn't a copy in Toledo?"

"We searched and found only fragments or inaccurate copies. We've even asked the libraries in Castile, Leon, and Galicia." Gonzalo grunted and shook his head. "*The Book of Healing* is massive. Twenty-two books. Very few complete copies exist in Iberia."

Yasin barked a hollow laugh. "I can't steal twenty-two books!"

"You don't have to. The library has most of them, but we lost the section called the *Metaphysics*. That's what I want you to acquire."

"*Metaphysics*." Yasin rolled the strange word around his tongue. "What does it mean?"

"It contains all Muslim knowledge about the soul, God, and the nature of existence." Gonzalo's lip curled into a sneer. "Discoveries far too important to remain in infidel hands. We need an accurate copy."

"Accurate?"

The Castilian's eyes widened. "We are the Library of Toledo. Can you imagine the disgrace if we distributed a faulty copy? Scholars and courtiers across Europe would mock the quality of our work and the king who patronized it." He crossed his arms and began absently scratching at his elbow. "The only known authentic copy outside of Muslim lands is in Valencia."

"Why not simply ask El Cid to borrow it? Isn't he a Castilian lord bound to your king?"

"Oh, Alfonso tried." Gonzalo grunted. "Diaz replied that his subjects would never permit his sending their precious treasures to Toledo."

"That sounds believable." El Cid had only captured Valencia a few months earlier, and shipping its treasures to Toledo would make pacifying the city more difficult. Yasin himself had left Almeria rather than watch the Almoravids destroy everything that made it beautiful.

"It's a lie," Gonzalo corrected. "Diaz likes his new kingdom and refuses to supplicate himself to his old master."

That also sounded believable. "So, the king asked you to acquire the rest of the *Book of Healing*?"

Gonzalo rubbed his hands together in a gesture that struck Yasin as more eager than irritated. "The king will reward whoever provides him with what his rebellious general won't."

Yasin bit at his lip. This nobleman expected a reward for his efforts, but he was carrying out this scheme without the king's knowledge. "Why not acquire it yourself?"

"I don't have the skills for thievery. I wouldn't know how to go about it."

Yasin's chest tightened. "And you lose nothing if I fail."

Humor tugged at Gonzalo's eyes. "Something like that."

Yasin admired the honesty, even though he'd be on his own if anything went wrong. He'd need to travel a dangerous route that skirted the edge of Almoravid lands. Bandits worked the trade routes between the major cities of al-Andalus. He'd have to steal from one of the most cunning men on the continent, then make that same journey back to Toledo. It would be incredibly dangerous.

And yet, he had little choice. If Gonzalo spoke true, Esteban had looted his room. "What are you offering?"

"A pardon of all crimes," Gonzalo answered at once. "As well as a small estate along the Tagus."

"An estate?" It was a generous offer. Evidently, Gonzalo recognized the danger as well.

Gonzalo shrugged. "One of my tenants died last year. Someone needs to work it; why not you?"

Beyond knowing nothing about farming, Yasin refused to entangle himself with an influential man who knew about his criminal activities. If Gonzalo could arrange a pardon, he could also revoke it.

This Castilian had already risked much by coming here. He had the need. Yasin decided to press further. "Christian and Muslim bandits ply both sides of that river. I left Almeria to avoid the Almoravids, not live beside them. I'll take gold."

Gonzalo scowled and turned toward the cot in the corner.

Yasin feared he may have pushed too hard. Surely the prisons of Toledo contained other smugglers. He could name a handful of competitors right now.

"Agreed." Gonzalo met his gaze again. "Fifty pieces." His tone carried finality.

"Splendid!" Yasin clapped his hands together.

Perhaps lifting Esteban's pouch hadn't been the mistake he'd thought it was. With that much gold, he could start his own workshop. He'd never have to worry about pleasing a master craftsman again. Starting over in another city would be easier, but the thought of stealing Master Iustez's customers one by one until he had no choice but to release Esteban and his friends was an appealing one. Oh, how he would savor that moment!

Yasin swallowed as he recalled the difficulty before him. "There is a problem."

"Problem?"

"I wouldn't know which text was which. I can't read."

Though Yasin knew no one who could read, the Castilian's condescending smirk filled him with burning embarrassment.

Gonzalo rubbed his chin. "I may have a solution."

SARAH

Sarah returned to her room after her day's chores. A shaft of moonlight shone through the high window, illuminating the dust floating on the air and washing the far wall in a silvery glow. Shivering, she reached for her shawl on the cot and wrapped it around her shoulders.

She had just lit a candle when a series of knocks rapped against her door.

"Enter."

Latch releasing, the door swung open and Gonzalo stepped inside.

At least he'd knocked instead of walking in on a defenseless woman in her shift. Yet, why was he here, after he'd made it painfully clear how little he valued her last time?

When the Castilian's searching gaze found her, he sucked in a breath and puffed his chest out. His eyes raced up and down her body.

Smug satisfaction strengthened her limbs. Despite having already tasted her beauty, he still hungered for it.

Perhaps she had discounted his interest too quickly. She now regretted reaching for the concealing shawl. She'd have to let it briefly slip to tease him with a glimpse of what lay beneath. She had kept her breasts covered during their last interaction.

"How may I help you, my lord?"

He pulled away from the door frame to stand squarely within the room. His gray irises ringed with black pinned her with an intense stare. "Did your training include Arabic literature?"

Her prepared seductions abandoned her. After their previous dalliance, he wanted to speak about literature? "Yes…as well as poetry, science, politics, history—"

"Are you familiar with Ibn Sina?" he interrupted with a hot intensity.

"I am." Her voice carried too much of her uncertainty at this development in the conversation.

"You've read his work? You'd recognize it among other texts?"

For a second time, hope of seducing him collapsed. If he couldn't offer her a way out of this library, she wished he'd leave her alone.

Yet, he was still a Castilian lord with free rein of the library. She was obliged to answer. "I've read his *Book of Healing* and *Canon of Medicine*, as well as the *Proof of the Truthful*."

The faintest curl of a smile tugged at his lips. "Do you enjoy wasting your talents on menial tasks?"

She adjusted her shawl to delay while she crafted a careful answer to the dangerous question. "I have never complained about any task my masters demanded." Memory of her terror at the guard's hungry gaze flashed into her mind. "I am thankful to have a place here, in any capacity."

"That wasn't my question. You are a trained *qiyan*, so you must speak and write Arabic. You're clearly fluent in Castilian. Do you know Hebrew as well?"

She bowed her head in a humble acknowledgement. The past five years had taught her that pride attracted trouble.

"Then you're more skilled than the scribes and priests within these walls." He raised his chin. "I ask again. Do you enjoy wasting your talents?"

Though he had embarrassed her and thwarted her seduction, it still felt good to hear him acknowledge her abilities. "Even a silent nightingale longs to sing."

He nodded and closed the door behind him.

They were alone. This time, though, she would not seek to cultivate his affection. He'd already shown her the futility of it.

"What if I could arrange for your freedom?"

Scraps of dreams knitted together again. Freedom. The word tantalized her. But even as her pulse leapt, Sarah fought against her excitement. Why should her knowledge of Ibn Sina win his favor after her companionship had failed?

She pulled her shawl tighter and raised her chin. "I would ask the cost of that favor."

He chuckled.

Sarah settled her hands on her hips. This was hardly the time for humor.

Lord Gonzalo raised a hand. "Forgive me. You're the second person to ask that question today." He sobered. "I need someone who can recognize the volumes that compose the *Metaphysics* section of the

Book of Healing in an unfamiliar library. It would require a journey beyond the city. Does this opportunity interest you?"

Her gaze fell to the floor. She recalled the texture of parchment and vellum on the tips of her fingers, the weight of the codices in Baghdad, the graceful curving script that caressed the paper. She could recognize any text in the four languages of this peninsula easily enough, but a journey beyond the walls was fraught with perils.

It didn't matter. She had to grasp this chance for freedom. She may never get another.

Yet, her liberation would also end her protection. Without the safety of a respectable marriage, she'd be subject to the evils of this vile city and the depredations of men like the library guard. Lord Gonzalo had already proven that no Christian of means would ever view her as a suitable wife. She would have to return to her fellow Muslims, to men who appreciated the value a *qiyan* could bring to their households.

But, where? Baghdad and the East would require another danger- ous sea journey, and her last one had ended in slavery. She could not risk that again. Even if she arrived safely, she'd be competing with every other *qiyan*. She'd already spent five years without fame or accomplish- ment, and younger competitors were being trained every year.

She would go back to the Muslim cities of the South. But arriving penniless would mean playing on street corners for pitifully few copper coins and no protection from venal men. Only by arriving in dignity with dresses, jewelry, oils, and perfumes could she present herself as Baghdad-trained *qiyan* and achieve the status she'd always desired. Without them, she'd be alone in a dangerous world, relying on the charity of others.

"I will need funds to start a new life."

Gonzalo scratched his chin with the back of his hand. "I would have thought your emancipation a sufficient reward."

"When we..." She forced herself not to look toward the bed where she'd seduced him. "I'd hoped to gain status through a respectable marriage. Without the means to settle myself securely, freedom is just penury and starvation."

He stared at her in withering silence for some time, but eventually his neck muscles loosened. "A small purse. Your freedom will already cost me."

Her fingers trembled as the excitement finally broke free. It would afford her the security she needed, if not the title and high status she desired. No longer would she waste her days as a slave of Christian priests. That was worth risking a journey.

"Then I will help you in any way I can."

He rolled his shoulders, straightening as he did. "Prepare yourself. I will arrange everything." After a perfunctory bow, he ducked through the door.

Sarah latched the door behind him and leaned against it, closing her eyes. She had hoped to elevate herself by making Lord Gonzalo her husband, but this was better. She needed not be bound to a Christian. She would abandon this wretched city with the means to arrive in the South in triumph. For the first time in her life, she would decide how she spent her time, with no one giving orders.

This city may be lost to Islam, but Allah had not abandoned her.

Crossing to the cot, she retrieved the wooden oud. As she brushed her fingers over the strings, soft notes broke the silence. She smiled. She had earned this instrument through her labors. It was the only object in this room she treasured. Music had kept her company through the darkness of this life.

She was going on a journey, and she would return as a free woman.

YASIN

The sounds of a city's streets had always spoken to Yasin, regardless of language or creed. Undertones of hurried excitement hinted at a full money pouch, and the clink of a sword hilt against mail warned of hidden guards waiting to catch over-eager thieves. But after three days of nothing but the muted muttering of distant prisoners and occasional footsteps to break the silence, the clamor of the early evening crowd thundered like a blacksmith's hammer in Yasin's ears.

The scarred Castilian guard in the brown tunic goaded Yasin with a hand on his back. "Keep moving. Lord Gonzalo expected us a quarter hour ago."

Grunting, Yasin muttered over his shoulder, "His nose will appreciate the delay."

Gonzalo had arranged the return of Yasin's possessions—including his ring knife—along with a basin of clean water and a small vial of scented oil. While they didn't compare to an afternoon soaking in the *hamam*, they'd removed the more fragrant reminders of his incarceration.

The man snorted. "Can't disagree with that."

They turned down a well-paved side street. The high walls flanking the complex to his left would have been impressive once, but the aged stone now bore enough crevices that he could easily scale them, even with a sack of plunder on his back. His escort pushed ahead of him when they reached the impressive oak doors.

A pair of city guards in yellow tunics moved to confront them, their muscles stiffening as if they expected trouble.

Yasin stepped aside to give them space.

"We have business inside," his escort grumbled. "Let us pass."

One of the yellow guards gave a smug grin before waving them off. "Run along."

His escort curled his fist around the hilt of his sword. "Gonzalo Martinez awaits us inside."

Both guards adjusted their stances, evidently having noticed the motion. One of them studied Yasin.

Having seen that look precede a brawl before, Yasin shuffled farther out of sword range. "I'll just wait over here." He waved his hands limply toward them. "You gentlemen are doing a fine job, by the way."

"Last warning," Yasin's escort growled. "Get the fuck out of my way, or when you wake back up, you'll be missing half your teeth and be reassigned to the southern border."

After sharing an anxious glance, the city guards stood aside. Yasin, shivering at the malice in the man's voice, couldn't blame them. Nonetheless, from the look of those ugly yellow tunics, he suspected proximity to Muslims would only improve their style of dress.

Assuming the Almoravids didn't massacre them, of course.

His escort marched between the unsettled city guards and gave the carved oak doors a great shove. They swung inward hard enough to bang against the walls with two echoing thuds. Yasin jogged to keep up as he crossed a large room with simple tables, no valuables of note, and hunched groups of men who probably wouldn't notice if he stole the quills from their hands. His fingers itched with anticipation of making an attempt, and he had to wipe them on his dark blue *jubba* to keep from trying. The fading light was perfect for an attempt.

Gonzalo, waiting near an open door to a side room, straightened as Yasin and his escort approached. He wore the same black tunic and patched boots as before. The nobleman smiled. "Come." He spun on his heel and stepped inside.

Within, three men sat at a long wooden table with inkpots, quills, and paper arranged before each of them. The two younger men on the ends wore simple robes of thick wool and the haggard expressions common to every apprentice. The elderly man between them wore a priest's habit and a long white beard. While eyelids and cheeks drooped with age, the eyes themselves studied Yasin with piercing and unsettling clarity.

"May God bless you, my son." The priest made the sign of the cross in their direction.

"Peace to you, Father." Gonzalo bowed his head. He was grinning when he straightened. "It's good to see you again."

Their easy familiarity unsettled Yasin. "Why do we need a priest?"

The priest cleared his throat. "Is this another criminal ready for execution?"

Gonzalo's hand clamped down Yasin's arm with surprising strength. Something wild and dangerous flashed in Gonzalo's eyes.

Yasin eyed the door. Gonzalo's man was probably still standing outside. Yasin doubted he could slip past, but perhaps he should try. He twisted to loosen his *jubba* enough to gain access to the ring knife in his belt as he tried to recall what crimes he had admitted to.

The Castilian watched him with an eerie stillness for a further moment before humor tugged at his lips and gray eyes. He tilted his head a fraction toward the priest. "A pardon, actually." He released Yasin's arm to fall limply at his side.

The release of Yasin's breath sounded over the clamor of the three seated men opening their inkpots and preparing their quills.

These men discussed death with a casualness Yasin would expect from only Almoravids. Lord Gonzalo held the power to send him to the noose or set him free. Yasin shivered but immediately regretted doing so.

Grunting with clear satisfaction, Gonzalo crossed the room to stand beside the table. "Father Efrain is a royal clerk and friend of my father. He'll draft your pardon and these scribes will make copies."

"I want one," Yasin warned.

"Of course." Gonzalo leaned against the wall and crossed his arms. "Another goes into the judicial records, and the last will remain in the library."

The ease of the Castilian's assent soothed Yasin. "Is it really that simple? I thought the king issued pardons."

"His Majesty doesn't concern himself with pickpockets." Gonzalo's tone held more than a little bitterness.

The scribes chuckled until the priest silenced them by rapping his knuckle on the table. Their mockery struck exactly the right tone of honesty and smugness he'd expect from a royal official, even a lowly scribe. If this had been an elaborate fraud, they'd have been more anxious.

"What crimes should I list?" The priest tilted his head toward Yasin.

The scribes held their pens above the inkpots, watching with similar intensity.

If this was his one chance, then he'd take full advantage. Esteban had lied once already; Yasin would ensure he never had the chance to do so again.

"Naturally, I'm an honest citizen who has never committed a crime"—he met the eyes of each man in turn, emphasizing the point—"but I've been accused of public drunkenness."

Three pens dipped into inkpots and began to scratch the paper. After a few strokes, they raised their eyes again.

"Violating water rights."

Again, the pens scraped the paper.

Yasin folded his hands before him. "Pickpocketing." He paused after each word so they could catch up. "Trespassing. Burglary. Smuggling."

With each crime, the priest's eyes grew wider. Against the wall, Gonzalo shifted his weight.

"Fraud. Dealing in stolen goods." He offered a resigned frown. "Selling faulty goods. Evading city guards."

The scribe furthest to the left cracked a smile and fell a little behind the others. Yasin halted until he caught up.

"Impersonating an official." He shrugged. "For that matter, impersonating a monk."

The elderly priest gasped. Beneath the man's outraged glare, Yasin offered a sheepish shrug.

The priest turned to Gonzalo for confirmation. Despite a faint grin, the nobleman merely nodded. The priest lowered his gaze again and dutifully scratched his pen over the paper.

Yasin cleared his throat. "Uh…laying with a member of the royal household."

Gonzalo barked a laugh that drew a look of horror from the priest. Ignoring it, the nobleman asked, "Which one?"

"I could not shame the lady in question." Yasin rubbed a faint scar on the back of his neck where her fingernails had scratched him. "But I can say she was lovely." Years married to a much older man had pent up quite a bit of passion. "Just lovely."

The grinning scribe chuckled until the priest whacked the back of his head. After the three men fell silent, the priest asked in a terse voice, "Is that all?"

Yasin considered inserting a few future crimes, but that would have required lying to a man of God. He had no intention of adding sacrilege to that list. That one, the priest might not write down. "That should cover it."

The scribes finished their copies and presented them for the priest's review.

As the three men huddled together, Gonzalo sauntered over to Yasin. "You're more suited to this task than I'd hoped."

Yasin pressed his hand to his chest and bowed his head. "I merely recount the slanders against me." Raising his eyes again, he gestured to the scribes. "I'd never dream of doing any of those dreadful things."

"I hope that isn't true, or you'll spend the rest of your days in darkness beneath the Alcazar instead of living in comfort." Gonzalo continued in a hushed tone, "If you fail or betray me, you'll learn that my influence isn't limited to a pardon."

The words carried more malice than he'd expect from a whisper. Yasin swallowed a rush of terror. Esteban, a mere apprentice, had arranged his first incarceration; he didn't want to imagine what a Castilian nobleman could do.

Yasin jumped at the sound of the priest's chair scraping against the floor. He clenched his fists, hating the naked reactions this nobleman induced. This man cut through all his self-control as only his father had. He didn't want to remain in Gonzalo's clutches a moment longer than necessary. Forget Toledo; when he finished this job, Yasin would take his pay to some other city, far from this dangerous Castilian lord.

The priest withdrew a seal attached by a cord around his neck as the scribes dripped melted wax on the seams of the folded pardons. One by one, he imprinted them, turning simple papers into official state documents. Selecting one, he circled the table and beckoned Yasin to advance.

"Kneel, my son, and be forgiven."

Obeying, Yasin lowered his head as the priest raised a hand above him. "*Te absolvo ab omni vinculo excommunicationis et interdicti in quantum possum et tu indiges in nomine Patris, et Filii, et Spiritus Sancti. Amen.*"

Though Yasin didn't speak Latin, he'd been forgiven his sins often enough to recognize the words of absolution. A flush of delight coursed through his veins. Gonzalo's warning faded away. He was cleansed in the eyes of God. This was a very good start to a dangerous journey.

He rose. With a deep breath, he accepted the pardon when the priest offered it. Behind him, the scribes sealed their inkpots and collected their materials.

Yasin studied the document in his hands. The rough paper felt stiff and smelled a little acrid. That seal, imprinted in wax, matched the official declarations he'd seen posted in the market. It seemed so strange that a simple piece of paper could erase three years of mischief.

The priest stepped past him without another word, and the scribes fell in step, chattering about their next task.

Gonzalo was studying him. "Are you ready?"

Yasin released a long breath. "Yes." He studied the pardon in his hand again. "Though I still can't read this any better than yesterday. It could be a list of insults for all I know." Eyes widening, he sucked in a breath. "*Ya salaam!* How do I know—"

Gonzalo crossed himself. "I swear before God that it's real. If it wasn't, I couldn't have arranged your release. You're no use to me as a fugitive."

Yasin saw no indication of deception in the nobleman's expression. Nor had Gonzalo's man demonstrated a strong relationship with the guards outside the library. Besides which, if the Castilian meant to deceive him into revealing his crimes, he'd accomplished that, or near enough. He had no further need for pretext.

Yasin folded the pardon in thirds again so as not to damage the wax seal. Reaching into his *jubba*, he released the buckle of a vertical leather strap sewn into the inside layer. Once opened, he slid the pardon behind his leatherworking toolkit, held in place by three horizontal leather straps sewn onto the fabric.

"How will I identify the right part of the *Book of Healing*, this *Metaphysics*?" Yasin fumbled to buckle the vertical strap again.

Smirking, Gonzalo patted him on the shoulder. "Come." He led Yasin through the door.

The swordsman was waiting outside, but Gonzalo waved for him to remain in place.

Yasin pressed his fingers to his lips, then his forehead as he passed. "Thank you for the pleasant walk."

He received a scowl in return.

Gonzalo led him back through the room with the tables. Someone had come through and lit the sconces. Though streams of wax hadn't yet begun to crawl down the candles, the air already smelled of beeswax. They cast enough light to illuminate the smooth walls. Old stone. This building was ancient.

A hooded figure stood near the library entrance. As Gonzalo led him closer, Yasin realized it wasn't a hooded cloak but a shawl. A woman, surrounded by priests and scholars in a library? Perhaps a servant had retrieved something to help with his task.

"Hello, Sarah," Gonzalo greeted in Castilian as he halted before her.

The figure lowered her shawl, revealing a cascade of hair that shimmered like the patina on flawless full-grain leather. The green eyes studying him sparkled like emeralds.

Yasin had rarely worked with gems; perhaps after she delivered whatever Gonzalo had prepared, he might have the chance to toy with this gem in one of these rooms. What a delightful way to depart Toledo!

Gonzalo gestured to her. "Yasin ibn Faraj, meet Sarah al-Bayda, a slave of this library."

Yasin was about to nod a simple greeting when the woman surprised him by concealing the bottom half of her face with her shawl and dipping her head.

He hadn't seen a courtly greeting since the parade in Almeria celebrating the victory against the Castilians eight years prior, long before the Almoravids had revealed their intentions to conquer al-Andalus. Where had a slave learned it?

Not to be outdone, he pressed his fingers to his lips then his head before resting his hand on his chest and bowing. "Peace be upon you, Sarah the Fair," he greeted in Arabic, translating her name.

"You speak Arabic?" she repeated in the same language as she lowered her shawl. Her eyes widened for only a moment before she masked her surprise. "Are you one of the faithful?"

So, she was a Muslim, yet associated with a Castilian nobleman. How that happened was probably an interesting story. "No, but I lived in Almeria for many years."

Her lips dimpled into a pleasing smile. "I come from Granada."

Yet another great city seized by the Almoravids. He'd heard rumors of a riot brutally suppressed there last year, but sorting truth from fanciful lies had become almost impossible.

All the more reason for finishing this job quickly. "What do you have for me?" he asked in Castilian so Gonzalo could understand.

Frowning, Sarah cocked her head. "Pardon me?"

"I could probably memorize the symbols of the title, but I'd prefer a written example I can compare to the original." Yasin glanced at Gonzalo, whose eyebrows knitted together. The reaction set his stomach churning. "I need some way to identify what I'm looking for."

"Ah, you don't understand." The low rumbling of Gonzalo's chuckle echoed in the foyer. "She's going with you."

"What?" The library, the scent of beeswax, and the scrutiny of both the Castilian lord and the Granadan slave pressed in on him. Not only had Gonzalo threatened him, but now he sprung a surprise like this. Unpredictable clients made for risky jobs. Yasin had always done his best to avoid them, but he was helpless here. "You never mentioned this."

"It shouldn't matter, unless you intend to betray me." Gonzalo's tone carried that hint of malice from before.

"I'll acquire this book for you," Yasin reassured, "but you said nothing about dragging a slave halfway across al-Andalus."

Sarah's eyes narrowed. "I'm more than a slave."

"She will help you," Gonzalo explained.

"Oh?" Yasin inclined his head toward Sarah. "Indeed, you are lovely, but I can secure my own companionship and wash my own clothing." He'd been robbed the only time someone else had arranged the former and suffered intolerable wrinkles when others did the later.

"I'm not just a—"

"She can find the *Book of Healing* and identify the correct volumes," Gonzalo interrupted.

"I didn't realize Castilians taught their slaves about Persian scholars," he countered.

Dipping his chin, the Castilian raised his eyebrows. "She was trained as a *qiyan*."

The objection died on Yasin's lips. "Was she, now?" She would certainly know how to read, and in fact probably knew more about the history of Almeria than he did.

He studied her again with fresh eyes. Beneath his gaze, she straightened and held herself with a stillness that suggested rigid control. She raised her chin enough to draw his attention to the long path from her neck to the neckline of her dress without exactly offering an invitation. Her hand pinched the two ends of her shawl just below her bust, accentuating the slope of her breasts.

It all happened in one smooth motion, effortlessly, as if she had practiced many times. Yes, he could see the signs now. The defiant pride in her eyes only confirmed what his senses now told him. The chance to spend weeks alone with her almost justified the trouble of dragging her along, and a couple would arouse less suspicion than a man traveling alone without goods to sell.

"You can identify this codex?" he asked.

"I'm much more than a simple slave." Anger flared within her eyes at that word.

Yasin knew that anger. He'd felt it when Almoravid armies marched through the central avenue in Almeria. He'd seen it on the face of every apprentice browbeaten by his master. He'd passed more than a few slaves glaring at the backs of their owners' heads with that same hostility.

Those defiant eyes and her dignified curtsey confirmed it: she would flee the moment they left the city, leaving him with no way to complete his task.

Yasin rubbed his hands against his *jubba*. Gonzalo had already threatened to revoke the pardon, and he needed this man's coin to start a workshop. A moment prior, the thought of bringing her along offended him. Now, the prospect of attempting this job without her expertise terrified him. He needed to bind her to the success of this mission.

But more than that, he had to maintain some control over this agreement. He was a free man, not a servant of the nobles like the swordsman who had escorted him to this library.

"I'll bring her on the condition that she gains her freedom when we succeed."

Other than a raised eyebrow, Gonzalo neither altered his expression nor his focus. Never before had Yasin observed such self-control. "I've already agreed to that, provided you deliver the volume as agreed."

This nobleman had dragged a priest and a pair of royal scribes to this library to draft a pardon. Even his swordsman had felt confident enough to threaten city guards. If Yasin failed to deliver on his promises, he'd have to run from this lord's wrath. He'd be a fugitive, first from Almeria, and again from Toledo and all of Castile.

He couldn't keep running.

At least, if he needn't keep an eye on Sarah to prevent her abandoning him, he could watch for chances for profit on this journey. Surely, someone between Toledo and Valencia could use a skilled leatherworker.

And if not, all corners of the world offered opportunities for a smuggler and thief.

SARAH

Sarah clasped Yasin's wrist and spun him around before he could reach the library's doors.

He recoiled at first, but upon recognizing her he calmed and straightened the lay of his blue *jubba*. "Oh, it's you."

Who did he think it would be? "Why?" she asked in Arabic.

"You tell me." His lip curled in a mischievous grin. "You reached for my hand."

She rolled her eyes, partly to deflect his weak attempt at humor and partly to look away from those lips. He had a pleasing smile, though he offered it a little too easily for her to trust it. "Why did you demand my freedom?"

"I couldn't abide a beautiful woman being bound to this community of unmarried men." His voice sounded huskier than before.

His interest was obvious. Lord Gonzalo had claimed this man was a thief and a rogue, and the thought of spending weeks with him made her shudder. If he forced his attentions on her, they would be far from any who might enforce the king's protection. She had to kill that possibility now.

"No amount of charm will convince me to share your bed on this journey." She arched an eyebrow and raised her chin, channeling all the disdain she could muster.

"That isn't my intention." His Adam's apple bobbed up and down. "I need your help to acquire this codex."

She subsided, satisfied that he posed no immediate threat. "Steal, you mean."

"Acquire," he repeated, as if the distinction mattered. His charming smirk irritated her as much for its timing, so soon after her rebuke, as for its pleasantness.

"How is that an answer?"

He shrugged. "I can't succeed if you flee at the first opportunity."

Was he a fool? Her accent, bearing, and skills would all expose her if she attempted to flee. She was a royal slave. Every noble, official, soldier, or subject could turn her in for a reward. And where could she go without money or protection? No woman would risk traveling alone.

The leering guards waiting outside this building flashed into her mind yet again. She shuddered and rubbed her shoulders. "You think I would escape?"

"I would, if I were you."

She had no doubt of that. Men could do as they pleased. No one would abuse or enslave them for traveling on their own.

"All who are oppressed yearn for freedom," he murmured.

A familiar emotion lurked beneath the bravado in his eyes. Anger, of course, but also irritation, grim determination, and…loss? The same look had reflected back at her in her washing basin. Her return from Baghdad had led to her capture, costing her the chance to return home. What did a thief and a smuggler value that could equal that loss?

This strange man unsettled her. Where was the respect for *adab*, for honorable behavior and decorum that the scholars and philosophers all agreed governed men's motivations?

The vulnerability lasted only a moment before his smile returned. "Meet me tomorrow morning at the Jews' Gate. We'll depart from there."

Depart. The word set her heart beating faster. "Why not now?" The sooner they left, the sooner she'd be free.

"No." He clenched his jaw. "I have business tonight."

She frowned. "You intend to punish those who put you in prison."

His gaze shifted to study something behind her. Lord Gonzalo, perhaps? "You're remarkably well-informed."

She ignored the implication. "Is that your intention?"

An easy laugh flowed from his lips. "Of course!"

"Don't do anything reckless."

He raised his eyebrows. "Your concern touches me."

"That's not…" She should have been more careful with her words. "My future depends on you remaining uninjured and at liberty tomorrow."

"Fear not, my lady." His grin broadened. "I wouldn't dream of missing the chance to spend time with you." He set his hand on the doorknob. "Tomorrow, second hour of the day, Jews' Gate."

Before she could respond, he opened the door and slipped through. "Sarah?"

She curtseyed to Lord Gonzalo when he approached. "My lord?" She kept her eyes downcast to prevent the Castilian from noticing the lingering irritation that surely showed within them.

He cocked his head toward the door. "How do you find our thief?"

She bit back her criticism. "He has great confidence in his skills."

Gonzalo's punctuated chuckle seemed forced and lacked the naturalness of Yasin's. "I pray such confidence is justified." He lowered his voice. "Your freedom depends on it." His voice carried a menacing edge.

She swallowed.

"Take paper, a quill, and ink from the library stores," Gonzalo said. "Write regularly about your progress."

It seemed a reasonable request from the man who had arranged this enterprise. "How should I send my letters?"

"Couriers collect official reports from every town hall. Mark your message as a royal dispatch and I'll receive it."

She gasped. "You have access to the royal dispatches?" Only the king's closest advisors and their agents normally held such power. Royal couriers could requisition replacement horses from any abbey or town and cross great distances quickly.

Gonzalo's fingers curled up to rub the fraying sleeve of his tunic. "My father's allies still remember how he aided them." His gaze became distant. "The king will restore my family lands when I bring him the final volume of the *Healing*." His eyes shifted, pinning her with a glare. "If you suspect Yasin intends to betray me or can't succeed, write to me. I'll revoke his pardon and hunt him down." The muscles of his neck tightened as he scowled. "Do this and you'll receive your freedom, even if he fails."

She nodded quickly. "I will, my lord."

But the nature of Gonzalo's request unsettled her. This Castilian nobleman clearly didn't trust a man whose freedom depended on his loyalty. Why should he trust a slave's obedience?

It didn't matter. If she needed to report on a thief, she would.

Unless this troublesome thief did something tonight to preclude their leaving on the morrow.

CHAPTER FIVE

YASIN

"WHAT'RE YOU DOING here?" Yasin's portly landlord leaned against both sides of the door frame. His cloak hung open, blocking the passage.

"I live here," Yasin stepped forward to push past him.

The landlord leaned in further, interposing him with his bulk. Yasin halted to avoid a collision. "I heard you were arrested." His breath smelled of wine, probably the same wine Yasin had gifted him.

Straightening, Yasin forced a smile he didn't feel. "That was a misunderstanding."

The landlord curled his lip into a smug grin. "That's not what your employer thinks."

Yasin's smile faded. "You spoke with Master Sanchez?"

"He came by when you didn't show up to work."

"What did you tell him?" The words spilled in a rush.

"I told him what the other leatherworkers said when they and a city guard came to look for their stolen property."

Esteban would have smugly repeated his lies, and now Master Sanchez had heard them, too. No craftsman would risk his tools and precious reputation by employing a suspected thief.

Yasin set his jaw. Though he intended to leave Toledo and would neither need this man's spare room nor work from Master Sanchez, he couldn't let this slander stand. "Those men lied." Yasin withdrew the pardon from his *jubba*. "Here's my proof."

Yasin restrained a pang of envy when the landlord ran his eyes over the paper with rhythmic ease. If only he could read, he wouldn't need to rely on a slave who could flee at any moment.

The landlord was staring at him with naked contempt kept at bay these past three years by regular bribes of exotic wine. "An innocent man doesn't need a pardon. I don't want a thief in my house." He pointed out into the night. "Go."

Bribery only ensured betrayal at the worst possible moment. "I'll gather my possessions and be on my way," Yasin said with a sigh.

"You can pick up tomorrow whatever the guards didn't take." The man's voice warbled with a momentary uncertainty.

Yasin recognized a lie when he heard it. Whatever Esteban hadn't taken, this man would, and Yasin needed the silver from his last job with the aspiring nun to reach Valencia. He certainly wasn't about to tell his landlord about his hidden cache.

Yasin had expected hardship when he'd first arrived in Toledo, but he'd dazzled Master Sanchez in a single day. Yasin had the skill of a master; any craftsman would be eager to have him…at least, until his incarceration.

Now, he understood that the real challenge had always been not in gaining a position but in keeping it. He would never be one of them. He was a Mozarab, a foreigner who had willingly lived among Muslims. That, they would never forgive.

Yasin eyed the street. A few people dotted the paved stretch in either direction, but the immediate vicinity was clear. The crowd was too thin to conceal theft but sparse enough to permit extortion. Yasin had just purged the stain —and any lingering bad luck—of his incarceration by visiting his usual church, but, evidently, he would already need to re-tarnish his soul.

"No, tonight." The other man bristled, but Yasin continued over his nascent argument. "Either you let me past to gather my things now or I'll return in darkness and choose from whatever I find inside." If this man considered him a thief and a ruffian, he would oblige him.

The landlord stilled, eyes narrowing. "I'll call the guards. They'll be waiting for you."

"Tonight, perhaps," Yasin admitted. "But they won't guard you forever, and I can be very patient."

"I thought you weren't a thief." The man scowled. "I thought it was all a misunderstanding."

Yasin shrugged. "If it was, you have no reason to deny me what's mine. If I lied, don't give me a reason to turn my skills against you."

The portly man leaned back, taking the pressure off the hands that still clutched either side of the door. Yasin watched those eyes fill with confusion, then irritation, and finally acceptance. It almost made him smile. No matter the language or faith, everyone squirmed the same way when trapped.

The landlord lowered his hands and stepped aside. Next, of course, would come the threat, the desperate attempt to salvage dignity.

"Retrieve what's yours and get out."

Happy to oblige, Yasin took the stairs two at a time. As a rule, he didn't linger in the clutches of anyone he'd threatened. He wanted to be gone before the landlord realized there must be something valuable inside to risk violence for its retrieval.

His room had been ransacked, true to Gonzalo's report. His table and chair both sat on their sides. A few tapers and half-melted candles lay scattered over the floor, including one pressed into the wood bearing a boot print. Yasin didn't see the half-dozen or so unused candles, nor the leather turnshoes he used on dry days. His chest was upturned in the middle of the floor, and shredded black and pale green clothing lay scattered around it, torn into jagged tatters by a knife too dull for use by any respectable leatherworker.

Reassembling the scraps together in his mind, he concluded Esteban hadn't bothered to steal very much. Dismissal and eviction hadn't been punishment enough. He'd tried to destroy everything Yasin had gained, both inside the workshop and on the streets, these past three years.

Yasin poked through the remains and retrieved a small scrap of brown cotton fabric from the satchel he'd brought from Almeria. He rubbed his fingers over the fraying edges. It still felt smooth to the touch, made by one of that city's finest Christian weavers. The bottom had torn last year. He had spent a week's wages to patch the precious cloth. None of that mattered now. It had been his last remaining piece of home, destroyed not by Almoravids but by a fellow Christian.

Yasin only prayed Esteban had done so out of impotent rage at not finding his stolen pouch.

Rising, Yasin crossed to the cot, a simple folding X frame with full-grain leather drawn taut over the top. Unable to resist, he ran his hand along the surface. Though it hadn't been specially treated, the fabric had only a few imperfections, probably the result of old wounds on the original animal. Despite the value of such a large piece of fine leather, Esteban's men hadn't scavenged it. They must have thought it belonged to the landlord.

But this cot was Yasin's. He'd saved for months to afford such a large piece of full-grain leather. Ever since abandoning his comfortable bed in Almeria, he'd learned the value of sleep. A good, supple leather cot made all the difference.

Yasin withdrew the ring knife in his belt and pressed it against the edge of the cot. With a single stroke, he sliced it off the frame, then pulled it taut and severed the other side as well. His stroke was smooth, straight, and true, traveling with the grain, the stroke of a true master. Satisfied, he rolled up the leather. He could get good coin for such a length, even a used one.

Yasin pushed the cot out of the way, and its feet scraped across the floor. Sliding his knife between two floor panels, he pushed until the corner rose enough to fit his fingers beneath. With another tug, it came away entirely.

Inside the small cavity separating his floor from the ceiling of the room beneath was the leather pouch. The weight felt exactly as it had three nights earlier in that lovely woman's room. The delightful jangle of coins clinking together had just the right pitch. But his luck had soured enough that he didn't relax until he opened the drawstring and saw the flash of silver.

It was still here. Hopefully, the contents of that pouch and selling the length of full-grain leather would get him to Valencia. He could almost kiss the landlord for safeguarding the furniture. Esteban hadn't even thought to check beneath that cot. The fool had missed two treasures.

Yasin fixed the pouch to his belt with a triple knot. He didn't intend to hold it as loosely as Esteban had.

He glanced around the room one last time. This had been his home. Now, it was only a filthy chamber in the house of an ungrateful Castilian. After stowing the scrap of fabric from Almeria inside his *jubba,* he wedged the roll of leather beneath his arm and departed.

The streets had cleared as residents abandoned the encroaching evening for supper. His sanguine mood began to lift while he walked.

Apprentices weren't supposed to turn on each other, not when their masters regularly exploited them. Esteban had broken the pact of brotherhood by involving the guards. And yet, because of that, Yasin wouldn't have to spend the best years of his life toiling for pitiful wages. He had the chance to earn his own workshop, to rise further than that cretin ever dreamed. Rubbing his success in that man's face would almost make up for his treachery.

Almost.

Esteban lived in a four-story *tapia,* rammed-earth tenement squeezed in the cramped crescent of the winding Tagus near the port and downwind of the dye tubs. Yasin walked for half an hour to reach it, during which the ramparts of the Alcazar crawled from being in front on his left to behind him. A window to Esteban's first-story room faced the shadowed alley between his building and the adjacent one. While a few candles illuminated the upper windows, Esteban's was dark.

Fortune was with him. The early evening light was perfect for theft: he could see, but the covering darkness would mask his subsequent escape. He would prefer to study his target for a while, but Esteban could return at any time and Yasin had only tonight to finish this business.

He waited until the area was clear before ducking into the shadow of the alley next to Esteban's building. Chips of *tapia* flakes from the crumbling walls covered the cobbles, and he had to choose his footing carefully to avoid grinding it beneath his boots as he crept further into the darkness.

Esteban's window sat at chest-level. Crouching beneath it, Yasin pinched the rolled leather from his cot between his knees and unrolled his toolkit over his thighs. Choosing a pointed awl and one of his long leather needles, he reached up for the lock on the window. It was so high that he had to stretch his arms almost straight to reach it. The angle was uncomfortable, but he couldn't risk standing and dropping everything on the filthy ground. Not only would the leather soak up God knows what smells, but the dampness might rust his iron tools.

Heart thumping, he searched for witnesses one last time. Satisfied that he remained unobserved, he inserted the awl into the lock and twisted while working the needle in the keyhole. After some initial probing, he found the latch inside and tripped it with a satisfying click. Now free, the shutters swung open a fraction, beckoning like a lover's arms.

He smirked in the darkness. Sheathing the tools, he re-rolled the toolkit and slid it back into his *jubba*. By now, his eyes had adjusted to the growing darkness. Squeezing the roll of leather in one hand, he swung the shutters open and rose enough to peek inside.

Now, Yasin understood why Esteban always traveled with two followers. Empty of occupants, the room had three cots with chests beside each. Each cot had linen sleeping surfaces stretched taut, and two of them showed evidence of repeated patching.

Yasin snorted. Esteban and his boys worked with leather all day, yet they couldn't afford to sleep on it? No wonder he'd reacted so strongly to Yasin's taunts: they cut too close to the mark.

After searching for witnesses one more time, he slipped through the window and assessed opportunities for mischief. A pile of empty pouches sat atop a table in the corner. A few were still attached to belts, all sliced haphazardly, that dangled over the edges of the table. The pouches looked empty, and he doubted he'd have time to search them all. Esteban and his boys must have been busy while Yasin was in prison. And they called him a criminal!

At the first chest, he found a carved ivory comb. It was too dark to see, but its texture suggested it was detailed, which meant it was expensive. Rather than taking it, Yasin snapped off a few teeth and deposited it in the second chest. Hopefully, Esteban and his friends would accuse each other of theft. It might even break up their little gang.

Rooting through the second chest, he found a pair of gloves. They had the feel of top-grain leather, not as valuable as the surface of his cot, but still quite an expense. They fit nicely beneath a long garment in the third chest.

As he stowed them, his fingers touched something long and wooden. He ran both hands along the length until he reached holes in both ends. A flute? He hadn't pegged either Esteban or his followers as musical. Snapping it across his knee with an alarmingly loud crack, he slipped it into the corner of the first chest.

As he did, his hand brushed against a length of leather rolled around several stiff objects. Esteban's leatherworking tools! They were a craftsman's most precious possession.

A creak sounded from the stairs. He sucked in a quick breath. Someone had probably heard the flute break and was coming to investigate.

Yasin grabbed the toolkit and leapt back through the window. A moment after he closed the shutters, the door to the room opened beyond them.

Picking up his pace, he squeezed Esteban's toolkit and grinned. He may have lost his position, but he'd taken Esteban's livelihood and sown suspicion among his companions. Both acts were sins, as was his subsequent satisfaction at them, but at least he'd profited from them. He could always atone later.

Sometimes, revenge was more satisfying than virtue.

SARAH

For the first time since being brought to Toledo, Sarah had the pleasure of waking to sunlight filtering through her tiny window. No one interrupted her before dawn with a list of chores or a pile of clothes to wash. Evidently, the priests knew she'd been assigned to Lord Gonzalo.

A smile lingered while she filled one of the library's satchels with the quill, ink, and paper for Gonzalo's reports, her comb, and her oud. Slinging it over her shoulder, she bounced out her door and down the hall, nearly dancing with excitement. Her fluttering heartbeat and the slap of her turnshoes on the stone floor would keep time with the fastest song she knew, but she tried to restrain her delight from breaking the silence of the library. Though a few priests and scholars working at the translation tables noted her passage, no one halted her.

She worked her way through the teeming crowd toward the Jews' Gate. Twice she swatted an unwelcome hand from her posterior. She doubted that sort of thing happened before the Christians took this city. Her people were more respectful than these shameful northerners.

Rickety stables crowded the wall on both sides of the gate, drawing knots of shouting northern traders outbidding each other for the few remaining mules and camels that could carry their wares to the markets deeper within the city. A tight collection of animals, wagons, and travelers clustered in the center of the square. Noticing that everyone wore several layers of clothing, Sarah began to doubt the sufficiency of her shift, dress, and shawl. How cold would this journey be?

Only one man among the sea of shouting and churning bodies

remained still. Inhaling a breath to steady herself despite the odor of animals, she marched over to Yasin in his dark blue *jubba*, leaning against the city wall between two stalls. He absently threaded a copper piece through his fingers while watching the crowd.

He straightened when she approached. "You found it," he greeted in Arabic.

Since the previous night, he had bathed and removed the wrinkles from his clothing. The morning light struck his face at an angle that accented the gentle curve of his nose and the slope of his neck. The pleasing aroma of faint sandalwood tickled her nose. He moved with an elegance that drew her in and almost allayed her concerns from the previous day.

After a moment, it occurred to her that he'd probably cultivated a disarming manner intentionally. She supposed his shadowy trade demanded it. She would have to guard against letting his cordial ease soften her to his charms.

"I'm pleased your revenge didn't delay you." Relief audibly tinged her voice.

As he rubbed his *jubba* near his chest, his hand exposed the outline of something beneath it. "You are a strange one."

She tilted her head. "How so?"

He shrugged. "I'd expect the thought of revenge to offend you."

"Not at all. The heroes of the great poems always punish those who wrong them." She folded her hands before her. "Usually by turning their enemies against each other."

"Is that so?" Yasin grinned so broadly that his eyes danced. They suddenly seemed much less offensive than the day before.

Lowering her gaze, she cleared her throat and focused on the rope in his hand. It led to the neck of one of the mules standing nearby, laden with a bulging, rolled blanket and a cloak slung over the animal's back. The blanket appeared new, with no snags or debris caught in the wool fibers.

"I don't know much about caring for animals."

"It'll be a dirty, uncomfortable journey." He patted the mule on the head. "Are you certain you want to come? If you drew the symbols I need to watch for, I could do this on my own. I promise you'll get your reward, all without needing to leave Toledo."

She wasn't about to trust a stranger's promise with so much at stake. Besides, his suggestion was an absurd one. "Every hand has a different script. Some scribes add a flourish, some write simply. The codex could be in Arabic or Hebrew or Latin. Even if I write examples of each, will you leaf through them all, comparing them to every book in the library?"

He turned to study the mule, giving her a profile view of the deepening creases of his frown. "Can I trust you?"

Sarah steadied herself with a few shallow breaths. "I said I'd help you."

He grunted. "Promises are worth the air that carries them."

And yet, he had wanted her to trust his promise only a moment ago. "I have some small investment in your success."

He broke into a broad smile. He had nice, even teeth, a rarity. "Now *that*, I trust."

She frowned. "What?"

"Self-interest. Oaths are easily forgotten, but a person will always follow self-interest."

He had not a drop of *adab*, no virtue worthy of appreciation. She exhaled a slow breath and glanced at the gates. So close. "Then shall we leave?"

He removed the cloak from atop the mule's back. Beneath it was a pair of dainty boots. He grabbed them, too, and gestured widely to encompass her clothing. "I figured even mumbling scholars wouldn't be foolish enough to provide their slaves with travel clothes. We've far to walk, and these should help."

She eyed the boots. "We're walking to Valencia?"

"To start, at least. I can't afford a horse in the city, but they should be less expensive on the road."

"But we have the mule," she muttered. "I thought—"

"You thought I'd let you ride while I walked?" A hint of humor tinged the question.

"It would be the courteous thing to do."

"From your perspective, certainly." He jutted his chin at the animal. "Bearing both you and our pack will exhaust the poor creature."

As she accepted the boots, he took the satchel from her.

"Careful," she pleaded. "My oud is delicate."

He raised an eyebrow. "Of all things, you bring an instrument?"

Cleaning himself had rendered him passably handsome, but he was still a brute. "You'd be surprised at the value of music."

Though he smirked, he said nothing.

Raising her skirt enough to see what she was doing, she replaced her turnshoes with the boots. They fit snugly but comfortably. When did he have the opportunity to gauge the size of her feet? The hem of her dress had covered them in the library, or so she'd thought.

"How do they look?"

She was still holding her dress aloft when he turned to her. Though she revealed perhaps more of her calf than necessary, his unmistakable blush offered a pleasing reward. She could taunt him, too.

"Good fit," he mumbled before unfolding the cloak, made of olive-green combed wool. "This will protect against the wind and cold. It won't help in a downpour, but we shouldn't face many of those on the way to Valencia."

As he flourished it to wrap it around her, she detected sandalwood again, rich and full like an oil, not smoky. She had initially judged him a filthy criminal, but only after he'd spent the previous three days in prison. He had since cleaned, pressed, and anointed himself. Both his dark blue cotton *jubba* and the fine weave of the linen *qamisa* beneath suggested both quality and expense. Though, she couldn't decide whether he was trying to impress her or he was truly more cultured than she'd believed.

His gaze shifted to something behind her. "It's time to leave."

She turned. A caravan, now clearly definable amid the crowd, was preparing to set out. Most of the travelers walked beside their pack animals and wagons, but a few armed men on horseback rode along the column. "We're going with them?" She lost count at around forty individuals.

He tugged the mule forward. "The roads beyond the city are dangerous." He eyed the caravan. "Very dangerous."

She suppressed a shiver at implications of the shadow covering his face. "Dangerous?"

He nodded. "Bandits work the scrublands between towns. They typically don't threaten large caravans, but even great numbers won't protect against Almoravid raiders."

She eyed the men and women filtering through the gates. "Such attacks are common?"

"Common enough that only the foolish or desperate travel alone."

She searched for some hint of deception, but his voice sounded even and strong, and his muscles showed no unusual strain.

She eyed the wooden gates, framed by iron at the corners, as they approached. She had always believed they were meant to keep slaves like her from escaping. She'd never imagined that they kept something terrible out.

What had she agreed to? Freedom wouldn't benefit her if she didn't survive.

No, Yasin had to be exaggerating the danger. Otherwise, so many traders wouldn't be clogging this square with their wagons. Supposedly, the king and his family migrated across the peninsula throughout the year. Anyone who wished to petition him would have to travel, as well. Such things wouldn't happen in a realm as dangerous as Yasin claimed.

"I suppose we'll need to speak Castilian, then."

"I don't see why." He raised an eyebrow. "Everyone speaks Arabic."

She surveyed the crowd milling nearby. "All of them?" The priests had to know the language to translate anything written in the last five hundred years, and Sarah assumed the vendors in the market knew just enough to communicate with customers. But…everyone? She gasped at the thought of Christians worshiping their god in a heathen tongue. Would he hear those prayers? Would Allah hear hers if she recited them in Castilian?

She fell into step beside Yasin as he led the mule to join the back of the caravan. The travelers ahead of them shifted, briefly revealing a pair of gate guards watching the column.

She sucked in a breath. They would see the iron bands on her wrists and stop her.

Yasin turned at the sound and dimpled his lips into a smile. "Don't worry. We'll be safe in this group."

He didn't understand.

She was so close. After all these years, she could smell her freedom in the scent of pine from the trees just beyond the walls. They smelled sweeter than all the fruit groves in Baghdad. Her feet itched to rush forward and indulge in that freedom.

But she hadn't achieved it yet. "The guards will stop me."

"You?" Yasin's voice sounded haggard, and he was breathing quickly. "Why should they stop you?"

The iron band around her right wrist began to itch. As she rubbed it, the other clinked against it. She jumped at the sound. "I'm a slave."

"I have rather more to fear." He flexed his grip on the rope. "They may leer at a beautiful woman, but they'll hang a smuggler. Lower your shawl and let your hair free."

She recoiled and pulled her shawl tighter. "You would have me be…immodest?" To proudly display one's hair offended Allah.

"They'll be so enthralled by your beauty that they won't notice your wrists." He cracked a grin. "Trust a thief about distraction."

Her hands moved to obey, but even as she lowered the shawl, the speed of her compliance made them shake. "I suppose I can beg pardon later." At his mere suggestion, she had broken *adab* without hesitation. His certainty had dispelled not only her doubts, but her decorum and obedience to Allah's law. "But only this once."

"Don't be so certain," he warned, eyes dancing. "By the end of this journey, I'll have turned you into a proper criminal."

She set her jaw, determined to prove him wrong.

The portcullis loomed like a massive whale, threatening to crush them with its menacing teeth. She needed to pass through these gates first. A transgression now would earn her freedom. Allah would understand.

One of the guards turned in her direction.

She held a tense breath. This was it. He would know she was a slave, would question her.

But he met her eyes for only an instant before looking away, cheeks reddening.

They kept walking with the caravan. Maddeningly slowly, the gate looming before her gave way to an open blue sky broken by a few puffy white clouds. Coiled anticipation released all at once, exploding in disbelief and joy. A smile sprung onto her face so widely that her cheeks hurt.

Tears sprung to Sarah's eyes as she admired the simple rammed-earth structures dotting the road beyond the gates on both sides. Though they looked identical to those within the city, she had never seen their like before. These ones lay beyond the wall.

With no greater effort than walking down a street, she had passed into freedom. Rapture swelled in her heart. It had taken five years, but she had finally done it.

The caravan snaked eastward, following the course of the Tagus toward far off Valencia. Shipping berths and warehouses dotted the northern shore. Every so often, the exposed mouth of a canal joined the river, feeding water to nearby neighborhoods.

Basking in the warm sunlight on her face, she closed her eyes and breathed in wild air far from the stolen city. The unencumbered breeze carried pine and fresh flowers and filled her lungs with reassuring strength. She no longer minded the long walk before her.

When she opened her eyes again, she was alone. Yasin had halted to stare across the river. His easy smile had faded into slackened wonder.

Trudging back to him, she prayed he didn't suffer from some malady that rendered him dumbstruck. "Are you well?"

He swallowed and nodded toward the river. "Look."

Frowning, she studied the piers and ragged ships clinging to the shore, the workers unloading crates that probably contained more ghastly northern dresses of itchy wool or the barely digestible bread of the mountains. "I only see Castilians."

He shook his head and pointed off to the east. "There."

Following his gaze, she saw it.

On the far side of the river, countless trees within a massive garden were organized by height like the cresting waves of the Mediterranean on her voyage east. A lattice of walkways and reflecting pools divided the groves, while a pair of visible water wheels and three gushing fountains added life to the distant garden.

She had seen trees poking out from behind the walls of some of the larger estates, but after so many years, she had almost forgotten what proper groves looked like.

"What is it?" Her hushed voice scratched.

Yasin took a step forward. "*Al-Munya al-Naʿura.*" His voice had drained of its smugness.

She gasped. "The Waterwheel Orchard." Her teachers in Baghdad had judged the *taifas* like Toledo to be pale shadows of the great caliphate of Cordoba, but even they had admired the wonder of this famous garden. Even viewing it from a distance filled her with vigor. She yearned to wade across the great river, even though its rushing current would surely cling to her dress and drag her down.

The fountains of al-Andalus continued to flow. The Christian conquest couldn't silence the beauty of her homeland.

"The great physician Ibn al-Wafid supposedly filled that garden with every plant and herb in pharmacology." She wondered if the rest of the story was true, that those paths passed every fruit and nut in the Muslim world.

"They say it contains figs that are half green and half white," Yasin offered.

"This city was home to so much beauty, so much knowledge and art, before the Christians came." She studied the profile of his face. "I wouldn't have expected you to care about such things."

His eyes lost their focus. "In Almeria, the scent of fruit hung on the air in the royal gardens. No matter how hot, I could always find relief beneath those trees." A wicked twinkle filled his eyes. "Relief and ripe oranges."

She gasped. "You could have been executed for stealing from the emir."

"Just being there was enough to get me arrested."

"Most people would avoid such risks."

When he grinned, lines around his lips suggested he smiled often. "Ah, but then I wouldn't have enjoyed the trees or the singing birds who lived in them." He adjusted the edges of his *jubba*. "My fingers may have ached from working in my father's shop, or my brother might have harassed me, but any day I could steal away to those groves was a good one."

In Baghdad, the floral scents of the gardens had soothed Sarah as she'd practiced her recitations for the songbirds in the shade of the fruit trees. "It sounds beautiful."

"It was. Perhaps a little too beautiful."

She frowned. "What do you mean?"

"The *taifa* emirs forgot the need to balance culture and strength." He grunted. "They neglected to protect their lands while they debated philosophy, and that bred resentment. When the Castilians attacked, their people rushed into Almoravid arms, and now all that culture you admire is gone."

The objection rang hollow. Countless priests in the library bemoaned the arrival of a Muslim power capable of resisting

Christian domination. "Muslims couldn't possibly inflict more damage than Christians."

"You didn't watch them destroy everything you loved about your home."

He had to be exaggerating. Honest Muslims could not do such a thing. Christian barbarians, yes. They'd enslaved her and inflicted misery. But her salvation depended on the South.

There, she would build her future, and this dangerous journey would give her the means to reclaim everything she'd lost.

III

LA MANCHA

AD 1094

CHAPTER SIX

SARAH

THE REFRESHING AIR Sarah had enjoyed closer to the city turned oppressive as the caravan crawled along the Spanish countryside. A dry heat permeated her dress and left her shift stifling. By the time they halted by a small stream in the late afternoon, Sarah had not only slung the cloak Yasin had provided over the back of their mule but had also taken to flapping the neck of her dress to let cool air in. If she once cared about the risk of accidentally exposing flesh before her fellow travelers, she could no longer remember. Her legs alternatively ached and throbbed and she yearned for a warm soak. Never before had she walked so far or for so long.

And this was only the first day of a journey that would take weeks.

While Yasin removed the rope tying the rolled blanket to the mule and began binding the animal's feet for the night, Sarah studied their fellow travelers as they set up camp. One man hammered wooden stakes on either side of his wagon's wheels with a rhythm that matched a song Sarah once heard over the palace walls in Granada. Beside him, the argument between a trader and two servants rose above the general chatter and braying of pack animals.

On the periphery of the camp, a group of women headed off in the same direction, their dresses fluttering in the faint breeze. Sarah tracked their progress for a moment before realizing they were heading to wash off.

Blessed relief. Allah be praised. Her fingers trembled at the thought of cool water rushing over her skin. She hesitated to prostrate herself before these people, but she could at least purify herself and pray silently.

"I'm going to the stream." She gestured to the empty waterskin sitting beside Yasin. "Hand me that and I'll fill it up."

"Good thinking."

She followed the women to a stream only a few strides wide that followed a depression in the surrounding plateau. In the distance, the southernmost peaks of the Central Mountains formed a deep purple backdrop for an endless sea of grass. Gaps in the foliage marked subtle shifts in elevation from the occasional slope or crevice.

Smiling to the others as she approached, Sarah slipped off her boots, lifted her dress, and stepped into the stream. The current was slow, but it felt heavenly as it caressed her aching feet.

"Mmm…"

After stuffing the hem of her dress into her belt, she crouched and submerged the waterskin. Water rushed up over the backs of her hands and wrists, sending a wave of relief up her arms. Already, the heat of the day began to fade. She began to hum a desert song about the comforts of a cool, comfortable tent.

Allah be praised.

Sarah rinsed herself without undressing while she prayed. The water chilled the iron bands around her wrists. Cooling them again in the morning might protect against the day's heat, at least for a time.

Yasin was stroking the mule behind its ear when she returned carrying the filled waterskin in both hands. He had finished tying the mule's feet together to prevent it from wandering off.

At her approach, he smirked. "There you are."

"I wasn't that long." She handed him the waterskin.

He slung it over the mule's back. "Come with me."

"Where?" She had walked enough for one day and just wanted to sleep.

He led her to a group standing near a wagon. One of them wore a belt with iron tools dangling from it. A craftsman of some sort? He stood among a few men and women in wool who wore wooden crosses on leather straps around their necks, probably pilgrims. Beside them stood a trio of priests in long black gowns, each recognizable by their tonsured heads.

But Sarah's attention was on the man in an expensive black and red muslin *jubba* and the woman who threaded her arm through his. Nobles wouldn't travel with a caravan like this, but perhaps they were a merchant and his wife? Or his mistress? She wore the most exquisite high-waisted, rich blue cotton dress. The expensive brocade along the neckline and hems looked as if it was softer than cat fur.

Sarah wanted one.

Then, she noticed the anvil on the ground before them.

Yasin leaned close. "Follow my lead."

"What is this?"

Instead of answering, he cleared his throat. "Under the eyes of God, I, Yasin ibn Faraj, a follower of Christ, wish to free my slave from all bonds of servitude."

Sarah gasped. What was he doing? He had no claim on her, no right to release her from anything. This…performance had no validity.

And yet, those listening watched her with solemn intensity. They believed this farce.

He turned to her. "Sarah al-Bayda, I hereby grant you your freedom."

She had dreamed of those words for so many years. The sound of them teased her ears and enfolded her in delight. It didn't matter that she would need to hear them again once they returned to Toledo. As far as these travelers knew, she would be a free woman.

Sarah glanced back as Yasin guided her toward the anvil. He pressed on her shoulders, compelling her to kneel beside it.

"Let her bonds be struck off," Yasin declared in a voice surprisingly well-suited for a poetic recitation.

Sarah felt at the bands around her wrists, pulse racing as the blacksmith withdrew a hammer and chisel from his toolbelt.

"God praises the man who frees a slave," said one of the priests, a portly man with a ring of gray hair encircling the bald patch atop his head. "May God bless you and all those who dwell in his grace."

"Amen." Yasin joined the others in making the sign of the cross.

She yearned to correct them, to declare her belief in the true faith, but just as she was about to speak, she stopped herself. These people would view her as a heathen who deserved slavery.

The blacksmith positioned her left wrist against the side of the anvil and laid the edge of the band along the top. "Hold still." His voice sounded like boots grinding on gravel.

The blacksmith's hammer seemed far away, as if she were watching the scene from beyond her body. *This can't be happening.* Any moment, they would laugh at her gullibility. Yet no one moved to interrupt when the blacksmith raised his hammer.

She glanced toward Yasin. Did he realize the punishment he risked by removing a slave's bands?

Defiance filled his eyes. He did understand, and he'd done it anyway.

Freedom.

The first strike of the hammer driving the chisel into the band made her jump. Her wrist jerked away from the anvil as the vibration traveled through the metal and tickled her wrist.

The blacksmith glared at her and repositioned it.

Holding her breath, she braced as blow after blow indented the iron band that had encircled her wrist since the slavers had affixed them in Barcelona. The blacksmith's muscled arm drove the wedge deeper and deeper, until the chisel finally broke through, severing the band. Easily twisting her wrist free, he cast the ruined length of iron aside and aligned her other band.

Sarah stared at her bare wrist, barely hearing the clinking of the hammer removing the other band. No longer would that rough metal burr tear her shawl. Her wrist felt so light that it seemed to ascend on its own accord. She had grown so used to the extra weight that she overextended as she flexed her liberated hand, making clunky and inelegant motions. She prayed she could adjust to regain her gracefulness.

"All done." The blacksmith flexed his shoulder and rubbed his arm.

She stared at her wrists as the assembled travelers offered their congratulations and departed, one at a time. Their words sounded like the mumblings of the scholars working in the translation room, dim and unintelligible. She ran her fingers along her arm from her elbows to her palms, retracing the smooth, unbroken path again and again, unable to believe it.

The iron bands that had marked her as a slave were gone.

YASIN

A half-dozen mercenaries stood by the edge of the camp with their hands wrapped around the hilts of their swords, staring out into the distance as the day's final light retreated in hues of pomegranate and red.

Yasin rubbed his smooth chin and watched them. When that many armed men looked anxious, he worried.

He approached them with a flagon from one of the pilgrims who now slept restlessly after overestimating his capacity for alcohol. The poor man thought Yasin was drinking as deeply as himself. "Peace be with you, gentlemen," Yasin greeted in Castilian.

The soldiers exchanged glances and frowned. One said something in a language that resembled Castilian but had too many differences for Yasin to understand.

The confusion melted from their faces when he repeated his greeting in Arabic.

"And upon you, be peace," answered one of them.

Yasin gestured beyond the campground. "Trouble on the horizon?"

A grizzled man with a scar that ran from his cheek to the top of his forehead turned. As he did, he smoothly adjusted the angle of his scabbard to avoid hitting his companions. He eyed the flagon. "That depends whether you're sharing your wine."

"Ah, but it's not mine." Yasin offered the same bright smile he'd given Sarah a day earlier. "It's yours."

Grunting and accepting it, the man raised the tip to his mouth.

Yasin jutted his chin at the wild grasses nearly concealed by the darkness. "Anything we should worry about?"

The man wiped his lips with the back of his hand and passed the flagon to one of his companions. "Bandits. Bears. Wolves. Boar."

Yasin's eyes searched the darkness. "You saw them?"

"No, but they're out there." The light from the dozen torches ringing the camp illuminated his narrowed eyes. "As are Christian *fuero* settlements and Muslim herders who regularly raid each other. They aren't particular about who they attack."

"Well…" Yasin's lip twitched. "I doubt they'd bother us with you fine gentlemen here."

"They won't." He shrugged. "But Almoravids would."

Yasin glanced south. The veiled ones were out there, somewhere between him and the sea.

"We're safe tonight, at least," the mercenary said. "A raiding party wouldn't risk traveling in the dark."

"Thank God." He'd sleep better tonight with that assessment. Perhaps these men simply tended toward the anxious. Yasin rubbed his hands together to banish the encroaching chill of night. He and Sarah had a long way to go, and he'd need his rest. "God keep you."

The man gave a perfunctory nod.

It was a good start, for the cost of another man's wine. He could do worse than having capable soldiers think well of him in case of trouble.

The dozens of animals and carts had trampled the tall grass enough that he could pick his footing through the makeshift camp without risk of a turned ankle. Travelers huddled around small campfires in cleared spaces. Bits of excited conversation suggested most didn't understand the hardship awaiting them. That would change. After a few more days on the road, weariness and frustration would douse their cheerfulness. It had for him during his long journey from Almeria. Travels began with eagerness and ended with gratitude.

The sharp baritone and bass of an argument from a campfire to the north set his heart thumping, and not even the subsequent laughter marking a harmless conversation could ease it. A quarrel could split the caravan, and that would be dangerous in a land so recently conquered. Nine years wasn't enough to pacify the uneasy subjects of the vast kingdom of Toledo.

Sarah sat beside a fire ringed by a number of tents. He made his way toward her.

Off to his right, two men were shaking their heads as they studied the harness affixing a chestnut horse to a wagon behind it. Yasin had seen that expression many times before.

They turned at his approach. One of them, a man with sunburned cheeks and a ragged beard speckled with gray, simply grunted when Yasin pressed his fingers to his lips, then his forehead.

Yasin suppressed a sigh at the reaction to his Mozarabic mannerisms, still so common after all these years. Well, he wasn't going to stop anointing his skin or begin wearing his hair like a shaggy mountain herder because these people assumed he was a Muslim.

"Peace be upon you." He made the sign of the cross. "Is there a problem, gentlemen?"

The other man, a few years younger than the first, relaxed. "This animal's been fighting me all day." He rubbed his arm. "My shoulder's throbbing from forcing it to walk straight."

Yasin studied the collar resting on the animal's shoulders and the series of straps that connected it to the wagon. The craftsman had cut costs by using split leather instead of the more expensive full grain, and a few of the straps were loose. One of them had rubbed the poor animal's stomach raw.

"This harness wasn't made for this animal, was it?"

The sunburned one narrowed his eyes. "You know of such things?"

"I do." Yasin reached into his *jubba* and withdrew his toolkit. "Adjusting the straps will make the horse more comfortable. He won't fight you." When he noticed their looks of surprise, he added, "As much."

"How much will that cost?" the bearded one grumbled.

"Not a thing." He needed friends on this journey more than coin. "Let me take a look."

One at a time, he adjusted the straps, threading new holes as necessary. He reassessed the fit after each adjustment until the entire harness was balanced and even. Finished, he rolled his tools back up and rubbed the horse's nose. He smiled when the animal responded with a happy whinny.

"See me if that doesn't help." With a wave, he departed for Sarah's fire.

Sarah had already claimed her satchel and kept it nearby. Her eyes followed him as he approached. "I don't understand you."

"Oh?" He rubbed his hands together above the flames. He hadn't realized how cold the night had grown until the heat banished it.

"You're a smuggler and thief, yet you help these people." She shook her head. "It's a contradiction."

He picked some stray grass blown by the wind off his *jubba*. "The world is filled with contradictions."

"So the histories suggest."

Yasin rose and crossed to the mule to escape the hellish thought that someone might one day record the events of his life.

She narrowed her eyes. "I can't decide whether you're a good man or a good liar."

A quick laugh burst from his lips. "Perhaps both." He retrieved the pack from atop the mule and laid it on the ground. "I only steal from those who can afford it. And men who spread lies about me."

She raised an eyebrow. "Were they lies?"

He unrolled the fabric, revealing four long wooden tent poles and two sacks of food. "As far as he knew, they were."

Her lips dimpled into a grin, and he had to remind himself that *qiyans* achieved that delightful effect only with great practice.

"These people are just trying to live their lives." He joined the poles to a common point to construct the tent frame. "If I exploited them, I'd be no better—"

"Than the Almoravids," she supplied.

He turned in surprise. She had been listening in Toledo. "Yes." He reached for the length of thick wool.

"Why are you reluctant to use your skills against the Valencians, then?"

He draped the fabric over the outside of the frame. Its fibers felt coarse beneath his fingers. The man who sold it to him insisted it would keep warmth in and the wind out. "I haven't met them."

She frowned. "Why should that matter?"

He recalled the young woman whose family had refused to let her join a convent and the officials who imposed restrictions on imports to line their own pockets. "It's all that matters." He tied the last knot.

"Why did you remove my iron bands?"

Her shift in topic had obviously meant to surprise him. He'd used the same tactic many times when probing for information.

He paused to consider his answer. "They almost led to trouble when we left Toledo, and I face tall enough odds without your status adding to them. The Valencians might restrict the movements of slaves. Your being free to move about the city could mean the difference between success and a trip to the noose." He offered a tentative smile. "I didn't accept our dear Castilian friend's pardon just to wind up in another prison."

Her eyes hardened as he spoke. "Is that your only reason?"

"Do you doubt it?"

She shrugged. "I'm not sure. As I said, I don't understand you."

When she resumed, her voice wavered, marking a striking deviation from two days of refined poise. "You don't behave as I expect, yet I must rely upon you. That's…unsettling."

She lowered her gaze to the fire. Yasin suspected this journey must be difficult for her. She deserved a more honest answer, if only to put her mind at ease.

He thought back to the circumstances that led to his first journey from Almeria. Did the markets of his home still remain silent, absent the poetry and music that filled his youth?

He sat beside her. "The thought of someone being compelled to act against her will does not sit well with me. Given the chance to prevent that, I had to take it."

She exhaled. "You're a better man than I first thought, Yasin ibn Faraj."

He chuckled softly, shaking his head. "You give me too much credit."

"How can it not be so, for you to worry about the plight of a slave?"

"You wouldn't say such things if you knew me in Almeria." He stared into the flames. "I used to believe slavery was the result of fool-ishness, suffered by men and women who made trouble for themselves."

The muscles of her neck tensed, but she confined her response to a simple, "What changed?"

He recalled his father's face contorted in rage in that alley. "Someone tried to take away my choice, about my faith, no less."

A man of principles would have objected long ago. No, he knew himself well enough to know the truth. Like all men and women, self-interest drove him. That deserved neither praise nor gratitude.

The heat from the dwindling fire made him squirm. Images of the past flickered in those flames. He sprung to his feet and approached the tent. "I note you brought nothing to sleep under at night."

"I expected to stop only in towns."

"Sometimes surely, but we'll be traveling through vast areas of wilderness."

"I didn't know." Stirring, she rubbed her shoulders. "You seem to know a lot about travel."

He shrugged. "You hear things, if you talk to people."

She arched an eyebrow. "I've never heard such things, and I talk to people."

He grinned. "Not the right people." He gestured to the tent. "It's undoubtedly warmer in there."

She rose and straightened her dress. "Thank you. That is most kind."

She strutted forward, only to halt when Yasin fell into step and started to remove his *jubba*.

"I intended to retire now," she said.

He savored her misunderstanding and offered his most innocent expression. "I agree. Tomorrow will be another long day. We should get to sleep." He pushed the flap aside and folded his *jubba* so they could both lay on it. He felt her eyes upon him as he stretched out on the ground. His feet and head nearly brushed either end.

"You intend to sleep inside?" Her voice dripped with alarm.

He almost laughed at her reaction. "Did you expect me to reward your lack of forethought by giving you my tent?"

"But you said—"

"That a young woman shouldn't spend the night in the cold."

She eyed the tent, then Yasin himself. "You wish to bed me, after all."

She did have a high opinion of herself! "I give you my oath I will make no overtures until you ask me."

Though she picked at the edge of her shawl, she made no move to enter.

He sighed. Now that he had reclined, his muscles felt the fatigue of every mile of the long walk. "Look, you can either sleep in the cold or share the warmth with me. Your choice."

She glanced at the fire. It had diminished in just the past few minutes. With a sigh, she crawled inside. As she settled down, she tugged her skirts away from him, carefully folding them so no part touched him. It took four attempts to arrange her hair before she finally stopped fussing and settled with her head upon his *jubba*. He hoped she slept more soundly than that.

"Your word?"

"My word," he promised.

"Good." She rolled over to widen the space between them.

Light and shadow from the campfire danced over the tent flap to the rhythm of Sarah's anxious breathing.

The mischief in him kindled. "You smell nice."

"Ugh." She scoffed and wiggled farther away.

His grin lasted until his body surrendered to fatigue and he fell asleep.

YASIN

Bleating animals and the hollow sound of wooden poles knocking against each other accompanied the arrival of morning. Fortunately, the chatter of the other travelers preparing for the day's journey lacked the cries of alarm that would have heralded trouble.

The scent of fresh stew hung on the air. As Yasin roused, a wooden spoon clanged against a metal pot. He'd have to charm a bowl out of whoever was tending it. Sarah would probably want some, too.

He stretched, but he withdrew his hands again when they collided with the fabric of the tent. Eyes snapping open, he surveyed the tent frame for any damage. He was a skilled leatherworker, but he knew nothing about joinery. If the heavy supports fell, they could land on Sarah and hurt her.

He tried to nudge her, but his hand came down on matted grass. Scrambling to his knees, he searched the corners of the tent.

She was gone.

He never should have removed her iron bands. Her *qiyan* training had fooled him, hiding the depth of her hunger for freedom. He had been so wrong to think he could appease it by negotiating her release upon returning to Toledo.

She had absconded in the night, and he'd have to find this codex alone. The indecipherable scribbles identifying it might as well be scratches on the bottoms of boots. The library would have thousands of books just like it. A quarter hour or a thousand years, it wouldn't matter. He'd never know which one it was.

He pressed his hand to his chest to still the thumping of his heart. Gonzalo's warning screamed in his mind. The Castilian would revoke his pardon and hunt him down.

He had to find her. If she'd stolen a horse, someone would notice. If not, she couldn't have gotten far. Someone must have seen her.

The sunlight blinded him as he pushed aside the flap and stumbled out into the morning. His mule was chewing on some grass nearby. She hadn't taken it. He'd have no choice but to ride it to pursue her, no matter how much it exhausted the poor animal.

The camp revealed no signs of agitation. Travelers packed their wagons and disassembled their tents. In the distance, the blacksmith kept time with the hammering of his anvil. He was probably repurposing Sarah's bands into new buckles for a harness or a pin for a wagon. A few cooking pots sat over crackling fires, but no outrage about a stolen animal rose above the muted morning chatter.

A woman's tinkling laughter caressed his ears and drew his attention. Which of his traveling companions produced such a delightful sound? He circled his tent, searching for the source.

He found it beside a wagon.

Sarah sat with legs folded to one side beneath her, pulling a comb missing several teeth through her hair. After finishing with one strand, she flipped it aside and moved to another. Her mouth alternated between bright smiles and silent conversation with a woman loading a nearby wagon.

Relief drained the tension from his muscles so quickly that it left a shiver in its wake. She had sworn her help, and while many might violate such an oath, clearly she would not. It seemed she had not only studied *adab* but also obeyed its principles.

She was picking at a knot by her right temple when he approached.

"Good morrow," he greeted.

"Good morrow." Her lips still bore a fading smile. She ran a hand through her hair, and it passed through smoothly, falling from her hand like a cascade of water.

"You woke early."

"*Sal—*" Her eyes darted toward the woman working by the wagon. "Prayer."

Yasin swallowed, comprehending the meaning behind that interrupted word. If she hesitated to mention *salat*, Arabic prayer, then she had decided to hide her faith from her fellow travelers. That decision couldn't have been easy for a devout Muslim.

Yasin swept his gaze over the camp. He wondered whether she realized how sensible her caution was. Almoravids occasionally infiltrated caravans to assess their value before attacking, and these people could eject them if they discovered her faith. He should have thought of it.

"Prayer soothes the soul." He forced a smile. "But it's shame to squander the rare gift of an uninterrupted night's sleep."

"I wouldn't know." She swept the comb through her hair without hitting a knot. Her lips dimpled into a smile. "Your snoring kept waking me."

He knelt on the ground beside her and freed his *jubba* from beneath his knees. "When I woke and you weren't there, I thought you might have fled."

Her hands halted. "Because of the bands?"

He nodded.

"You said something similar in the library." She pulled the comb through her hair yet again before turning to him. "But I would never do such a thing."

"Because of *adab*?"

Her lips drew taut. "Because those bands weren't what prevented my escape."

That wasn't the response he'd expected. "What did, then?"

"For all your charm, you know nothing of a woman's troubles."

He repressed a swell of pride. She thought him charming! "What do you mean?"

She lowered her hands. "Men can wander through the world without any care for their safety."

"That's not true—"

"You told me you came from Almeria. Did you travel with others?"

He frowned. "I was supposed to."

"Oh?"

"My brother and sister. At the last moment, they…" He swallowed, remembering his father's taunts. "They didn't join me."

She raised an eyebrow. "Did that stop you from leaving?"

He lowered his gaze, conceding the point.

"You can work, fight, travel." She shook her head. "That's why I admire the boldness of *adab*. The freedom of unleashing one's spirit so completely."

"Surely a woman can do the same." The fragments of understanding he'd gleaned from their exchanges in the library and in the square conflicted with her words now. "Neither horse nor trail considers one's sex."

"But people do. People suspect a woman of evil if she travels on her own. With no one to avenge or defend her, anyone she passes might accost her without fear of retaliation." She glanced around before lowering her voice. "And I'm still a slave. If I fled, I'd spend every day fearing capture. If I was captured, I'd be flogged and sold to a brothel." She looked away. "Men need not worry about such things."

Sarah's words filled Yasin with a growing disquiet. She referenced those horrors as calmly as she might describe the weather.

"If I help you, I'll have the means to make a respectable match and build a life for myself." Her eyebrows knitted together. "Freedom alone isn't enough. The discomfort of living under heathens is nothing compared to the danger an unaccompanied woman faces in this world."

He thought back to his sister, Amira. For three years, he'd thought fine words had weakened her will. Perhaps he'd judged her too harshly. He would have protected her and remained at her side, but what if something had happened to him? She would have been alone in Toledo. In Almeria, she had her family, their community of Mozarabs, and even, perhaps, the families of the Muslim leatherworkers and their neighbors to safeguard her. Yet, he had expected her to abandon it all with him.

"I don't expect you to understand," Sarah said. "Your life is different than mine."

It was, he admitted to himself, in more ways than she meant. But perhaps he could understand enough. "It couldn't have been easy to leave Toledo with a stranger." He regretted taunting her last night.

She pressed her hands against her stomach and smoothed out her dress. A wave of emotions passed over her face too quickly to identify. "It was necessary."

Necessary. What had she thought of him when she'd first heard about this mission? She had every reason to judge him a criminal and a villain who would exploit her. No wonder she'd made it clear she wouldn't lay with him.

He rose and placed his hand against his chest. "I will never abuse or harm you." He tried to pour his sincerity into his words, both to ease Sarah's mind and to atone for the discourtesy he'd carried for his sister all these years.

The humor pulling at the corners of Sarah's lips suggested he had failed, but her words filled him with an unexpected thrill. "I'm beginning to realize that."

SARAH

Before the caravan departed the verdant grasses of the Tagus Valley, the mercenaries organized a hunting party. Yasin insisted he was useless as a hunter, but he offered to bind any damaged spears and repurpose his leatherworking tools to craft arrows.

The hunters rode ahead, leaving the caravan to crawl out of the tall grasses and onto the more arid plateau of La Mancha. The flat scrubland stretched out in all directions, broken only by the mountains of central Iberia, barely visible to the north. A breeze rolled across from the south, bringing the scent of olives to tantalize Sarah's nostrils, though the source remained frustratingly out of sight.

Not everything remained so hidden. A pair of scorched wheels and the splintered remains of a wagon lay spilled along the caravan route.

"Can you imagine your wagon catching fire out in this wilderness, all alone?" she asked.

"I doubt they were alone." His voice sounded like an ill-tuned oud.

"What do you mean?"

"They were attacked."

"Attacked?"

"Fear not." He pointed to the weeds growing between the spokes of the wheels. "It happened some time ago, probably last year."

That answer did not reassure her.

By the time the caravan caught up with the hunters, they had killed a boar, a stag, and a mountain sheep with long, curling horns. The small quantity of available salt preserved some of the meat, but Sarah helped the other women cook and dry the rest. Between Yasin's services and Sarah's labor, they earned a share of the food sufficient for many days.

Though, Sarah earned more than a full belly. The next night, one of her fellow cooks invited her and Yasin to share a campfire with her group of pilgrims. Her skin tingled with excitement at the offer. Not since her time in the palace of Granada had Sarah received such an invitation, albeit from another servant. She wouldn't squander the opportunity for companionship, even with a Christian.

Two men and a woman chatted together on the other side of the fire, ignoring her. Yasin sat out of earshot beside their mule with his toolkit unfurled on the short grass before him. His attention was fixed on repairing a damaged belt laid across his lap.

She had a little time, at least, alone with the young woman who had invited her. Sarah approached with her comb in hand. "Thank you for your hospitality."

The woman tucked a stray lock of blonde hair beneath her hood and gave a quick smile. "The Lord says we should offer generosity."

"Then let me repay that kindness." She raised the comb and gestured to the tendril, which had fallen back out again. "Your hair is beautiful. May I comb it out for you?"

Eyes brightening, the woman cast a hesitant glance across the fire toward the other pilgrims. After a moment, she nodded and removed her hood, releasing a cascade of fine hair the color of wheat.

Sarah settled beside her and raised the comb. "It's missing several teeth, but it should serve." She began to pick at the tangles accumulated from being constrained all day.

The pilgrim jumped as Sarah touched her hair, but after a few strokes, she began to settle. Her eyes remained fixed on Yasin in the distance. "Your former master dresses like a heathen. Is he truly a Christian?"

Sarah suppressed a smile. The question would undoubtedly unsettle Yasin, given his flight to preserve his faith. Yet, the short cut of his kinky hair and his Islamic *jubba* rendered him indistinguishable from the Muslims of Granada. He needed only line his eyes with kohl to be the very image of Ziryab, the great poet.

"Yes," Sarah reassured. "His faith is genuine."

The tension drained from her companion's face and shoulders, making her slouch. Though her face bore no blotches from laboring in the sun, her posture showed no sign of refinement either. Her hair, however, was magnificent, untangling with the lightest tug. Sarah wished hers did the same.

"How do you come by the caravan?"

The pilgrim grasped the crudely carved cross hanging from her neck and pressed it to her lips. "We made a pilgrimage to Toledo."

Sarah's hand halted at the end of a stroke for a long moment before she remembered to resume. The men who had enslaved her and the priests who commanded her bore crosses like that. She would have to guard her words and actions carefully. Who knew how these pilgrims might react to discovering her faith?

"I wasn't aware Toledo attracted pilgrims."

The woman bobbed her head up and down, causing Sarah to lose her grip on the comb. It dangled for a moment at a knot before falling away.

"It is a holy city, the first reclaimed from the heathens." Her words came quickly now. "I wove an extra length of cloth each month and squeezed an extra serving out of my food for four years, all to afford this pilgrimage."

Sarah was glad the woman couldn't see her eyes to read the surprise in them. This woman had spent nearly as much time earning her way to Toledo as Sarah had spent escaping it. Why would anyone wish to visit Toledo when they could instead visit Granada, Seville, or Cordoba?

With her comb, Sarah parted the woman's hair on the other side. After a few adjustments, she studied her work and gave a curt nod. "If you put your hood on the right way, you can let just a little show."

Yasin arrived with the repaired belt hanging from his fist and knelt before the fire. "Good evening, ladies," he greeted in a throaty voice. His lips curled into a smile as he eyed the pilgrim.

The woman bowed her head in a greeting but showed no sign of warming to his attention. Sarah smirked. Evidently, not everyone found him irresistible.

Mirth tinting her voice, Sarah asked the woman, "Did you find what you sought in Toledo?"

A sigh turned into a faint smile as the woman stared into the fire. "God was present in the buildings, in the streets. Even the water flowing down the river tasted refreshing and cleansed my soul."

Yasin cleared his throat. Mischief glinted in his eyes.

Sarah bit her lip, recalling the sewers that carried the city's filth away and deposited it in the Tagus. Hopefully, the woman spoke of clean water flowing into the city.

"I shivered with wonder when I entered the cathedral," the pilgrim continued. "Some of the others wept. I couldn't believe its beauty."

Sarah's nostrils flared in jealousy. It wasn't fair that the people who had created such a wonder could no longer enjoy it. "The cathedral was the Great Mosque before the conq—capture of the city."

She regretted the words the moment she uttered them. Discussing that subject was reckless. She risked everything out of pride.

However, the young pilgrim neither recoiled nor bristled. Instead, she simply twisted to face Sarah. "Is that why so many heathens prayed in the square outside?"

Sarah forced the muscles of her neck to relax. "It is."

The young woman spared a glance for her companions before leaning closer. "The priest in my village teaches that Muslims are corrupted by the devil's lies." Head dipping closer, she further lowered her voice. "But no faith that creates something so heavenly can be truly evil."

Sarah would never have expected such a sentiment from a Christian pilgrim. The priests who had witnessed her fraudulent emancipation would likely declare this woman a heretic for those words. Sarah glanced at the other pilgrims across the fire. The crackling flames filled the silence, punctured occasionally by their conversation. They didn't seem to have overheard.

The part of her that had blossomed in Baghdad yearned to encourage this woman's doubts. Sarah could reveal her faith and ask whether this woman found her evil or depraved. Sarah might very well sway her, just as others had done for her in Baghdad.

But that was too dangerous, and she wouldn't make the same reckless mistake as earlier. Silence was safer.

Yasin, however, evidently hadn't learned that lesson. "The Muslims created much of worth," he said loudly enough to draw the attention of the others.

"You admire them?" a balding man asked in a shrill voice.

"I admire beautiful things, no matter their source." Yasin gestured toward Sarah. "Consider my companion here."

She gasped, unable to believe he would expose her in such a way. Did the man have no sense, to call her a Muslim among all these devout Christians?

Yasin continued before she could respond. "Despite her humble attire, she possesses the most exquisite oud I've ever seen. Firm horse-hair strings, and the smoothest hardwood."

Her oud!

The balding man leaned forward, eyes bright. "Are you a musician?"

The danger having passed, Sarah bowed her head as she exhaled her fading anxiety. "I can play a little."

"She's being modest." Yasin turned to her. "Why not show them your skill?"

Glaring at him, she resolved to poke him awake tonight. His words had nearly caused a religious argument, and now he was using her to deflect it. She was here to identify a text, not save him from his mistakes.

"Please?" Yasin spoke the word softly, yet with a vulnerable tenderness.

The sincerity in his eyes made Sarah pause. He had undoubtedly used her to distract the pilgrims, but she now recalled his curiosity at her bringing the oud. Could he possibly want to hear her play, too?

"Oh, please play," the blonde pilgrim pleaded.

Every eye waited on her response.

"Very well." She could hardly refuse.

A ripple of excited chatter spread among the pilgrims. Two of them shouted others over.

Rising, she crossed to the tent Yasin had erected along the periphery. It sat close enough to benefit from the light of the campfire, but far enough that crossing the short distance gave space for her irritation to grow.

These pilgrim fanatics couldn't possibly appreciate the nuance in her tonal blending or the deftness of her chord transitions. In fact, her courtly compositions would probably offend them for being too Islamic.

Her oud sat just inside the tent flap. She frowned. She had placed it along the back by where she'd laid her head. Every night before she fell asleep, she protectively looped her arm around the strap. Yasin must have moved it.

This was no panicked tactic to sidestep trouble. He had arranged circumstances to hear her perform, even risking a quarrel to do it.

The thought filled her with a strange excitement. He wanted to hear her play? Then she would ruin him to every other musician.

Several others had approached the fire by the time she returned. As she approached, a hush descended, broken only by the occasional crackle of the burning logs. They were open to her, waiting to receive the magic she would weave. Their eager attention intoxicated her. She felt unstoppable, infallible, beneath their gazes. She settled her legs beneath her and nestled the oud on her lap. Her fingers tingled with anticipation.

In the Great Market, she'd been surrounded by shouts and negotiations and entreaties in half a dozen languages. Not for many years—since her trials in Baghdad—had so many waited for her in silent anticipation. She would have never expected to experience it in a camp filled with Christians.

She could live within this sensation forever.

Closing her eyes, she began to dance her fingers across the strings.

YASIN

In the summer of Yasin's twelfth year, a young Egyptian arrived in Almeria after fleeing the jealous husband of his lover, the daughter of one of the sultan's chief advisors. Rumors swirled that he had belonged to an ancient noble house and once owned three estates, but he had arrived with only the worn clothes on his back and an oud with a missing sliver of wood from its neck.

Yasin would often listen in hushed reverence to that Egyptian's playing in the busy marketplace. Chords of airy delight and the deepest, soul-breaking sorrow would drip like blood from the wounded instrument and sting Yasin's very soul. That music had shown him the magic of a vibrating string. It was the most beautiful sound Yasin had ever heard, better even than a woman moaning in delight.

Until tonight.

Sarah's fingers flew over the strings like a breath of air rippling over fine fur. The instrument sighed and cried out in her delicate grasp, filling the air with plucked chords that set Yasin's heart beating faster and faster. Though he had witnessed an instrument weep and rejoice in the hands of a master, his heart leapt with every rise and collapsed with each fall of the rhythm.

Her voice, strong and smooth, sang the lament of a young woman who had lost her lover. It followed the blended Andalusi style, mixing airy metaphors and allusions of classical Islamic music with the repeating refrains more common in the peninsula's provincial towns.

No one spoke. The flames of the fire reflected in their glistening eyes. Even the normally restless animals stilled at the delicate work of her lips and fingers. Nothing dared to interrupt.

Yasin had heard this song often in Almeria, but when Sarah played it, he felt the longing ache of separation. The hollowness in the soul of the woman in the song resonated within him, stoked by notes that set his breath rushing. The lament on her lips reminded him of the agony of his own exile, the fear that he would never again see his sister or mother. He had lost those who loved him best of all.

Sarah transformed before his eyes as she played. Gone was the irritation at his barbs and the wounds of her slavery. Those cares had faded from her expression. Her posture grew more confident with each note until she glowed more brightly than the flames beside her. He could not look away.

What strange arts had taught her such skill?

She had been right about the oud. In her hands it wove powerful magic that quickened the heart and squeezed the soul. He imagined that the Almoravids could hear it all the way back in Almeria, that it made them clutch at the sky in impotent rage. They had destroyed his home, but Sarah's music defied their power.

And that thought made him smile despite the ache in his heart and the sad tale of love denied.

CHAPTER SEVEN

YASIN

They saw the smoke on the horizon three days later, a column of healthy, white puffs that blended with high clouds. A wave of excitement spilled through the column as the travelers prepared for the town ahead. They would reach it before nightfall.

Yasin greeted the news with an exhausted sigh. They couldn't arrive a moment too soon. He'd thought his previous flight had prepared him for the rigors of a long journey, but after six days on the road, his feet throbbed and his back and shoulders ached from leading a mule that kept trying to chew grass instead of advancing. Evidently, crafting leather hadn't kept him as fit as he'd believed. Acknowledging that unfortunate fact only added to his list of woes.

When the sixth rider broke from the main body to gallop ahead, Sarah tugged on Yasin's arm. "Where are they going?"

As the well-muscled horse receded into the distance, the rider's money pouch bounced heavily against his leg with each stride. Yasin would give anything to relieve the aches in his feet with just a few hours' use of that horse. "They're riding ahead to arrange lodgings."

"Should we do the same? I miss sleeping on something other than hard earth." Sarah's hair spilled away as she stretched, exposing the silky, unblemished skin where her neck met her shoulder.

His fingers twitched, and he restrained the desire to caress it. "I don't have a horse."

She patted the mule on the head. "What about him?"

"I won't risk overloading the poor animal."

She eyed yet another rider rushing ahead of the caravan. "I would."

"We'll make do." Yasin rubbed his chin and recoiled at the stubble. If he didn't find a razor, he'd soon resemble one of these Castilian mountain herders. His *qamisa* was horribly wrinkled, too. Many more days of sleeping on the ground and he'd have no refinements left.

An hour before dusk, the caravan reached the town, a collection of two-dozen *tapia* rammed-earth buildings and a single stone abbey. The absence of wood-framed structures didn't surprise him. Earthen buildings offered blessed relief in the hot summers, and while he'd seen plenty of grass and bushes the previous six days, they hadn't passed a forest large enough to supply timber framing.

The settlement appeared to be only a few years old and was probably one of the *fuero* towns the Castilian king had authorized in the wake of Toledo's capture. No moss grew on the structures, and the stone of both the abbey and the central well bore no damage. A pungent wave of animal urine suggested a nearby tannery, but despite the unmistakable outline of a brick kiln, Yasin saw no craft stalls.

Sarah's head swiveled as she studied the structures. "Perhaps we can still find a room."

Groups of travelers splintered off, and waiting residents welcomed them inside after receiving handfuls of coins.

"I doubt we could afford it, considering these prices."

"You can tell what they're paying from here?" Her voice contained a satisfying awe.

"Oh, yes." Having learned to distinguish silver from gold across a crowded market, he had no trouble counting the clinking silver across this small square.

"Impressive." She rubbed absently at her thigh. "Where's the inn?"

"Safely tucked away in Valencia." He shook his head. "You won't find them outside the great cities."

Her eyes widened. "Travelers' rests?"

"I'm afraid not."

She turned when another group peeled away to greet its local hosts. "A tent again, then." The weariness of her sigh matched that of his throbbing feet.

"God provides." He offered a broad smile. "And if not, Yasin ibn Faraj will." He swung the mule around and headed for the abbey.

"Blasphemer." Her eyebrows peaked just enough to suggest skeptical curiosity rather than outrage.

What wood the town had was concentrated in a fence surrounding an extensive garden on the northern side of the road. Within it, a grove of fruit trees wrapped around one face of a long, squat limestone building with a wooden cross topping its peaked roof.

Yasin grunted and shielded his eyes from the unnatural brightness of the reflective limestone walls. He hadn't seen such an unblemished building in years: the brown *tapia* of Almeria and Toledo absorbed sunlight. This abbey couldn't be more than ten years old, with no mossy growth to soothe the eye.

"Is something wrong?" Sarah asked.

"Nothing."

A few tonsured monks in black habits tended the garden. Unlike the fine cotton robes and high-quality leather boots of most religious orders in Castile, these monks wore simple homespun wool and leather sandals that bore the scuffs and tears of hard use and frequent mending. They paid Yasin and Sarah no attention as they approached the great wooden doors of the abbey. Nor did they look up when a third monk positioned a wheelbarrow nearby and filled it with withered vines and prunings.

Yasin smiled. He'd shown similar concentration more than once as he skived or beveled a piece of leather. Though he could never embrace their celibacy, he could admire their dedication to their craft.

He glanced back at Sarah and swallowed. "Follow my lead." He tied the mule up to a post embedded in the ground and knocked on the wooden door.

An elderly man with tonsured gray hair answered. Despite his age, his eyes seemed alert. "God's blessing upon you."

Yasin bent and kissed the monk's hand when it began to rise. "And upon you, Brother."

"You aren't from the village." He frowned when he lowered his eyes to Yasin's empty hands. "Why do you disturb our contemplation?"

"We are travelers from Toledo. Our caravan just arrived." He lowered his gaze and folded his hands before him. The sounds of horses being led to stables and hitching posts tickled his ears. "We beg your hospitality."

The ancient eyes widened, and the monk glanced beyond them at the square. "You are traveling alone?"

"Myself and my wife."

Sarah gasped beside him.

"Please forgive her," Yasin added. "We are recently married, and being referred to as a wife still surprises her."

The man settled his gaze on Yasin's *jubba*. "You…are a Christian?"

He repressed a sigh. These Castilians seemed incapable of separating a man's faith from his choice in clothing. Reaching beneath his *qamisa*, Yasin withdrew the cross at his neck. "Yes, Brother. As is my wife."

"And yet you lack the coin to afford lodgings in town." The monk's lips carried the hint of a scowl. "What circumstances caused you to leave Toledo?"

Yasin caught the implication. "Almoravid raiders attacked our village beyond the Tagus three weeks ago."

"Muslim devils!" The monk crossed himself.

Yasin clenched his teeth to keep from smiling. Mentioning Muslims made most Christians—particularly those who had never lived beside them—forget everything else, even suspicions about a potentially scandalous couple.

Beside him, Sarah glared at him with all the rage of a Mediterranean storm. He wondered which of his comments she would harangue him about first.

But he still had to address the man's suspicions. "We passed through Toledo with our few possessions that weren't burned or looted. I'm a master leatherworker and hope to start over in the village of my wife's family, near Valencia."

"Leatherworker?" The man flexed his fingers at his side.

Yasin seized on the interest and reached into his *jubba*. "Indeed. I'd be honored to do any mending your community may require." He withdrew his rolled toolkit.

"On behalf of my order, I offer you hospitality." The monk again made the sign of the cross before beckoning them inside.

Only the structure's exterior was limestone. The interior walls were made of the same mix of *tapia* as the other buildings in the small town. Yasin suspected the monks themselves had constructed them, for they were irregular enough that the trio's footsteps didn't echo off the textured walls.

The monk led them to a simple wooden door with a latch that slid into a groove in the wall. It had no lock, but even if it did, the effort of a few minutes would flake away enough of the brittle wall to expose the entire latch and render such a lock useless. The room itself had a single cot and no other furniture, but it was dry.

"Thank you," Yasin said.

The elderly monk nodded. "I'll return after I've collected sandals from my brothers for you to mend."

Yasin raised his fingers but halted before performing his usual salutation. These up-country Castilians had likely settled here after the capture of Toledo and probably weren't used to Andalusi gestures. Instead, he simply bowed.

Without another word, the monk exited and closed the door behind him.

When Sarah inhaled to speak, Yasin raised a hand and pointed to the door. The footsteps softened as the monk receded down the hall. Only when they had faded entirely did Yasin lower his hand.

"Your wife!" Her voice was somewhere between a whisper and a hiss.

Laughter bubbled up from deep in his chest.

"What's so funny?"

He sobered after a long breath. "Monks would never permit unmarried men and women to stay together under their roof."

"You could have called me your sister."

He grinned. "That wouldn't have gotten a reaction from you."

She grunted.

He rubbed his hands together. "I expected you'd take more offense at my exploiting their hatred of Muslims."

"That part, I understood. You needed to prove you aren't an Almoravid devil." She had taken offense, after all.

"It got us through the door."

She sighed. "I just wish it didn't involve stoking prejudice against Muslims."

Yasin raised a finger. "Not Muslims. Almoravids."

"Is there a difference?"

"Oh, yes."

She shrugged and glanced away. "I doubt they recognize it."

He crossed his arms, though it likely wrinkled his *jubba* further. "You're probably right."

Some of the tension drained from her stance. "I am thankful to sleep indoors," she said in a friendlier tone.

He couldn't help himself. "And since there's only one cot, you'll be warm, snuggled up against me tonight, dear wife."

She scoffed and rubbed her shoulders.

He grinned at the reaction. "Collect our things while I see what work these monks have for me."

Her fingers picked at a crease as she straightened the folds of her dress. "Will you be long?"

His eyes widened. "I knew you'd grow fond of me."

Her sigh echoed. "Yasin…"

"You'll have time," he reassured. "After I've finished with the monks, I'll visit the local church."

She wrinkled her nose. "The church?"

Though he smirked, the expression didn't reach his eyes. "Every soul needs refreshing from time to time." He looked away quickly. "And I'll visit the alehouse afterward, so I'll probably be quite late. If you get hungry, eat some of our provisions."

"How do you know there's an alehouse?"

He chuckled. "There's always an alehouse."

Her expression darkened. "And you're the kind of man that must always find it?"

The implication grated on him like a smooth boot on gravel. "I need to know what dangers lay before us, and the people of this town can tell me, particularly when they're drunk. So, I go where I must."

She sighed. "I only meant—"

"I know what you meant." He interrupted her with a raised hand. "I scorn nothing that brings joy, but nor does it rule me as you fear."

She paused. "I hope that's true."

"Judge that once you hear what I discover." Yasin grinned. "And whether I can remember it in the morning."

SARAH

Sarah closed the door on Yasin and breathed a sigh of exhausted relief. She stood with her hands pressed against the smooth wood until his footsteps faded entirely.

Finally, alone.

She scraped her fingertips over the solid smooth grain of the door. It felt reassuringly substantial and separated her from the noise of the caravan, the stench of animals, and the rough stranger upon whom she now utterly relied.

Sighing, she hiked up the skirt of the itchy woolen dress and slipped off her boots. The cool floor soothed her sore toes as she padded to the center of the room. She would have to find a stream to soak in later. Perhaps she might even find cotton wraps to protect them from further blistering.

Retracing her and Yasin's steps into this room, Sarah identified East and raised her hands, palms-out, on either side of her head. She could conduct the full prayer now, even if she couldn't cleanse herself properly. The Asr prayer was a silent one.

Allah is the greatest.

She shifted to clasp her left hand with her right before her. A thrill of delight filled her as she noticed the absence of the iron bands on her wrists.

In the name of Allah, most gracious, most merciful. All praise is due to Allah, lord of all that exists...

She progressed through the prayer, accompanied only by the sound of her shifting wool dress as she first bent at the waist, then knelt and prostrated herself. Each gesture and phrase filled her with strength and eased the burden of her travels.

Finishing, she leaned back on her folded legs and exhaled a relieved breath. Allah was still with her on this vast plateau, surrounded by heathens and far from any mosque.

Imagining how these monks would react to learning that a Muslim prayed to Allah inside their abbey made her smile. They'd assuredly revoke their hospitality, and she'd have to sleep in that tent again. It might be worth it, if only to gloat over what she'd done.

But then she thought of the grass reclaiming the burned wagon wheel. The pilgrims might shun her if they learned her religion, and she didn't want to face the dangers of the road alone. Concealing her faith seemed wrong, but it was necessary. Yasin would probably congratulate her for the practicality of that thought.

Yasin. His smug smirk and casual manner more resembled a bather at the *hamam* than the manly strut of the emir and his courtiers. Yet, alone among Christians, Yasin hadn't mistreated her for her faith. He spat vitriol about the Almoravids at every opportunity, but not for their beliefs.

Raising her hand to investigate tension around her mouth, she discovered she was smiling. What was happening to her?

Though he could turn a phrase, he used that skill to lie and irritate. His every word seemed designed to grate on her, and his recklessness frightened her. When Allah had blessed him with his freedom, he had endangered himself further by revenging himself upon his accusers. As much as she relished the removal of her slave's bracelets, he had risked punishment with that act. He lived on the edge of oblivion, and she feared what would happen if he fell off.

And yet, despite his taunts, he had behaved respectfully at night and had paid no heed to her faith. Those facts distinguished him from every other man in Toledo.

She eyed her boots lying on the floor, gifts from him along with her traveling cloak. He had provided for her comfort after only a brief meeting. And the way he'd soothed the poor beast whose harness he'd adjusted, he evidently possessed a degree of compassion.

She raised her eyes to the ceiling. She was in Allah's hands, far from the great cities that had been her home. She only prayed that the hints of virtue within Yasin were strong enough to see them through this quest.

YASIN

Yasin barked a laugh and raised his wooden mug quickly enough that a little ale sloshed over the side and dampened his fingers. He licked them clean before drinking. The bitter ale had a pleasing apple aftertaste but stung as it surged down his throat.

Over the rim, he studied his two new friends. Shaggy hair in the style of the northern mountains hung down over the forehead of the closer one, a Castilian with a thick beard flecked with gray. The Leonese man beside him bore a perpetual sneer and whistled from a missing canine when he spoke. Yasin suspected either could crush his bones; albeit not a difficult task, but one made easier by their thick forearms.

They were exactly the sort of men who knew the dangers—and opportunities—of the area. Though wary at first, they softened when he flashed a few copper coins for a round of drinks. In Toledo, he'd have had to flash silver.

That was good. His coin pouch was draining quickly. The mule and tent had cost more than anticipated. Nor had he expected to buy Sarah boots or a traveling cloak when he'd shaken Gonzalo's hand, but those expenses were necessary to get her to Valencia alive.

Once again, he imagined his promised reward. Would gold shimmer in the light more brightly than silver? Only once before had he heard the intoxicating clink of two gold coins striking each other. A tingle crawled up his back as he imagined a cascade of it.

His companion's mugs gave a hollow thud as they struck the wooden table. Yasin lowered his own, still half-full. His fingers were beginning to tingle, and he hadn't even finished his second drink. He'd have a headache in the morning without some small ale to keep it at bay, but Yasin doubted this alehouse had any. The dozen other customers were all drinking the same strong brew.

"Growin' wheat ain't like herdin' sheep." The Castilian's thick accent bore indications of Aragonese and resembled that of an apprentice of Master Sanchez who hailed from Burgos.

"In what way?" Yasin pulled his eyes away from a woman in a delightfully thin shift who was circulating through the crowd. Even the most mundane conversations could yield important information, and he'd finally loosened their tongues.

"You gotta feed sheep, keep 'em from wandrin' off. Takes attention and a keen eye. Then there's sheerin', slaughterin' and preservin' the meat." He jutted a finger toward the door. "But wheat don't go nowhere. After you plant and make sure it's got water, you just sit and worry."

"I hate the worrying," the Leonese echoed. "If it isn't drought, then it's travelers tromping through my fields." His missing tooth made him whistle his *s*'s.

The alcohol had begun its work for them to say such things to traveler. "Why not bring sheep down from the north?"

The Castilian chuckled and gave the Leonese a bemused grin. "Can't herd and farm jest by meself, and wheat makes more coin than sheep. The man recruitin' for this *fuero* spoke true 'bout that."

The Leonese grunted. "But it's only profitable in years without Muslim raids."

Yasin clenched his mug, but he restrained a flare of anger at the Almoravids as he drained the remainder of his ale. The mug struck the table with a dull thud. "They raid often?"

"Often enough that I'm counting seasons," the Leonese said. "Two more years and I can head north again free and clear."

The king's *fuero* charters filled the lands reclaimed from the Muslims with Christian settlers. While each had different terms, few prevented settlers from selling their lands. Criminals, however, needed to reside in a *fuero* for ten years to have their crimes expunged. Only a truly dark past would induce this man to risk his life on the unstable border.

And Yasin had started to suspect he was wasting his time tonight…

"They watch the roads?" he pressed.

The Leonese nodded. "No warning, either. They'll ride through the night, hit a caravan, then head south with plunder and slaves. The bigger the caravan, the more interest it attracts."

"Shame, thinkin' o' those fine things headin' south."

"And those poor ladies as heathen slaves," said the Leonese.

The Castilian grunted and pushed his chair back. "I'll get the next round." Rising, he gathered the mugs.

As the man turned to leave, Yasin noticed familiar scratches marring the smooth leather of his belt on the left side. Scabbards made such marks. Yasin had seen them many times when Master Sanchez did repairs for the city guards.

These man wore swords, and often.

Yasin supposed *fueros* would need to defend themselves from bandits, and these men certainly looked fit enough to serve in a town militia. Toledo, Cordoba, and Valencia were too far away to protect them. Still… Swords were expensive and required a sharpening stone and oil. Arrows and spears were both cheaper and better suited to defense, or so soldiers in the Toledo alehouses claimed. A man owned a sword only if he intended to live by it.

And yet, here they were, in the middle of nowhere.

The Castilian was approaching again with three brimming mugs when a brawl erupted across the room. The man halted and, like everyone else, turned to watch. Yasin, though, instead reassessed the Castilian. Both his undyed wool tunic and pants bore the rips and stains he'd expect from field work. His boots, however, stood out. These were no simple turnshoes of soft leather. A master craftsman had shaped and trimmed the tops of those boots out of a single piece of flawless full-grain leather. The skived edges attached to the sole, a shaped piece hardened by boiling so skillfully that they bore no cracks.

Yasin could work leather extremely well, but even he could produce this quality of work only once out of every three tries. The fine-quality material alone would cost a year's apprentice wages. Even with Gonzalo's promised gold, Yasin wouldn't risk so much money on a single piece of material. Yet here they were, on the feet of a *fuero* farmer living on the raiding routes halfway between Valencia and Toledo. It made no sense.

The brawl lasted only a few punches, and the Castilian distributed the mugs after the loser was dragged away, unconscious.

Before drinking, Yasin breathed in the aroma to confirm the man hadn't added anything to addle him. That trick caught the incautious in Toledo all the time. "I notice the fine craftsmanship of your boots," he began. "Did a cobbler in town make them?"

Of course not. A man with such skill would be working in an emir's court, if any emirs remained.

The Castilian's eyes wobbled, as if they yearned to consult his whistling companion. Yasin was impressed he resisted the temptation. Such self-control took discipline.

"No. From a peddler come this way last season."

A lie. No merchant would barter them here when he could earn a pile of gold in any city on the peninsula. Given the lack of wear, if this man bought them even a season prior, Yasin was an olive farmer from Granada.

The Castilian's voice grew stronger. "Cost me a year's coin, but perfect fer field work."

They were perfect for a palace's marble floor. Squandering such beauty on field work in a *fuero*? Unforgivable.

Despite his discomfort, Yasin forced a smile and acknowledged the answer with a tip of his mug. Something was going on here. By the time they'd finished their mugs, he'd decided on a risky strategy to discover what it was.

As the Leonese farmer stood to buy another round, Yasin halted him. "Let me pay for this one." He tossed two silver coins on the table.

His companions watched as the coins bounced and clattered together before rattling to a halt. The unmistakable sound had drawn the attention of a few others, who were now watching Yasin's table with naked greed. Each looked strong enough to deliver a vicious beating. He had certainly attracted attention.

Plucking one up, the Leonese rubbed the coin between his fingers, gauging the weight and composition. Yasin had done the same a week earlier. "You'll be a popular man indeed if you keep flashing silver like that," he said softly enough that he didn't whistle.

"Unfortunately, they're my last ones," Yasin lied, shrugging. "I'm not likely to have more until I reach Valencia.

"Issat so?" The Castilian shifted his posture for a better look at Yasin's waist. "How come?"

Fortunately, his money pouch was concealed by his *jubba*, yet another advantage of Arabic fashion. Yasin curled his lip into a smirk.

"Let's just say my fortunes rely on rulers thinking they can dictate what their subjects can possess."

The Castilian smirked. "Some folk have funny ideas."

"Indeed, they do."

The Leonese jutted his chin at him. "And you expect to smuggle past El Cid in Valencia?"

"Why not?" Yasin shrugged. "Fancy reputation or not, he's only a ruler. I did fine in Toledo under the king's nose."

The Leonese grunted. "The king's a pup. Diaz beat the Almoravids. He set himself up as an emir like the heathens. Smart as they come, sneaky, and utterly intolerant of betrayal."

Yasin rubbed his chin until the whiskers scratching his fingertips became as unsettling as the implications of the comment. His mission would be that much harder if this man wasn't exaggerating. "He's still a noble, and nobles always underestimate people like us."

That brought a round of nods. "Try not to get killed"—the Leonese raised his mug—"and we'll visit the next time we're in Valencia."

Yasin raised an eyebrow. "Oh?" After three strong ales, he'd finally reached the point he'd hoped for.

"It's useful to know a man who can get certain things past the gates."

He leaned forward and narrowed his eyes. "You have goods here worth the cost of smuggling?"

The Castilian chuckled through a grin. "During pilgrim season, we do."

Yasin forced himself to smile, even though he felt sick. He tightened his abdomen to avoid vomiting across the table. Now, he understood why these men owned swords. They scouted the caravans that passed through their *fuero* and attacked those with too many valuables and too little protection.

He only prayed these men had struck the buyer of those beautiful boots, not the master cobbler who had crafted them. The thought of such talent moldering beside a burned wagon was too tragic to endure.

Attacking Almoravid raiders or murderers was one thing, but only true villains would attack innocent travelers. For all he knew, every *fuero* between here and Valencia could do the same. These *fueros* formed militias to defend themselves, but so far from the cities, such an armed band could do what it pleased. The nobles didn't care enough, and the city guards were too far away. How many of the raids reported in the alehouses and markets of Toledo weren't committed by Almoravids, after all?

"Isn't attacking caravans dangerous?" He kept his voice low so it wouldn't carry beyond his table. "They have guards."

The Castilian grunted. "Only the smart ones."

At least he and Sarah would be safe, thanks to the mercenaries accompanying them. A day earlier, he took comfort that their skill would repulse Almoravid attacks. Now, he realized their true value lay in deterring Christian treachery.

But the thought of all those pilgrims traveling these roads, too poor or foolish to travel in armed groups, haunted him. They came to nourish their faith. How many of them had died because they'd trusted the honor of fellow believers?

SARAH

Sarah awoke to morning sunlight peeking through the small window. Lifting aside the cloak serving as her blanket, she stretched atop the cot. Though a few passing monks and a pair of nearby amorous cows meant her sleep hadn't exactly been uninterrupted, she still felt refreshed. Whether the cause was a night beneath a proper roof or something other than hard ground as a bed, she couldn't say. Perhaps her body had simply responded to the similarity between this room and her chamber in the library.

She rubbed her eyes in an attempt to purge the hellish thought. Her room in Toledo was a prison, not a sanctuary.

It was hard to tell the hour since the shutters were oriented to the south, but there was enough morning light for Sarah to see the room clearly. Yasin was curled in a ball on the floor with the tent cover stuffed beneath his head. Though last night had been chilly, his *jubba* lay on the floor beside him, carefully stretched to lie flat. It seemed he cared more about avoiding wrinkles than banishing the night's chill. Yet, he had asked her to judge him by the manner of his return, and he'd given her no cause for objection. He hadn't woken her when returning late the previous night, and it seemed unkind to wake him now.

Choosing her footing carefully to avoid nudging Yasin, she retrieved her satchel, then tiptoed to the door. The latch, thankfully, didn't squeak when she lifted it.

The muffled sounds of muted conversation and the clatter of wooden utensils led her to the kitchens, where two tonsured monks were scrubbing bowls by a basin while a third bald one did the same to nearby mugs. A counter ran along the long side of the room, topped by all manner of wooden utensils and a pair of large cooking pots. A table with a pair of long benches separated her from them. The aroma of onion soup and small ale hung on the air.

They turned and gawked when she cleared her throat.

"I beg your pardon, but can you tell me where you store royal dispatches?"

They stared at her with the widened eyes of a deer. Eventually, the bald one wiped his hands and advanced. "Dispatches?"

She folded her hands together at her waist. "Yes, sir. Royal messages bound for Toledo or north to Burgos or Santiago de Compostela."

At mention of the last name, the monks crossed themselves and bowed their heads. That city far to the northwest had a shrine to St. James, the Muslim-slayer. Of course, these men would respect such a barbaric legend.

"Royal riders stop here for a blessing before continuing to Toledo."

She reached into her satchel. "Might I leave something for the next rider?"

"You have a message for the king, do you?" He chuckled, and his companions soon joined in.

She restrained her reaction to an arched eyebrow. "No, for one of his agents." Withdrawing the contents of the satchel, she set the pen, inkpot, and a sheet of paper on the table.

She tried her best not to smirk at the monk's subsequent gasp. A literate woman surprised most men.

Dipping her pen in the inkpot, she hesitated. These monks would undoubtedly read anything she wrote, and chances were good one of them knew both Latin and Castilian, perhaps even Arabic. She would have to keep her missive vague.

Careful to take only a little ink to avoid drops that might stain her fingers or dress, she began to write in Latin.

To Lord Gonzalo Martinez,
Day seven since departing Toledo. We continue east with the caravan. No signs of trouble. Expect to reach destination in two weeks. Peace be with you.

Sarah al-Bayda

Once it had dried, she folded it and wrote Gonzalo's name across the front before presenting the missive to the bald monk. "May I rely upon you to impart this missive to the next dispatch rider headed toward Toledo?" She bowed her head in the submissive way the library priests had always enjoyed.

Skepticism having replaced the humor in his expression, he accepted the letter. "You may rely upon me."

Sarah prayed that was true. Hopefully, Lord Gonzalo would receive enough of her messages that he didn't suspect treachery and send men after her and Yasin.

Swallowing, the monk made the sign of the Christian cross with a sweeping motion. "God bless you."

A chill ran over Sarah's skin, but she forced herself to receive the blessing with a bow before turning and leaving the kitchen. Only once safely in the corridor did she shiver to cast off the heathen gesture.

The walls of this abbey suddenly seemed to squeeze in on her. She felt their messiah in every surface. It dragged at her shoulders, smothering her. How could Allah penetrate so much blasphemy? She needed to get out, to taste the fresh scent of free air, to bask in the sunlight. Perhaps she could cleanse herself at the local stream before the other travelers roused.

Passing the door to her and Yasin's chamber, Sarah cracked open the abbey doors and stepped outside. The sunlight stabbed her eyes as she emerged into the courtyard, and she squinted them shut. Sage, mint, and ripe apples filled her nostrils, even though she hadn't noticed them when they'd arrived the day before. Perhaps the abbey would let her take a few sage clippings to clean her teeth, or some mint to keep Yasin's breath tolerable on this journey.

She risked cracking her eyes open. As the image before her resolved, she gasped and widened them, ignoring the burst of pain. The caravan, with all its animals, vehicles, and milling members, was already assembling in the square. She located the sun, only to find it halfway up the sky.

They had overslept.

Amid a twirl of her skirt, Sarah charged inside toward her room. Yasin was still asleep when she burst in. "Wake up!"

He shielded his eyes. "Softly!"

"We don't have time for 'softly'. The caravan is leaving."

He bolted upright. His eyes appeared lucid, none the worse for his night at the alehouse. "Impossible! I never sleep through the night."

"Tell that to the sun, four hands above the horizon." She untangled her riding cloak and flourished it onto her shoulders.

"We can't miss that caravan." He lifted his *jubba* more carefully than the situation justified.

"That's why I shouted."

Outside, while Yasin collected their mule from the abbey's stable, Sarah cast a longing glance at the buildings surrounding the square. The wind caught her shawl and tangled her hair more often on this plateau than within the shelter of Toledo's buildings. She had hoped to buy a new comb, but she'd have to wait for the next *fuero*. A simple wooden one wouldn't cost much, and she doubted a man who worried about his appearance as much as Yasin would begrudge the expense. He'd probably use it, too.

"Good, they haven't left yet." Yasin twisted his arm within his *jubba*. The motion pulled the lead rope taut and caused the mule to bray in annoyance. "Did we forget anything?"

Sarah turned to say they had little enough to remember but froze at Yasin's firmly set jaw. His anxious eyes darted back and forth across the square.

"What is it?" she pressed.

"Where are the rest?"

"Rest of what?" Searching the column, she found the pilgrims, the priests, even the merchant and his wife.

He marched forward with long, determined strides, tugging the mule behind him.

Sarah scrambled to keep up. "Yasin!"

Instead of joining the rear of the caravan, he approached a well-muscled caravaneer who was adjusting a strap on one of the wagons.

"Where are the mercenaries?" Yasin demanded despite the difference in their sizes.

The man didn't turn. "Left this morning."

"Did they ride ahead to Valencia?" His words came quickly on a strained voice. His drinking last night must have caused more harm than a headache.

"They were bound for Barcelona, not Valencia," he supplied before departing further down the column.

Yasin's eyes lost their focus. "Barcelona." His voice was no more than a whisper.

"What's wrong?" Sarah had never seen him look so unsettled.

He stared at the ground.

"Yasin!"

His eyes snapped toward her, twitching with uncertainty.

She placed a hand on his forearm. "What is wrong?"

He frowned. "We aren't going with them."

She gasped. "You said the roads were too dangerous for us to travel alone."

"That was before last night."

"How does your getting drunk change—"

"I wasn't drunk," he hissed. "And you should thank God I went to that alehouse." Abruptly, he swung the mule around and followed after the caravaneer with long strides.

Sarah followed after, clutching at his *jubba*. Though she expected him to squirm out of her grip and straighten the wrinkles, he ignored her.

Instead, he spun the caravaneer with a tug on his shoulder. "We're staying for another day. We'll catch up with you."

"What?" Sarah cried.

Glaring, the caravaneer shrugged off Yasin's hand. "That's your business."

Yasin pinned him with a stare. "I advise you to make for the next town with speed."

The man eyed Yasin for a moment before grunting and walking away.

Sarah turned Yasin with both hands. The effort of spinning him strained a muscle in her upper arm. "Stop. Explain this to me."

"We can't join this caravan without those mercenaries." His eyes didn't appear addled and his voice seemed strong and clear, yet he spoke nonsense.

"Why?"

Sighing, he drew her further from the caravan, toward the abbey. "Last night, I met some men of this town's militia. After a few"—he shook his head—"several drinks, they gloated about attacking travelers on the road. Judging by the numbers in the alehouse, they have a few dozen men."

"*Ya salaam!*" A few of the travelers turned in her direction. She lowered her voice. "Your people do such things?"

"These aren't my people."

"Thieves, I mean."

"These men aren't thieves." Yasin chopped the air with his hand. "They're murderers."

Sarah decided not to press the issue. "In Toledo, you said traveling alone was dangerous."

"Without mercenaries to guard it, a group this size will invite attacks. It's a liability, not a safeguard." He shook his head. "And this town had a whole night to browse the caravan's valuables."

She gasped. "You're abandoning them to their fate."

That brought a glare. "What would you have me do? I don't have a sword, and I doubt you're hiding one under that dress. This knife is the closest thing I have to a weapon." He raised his finger to reveal a thin ring around it, with a small blade the size of her smallest finger attached to it.

She took a step back. "Where did that come from?"

He lowered his finger to his belt. "A slit lets it slide between the layers of my belt." To her surprise, the blade disappeared, leaving only the ring visible.

"But you do have a weapon."

"Weapon?" He grunted. "It's a tool to cut the drawstrings of money pouches." He crossed his arms. "Besides, I've never been in a bar fight, let alone a battle."

Just when she glimpsed the faintest glimmer of *adab* within him, he proved her wrong. "They have to be warned."

"I've done what I can." He nodded toward the caravaneer. "Both now and last night."

"Last night?" She wrinkled her nose. "In the alehouse?"

"Yes." He rubbed his forehead. "My drinking companions left in far worse condition than I. They'll be sleeping it off all morning."

"Is that help?"

He nodded. "Avoiding trouble is the wiser path. I can't help these people once they leave, but I may have saved their lives by delaying pursuit for a few hours." He swept his gaze over the caravan. "We'll follow once I'm certain no one is trailing them."

Sarah stood watching the caravan while Yasin led the mule back to the abbey. Her thoughts lingered on the merchant's wife in the beautiful blue dress and the pilgrim who had shared her campfire. They were Christians, but they were also honest, kind people, not at all like the slavers or lecherous guards of the library.

She could warn them of danger and beg them not to leave, but they'd never believe her. Yasin had no proof to openly accuse the *fuero* settlers of planning an attack, and a vague warning would only raise questions about where her information came from. They might even suspect her loyalties. She was a Muslim, and Yasin looked like one. In a world where town militias attacked the travelers they were supposed to protect, Sarah couldn't predict the caravan's reaction.

When she'd agreed to this quest, she'd thought only of the opportunity. But now, surrounded by bandits with the safety of Toledo's walls a week away, she felt vulnerable and alone with only a thief without a hint of *adab* to rely upon.

YASIN

Yasin watched the town square from the grass of the abbey courtyard as the day matured. When Sarah began asking questions, he handed her half of his remaining silver coins and told her to buy a flint and whatever other supplies she needed. She accepted immediately and headed into town. While it delivered some much-desired quiet, in truth he trusted her to understand their needs better than he did.

Though his money pouch had lost much of its heft, the remaining towns on their route would probably have unlocked chests and doors. After all, those who didn't properly secure their valuables deserved to lose them. Burglary would draw attention, but he and Sarah would move along before it caught up with them.

Sarah returned with fingers stained by cherry juice, followed by a strapping young man who carried a full satchel and eyed her breasts and posterior a little too often. Yasin couldn't blame him, but he'd be sadly disappointed, if not by Sarah, then by her supposed husband. They had to maintain appearances for a few hours more, at least.

The aroma of stews and freshly baked bread drew the townsfolk away from their labors and back to their earthen homes for the day's main meal. Only then did Yasin decide the caravan was safe. As the last of them stumbled inside, he and Sarah departed.

He led Sarah around the back of the abbey and circled the town far to the north before turning east. They followed the seams between fields far enough from the road that they could avoid other travelers but close enough to identify any large groups moving in either direction.

An hour into the journey, Sarah sighed. "I wish you would stop that."

"Excuse me?" She hadn't spoken since leaving the *fuero*.

"You keep looking behind us."

He'd been feigning interest in their surroundings, but it seemed he couldn't fool a trained *qiyan*. "I'm making sure we're not being followed."

"I know, but they'd have overtaken us by now if they were."

The insightful comment surprised him. For having spent her life studying courtly arts, she understood the mind of a brigand. "We were fortunate."

She arched an eyebrow. "Or, you misread the danger."

He suppressed a flare of irritation only because he had considered the same possibility.

Scurrying in the underbrush drew his attention. He focused his senses in that direction, blood pumping at the potential threat, but heard only the wind blowing through the wild grasses and the distant calls of an animal. He had too little knowledge of these wilds to identify which kind. The sounds didn't come from men, though.

He took a cleansing breath. "I was wrong. But that doesn't mean I was mistaken."

"I don't understand." Her look of confusion delighted him.

"Though nothing came of it, my caution was justified. I'd rather avoid imaginary trouble than stumble into danger."

"Well-phrased." She drew in a breath. "It just surprises me, seeing how much you risked to punish the man who had you arrested."

Yasin shrugged. "We're far from Toledo. A mistake here will cost us our lives."

He led them further south toward a mountain ridge running east. Despite the encroaching sounds of wildlife circling closer in the fading light, Yasin kept moving, eyes searching the crags.

She glanced behind. "I saw a nice stream over the last ridge. We could probably go back and reach it before full dark." Her tone carried a subtle hint of persuasion that another man might have missed.

Though she had a *qiyan*'s subtlety, Yasin had survived by detecting nuance. His lip curled upwards. "No bathing tonight, I'm afraid. Not when the militia could be nearby."

"That wasn't what I meant," she insisted a little too forcefully. "Only that we could refill our waterskin."

Yasin shifted the weight on the sloshing oiled leather bag slung over his shoulder. It felt full to him.

He halted at a small cave halfway up a ridge that had the jagged look of a block of cheese torn in half by a giant. The combination of a few trees with low, full branches and a scattering of moss-covered boulders had obscured the entrance until they'd passed, even though it was wide enough to admit both them and the mule. Yasin saw it only because he was searching for such a feature.

Sarah shuddered, staring at the cave. "We aren't setting up camp?"

"Not tonight. Not alone." He swallowed. "The soldiers kept watch every night, and they were among a group of fifty. These lands between the Christian kingdoms and the Andalusi city-states are the most dangerous on the peninsula."

"Perhaps we should have gone over the mountains to the north, then followed the coast down to Valencia instead."

She was probably right. "What's done is done." He adjusted his grip on the lead rope, causing the mule to bray. He spared a moment to pat its neck. "It's only one night. We'll catch the caravan tomorrow."

After crafting a torch from a nearby branch and some parched moss, he entered the cave and led them down a short tunnel. He nearly collided with a wall when the path twisted sharply to the left before opening into a wider chamber.

He released a satisfied sigh. "Perfect." His voice dissipated without echoing off the uneven ceiling a few handspans above his head.

Sarah studied the rocky floor. "It'll be an uncomfortable night." She sniffed the air. "And cold." She pulled her cloak around herself and rubbed her shoulders.

"We can start a small fire," he offered.

"It won't be seen?"

He pointed back toward the tunnel. "The bend will hide the light, and you'll welcome the heat tonight."

CHAPTER EIGHT

SARAH

THE NEXT MORNING, they returned to the road to make up time. Yasin insisted some marks in the dirt proved they were gaining on the caravan, but when Sarah pressed for specifics, he offered none. She doubted he knew the faintest thing about tracking, but lacking a better suggestion, she said nothing.

A few hours later, they stopped at a stream a short distance from the road to refill their waterskin. Sarah was glad for the respite. Her feet ached and even the faintest motion left her muscles feeling stiff and heavy.

The babbling of the shallow water running over the rocks made it difficult to place other noises. At first, she thought the slurping to her right was Yasin guzzling water. But he was to her left, splashing as he struggled to position the mouth of the waterskin into the trickling current.

Something was definitely hiding in the tall grasses. "Yasin, listen."

At a splash downstream, he froze, eyes focused beyond her. He held his finger to his lips.

They hadn't approached the stream with any particular caution or discretion. A raider wouldn't make a noise like that before attacking and another traveler would announce himself. It had to be an animal. She had neither the protection of a winding cave passage nor a fire, only a man with a hidden knife the size of her smallest finger.

A strong gust of wind bent the grasses over. As it did, a chestnut head with dark brown hair poked into view.

A wild horse in the wilderness! The chances of stumbling upon one were impossibly small, yet here it was.

Behind her, Yasin began to laugh.

Bristling, she raised her chin. "I may have been wrong in my fears"—she shook the water off her hands—"but that doesn't mean I was mistaken."

"No, no… I'm thankful for your caution. That's not why I'm laughing."

"Why, then?" She wiped her hands dry on her dress.

A twinkle brightened his eyes. "I'm just pleased I'm filling our waterskin upstream of that horse."

Her cheeks threatened to pull her lips into a smile, but she resisted. If she encouraged his humor, she'd have to endure it all the way to Valencia and back.

Yasin set the waterskin down and crept toward their mule, which was drinking even further upstream.

"What are you doing?"

He retrieved the rope tying his pack and Sarah's satchel to the mule's back. "I'm going to catch him."

Leather and thievery wouldn't help him tame a wild animal. "You'll get yourself killed."

Rope dangling from one hand, he pressed the other to his chest. "Darling Sarah, are you worried about me?"

In fact, she was. "Wild animals are dangerous." She straightened a lock of hair blown across her face by the breeze and repositioned her cloak. "What will I do if you're kicked to death?"

His smug smile gave way to an unsettled frown. "Worry instead about the saddle sore you'll have after I succeed." He brushed past her.

She clasped his wrist, halting him. He may be a thief, a fool, and entirely bereft of *adab*, but she didn't wish to see him injured. A fluttering filled her belly. "Be careful. The emir had many horses, and more than one stable boy came to harm by them."

Yasin swallowed. "Perhaps you should try."

She withdrew her hand. "I'd never be so foolish."

With a grunt, he advanced along the edge of the stream silently except for the gentle hiss of the swaying grass brushing against him. He neither stumbled on the uneven ground nor splashed a misplaced foot in the water. Evidently, he could be silent when he wished, as rare as those occasions were.

The wind changed and the horse raised its head, turning toward Yasin. He crouched to shelter in the grass.

Sarah recalled fragments of overheard conversation from her time in the emir's palace. "Don't hide," she whispered as loudly as she dared. "Let him see you."

He'd evidently heard, for he straightened and continued his approach, hands spread out at his sides. The wind carried the brushing swish of each step through the grass like the slithering of a snake. As he advanced, she prayed the animal merely bolted instead of rearing and charging.

The horse had abandoned its drinking and stared at Yasin with a motionless intensity broken only by the occasional twitch of its ear. Its smooth, almost silky, mane looked as soft as the fur blankets of the palace that she could now only dimly recall. She yearned to reach out and touch it. How could a wild animal keep itself untangled when Sarah struggled to keep her own hair tidy and unknotted? It wasn't fair. This creature cared nothing for modesty. It knew only wild freedom, and yet its mane looked pristine and orderly. Perhaps she, too, should let her hair loose.

The very thought of baring her naked head to the world compelled her to pull her cloak around her more tightly. No, she couldn't surrender to such wild impulses and leave modesty behind. Such brazen liberality was an offense against Allah, even if it eased her grooming.

She drew in a tense breath as Yasin took his last step and reached for the animal's nose.

The horse darted its head forward. Sarah's shaking hand flew to her mouth as she turned away.

Allah, be merciful. Keep him safe.

Tinkling laughter made her turn again. The horse was rubbing Yasin's face with its muzzle. He had done it.

She approached with quick steps, nearly stumbling several times as she struggled with the uneven ground. By the time she reached them, Yasin was feeding it a fistful of grass. He'd coiled one end of the rope around his wrist and looped the other around the animal's neck.

"How is this possible?" She shook her head. "That's a wild horse. You should not have been able to do this."

"And yet, I have," he crooned. "And because of my magnificence, you will ride like a princess tonight."

The thought of approaching Valencia like a civilized person filled her with a giddy excitement. "You would let me ride while you walk?" She regretted her words the moment his eyes softened into the start of a smile. He would taunt her now that he knew how badly she desired it.

But the taunt never came. He had turned back to the animal, rubbing its back with smooth, almost sensuous strokes. He had a gentle touch. "I'll ride the mule."

Indignation rose as she recalled their conversation back in Toledo. "If it can't bear my weight, it surely can't bear yours."

"I said it couldn't bear both you and our possessions, but a proper horse can."

Allah had delivered her from the pains of her sore feet. There could be no other explanation. Yasin alone could not have overcome this beast's wild nature unless the Maker had stilled its heart.

"You two act like old friends." Humor lifted her words, rushing them.

Yasin's hand stopped, and he lowered his head to study the horse's belly. When he spoke, the pride had drained from his voice. "There's a reason for that." His eyes darkened by some unknown burden.

"We've found your equal, at last!"

He didn't respond to her jest. Instead, he pointed a shaking finger at a raw spot along the horse's stomach. "That's caused by a loose harness. I've seen it before."

She released a faint chuckle. "I guess it isn't a wild horse, after all."

He wasn't laughing. "No, Sarah." He pointed again. "I mean I've seen this very injury before. This is the horse whose harness I adjusted the first night of our journey."

"Then, we're close to the caravan!" She felt exposed out here alone, but all that would change once they reached the safety of others. "Did it get lost?"

He shook his head slowly, deliberately. Without another word, he heaved himself onto its back.

She clasped his arm. "You promised I could ride it!"

He ignored her except to free his wrist from her grip. Shielding his eyes from the noonday sun, he swept his gaze across the surrounding plains. After perhaps a quarter turn to the south, he halted, eyes fixed on the distance.

"What is it?" She turned in the same direction but saw only grass.

When he slid off the horse, the eyes that greeted her had aged. His throat bobbed with an audible swallow. "I see an overturned wagon in a clearing up ahead. Bring the mule." His voice vibrated with an intensity that belied its softness.

The terrifying contrast silenced her many questions.

Yasin guided the horse south along the stream. Sarah followed in silence behind, leading the mule. The faithful animal brayed any time she guided him too close to the horse. Hopefully, it would grow accustomed to its new companion, or they'd struggle to manage the animals.

Perhaps a damaged wagon had to be abandoned and the horse tethered to it had bolted.

As they approached the clearing, a pungent odor permeated the air: animal dung, probably, from so many beasts halting in one spot. Yet, she heard no animals grazing or travelers shouting instructions.

Though it had passed by here recently, the caravan must have already moved on.

When she stepped into the clearing, she realized how terribly wrong she was.

Ash and the charred remains of cindered wagons and carts blanketed the clearing like ink splashed across a page. Their ransacked contents lay scattered beside upturned chests and shattered locks. Dried flows of ale left stained lines in the dirt leading from discarded, cracked casks to the stream.

"Saints preserve us." Yasin crossed himself.

Sarah followed his gaze to the source of his attention. The burned bodies of the priests who had witnessed Sarah's emancipation lay in a pile at the center of the clearing. Their crosses, though charred and stained with ash like the rest of them, still retained their distinctive shape. Half a dozen others lay scattered across the smear of devastation. Their unblemished state preserved the gruesome clarity of their flesh, split open like peaches sundered by a dull blade. And the blood…so much blood.

She shut her eyes, but images of these poor people haunted the darkness behind her eyelids. She wished she hadn't seen them.

The wind changed and carried a sickly, fruity odor that clung to the top of her mouth. The scent of death. It was worse than the sweaty, earthy smell of bodies packed in the hold of the stinking ship that had taken her as a slave.

Though she clutched at her stomach, it was too late. Doubling over, she voided its contents on the ground. Seeing the remnants of her morning meal before her brought another convulsion that shook her entire body. The people lying slaughtered around her had helped prepare that meat.

Hands on her shoulders anchored her.

Yasin. If not for his caution, they would have shared this fate.

She steadied herself with a breath. Now that she was prepared for it, she could endure the stench. Opening her eyes, she rose and shook her head at the ruin around her. "This is an abomination. A crime against Allah."

"Morality doesn't grow in the soil of this land." His voice rose and fell from behind her, as if he were looking around. "Out here, men do what they can with little regard for what they should."

"Men of the *fuero* would have passed us." She gasped. "The mercenaries did this. They never left for Barcelona!"

Yasin crossed to a slain horse lying near one of the wagons. He ran his hands along the tack, then down to the stirrups. "No Christian did this." He showed her the stirrup, but it appeared unremarkable. "Muslim raiders from the South."

"You can tell that?"

He nodded. "The leather is superb. Very high quality." He sighed. "This horse was fit, and I don't see any flaws except for the wound that killed it. It did not belong to a bandit."

The caravan must have fought back, then. "How can you tell their faith?" Yasin had already shown contempt for the Almoravids. Perhaps he saw what he wished to see.

"I've crafted stirrups for both Christians and Muslims." He stretched the stirrup taut. "Muslims ride *a la jineta* with short stirrups for better speed." He extended his hand to measure out a distance two handspans beyond the end of the stirrup. "Very different from the Christians who ride *a la brida* for stability." He closed his fist around the stirrup, twisting it in his grip. "Only an Almoravid warband would use short stirrups of such high quality."

The *fuero* farmers had the opportunity to review the riches and defenses of caravans before attacking. They risked very little. But Almoravids would have to travel for several days into unfriendly lands without a hint of what they might find. "Why would they risk so much?"

Yasin rose and wiped the soot off his hands. "Slaves." He gestured lazily over the goods spilled across the clearing. "They certainly didn't want plunder." He shrugged. "My guess is they gathered the captives for the slave markets, looted the gold and silver, and destroyed the rest."

She searched the bodies for familiar faces. Beside a burned wagon, she found the kind woman who had been loading her wagon, but she found no sign of the merchant and his wife, nor the pilgrims. The young woman who had been awed by the artistic piety in the Great Mosque of Toledo had started to doubt the zealotry of her local priest. Those doubts would disappear after a single day as a slave.

"A terrible fate," she murmured.

The eyes Yasin turned on her carried both rage and pain in equal measure. "The claim of holy war justifies many evils, and the men who believe God commands them to kill spare little thought for your *adab*."

She had once believed only the most depraved man could sell another into slavery. The Christian pirates who had seized her on her way back from Baghdad had been unkempt ruffians with no place among civilized men. They deserved to be wiped clean from the seas. But a believer who prayed five times a day to Allah? The Almoravids claimed to follow a purer interpretation of the prophet's faith, yet they had ignored the protections of *dhimmis* and succumbed to the same base impulses as misguided Christians.

Yasin followed a path of crushed grass leading away from the clearing to find a bay horse chewing at the tall grasses, still harnessed to a perfectly undamaged wagon. From the amount of dung nearby, it had been standing there for some time.

"They attacked last night," Yasin concluded. "It's the only way they could miss a wagon of this size. The horse pulling it fled at the first noise."

Sarah rubbed her arms to banish a sudden chill. "This is the second horse they missed."

"They didn't miss the one by the stream. It had no harness or saddle. They deliberately released it."

"Why would they do such a thing?"

"A riderless horse is a burden, and they already had slaves and plunder to manage. They need to get south before the Castilians could react."

"Why go to the effort to free it?"

Yasin scowled. "Because they'll be back. Why kill today what they can steal tomorrow? Someone will find it, give it a new saddle, and bless their good fortune, right up until a veiled rider loots it."

"Allah bless these poor souls."

"Amen." After a loud inhalation, Yasin approached the closest wagon, abandoned with the slashed harness still attached to the front. The wheels of the closer side had splintered, leaving the bed of the wagon tilted to the side. Leaning in, he began searching the spilled contents.

"What are you doing?"

"Salvaging anything of value." He swept a limp hand over the wreckage. "If I can find a dual harness, we can hitch both horses to the wagon."

She drew in a sharp breath. "How can you do that? These people were murdered."

"Not by me. Neither they nor the boar that roam these lands will have use of these things anymore." Eyes strained, Yasin stepped back. The muscles of his neck and jaw were drawn tight. "I can't change their fates, but I can change ours. My pouch is nearly empty. We need the coin these goods can fetch in Valencia."

She crossed her arms. "This is wrong."

"Perhaps," he admitted. "But it's also necessary." He stepped back and unfurled a blue high-waisted dress.

Sarah's fingers crept forward to touch the fabric, but she halted as she remembered the merchant's wife who had worn it. The poor woman was probably bound for the South to serve in some nobleman's estate…if she were fortunate. Sarah had made that same journey once before. That poor woman's struggle was only beginning.

YASIN

Yasin searched the remnants of the caravan with a practiced eye for value and the diligence of a Castilian tax collector. Clothing, supplies, spices, cooking utensils, tools, needles, grain, spare wagon wheels and axles… It would all fetch a good price in any market. Within the hour, the wagon held as much as he dared to load.

Best of all, he found not one but two fresh razors and a small copper mirror. A quick trip to the stream removed over a week's growth from his chin. For the first time on this journey, he felt like himself, a barbarian no longer.

He also found a discarded dual harness that needed only a few repairs. More than enough spare leather straps lay scattered through the clearing to replace those the Almoravids had cut when freeing the pack animals. It wasn't his finest work, but he intended to bring this bounty into Valencia intact and two horses would let them travel faster with fewer stops.

With two horses and a wagon to manage, he had little choice but to release the mule. Free of its lead rope, the relieved creature gave a shake of its head and wandered off to eat the abundant grass.

Traveling by wagon filled Yasin with an invigorating excitement after a week of walking. The breeze diminished the afternoon heat, and the vibrations of the wagon massaged his aching feet.

Between enjoying the ride and assessing how the horses were taking to their makeshift harnesses, Yasin didn't notice Sarah's silence until the sun started to set. Not only did she say nothing, but she moved only in response to particularly violent rocking. Otherwise, she spent the day staring at the horizon.

Her stony silence was unsettling. His salvaging of the caravan had upset her, and that knowledge left a knot in his stomach. Despite her constant complaints about his integrity, he had started to enjoy their time together. He could have sworn she was starting to soften to him, as well. He had even begun to wonder if *qiyan* training extended to ostentatious lovemaking as alehouse rumors suggested.

He may have ruined all that, though he had little choice in the matter. Reaching Valencia was costing more than he'd anticipated, and they would also need money to live on while he determined how best to acquire the *Book of Healing*. His actions hadn't offended any Andalusi Muslim customs, and surely Sarah didn't expect perfectly serviceable goods to rot when they could be useful.

The gruesome memory of those burned priests haunted Yasin. They had been healthy and incapable of resistance, the perfect characteristics for good slaves. Killing them had thrown away the chance for profit. Such brutal and senseless murder was an offense against every god, except perhaps those of the devils from the north seas who raided the ports.

People of the Book were supposed to be protected from such brutality. The emir of Almeria would have never done such a thing, even immediately after the fall of Toledo when everyone feared the Castilians would sweep across the peninsula. Many things wouldn't have happened under the emir. But he was gone, exiled by the Almoravids to some fortress in the Maghreb of northern Africa.

Perhaps not everyone thought in terms of profit. What a hellish thought! Yasin shuddered but covered the reaction by leaning forward and pretending to adjust a section of the harness.

Sarah didn't seem to notice.

When they stopped for the night, she fed and watered the horses while he erected the tent and began a fire. She smiled when he handed her a piece of meat from the mercenaries' hunt. The spark of light in her eyes after the long, cloudy day emboldened him.

"You were quiet all day. I was concerned."

She nibbled her food with hesitant bites. After the day's travel, she must have been famished, but she ate as if the meat disgusted her. He had found some supplies and a cooking pot in one of the wagons. Perhaps she would enjoy boiled eggs in the morning.

"I was thinking about the caravan."

"It's a hard thing to face death like that."

His thoughts returned to the bodies, but before the haunting image returned, he searched for something more pleasing to distract him. He settled on her hair, unbound and uncovered within the safety of their camp. Firelight painted it in an auburn glow, and the shadows only served to accentuate its softness and shimmering beauty. He longed to feel it tickle his fingertips, but of course, he could not. He'd made a promise, and she would ever ask.

"I'm sorry if my actions in the clearing offended you." His words carried a sincerity that surprised him.

She frowned. "Actions?"

"Gathering what items could be saved."

She shook her head. "No. Your reasons made sense." Her words came slowly, as if weighed down by exhaustion. "They just hadn't occurred to me."

"Ah." He fell silent, struggling to reconcile this answer with her behavior.

When he glanced up again, she was smiling at him.

"Was that bothering you all day?" Her voice carried a hint of humor that tickled his ears as much as good Almerian wine would his throat.

"Partly." He swallowed. "I can't help thinking about those priests."

"It will be worse for those bound for the slave markets." She lowered her food and stared into the fire. "No one is ever prepared for that life." The haunting reminder of trauma shadowed her eyes.

Yasin set his food aside. "Did something similar lead you to Toledo?"

"Not exactly." The words sounded hollow. She raised her knees to her chest, hugging them. "My family lived on a small farm outside Granada. I had a sister and three older brothers. When I was very young, my parents sold me to the emir."

He drew in a sharp breath. Even after the looting of the Christian quarter in Almeria and the lack of business after the fall of Toledo, his father had never considered selling his children. "How could they do such a thing?"

She shrugged. "They were Christians. After two seasons of drought, they couldn't afford food, let alone the *jizya*."

Yasin fell silent. The tax on Christians had altered the course of both of their lives. At least it had affected him as an adult, when he could choose how to react to it. "I can't imagine sending a child into such a life."

"It wasn't as bad as you imagine. The emir, Abdallah ibn Buluggin, was a young man, young enough to prefer proving his virility on older women instead of younger. I grew up as a servant to his harem." She drank from the waterskin and set it down again. "One day after the fall of Toledo, the *agha* heard me singing for the concubines. He brought me before the emir and recommended me for training as a *qiyan*."

"What was the emir like?" Other than a shadowy dalliance with a lovely lady of the royal family eager to enjoy the seedier side of the city, the closest Yasin had ever gotten to any noble was stealing fruit from the royal orchard.

A smile crept onto her face. "I met him only twice. The first time, he closed his eyes while I sang. Every emir desires—desired—music in his court, but ibn Buluggin truly loved art and poetry. The second time was when I departed for Baghdad. Through Valencia, actually." She started to chuckle. "He told me I was a nightingale of Granada, and that I should return when I learned to sing with the beauty of twilight."

Yasin found himself smiling, too. "A lovely sentiment."

"I thought so. When I reached Baghdad, I realized he meant something deeper, though." Her smile faded a little. "My teachers called him a lesser son of Berber goat herders, controlled by Jewish advisors. They called the *taifas* a fading echo of the glory of Cordoba." She bit her lip. "I saw such beauty in Granada, and I think the emir did as well. It deserved to be celebrated, and I was honored by the chance to praise it."

"I've heard many rumors about *qiyan* training," Yasin said. "What did it really entail?"

Sarah took another bite of the meat and swallowed. "Music, poetry, debate, mathematics, writing. How to recount the lamentations and exaltations that give our history meaning."

He rubbed his chin. "And…lovemaking?"

"No, not that." She shook her head. "But we do learn how to infer intention in others and convey meaning with our movements. You could call that seduction."

So, the rumors of mystical sexual training were just that. "Convey meaning?"

"One uses different gestures to cultivate a suitor or discourage his ambitions. The goal of every *qiyan* is to accumulate fame so she might marry well, and thus gain the security that allows her to continue to hone her craft."

Yasin grunted. "You've certainly honed your craft."

Her eyes danced with humor, the first time all day. "I was a very good student."

They both started to laugh, and the air between them grew lighter. The grim shadow of the caravan's fate faded. They had survived, and life was filled with more than sorrow.

"I learned so many wonderful things in Baghdad," she continued. "More than I ever imagined while living on a farm outside Granada. A year into my training, I converted."

In the flames of the campfire, he saw the slopes of his father's face. The indignation of those last few nights in Almeria came rushing back. He clenched his fingers until they ached. "No one should be forced to sacrifice their faith."

"It was my choice," she insisted. "A faith that inspires the poetry of Wallada bint al-Mustakfi and the music of Ziryab must surely enjoy divine blessing."

"It also slaughters innocent pilgrims," Yasin countered.

"As do the Christians."

"True enough." He swallowed. "What does your family think of your conversion?"

"They surrendered the right to an opinion when they sold me to the emir." Her voice dripped with bitterness, albeit tempered. She fell silent for a few moments. "When my training was finished, I was eager to return to Granada to praise the country that had given me so much. I boarded a ship for home." Her eyes lowered to focus on her knees. "It never arrived."

Every instinct honed by a life of theft, deception, and persuasion told him she was reaching the climax of her tale. But it was hers to tell, and he waited her out.

After a long stretch of silence, she drew in an unsteady breath. "Sicilian pirates took everything we had and carried us to Barcelona in chains. I spent the next three weeks caged like an animal, surrounded by filth. I will never forget the humiliation, the hopelessness."

She rubbed her wrists, and Yasin realized they had probably been encircled by cold metal from that day until the blacksmith had struck them off a week prior. Her horror at the fate of the captured travelers and her silence throughout the day made more sense now. Yasin's family had never owned slaves; it was forbidden to *dhimmis* in Almeria. Those sold in the marketplace seemed clean and well-groomed, but he now wondered how many sellers treated their captives as Sarah described and simply cleaned them up for auction.

She stirred and finished her food. "A passing priest from the library in Toledo was looking for a woman to cook for him on the way home. He bought me."

She was fortunate for that fate; he suspected most women taken as slaves ended up in brothels or were used to satisfy their owners' base desires.

Yasin gestured for her to pass the waterskin and took a sip when she did. "You could have lied to gain your freedom, told them you were a Christian."

"Silence is one thing, but denying my faith would have been an unforgivable sin, even to thwart the tyranny of Christian slavers."

Yasin barked a laugh before slapping his hand over his mouth.

"Do you mock me?" Ice reinforced her words.

Sobering, he shook his head. "Never. It's just… That same sentiment sent me into exile." A log fell in the campfire, collapsing the structure of the remaining tinder.

"I didn't know you were exiled." Sarah wrapped herself in her riding cloak.

Yasin crouched and added a trio of thick branches, angled atop each other, to the fire. The flames embraced the new firewood, throwing up fresh heat that drifted in Sarah's direction.

He settled down closer to her than before to keep warm, legs crossed in disregard for his wrinkled pants. Cotton replacements were among the scavenged items in the wagon, but donning them now would only ruin them, too.

"The day the Almoravids marched into Almeria, they tripled the *jizya*. My father commanded us to convert to escape the tax." He threw the remainder of his meat into the fire. It struck one of the mostly burned branches amid a flicker of ash and spark. "I refused to let him take my faith from me, so I left."

"And you live with the consequences, as I did."

He rubbed his hands before the fire, conscious of her gaze upon him. "When the Almoravids first arrived in Spain, even the Mozarabs celebrated. Toledo had just fallen. We feared Valencia would be next, then Almeria. We were Christian, but we were also Andalusi. We didn't want to lose our *hamams* and spices and performers."

"The Christians of Granada felt the same."

He'd heard as much. "Yet it happened anyways, taken away by the very people who were supposed to save us. In the first three days, the Almoravids drove out the dancers and musicians and forbade women from traveling unescorted through the streets." He shook his head. "They destroyed everything that made our city great."

She turned back toward the fire. "It must have been hard to leave your family."

"My brother and sister were supposed to come with me." He leaned back, resting his hands on the ground behind him. "My father convinced them to stay."

"Have you seen them since?"

He shook his head. Sometimes he would wonder whether Amira ever married, or if Salim had a passel of children. He probably ran the workshop with father now, all because he'd submitted to the Almoravids. The coward.

"Do you ever regret your decision?"

He grunted. "Never."

"Truly?"

"I'd rather live free in poverty than spend my days in an Almoravid palace." He leaned forward again and wiped his hands clean of the dirt clinging to them. He wished he could wipe out his memories as easily.

Out of the corner of his eye, he noticed her studying him.

"Do you doubt it?"

She sighed as his mother used to after catching him in some mischief. "The day I met you, you'd just been released from prison and immediately committed another burglary."

"And?"

"That suggests a dissolute life, not a content one."

He started to chuckle. "You're wrong about that."

She cocked her head. "Am I?"

"Put me against any leatherworker on the peninsula and I'll beat him, regardless of material, grade, or technique. I don't smuggle and steal and defraud out of desperation."

"Then why?" She leaned forward over her knees. "Why do you defy the lords of the city?"

He grunted. "Because I refuse to let others tell me how to live. This bottle of wine is legal, that one gets you imprisoned? A beautiful daughter must marry a man twice her age because her father orders it? If I tolerate these things, I might as well have converted and bowed to the Almoravids." He shook his head again. "Every mug of ale and song and woman I enjoy defies their tyranny."

"You hate them." She spoke the words without condemnation, a mere statement of fact.

He could guess at her implication, though, and refused to let her view him as another zealot. "I hate what they did to my people. I hate the way they destroyed Almeria."

"The city still stands."

He recalled its receding walls as he'd ridden away on a rented horse he'd had no intention of returning. "Not as it once did. It was a place of beauty and sophistication, where Christian and Jew and Muslim could trade songs or barbs or caresses."

Slipping a hand into his *jubba*, he withdrew the scrap of the satchel he'd brought from Almeria. A loose thread must have snagged on his toolkit, for it had begun to unravel. He rubbed the soft material between his fingers. "But that Almeria is gone forever."

A smile brightened her face.

"The one time I don't intend a jest, I amuse you."

"It's not that." She wiped the smile away with surprising speed. "You just sound like Ibn Hazm. The disintegration of the Caliphate of Cordoba into the *taifas* broke his heart. His laments are famous to both scholar and *qiyan*."

He very much doubted anyone would ever read his thoughts about Almeria. He would have to learn to read first, then write, and then compose poetry. A hundred other tasks interested him more.

"I was wrong about you," she said.

Now, that piqued his curiosity. "Oh?"

She twisted to face him. Though the fire silhouetted half her face in shadow, her eyes carried an unmistakable sincerity. "I believed you to be immoral and vulgar, void of merit. But that isn't true. You live according to your will, in full command of yourself. This is *adab*, too."

The compliment warmed his heart, banishing the emptiness of

his memories and his unease from the traumas of the day. He replaced the scrap in his hidden pocket.

This burden Gonzalo had forced him to bring along had proven to be welcome company, after all. "Thank you, Sarah."

She smiled, brightly and broadly enough to reach her eyes. "You're welcome, Yasin."

CHAPTER NINE

YASIN

THEY KEPT A good pace as they rode through La Mancha's sea of golden grasses, interrupted by occasional shrubs and jagged rocks. Game was sparse, which pleased Yasin well enough. He had neither a bow nor the skill to use it, and animals would attract wolves and bears that would endanger the horses and ruin any hope of bringing these goods into market. Without friends in Valencia, he would need that money for bribes.

But, he was getting ahead of himself. Fishing a hand into his *jubba*, he withdrew the folded document behind his toolkit and handed it to Sarah. Last night had reassured him that she would answer him honestly. "Can you tell me what this says?"

She peeled back the folds with the same care she showed when handling her oud. Her eyes raced across the scribbles atop the page, fast enough to spark a pang of jealousy. It came so easily to her.

"This is your pardon."

"Is it?" He searched for the truth in her eyes. "Gonzalo made a fine show of it with a trio of priests, but I had no way of knowing what it said."

"You doubted, yet still you came?"

He gave an uncertain shrug. "Not doubt, exactly. Good sense told me it had to be real, but there's no replacement for certainty."

Her eyes widened as she continued to read. "Yasin!"

Scanning the horizon for danger, he found only empty wilderness. "What?"

"You bedded a member of the royal household?"

He snatched the parchment from her grasp. "That's enough of that."

It was genuine, after all.

After camping alone among the rocky outcropping of broken hills for one more day, they came upon a small village of a dozen cultivated fields. The handful of buildings nestled in the bend of a wide stream composed a far smaller settlement than the first *fuero*. Lush, bushy trees hugged both shores of the water, offering a striking contrast to the golden grass, wheat, and barley like a green damask ribbon draped over a golden *qamisa*.

"God be praised," he exhaled.

"Seems little more than a collection of homes."

"Perhaps, but it's better than camping in the open another night."

"I appreciate sleeping with a roof over my head, too," she began, "but if all these settlements harbor ruffians, shouldn't we avoid them?"

"A settlement this size poses less risk than camping on our own." He gestured at the farmsteads. "They'd need all their men to guard them, not ranging a-field seeking mischief."

"*Less* risk?" Sarah turned an icy gaze on him. "Earlier, you said the *fueros* attacked only rich caravans. Do you mean to say we were in danger every moment of the past few days?"

"Very much so."

She gasped. "Why didn't you tell me?"

"Telling you would have only made you worry."

"I'm worried now!"

"Yes." He offered a sweet smile. "But instead of your fretting, I've enjoyed three days of pleasant company."

Yasin guided the wagon toward the settlement. He doubted he was still on any of the caravan paths. Without maps, he had simply set out east along water, intending to hug the coast once he reached the sea. Though disastrous for a large caravan, it was probably safer for a pair of travelers eager to avoid ambushes.

Sarah funneled her lingering resentment into a sharp nudge of his arm. "We have an audience." She pressed something into his palm.

"Eh?" He opened his hand to find a few sprigs of mint.

"To make a good impression."

He quickly stuffed them into his mouth and began to chew.

A knot of people had gathered outside the largest building, a single-story *tapia* structure with a straw-thatched roof. A pen constructed of tangled driftwood wrapped around one side, but a few chickens were pecking at the ground in front of the threshold.

He saw no church, let alone an alehouse. He licked his dry lips.

The villagers followed his movements as Yasin drew the wagon to a halt. Most were women, but the men found reasons to hold farm instruments: one scythe and two pitchforks. They clearly didn't see strangers often. Yasin held a tense breath until a group of curious children ran between the adults, giggling and halting to stare at him.

Descending, he made the sign of the cross before approaching with his empty hands extended. "God's blessings upon you."

"And upon you, stranger," answered a woman with a hint of gray at the temples of her long, backswept hair. Her sun-worn skin and the deep creases at the corners of her eyes spoke of considerable age, but those eyes retained their vitality as they searched the horizon before settling on Sarah, still seated on the bench of the wagon. "What brings you here?"

The men's nervous shifting suggested they weren't used to conflict. Though the burly man with the scythe continually adjusted his grip, he leaned back on his heels, showing none of the alert, coiled tension as the guards in Toledo. Yasin's instincts didn't tingle with danger. He doubted they would attack him or Sarah for their goods.

He could risk a little honesty. "Misfortune, I'm afraid. We were part of a caravan from Toledo that ran into Muslim raiders."

"Devils, here?" said another, younger woman with raven-black hair.

Bless her heart, Sarah didn't react to the insult. He'd have to praise her self-control later.

"No. Two days to the west. I doubt you need worry. They will have headed south, laden with slaves and plunder." Yasin crossed himself and wasn't disappointed in his assumptions when every last one of the adults did the same.

"Did no others escape?" the elderly woman asked.

"No." Visions of the priests conjured like phantoms in the empty space between himself and these villagers. "You don't forget a sight like that."

"No, you don't," came the soft reply. She dropped her chin and shook her head like a ripe apple shaken by the wind. "A sorry fate." From the freedom of her tongue and the way the others arrayed themselves around her, Yasin judged her some sort of village elder.

"And how did you find your way here, with a wagon and two horses, when so many others did not?" the raven-haired woman demanded.

"Maria!" The elderly woman's voice could cut leather cleanly. "A couple traveling the roads alone is no threat to us. Just look at them!"

Yasin nodded before the implication of her words sank in. Was she saying he was helpless?

"We're all thinking it, Mother." Maria jutted her chin at Yasin. "He dresses like a Muslim."

As did half the peninsula. Did it escape her that they were speaking Arabic? A flash of anger inspired a series of biting retorts to defend the finest fashions of his Almeria from this woman's ignorant assumptions.

Nonetheless, his better judgment quenched his anger almost as soon as it flared. Though these settlers were few, and he and Sarah were fewer. In any case, he should have anticipated this reaction and concocted some story about traveling alone. Bandits of all types probably plagued these farmers, and the only thing that bothered them more than a nearby attack was discovering that a pair of survivors had mysteriously escaped unscathed. He'd be suspicious, too.

He would need to concoct a tale and inflect his tone so they believed it. But what could he say, now that he had already mentioned the caravan?

Sarah cleared her throat. "If he were a Muslim, we would both be dead."

What a peculiar thing to say! Despite turning it over in his mind, Yasin couldn't fathom what chain of logic produced it. He swallowed to clear his throat of the sudden lump.

He wasn't alone. Squinting, his raven-haired inquisitor folded her arms. "What kind of answer is that?"

Sarah's lips dimpled into a condescending smile that made the woman fidget. Yasin wished he had that skill!

"A night of heavy drinking caused us to miss the caravan," she explained. "Otherwise, we would have shared its fate."

That much was true, though not quite for the reason she implied. He would have thought her precious *adab* forbade twisting the truth into a knot like that. Yasin repressed a smile. She would be utterly disreputable by the time they finished this journey.

The elderly woman wiped her hands on her apron and passed Yasin to approach Sarah. "Even the Lord's afflictions can sometimes be a blessing, my dear."

Yasin couldn't help but grin. This was a woman after his own heart. If he'd only met her two decades earlier…

"I'm discovering how true that is." Sarah met his gaze with the faintest hint of humor. Just what did that expression mean?

The woman extended a weathered hand to help Sarah down. "This isn't easy country. After the time you've had, I wager you'd enjoy a nice clean bed, yes?"

"Yes, thank you."

"Then allow me to extend my hospitality to both you and your husband. My name is Esmeralda."

Yasin swore her face reddened, but Sarah sank into a shallow curtsey without hesitating. "Sarah." Whether it was the fate of the caravan or their time alone together, something over the previous six days had tempered her reaction to being named as his wife. "Thank you for your kindness."

They disappeared, arm-in-arm, into the largest home. Yasin watched them with a mix of humor and disbelief. Perhaps *qiyan* training provided some value beyond fine music and arrogance, after all. What an intriguing possibility!

SARAH

The flames of the bonfire were large enough to warm the settlers lounging around it but not so great that a stiff wind would blow sparks to ignite the few remaining crops awaiting reaping. From the ring of stones surrounding it, Sarah supposed the settlers often gathered beneath the bowl of brilliant stars.

On the far side, Esmeralda beckoned Sarah over to her, despite the gesture provoking a look of disapproval from Maria, her companion.

Nodding to acknowledge the silent invitation, Sarah circled the fire's warmth. Some distance away, Yasin was entertaining a dozen enraptured children with wild gestures like the storytellers in the marketplace of Granada. Of course he, who so often acted like a reckless youth, would relate well to children!

No, that wasn't fair, for the adults listened with the same attention. Sarah was too far away to hear his words, but the curved smiles of good humor suggested most didn't believe a word of what was surely a fantastic story.

A wave of heat carried cinnamon from the burning fig firewood. The familiar scent invoked memories of the *agha's* overwhelming perfume back in Granada. She had hated it at first, until one night a week after she had arrived at the palace. She had been crying, missing her home as an eight-year-old girl did. But as the eunuch held her in his arms, soothing her worries, she had gotten over both her distaste at his perfume and her loneliness in the strange palace. In that moment, Granada had become her home.

A smile lingered as laughter from a young couple some distance beyond the revealing glow of firelight drew her attention. They were whispering together with self-absorbed attention, and the young man was stroking a lock of his companion's hair as she rested her hand on his thigh.

His thigh!

She couldn't help but stare. Never had she seen a couple act so brazenly, and in public, no less.

These people behaved far gentler than the brutish men who had frightened Yasin in the first *fuero*. The people of Granada would show such kindness, but Sarah never imagined a Christian doing so. They gave freely the hospitality for which the other village charged dearly. Despite sharing the same daily struggles on this limestone plateau, they had reacted differently.

When Sarah came near, Esmeralda patted a stool beside her. "Enjoy the warmth beside us. We so rarely see travelers."

Sarah smiled at the fond gesture. The elderly matron who had watched over emir's women would pat the benches in the harem like that.

"I'm surprised at that, considering how close you are to the caravan routes."

"Why should they come here when they can reach larger *fueros* with a few hours' travel?" Maria remarked.

Esmeralda merely shrugged. "It's just as well. We can accommodate the occasional couple or royal herald, but we can't supply an entire caravan. So many wagons and animals would trample our fields and strain our resources."

Sarah cocked her head. "Do royal heralds pass through on their way to Toledo?"

The elderly woman squinted before relaxing again. Though it

lasted less than a heartbeat, the brief gesture warned that this woman's welcoming demeanor didn't come from simple-mindedness. "Yes, from time to time."

She had sent only one message to Lord Gonzalo, and it might not have reached him if Almoravid raiders were operating nearby. She had to send another. If he suspected they'd betrayed him, he wouldn't hesitate to send men to kill Yasin and drag her back in chains, probably after using her to satisfy their depraved urges. A shiver crawled over her arms and down her chest as if she could feel their hands upon her.

Lord Gonzalo had undoubtedly known the dangers she'd face on the road and had deliberately neglected to warn her.

"My dear, you're shivering. Let's move closer to the fire."

A fire wouldn't banish this dread, but Sarah forced a breath to still the fear. She was safe for the moment, and she had time to prevent that fate. "Might I ask you to see that a message reaches Toledo?"

One of Esmeralda's eyebrows shot up. "My memory isn't what it used to be, I'm afraid."

"I would write it down for you." Sarah rubbed her fingers together self-consciously. She would have to avoid staining them with ink, or Yasin would ask questions.

"You can write?" Maria challenged.

"Yes." Sarah doubted either of them could read, but she'd keep the contents innocent, regardless. "You need only instruct the next rider to deliver it to any city official."

"Official, eh?" Esmeralda's lips curled into a satisfied smile that would have alarmed Sarah if not for the kindness clinging to her eyes. "That man isn't your husband, is he?"

Sarah sucked in a breath. Priests in Toledo condemned wantonness between the sexes with the same verve as the strictest imams in Granada. These settlers might eject them as adulterers, regardless of Yasin's entertaining stories.

Up came one of Maria's eyebrows. "Mother?"

Esmeralda patted the woman's thigh before turning to Sarah. "Do you imagine you're the first young woman to run off with an unsuitable man against her father's wishes?"

Sense held the panic at bay. Yasin was assuredly unsuitable. Memories spilled out in a frenzied jumble. Yasin looking like a dirty, disheveled ruffian in the library. His feeble jests that would see him ejected from any feast in Granada.

Yet she also recalled the clean lines of his *qamisa* and his fresh scent when they'd left Toledo, and the tender affection in his eyes and on his lips when, over the campfire, she had glimpsed the *adab* hidden beneath layers of canniness and cold pragmatism.

Still… Begrudging respect was a far cry from passion.

Esmeralda patted her hand. "Write your letter. I'll make sure your father knows you're well."

Sarah disliked repaying this woman's kindness with deceit, but confirming Esmeralda's misunderstanding neatly sidestepped any uncomfortable questions about them traveling together. It would even explain their full wagon. They had gathered everything they owned and fled to start a new life together. Neat and tidy. Plus, Esmeralda would take every pain to deliver her letter to Toledo if she believed it reassured a worried father.

What could she say, in any case? That she was a slave who had removed her bands and traveled with a thief to steal from El Campeador, a great ruler and relentless enemy? That would only borrow trouble they didn't need.

"You would do such a thing?"

The elderly woman cradled Sarah's hand and gave her a kindly smile. "Of course, my dear." The woman glanced at Yasin, still encircled by the children. "I made the same decision as you, long ago."

Two weeks earlier, she would not consider such a cruel deception. This journey was changing her. Little by little, he was corrupting her.

No, that was too simple of an answer. He hadn't created the dangers they faced, merely reacted to them as best as he could. Nor had he forced her actions. She had chosen them herself.

In Granada, Baghdad, and Toledo, she had been constrained, bound. But here in La Mancha, she'd traveled as a free woman. Why shouldn't that affect her? Great quests always changed the heroes in the poems, and sometimes a lie avoided terrible consequences.

She had believed her training had prepared her to face the world, that *adab* and education would overcome any challenge. She had been terribly wrong. There were no simple answers to some problems, only uncertain choices and complex truths.

"Father proved himself worthy of your trust, Mother." Maria raised her chin with swelling pride. "And you knew every skill a woman needs to manage a household."

Esmeralda smiled at her daughter. "And I made sure you did, too."

Maria offered a tight smile shaded with bitterness. Sarah suspected that training hadn't gone smoothly. She turned to Sarah. "If you're eloping, I hope you're similarly prepared."

"What sort of preparation do you mean?"

Eagerness flashed in Maria's expression. "Can you slaughter a sheep, weave cloth, or tend a garden?"

Sarah frowned. "No…"

"Forage for herbs, either for seasoning or medicine?" Maria raised an eyebrow. "Harvest crops? Care for chickens?"

Sarah remained silent. She had none of those skills.

Maria sighed. "What *can* you do, then?"

"Maria…" her mother warned.

Anger flaring, Sarah retorted without thinking. "I can read and write in four languages and recite the history of Iberia." Sarah doubted this woman could even name all the peninsula's regions. "I play several instruments and sing remarkably well."

Out of the corner of her eye, Yasin straightened and craned his neck toward her.

Far from being impressed, Maria merely scoffed. "Ornamental emptiness. Music won't clothe your children or keep your animals alive. You can't appease starvation with a song."

"Maria!" Esmeralda's voice struck like the blacksmith's hammer hitting his anvil. "That's enough." She patted Sarah on the hand. "Fear not, my dear. You're young. You still have time to learn the things a woman must know."

How dare these women casually discount those refinements treasured by every courtier and emir in *Dar al-Islam*! She had worked for many years to master skills that few could.

"Sarah?" Yasin's call drew her from her reverie. "Will you play for us?"

She would prove how wrong these women were to laud common labor over music and art. "I'd be delighted."

By the time she'd retrieved her oud from the wagon, the townsfolk had gathered their stools around the children, closer to the fire. Even the young couple gave her their attention. Yasin had reserved her a stool set apart from the rest, and she settled herself onto it.

Out here in the wilds of La Mancha, far from the great cities of al-Andalus, these settlers had probably never experienced the performance of a trained *qiyan*. They had abandoned such refinements to strike out on their own among the grasses of this dry land.

The desire for freedom had brought them here, as it had brought her, so, she began a song of liberation and celebration.

She plucked the strings with quick motions to weave a trilling song that danced on air like the flames of the bonfire. Her grip relaxed, leaving her fingers nimble and precise as they touched the strings. The settlers faded away until she saw only the smooth wood and the taut strings of her oud and her fingers, moving with confidence and precision.

The music flowed over her, bringing reassurance and peace. This trip wasn't what she'd expected, but she had at least as much fortitude and determination as Yasin. If he could cope with it, then so could she.

Gradually, she became aware of Yasin singing beside her, a strong and clear baritone that complemented the oud's vibrations. His voice warbled from weak abdominal muscles on the high notes and a rhythmic imprecision that would have earned the ire of her teachers, but passion and longing hung on each note, exposing the same deep emotion as when they had admired the gardens of Toledo.

She adjusted her tempo to match the drag-and-hold cadence of his syllables, the distinctive rhythm of Almeria. Belatedly, Sarah recalled that this song came not from the East, but from al-Andalus itself. The words obviously held a special meaning for him.

Her world contracted to include only the music connecting them. Her heart leapt in time with the rhythm. Why hadn't he shared his voice sooner? They could have filled all those days on the road with joy and beauty.

When she'd finished, the *fuero* came back into focus with a round of applause and excited chatter. She offered a bashful smile to acknowledge the praise.

But it lasted only a few moments before someone, inspired by her performance, began singing a crude Castilian song. Despite the roughness of the voice, others joined in, and soon the entire assembly was chanting together and excitedly clapping.

For a moment, her breath caught in her throat. Yes, she had entertained them, but only as much as the next singer. These people didn't know enough to appreciate the skill of her transitions and the difficulty of the piece. She doubted anyone outside a cultured court in one of the major cities would recognize the sophistication of her artistry.

Well, that wasn't entirely true, for Yasin watched her with vulnerable, intense, eyes. They were open windows, exposing sorrow and joy and memory and surprise in a confusing, overwhelming jumble. Here, among this settlement of a half-dozen families, she had met the real Yasin, not the man of jests and smirks who had accompanied her thus far.

He swallowed, but the motion didn't restore his bravado. "It's the music from home that I miss the most." The lilt of his words carried none of the complex emotion in his eyes, only sorrow.

She knew that feeling well.

YASIN

Yasin adjusted his grip on the reins from atop the wagon while Sarah bade Esmeralda goodbye. The farmer who had tended to their horses reported that the animals had eaten heartily, and Yasin could believe it from their whinnying and excited stamping.

Amid this peaceful settlement, Yasin felt some of their contentment. The early autumn crops, caught in the middle of reaping, swayed in a rhythmic dance with the wind blowing across the plains. Even the tufts of smoke rising from early morning fires seemed bright and cheerful.

The *tapia* homes all had crisp edges and well-patched walls smooth enough to leave no scrape if he ran his hand over it. These people had crafted every corner with precision. That was love, love not for a building, but for a home.

He closed his eyes. The babbling water trickling over the rocky stream bed and the calls of livestock scampering through the paddocks soothed him. The scents of baking bread tickled his nose without the noise of shouting vendors and pedestrians. Last night, he hadn't needed to listen for a thief slipping into his room, nor the scraping of his landlord unlocking his door at the demands of the city guard.

He released a long sigh. He'd left home to preserve the pleasures and freedoms he cherished. No matter the peace it brought, he could never live in a village like this, hidden away in the bend of a stream far from the markets and musicians and craftsmen of the great cities. At least in Toledo, he could retain some of his valued traditions.

The wagon rocked when a young man helped Sarah climb aboard. He smiled like a fool as Sarah thanked him.

A part of Yasin wished his desires were as simple as yearning for a pretty woman. But he searched for a way of life that drifted further out of reach with each passing day. He'd fled Almeria because of the Almoravids, and he'd left Toledo under the pall of infamy. Was this his life now, drifting from city to city until he'd used them all up?

"Shall we continue on?" Sarah asked in an airy voice unburdened by the troubles of the past few days.

He surveyed the small crowd of waving villagers. Perhaps, one day, he might find such contentment.

That task would become much easier with a pouch of gold. Valencia beckoned, with its great library and a dusty book that would unlock everything he desired. He needed only grab it from beneath the nose of Rodrigo Diaz de Vivar, the most cunning man in the world.

This would be his greatest triumph.

"It would be my pleasure." He guided the horses eastward, toward the sea.

IV

VALENCIA

AD 1094

CHAPTER TEN

SARAH

THE MONOCHROMATIC GRASSES of the plateau gradually gave way to lush green as Sarah and Yasin descended into the Kingdom of Valencia. Every time her ears popped, it seemed the landscape infused more color. Farmhouses encircled by cultivated fields dotted the landscape, packed so densely that she lost count. Vineyards and groves of fruit and olive trees separated the wide strips of golden wheat irrigated by the muddy brown water of the canals weaving through them like lace. Fragrant flowers and sweet-smelling fruit buried the odor of horse for the first time in more than two weeks.

A lightness lifted Sarah's heart as they continued east. The emptiness of the Castilian plateau had filled her with looming dread, as if raiders could spring upon them at any time. These lands, on the other hand, teemed with fields, livestock, and happy tufts of white smoke. Sense told her that more people increased their danger, yet she felt no apprehension, only affinity for this land that so resembled Granada.

They passed no further *fueros*. Castile may have needed to persuade settlers to populate the scrub lands around Toledo, but no such desperation drove these farmers. They graciously accepted the pair of weary travelers each night, bearing no suspicion nor asking anything in return. That price seemed to please Yasin.

And then, the gentle hills and wide valleys broke and revealed the city itself, nestled within the final bend of the Turia River as it met the sea.

"We made it." The weight that had settled over her since stumbling upon the ruined caravan finally lifted. They had survived.

"That we did." Yasin's voice was thick with relief. "Ibn Sina's *Book of Healing* is somewhere in that tangle."

"It'll likely be richly decorated, possibly with gold or silver."

His eyes seemed to twinkle, but Sarah supposed it was simply a trick of the morning sunlight. "Let's go get it."

Tall stone walls stretched from the northern shore of the river to sweep around the center of the city. Rickety scaffolding encased one section where hundreds of workers repaired a segment that had collapsed into a rockslide of loose debris. She did not envy the men who had to labor atop that swaying, wooden structure.

The walls couldn't contain the city, it seemed. Districts not only spilled out beyond the gates but fully encircled the walls as densely as those neighborhoods within them. Those outlying districts had one grim disadvantage. At several points, collapsed buildings, cleared expanses, and debris mounds testified to the two-year siege that had delivered the *taifa* to El Cid. The exteriors of the closest buildings bore imperfectly removed soot from recent fires and the too-clean planks of recent repairs.

Unlike Toledo or Granada, Valencia wasn't a sea of rammed-earth *tapia*, but a mixture of wood and earthen structures with a heavy concentration of stone buildings in its center. The panorama of white, brown and tan, ringed by rows of color from orchards, fields, and pastures, reminded Sarah of the mosaics on the Great Mosque in Toledo.

Yasin steered the wagon to join a line of travelers and merchants approaching the western gate. His eyes widened. "Look at that!"

The perfectly straight street before them ran from the outskirts through the gates, all the way to the Great Mosque at the city's core, visible over the walls. Trees and gardens flanked the road sporadically, dotting the mix of *tapia* and wooden buildings with bursts of color that made Valencia seem like a living creature.

Sarah couldn't help but smile, recalling her own wonder at Valencia's famously straight streets when she'd passed through on the way to Baghdad. No other Andalusi city had anything quite like it. Some said they were unchanged from Roman times. Whatever their origin, they looked like an endless portal beckoning her to her destiny.

"Wait until you see the markets," she promised.

Yasin nodded toward the approaching gate. "First, we need to get inside."

A dozen guards stood on either side. Most searched travelers as they approached, but a pair stood back from the rest, watching with quick eyes and hands resting on the hilts of sheathed swords.

"Be at peace." She rested her fingers on his wrist with a feather touch. "We've done nothing to warrant suspicion."

He rolled his shoulders and stretched his neck. "Not yet."

She forced herself to smile. The circumstances of their departure might differ considerably from those of their arrival, depending on how their stay in Valencia went.

A guard with long shaggy hair interposed them with a raised hand. "Halt," he instructed in Arabic. "Submit to a search."

Yasin obeyed, and another guard began poking through the goods piled in the wagon.

"What brings you to Valencia?" the long-haired one asked.

Yasin offered no smile this time. "A new beginning, far from the Almoravids."

"Is that so?" The guard ran his eye over first Yasin, then the horses, and finally Sarah. "Attacked?"

"Thank Jesus, no." Yasin crossed himself. "But, it happened to enough neighboring *fueros*. It was only a matter of time before our turn came."

"Finally saw the foolishness of old Alfonso's settlements, did you?" He grinned. "Well, El Campeador hanged the Almoravids who lived here. No worries on that account."

"Now, that *is* good news," Yasin answered with a vehemence Sarah was beginning to realize indicated honesty.

The guard narrowed his eyes. "You weren't bound to the land, were you?"

"No, sir." Yasin's reply carried the same vehemence as before.

"And your trade?"

Yasin retrieved his tools from his *jubba*. "Leatherworking."

The man studied the roll and grunted. "Lord Rodrigo can use all the craftsmen he can find." He gestured to the horses. "Is this your work?"

Yasin shook his head. "I bought these horses in Toledo with full tack." He patted the rump of the closest one before shrugging. "I'd have designed the straps differently."

"Hmm…" The guard probed the leather with a finger.

The other guard finished his examination and approached his partner. "Some mighty fine things back there, but nothing illegal." He turned to Yasin. "These are all your goods?"

"Only the ones we could bring with us." Yasin released a long sigh.

Sarah spent a few moments trying to decide whether Yasin had deliberately misinterpreted the use of *all*.

However, his answer seemed to satisfy the guards. The long-haired one stepped aside and waved them forward. "Move along."

"Ah, thank you, sir. Thank you." Yasin bobbed his head like a fool and guided the horses through the gates.

The noise of residents, street sellers, and pedestrians enveloped them quickly. People pressed in close enough to touch her. After so many days with only Yasin on the road, the sudden rush of squirming bodies felt unsettling. She pulled her cloak tighter, wishing it could shut them out completely.

Yasin glanced behind before muttering, "They're good, these

guards." After a quick breath, he nodded toward the back of the wagon. "Watch for thieves."

She twisted so she could keep an eye on the back of the wagon. "What do you mean?"

"They tried to catch me off guard."

She frowned. "You told the monks at the abbey that Almoravids attacked our village. Why change your tale now?" If those settlers came to Valencia to trade, they could expose the lie.

"These guards see travelers every day. They can tell the difference between refugees and immigrants. I salvaged too much from the caravan for us to be the former."

He was probably right. "Then, why not take credit for your harness?" He had worked hard to lash together the remnants of leather at the caravan. "Wouldn't a leatherworker seeking a new start celebrate his work?"

"True, but they see a lot of horses. They might ask why ours aren't appointed the same way. Maybe they'd think I stole them." He flashed a wry grin. "It's best not to linger near those who can control your fate."

Considering both of their experiences, she couldn't disagree.

Yasin sold the wagon and horses after a lengthy conversation with the owner of a stable just inside the gates. She had packed the blue dress, oud, writing supplies, and a few necessaries in a spare satchel by the time he'd returned. Her shoulder was already starting to hurt from the weight.

"This is all I can carry." She eyed the back of the wagon longingly as its new owner inspected it.

"They'll watch the rest until we find buyers," he explained. "You can leave that, too, if you like. They won't steal it. It'd be bad for business."

She shifted her weight to take the strain off her shoulder. "I'd rather not."

"Then at least let me carry it. You look like you're about to collapse."

She happily handed it over. "What happens when we're ready to leave?"

"You won't have to walk to Toledo." He patted the chestnut horse on the back. "We'll buy new ones. It'll be cheaper than stabling them for however long we're here."

She bit her lip. "How long do you think that'll be?" She would only taste true freedom after their return. At the thought, she resolved to write again to Gonzalo. Surely El Cid still sent messages to Toledo, even if he refused to supplicate himself to his king.

Yasin scratched his nose. "As long as it takes. Now, come. I got directions to an inn."

"An inn?" Her voice fluttered with excitement.

"I promised you an inn."

She frowned. "Did you?"

He narrowed his eyes for a moment before shrugging. "Close enough to it."

They continued deeper into the city. Sarah took comfort from the Great Mosque looming ahead of them, beckoning them closer. Even from a distance, she could tell it hadn't been defaced or pillaged, nor did any crosses stand in triumph upon its minarets. Majestic. Untainted.

The central avenue, running like the string of an oud through Valencia, seemed spacious compared to the twisting streets of Granada and Toledo. Wagons, carts, and riders filed past in two long lines down the center of the avenue, relegating pedestrians to the raised cobble sidewalks, a space too small for the traffic.

Yasin kept one hand clenched tightly around his money pouch and the other against her back to avoid being separated by the jostling crowd. To her surprise, his touch comforted her. When she'd first met him, she hadn't believed him capable of evoking anything but revulsion. That was before the caravan, their campfire conversations, his singing, the clearing… Now, only he and her oud seemed familiar in this strange city.

She twisted to confirm that the satchel was still safe, slung over his shoulder.

They crossed an intersection, and Sarah glanced down the side street. The long row of houses and shops extending into the indistinct distance was jarring after a lifetime spent among awkwardly twisting alleys and cozy, private spaces. She felt the eyes of the entire city upon her.

And yet, despite the straightness of the streets, they reminded her of Granada. Music danced on the air, woven by itinerant musicians standing at the street corners. Jugglers flung knives into the air and caught them with quick motions, and dancers twirled in rhythm. Topiaries and mosaics adorned the buildings with a riot of color. Accents, languages, and inflections battled for primacy in her ears, but most of the words were in delightful Andalusi-accented Arabic. She even caught a Granadan accent like that of her father. Though she twisted to seek out the source, the crowd shifted too quickly and she didn't hear it again.

The chatter carried a hint of excitement, not at all like the anxious desperation of Toledo. Fragments of conversation spoke of new clothing and feasts. Groups of women—both veiled and unveiled—haggled with shopkeepers and chatted lazily, unburdened by urgency or the fear of outcry at their presence. An official argued with a butcher about inaccurate scales, but even the onlookers heckling the crooked shopkeeper did so with humor rather than anger.

At the corner of another intersection, a group of priests, imams, and a single rabbi wearing a kippah cap stood in a cluster, wrapped in an intense discussion. One of the imams shook a scroll at the priests and gestured boldly with his free hand. Though she expected the priests to begin haranguing the others, they only nodded and shook hands with the faithful. One even raised a hand to concede a point.

Along with the occasional tuft of perfume-scented steam from a nearby *hamam*, the aroma of spices grew stronger, teasing her nostrils and stinging her eyes. Turning the corner onto another long, straight avenue, they confronted a riot of color from an endless chain of spice sellers. Opened leather sacks revealed cinnamon and nutmeg, cardamom and turmeric, cumin, oregano, and a dozen other spices she hadn't tasted in many years. Her mouth watered at the few grains that spilled each time the ladle deposited some on a scale.

The spice street opened up into the main market. Several stalls in a cluster contained bottles of perfume and scented oil to adorn the skin. Beyond them sat pigments and dyes: lac, kohl, indigo, and a dozen other powders. Another held fine platters and goblets, glasses of Iraqi crystal, bronze forks from Byzantium, and silver spoons intricately carved with Islamic prayers. One stall selling hourglasses even had a weight-driven water clock, the gears and moving weights of its design very much like one she had seen once at a noble's estate in Baghdad. Unlike the one in the gardens of Toledo, this one could fit on a table. Imagine mastering time in such a way!

Was this truly a Christian city, with such…civility? Where was the fanaticism Yasin insisted was sweeping the peninsula?

She longed to indulge in all the wonderful luxuries surrounding her, even as she realized how impossible that dream was. Yasin had provided necessities on the journey—including for her monthly *haidh* which was, Allah be praised, nearly over—but hadn't wasted a coin on luxury. Now that they'd arrived, all their money would go toward their mission. And, as much as she hated to admit it, even scented oil wouldn't comfort her as much as a signed emancipation order.

Of course, if she had her own money, enough to establish herself in proper status to attract a worthy husband, she wouldn't need a noble in Toledo to grant her freedom. She wouldn't need to return to Toledo at all.

"My, oh my…" Yasin grasped her hand in a firm but callused grip and led her through the crowd to a stall filled with fine silks, cotton brocades, and the finest-grained linen she had ever seen. He traced his trembling fingers along a reddish-brown cotton *qamisa* folded near the front.

His eyes were dancing. "This is Egyptian cotton. Look at the weave." He crouched to study it. Eyeing a bolt of rich blue silk, he barked a laugh. "And the silk… I've not seen its quality since I left home." He stroked the fabric as he might a kitten.

"I told you you'd love the markets." Humor added breath to her voice.

At the end of the next side-street, they found the inn, a two-story stone structure with a double-door entrance. After a quick negotiation on price, the owner escorted them to a second-floor room. The light seeping through the cracks of a shuttered window illuminated a table, bench, and a single, glorious, platform bed with a mattress as thick as her wrist.

Relief washed over her as she pressed her hand into that blessed mattress. The surface gave just a little, but that modicum of cushioning thrilled her after two weeks of stiff surfaces. Her feet still ached from walking, sitting on the wagon bench for consecutive days had left her legs and bottom sore, and her back throbbed from nights on the hard ground. Through it all, she had dreamed of a bed.

Yasin had thanked the innkeeper and was setting the satchel down on the table. She inhaled to remind him to be careful with the instrument, but he had already positioned it delicately, without making a sound.

Dodging raiders, greedy settlers, wild animals, and the elements, they had crossed half of al-Andalus and had arrived safely, if not soundly. Somewhere in this city, a wood-bound codex sat in a corner of a library, waiting for them to steal it.

She took a deep breath. "Now that we're here, how do we begin?"

He grinned. "You can start by finding us somewhere to live."

She glanced at the soft bed she'd spent weeks dreaming about. "Somewhere other than here?"

"An inn will suffice for a few days, but we presented ourselves as a respectable husband and wife looking to start a new life. The guards saw us arrive with a wagon filled with valuables. We'd raise suspicion if we don't set up a household, and that would make our task harder."

He spoke matter-of-factly, as if such reasoning would occur to anyone. The details of deception bewildered her. Had his mind been calculating the implications of every interaction and each of their lies this whole journey? If so, she had seriously underestimated him.

She nibbled at the inside of her lip as one of those implications gnawed at her. She had only known one married woman, and memories of her mother had dimmed with time. "I've never set up a household before." She sighed. "I wouldn't know what to do."

"Now that the siege is over, there should be plenty of rooms for let."

"Yes, but what should I look for?"

He shrugged. "Just think about what a woman starting a family would value. Security, comfort, proximity to the markets for food. Visit a few places and pick the best."

They'd passed plenty of women on their way here, so she doubted traveling alone in daylight would be dangerous. In fact, she looked forward to a little time by herself.

Recalling their journey returned her thoughts to their purpose. "Where will you start?"

He crossed his arms and leaned against the table, though on the other side from her precious oud. "I have to solve two problems. First, I need to find the *Metaphysics* section of the *Healing*."

Sarah nodded. "We know that. In the library."

"I need to verify that. Even if it's there, it's surrounded by El Cid's toughened mercenaries. I'd be a fool if I didn't look for another copy first."

"An authentic copy," Sarah reminded.

He swallowed. "Lord Gonzalo was very clear about that."

"And if you can't, then you'll steal the one in the library?"

"El Cid isn't a forgiving man. I'd rather not steal from him." His Adam's apple bobbed up and down. "There may be safer ways."

He sounded confident, but she remained skeptical. "What other ways?"

"Leatherworking, for a start. Someone has to maintain the leather covers, and my skill could get me into the library. Failing that, fraud, smuggling, bribery…" He shrugged, but a smirk tugged at his lips. "All of which are less risky than burglary."

"And if there's no other way?"

He abruptly took her hands. Startled, she began to pull away, but he bent down, drawing her gaze. Her resistance faded as she met eyes filled with sincerity, not desire.

"I promise I will bring a copy back to Toledo. I need this as much as you do."

She drew in a silent breath. He had kept his word so far, and she doubted he would lead her to Valencia only to break faith now. But it sounded like this process would take more than a few days. She'd have to explain Yasin's plan carefully in her next message to Lord Gonzalo. "You mentioned a second problem?"

He released her hands, and they felt cold after the warmth of his fingers. Leaning against the wall, he rubbed the side of his neck. "Escaping the city without being caught." He ticked off the points with his fingers. "I need to learn the streets, find the secret ways past the walls, and determine which officials will honor a good, sturdy bribe."

Theft involved more preparation than Sarah had guessed. She began to understand Gonzalo's reasons for approaching a thief for this task. "How can you do that?"

His smile transformed into a grin. "I'm going to the alehouse."

This time, his pronouncement evoked no flare of disapproval. His last visit had saved their lives.

"I don't have contacts here," he continued. "I need to find someone desperate enough to risk working with a stranger. And there's no finer place to find desperate men than the alehouse or the marketplace."

"Why not start in the marketplace?"

His smile widened. "Because I have Almoravid executions to celebrate."

YASIN

While Yasin's first descent into the taverns of Valencia revealed no easy path into the library, a drunken clerk confirmed that the library had survived the siege intact. However, he also revealed that only royal craftsmen maintained the manuscripts' leather binding and covers. His respectable trade wouldn't put Ibn Sina's codex in his hands.

A local baker's comment about visiting the port to secure some spices forbidden by El Cid's regulations hinted at a healthy smuggling network. Insinuating himself within it would fill Yasin's coin pouch, too. Though selling the wagon and his salvaged goods would help, lodging and bribes would quickly deplete his funds.

The next morning, a layer of clouds blocked out the sun, but a warm ocean breeze compelled Yasin to leave his blue *jubba* at the inn. That suited him just fine: the expensive garment would attract too much attention. He elected to wear the dirty *qamisa* that still smelled of cinnamon from the *fuero* bonfire instead of the clean one he'd salvaged from the caravan.

Stepping through the double doors of the inn, Yasin watched the crowds to orient himself. He could have asked directions to the port easily enough, but if acquiring the *Healing* led to trouble, he'd rather limit the number of people who knew his interests and business. Fortunately, even without the sun to navigate, the motion in the streets spoke to him. A good number of the mules hauling laden carts were coming from the same direction, and the grimy, wrinkled *qamisas* of the burly men leading them identified them as dockworkers.

He grinned. Sarah could read books, but he could read people.

He followed the carts to their origin, weaving through the crowds with a comfortable ease. Much about Valencia reminded him of the Almeria he loved. Oils and perfumes of sandalwood, agarwood, and musk followed in the crowd's wake. Bobbing veils of silk and lace wove through the crowds, so unlike the brazen exposure of Christian faces in Toledo.

In the distance, a rebab played the jaunty tune his mother used to sing to help him fall asleep. A stab of pain steadily grew in his chest as he remembered her sitting on the edge of his bed, stroking his head. He recalled her hair most vividly, long locks of nearly black that swayed with the subtle movements of her head as she sang. As a child, he had so rarely seen unbound hair.

Pushing the memory aside, he checked his coin pouch. He wore no *jubba* today, and a wandering mind could make him a victim of the city's pickpockets.

Amid creaking wheelbarrows and pulleys carrying bricks, squads of workers were busily repairing several sections of wall damaged in the recent siege. Near one section, a mason covered in clay and a smith with a belt of dangling tools discussed repairs to a rusted semicircular grate atop a drainage canal. The stones of the archway above the canal had loosened and spilled out of place over time, forming a pile of debris beneath a hole perfect for smuggling.

Yasin shivered at the implication. Elsewhere, such weathering was usually overlooked. No wonder the smugglers focused on the port: El Cid was sealing the walls of Valencia up tighter than a bottle of fine Almerian wine, which Yasin suspected he'd struggle to slip past them.

El Cid's men were everywhere, and they moved with discipline, wholly unlike the lazy guards of Toledo. When they spoke to someone, they slid into a defensive stance and rested their hands on their swords, ready to draw cut. Not once as Yasin followed them did they shout at a street urchin or harangue a vendor. They didn't carouse or taunt each other. Yasin kept his distance, lest he attract their scrutiny.

Finely painted and stuccoed buildings slowly gave way to uneven steps, rotting wood, and threadbare awnings as he approached the port. Gruff laborers replaced the well-dressed residents. Even the air changed. Damp wood, humidity, baking bread, and seared fish replaced the oils and perfumes.

The port itself stretched across the shoreline as far as he could see in both directions. Across the river, little wooden and *tapia* houses on the far shore looked squat and simple, much like those he'd passed upon entering the city. A few men splashed each other by the riverbank, their faces twisted in laughter rendered silent by the calls of nearby dockworkers. Far to the east, horses' heads and men sitting atop carts bobbed in and out of view as they traversed the great stone bridge spanning the river. Its arches blotted out Yasin's view of the sea beyond. Through the haze of distance, the high, covered platforms of wooden watchtowers rose above the southern districts. Yasin counted four of them before he could no longer discern their silhouettes from the horizon.

This port was busier than Toledo's. Lines of dockworkers trudged up and down wharves, unloading barrels and crates from the moored ships in an endless procession. They caught an earful on both ends, first as the sailors shouted threats should they mishandle the merchandise and again as *jubba*-wearing officials complained about how they stacked the cargo. Boys scampered about, carrying bowls of water and feed bags for the wagon mules. One ducked beneath a pair of dockworkers straining under the weight of a rolled carpet, then dashed out of reach as they cursed and grabbed for him.

Groups of men waited safely out of range of the laborers. Each party included a single finely dressed merchant's factor in cotton brocade and supple leather boots surrounded by gruff craftsmen hovering nearby, inquiring after their goods. They all bore marks of their trades, whether flour or soot clinging to their beards and clothes or stains on their fingers.

A well-groomed tax official marked wax tablets, occasionally counting cargo with a wooden stylus. Only after approving the shipments did the official allow the dockworkers to load the exports or the carters to disseminate the imports throughout the city. Thick-necked enforcers in black *qamisas* stood behind him in case anyone tried to evade paying their port fees.

Within the mostly innocent activity, Yasin recognized the subtle signs of mischief. Three wharfs down, a dockworker who stood half a head shorter than the others set a barrel back a little further behind a railing, only for another passing laborer to pick it up and disappear down a side street. A sailor skipped past the dockworkers and flagged a woman peddling fresh bread to the laborers. As he waited for some, he casually slipped a pouch to a passing wagoner, who boarded his cart and guided its mule forward. Signals, gestures, handoffs during chance encounters, actions that broke pattern… Oh, yes, smugglers were thriving in this port!

After half an hour of observation, Yasin noticed only one passing guard patrol. He'd wrongly assumed El Cid had repaired that crumbling drainage grate to prevent smuggling. El Cid was a soldier, and a weak drainage grate could admit a force of Almoravids into the city. Walls were military assets worth guarding and repairing, but a port was merely a source of revenue. Why should he guard the port when it was protected by that wall of watchtowers to the south? El Cid had sealed the flow of illegal goods through the gates purely by accident.

With the right introduction, this port was Yasin's way out of the city.

After buying a loaf of apricot bread from the peddler, he sat upon a crate free of pigeon droppings by an unused wharf and waited for his chance.

SARAH

Freedom!

In the short distance between her room and the beckoning morning sunlight seeping through a crack in the inn's great doors, Sarah's self-control unraveled. By the time she erupted through the doors and onto the street, her cheeks hurt from smiling.

She laughed as she twirled, unfurling the skirt of her salvaged blue cotton dress. After years of homespun wool tugging and snagging, the free-flowing fine cotton filled her with a quiet rapture, even if the adjustments she'd made over the years to account for the weight of her wrist bands felt clumsy and unnecessary now. By the end of her third liberating spin, though, her grace had begun to return.

Yes, she had felt free beneath the great dome of unbroken sky on the grassy plains of La Mancha. But only now, wrapped in a flowing dress deserving of a *qiyan* in a great city, did her burdens yield to sweet, unbridled relief. Here, she was neither slave nor bound servant. No priests would take her by the arm and drag her back to sweep out a room or empty a chamber pot. She was a free woman for the first time in her life, and she intended to enjoy herself.

But Yasin had entrusted her with the vital task of maintaining their role as relocated *fuero* settlers, so she sobered quickly. She refused to let him down. He'd suggested starting near the markets, sensible advice that Sarah, who hadn't previously contemplated life as a wife, decided to follow.

Every face she passed bore the finest cosmetics around their eyes and the reassuringly darkened complexion of the faithful, not the pale skin of those northern goat herders. A few quick inquiries at the nearest stalls directed her toward a *tapia* building one street off the great market.

The man who opened the door studied her with narrowed eyes, attention halting ever so briefly at her bust and her hips. He leaned a forearm on the door frame, and as he did his *jubba* draped open. "May I help you?"

She had never negotiated with a landlord before and knew nothing about what was expected of her. Was it even appropriate for a Valencian woman to conduct business that would put her unchaperoned in a room with strange men?

After a moment's hesitation, she slipped into her usual, cautious pose. Folding her hands before her as an added layer of separation, she raised her chin a fraction to meet his gaze. "Good morning. I understand you have rooms to let."

He studied her a second time. Evidently, she presented a convincing approximation of a respectable wife, for he stepped aside. "I do. Allow me to show you what I have available."

The entryway and stairs leading to the second floor showed the age of the building; twice, she had to brace against the wall when her foot landed on a divot in the steps. A muttering conversation and the noise of servants beating a rug echoed off the walls. While living here wouldn't be quiet, at least she needn't worry about this landlord taking advantage of her without witnesses.

He led her to a door at the far end of the upstairs hallway and entered. The sound of hurried footsteps and the fluttering of his coat indicated some burst of activity within, though Sarah couldn't see what.

She had no trouble seeing the rat that scurried out a moment later. Shrieking, she lifted her skirt a few fingerspans and jumped to the side as it passed.

Opening the door fully, he swept his hand to beckon her inside. "Here we are."

Sarah halted at the door. The modest room contained a bed and a simple pine table and was barely larger than their borrowed chamber at the *fuero* abbey. More concerning to Sarah was the series of sizeable cracks in the *tapia* walls…and the scraggily, unwelcome guests they evidently admitted. Even if the claw-scratched hole at the base of one of the walls hadn't immediately disqualified it, the ridiculously high price the landlord quoted would have.

She forced a smile to conceal her disappointment. "Thank you. I will discuss it with my husband."

She hoped that the second property, further from the markets, would be more affordable, but Sarah rejected it before even entering. The odor of emptied chamber pots extended from beyond the nearby alleys, baking in the warming sun. Investigating, she noted that the closest sewer was two streets away. While Sarah was willing to walk the distance to dispose of her waste, the building's other tenants evidently weren't.

She was learning, though, and as she did, she reassessed her priorities. Privacy seemed more vital to their purposes here than proximity to the markets or *hamams*. And rooms on the first floor would let them come and go more easily if they had to make a quick escape.

She released a tiny gasp. She was thinking like a thief, not a *qiyan*. Like Yasin.

Her surprise lasted only a moment. Why shouldn't she? She and Yasin were partners in this heist. Had the victim been a Muslim instead of a Christian warlord, that thought might have disturbed her.

Her inquiries in the port led her to a three-story structure made of weathered elm whose door bore no intricate carvings or adornments. The street and alleys surrounding it looked blessedly free of refuse. Hopefully, the inside was as suitable and the landlord didn't demand an emir's ransom.

After adjusting her white cotton shawl to cover as much of her hair as she could, she knocked on the door and prepared herself for the same disappointment she'd experienced all morning.

A Muslim with neatly trimmed hair swiveled the door open. He eyed her for a moment before pressing his hands to his lips, then his forehead. "Peace be upon you, dear lady."

"And upon you, be peace." Sarah stiffly bowed her head. "I wish to speak to the landlord."

"Ah…of course." He stepped back to allow her entry. "If you'll wait a moment?"

The man led her inside, then retreated further into the building. That the landlord was present at this time of day suggested a well-kept property, and Sarah's observations while she waited seemed to confirm it. The faint scent of flowers drifted on the air, but not so intensely as to conceal mold. Nor did refuse collect in the corners.

A woman wrapped in a burgundy shawl emerged at the other end of the hall. Sarah stepped aside to permit her to pass, but the woman halted before her. "Peace be upon you. How may I help you?"

"I wish to speak to the landlord."

The woman raised her chin. "You are."

Mouth falling open, Sarah needed a moment to recover. She'd seen women working in family shops, but to manage an entire property? Neither her experience in the emir's palace nor in the library had prepared her for that. And yet, for all she knew, such a practice was common. She could hardly claim to know better.

Stirring, Sarah bowed her head. "I would like to inquire about lodging for myself and my husband."

"Your husband?" The landlady studied Sarah's shawl, dress, and boots. "What is his vocation?"

"He is a master leatherworker, having trained both in Almeria and Toledo."

"A nice, clean trade." Eagerness replaced suspicion in the woman's expression. "I have a few rooms. Come." She gestured deeper into the building.

When the woman approached the steps, Sarah interrupted, "Do you have any on the first floor?"

Halting, the woman raised an eyebrow. "Yes, though they're more expensive."

As he'd done throughout their journey, Yasin had graciously slept on the floor last night, letting her use the lone bed in their inn room. It had been a kind gesture, but Sarah couldn't let him continue that way. "And, if possible, I'd like one with two beds. Cots would suffice."

The woman's eyebrow sprung up. "Two beds?"

Sarah had only meant to provide Yasin with some comfort; she hadn't thought through the implications of the simple request. Now, the mistake of a loose tongue had exposed her deception. What married couple needed separate sleeping surfaces? The landlady would tell her friends, and word would spread. The gossip would attract exactly the kind of attention Yasin had wanted to avoid. The port was a small place, and she and Yasin likely couldn't afford another district.

Damn her ungoverned tongue! She should have considered these implications. Catching her breath, Sarah pressed her hands against her stomach to still their sudden shaking.

The landlady's gaze followed the motion and settled on Sarah's belly. After a moment, her face brightened. "Oh, of course!" She reached down to place a hand on Sarah's midsection. "How far along are you?" She released a girlish giggle. "It'll be so nice to have a baby in the building again!"

A baby. Sarah heard the word as if from a great distance. She hadn't imagined ever having children. Never before had her circumstances permitted it. Marriage had been an unwelcome threat when she'd been a slave in Granada. Not even in Baghdad, when her growing collection of refinements had made the possibility of a worthy match more likely, had she thought beyond courtship and the pleasures of an attractive young suitor. In Toledo, marriage had been a desperate hope to free her from her bondage.

And yet, once she and Yasin returned with the final volumes the library needed to complete the *Book of Healing*, her circumstances would be forever changed. She could buy a home in the South, dress finely, and afford perfumes and tinctures. Presenting herself as the accomplished *qiyan* she was, she could finally make a suitable match. And children would naturally follow, wouldn't they?

The landlady led Sarah into a first-floor room and began to rattle off the features. "As you can see, this room has a hearth suitable for cooking. I'll even stock it with basic staples and allow you to use my pots, if you clean them afterward." She giggled. "You need to keep up your strength for the baby, after all."

Sarah's thoughts swirled with vivid images of strange, new possibilities. For the first time, she could see a future with a family of her own. She imagined herself rocking a child back and forth in her arms beneath the room's small glass-encased window. Snuggling nestled in the embrace of her husband on one of the room's cots, watching the baby sleep in the impression of the other. Sitting on one of the stools accompanying the simple table, singing to her child as she nursed.

She could almost feel the weight in her arms, the softness of the baby's skin. It was all within reach. For the first time in many years, her future was filled with possibilities and no longer frightened her.

YASIN

After half an hour of waiting, Yasin got his opportunity.

In front of an abandoned corner house with a collapsed roof, a broad-chested dockworker with a neatly trimmed beard flipped over a barrel. Withdrawing a knife from a sheath at his waist, he wedged it between two bottom planks. After a few moments' effort, one of the panels popped open to reveal a hidden compartment.

Watching from across the port, Yasin beamed with professional delight. Concealment was tricky. He had gone through three belts before crafting the perfect hidden sheath for his ring knife. A true master must have designed that barrel for the panel to remain sealed under the weight of its contents yet open with the pressure of a simple knife.

The dockworker was struggling to wedge a cloth-wrapped parcel into the newly exposed compartment. Out of habit, Yasin surveyed the area for witnesses. A group of laborers stood nearby but directed their attention to an unveiled woman in a low-cut dress selling ale from a hand cart. The tax official and his men stood two wharves over, assessing a collection of cargo destined for an Egyptian ship that had just docked.

But up the street running alongside the abandoned house, a pair of city guards sauntered toward the docks. In a few moments, they would round the corner and catch the smuggler, who was still struggling with his package.

In Christian cities, being caught would cost him a month in a dank prison. Muslim cities would sever his hand. Yasin couldn't guess the punishment a man like El Cid—so familiar with both worlds— would exact.

Jumping to his feet, Yasin cast aside the heel of his bread and wove through the crowd. A number of wagons had just set out from a nearby wharf, and Yasin slipped between two of them. One of the horses stopped short to avoid Yasin. The trailing driver shouted and tried to strike him with his whip, but Yasin dashed out of range and the cracker struck empty air.

The guards had already reached the back corner of the building. The smuggler had squeezed most of the parcel into the false-bottomed barrel and was trying to replace the wooden panel. He needed only moments, moments that would mean the difference between prison and profit.

Yasin intercepted the guards two steps before they turned the corner. "Help…please…" He rested his hands on his knees, feigning exhaustion.

Visible in Yasin's peripheral vision a couple strides away, the startled smuggler halted and gawked. He couldn't possibly know what danger lay around the corner.

"Thank God I found you guards," Yasin continued before the startled smuggler said something to reveal himself.

Around the corner, the guards rested their hands on their hilts. The one closer to the corner home raised his left hand to halt Yasin. "What is the meaning of this?" He had an Aragonese accent.

The hand must have extended past the corner of the building, for the smuggler shifted his gaze to it before resuming his efforts to snap the panel back into place.

By God, this was close!

"A thief stole my sack!" Yasin pointed down the street to the west. "A boy, no more than ten years. Snatched it right off my shoulder."

The guards gawked for a moment before erupting with deep-throated laughter. The Aragonese released his sword and pressed his hand to his chest to steady himself.

The laughter nicely concealed the click of the smuggler's panel and the sound of him flipping the barrel over.

"Hear that, Diego?" the Aragonese asked. "An urchin robbed him."

"You don't say?" The other grinned broadly enough to contort his words. "This is news Lord Rodrigo must hear!"

Finished, the smuggler leaned against the sealed door, staring off toward the wharves as if uninterested in the barrel beside him. Though Yasin questioned his judgment in opening a false bottom in public, at least the man could blend in.

The Aragonese pushed Yasin back. "Stop wasting our time."

"But my sack—"

"Consider it a lesson. Keep a closer watch on your things next time." He brushed Yasin aside with his outstretched arm.

The force caused Yasin to stumble a few steps, and he used the motion to keep himself between the guards and the barrel as they turned the corner and continued their patrol along the row of wharves. He watched them until the crowds interrupted his view.

Yasin flashed the smuggler a wry grin. "That was a close one," he muttered in Arabic.

The smuggler unfolded an arm and rubbed his whiskers. "I'd be done for if you hadn't delayed them." He had a thick Andalusi accent. The man's jaw contorted as he chewed the inside of his mouth. "Why?"

Yasin considered his answer. The smuggler's accent, grooming, and familiar *qamisa* and baggy *sirwal* pants—albeit dirtier than those Yasin would ever wear—suggested he was almost certainly a Muslim. That hidden parcel could be anything from stolen jewels to reports about Valencian defenses bound for the Almoravids. Yasin prayed it wasn't the latter.

But smugglers always took exception to those in power. "I don't like the idea of a Castilian dictating what a Valencian can trade."

The man gave a toothy grin. "Then you have my thanks." He pressed his hand to his chest and bowed at the neck. "I am Hisham al-Hasan." Hisham the handsome, a judgment only a mother could believe.

Yasin pressed his fingers to his lips and then his head. "Yasin ibn Faraj of Almeria."

Hisham jutted his chin at the barrel. "You aren't curious what's inside?"

Yasin fought not to look. This was a test. "I'm looking for work, not trouble."

"What kind of work?" Hisham's lip curled as he eyed Yasin. He would notice the stained and wrinkled *qamisa* and the calluses from years of working leather.

"I have experience driving wagons." Yasin had gotten quite the education this past week. "They go where I want them to."

"So you know horses?" Hisham stroked his finely trimmed beard. "Perhaps I could have a word with the harbormaster. We can always use a good wagoner."

Yasin narrowed his eyes. A smuggler might exploit a man he believed to be desperate for work with no other options. "Why would you do that?"

"I owe you, and I settle my debts." Hisham sniffed and rubbed his nose. "And I'd rather have you delivering cargo than a man without discretion."

That was an answer Yasin could appreciate.

SARAH

"You wish to be a dockworker?" Sarah frowned as she plucked the wrong string of her oud.

"Not a dockworker, a wagoner," Yasin took a bite of a pear. A drop of juice rolled down its side and he licked it up. "Delivering cargo throughout the city."

She lowered the neck of the oud. "Forgive me, but I thought you were a leatherworker."

"Leatherworking won't get me the *Healing*." He finished chewing and swallowed. "The library uses their own craftsmen to maintain the codices."

She flexed a cramp out of her fingers. "Delivering crates provides more opportunity?"

"Hisham expects me to deliver his smuggled goods," he continued, "but once I learn where the real demand is, I can establish my own customers. Then, we'll see more coin."

Gonzalo's warning echoed in her mind. Her finger slipped and brushed against a string, filling the room with an inadvertent note. "Please take care. If we don't deliver—"

He raised his hands defensively. "I know, I know. I'm not here to make money. But information and supplies aren't free." He took another bite of his pear. "And it'll introduce me to people. I need to find someone—a scholar, a servant, maybe even one of the city craftsmen—who can lead me into the library." He shrugged and took another bite. "If I'm very lucky, one of my deliveries will take me there. I could dress you like a laborer and we could slip away while unloading."

She stirred at the comment. "I thought you didn't want to resort to burglary."

He raised a finger. "I *hesitate* to resort to burglary. It too often leads to encounters with armed soldiers." He crossed himself abruptly. "But nor would I ignore a chance that falls into my lap." His eyes became distant. "It might help with the other problem, too. Smugglers know the ways in and out of every district. If I can avoid those who'd slit my throat for a copper coin, they might help us escape."

"Yasin!"

"You do worry about me, don't you?" He grinned broadly enough to reveal the piece of fruit he was working on. "I'm sorry if it upsets you, but it's a danger. I have nowhere to run if trouble comes. Not yet, at least."

"Well, you'll have somewhere to rest your head, at least. I found us a new home."

"So quickly!" His eyes brightened. "Well done."

"Thank you." Feeling a blush begin, she looked away. "It's close enough to the port that I could hear dockworkers laboring, but it isn't too loud. Plus, it's some distance from the closest guard post."

"I hadn't considered that. Good thinking."

Distracted by the compliment, her finger slipped and she missed a note. Embarrassed, she rested the instrument against her chest and massaged her fingers. "And I thought of another way I can help our cause."

He cocked his head and took another bite. "Oh?"

She nodded. "The taverns offer entertainment to draw customers in. A trained *qiyan* can earn good coin with her music. As you said, we have expenses."

He halted in mid-bite. "You would use your labor to help cover our expenses?"

"I value my freedom as much as you value your workshop. If I share the rewards, I should share the burdens." She set the instrument down. "I'm an equal partner in this venture, aren't I?"

"That's true." He finished his bite. "But such places can be dangerous for a woman on her own."

"I wouldn't be alone if you escorted me. You could have your conversations—"

"My conversations?" His lips curled into a grin.

"Yes, where you charm people into telling you what you really want to know."

His eyebrows shot up. "You're saying I'm charming?"

She ignored the goading. "You could ask around for news that might help us while I play."

The mischief in his eyes faded, and his gaze assumed the distance of thought. "That's a good idea." His attention returned to her. "And you can keep your ears open, too. You know more about libraries than I ever will. You might notice something I'd miss."

She drew in an unsteady breath. "You would trust your fate to information I gathered?" If exposed, Sarah could always plead her sex and claim obedience to Yasin, but he had no such defense. He was putting his fate in her hands.

He shrugged. "You're intelligent and cautious." The soft words echoed through the quiet room like the voice of Allah. "Your quick thinking soothed the farmers' suspicions at the *fuero*." His eyes bore no veil of charm or irony. "I trust you."

Ya salaam!

This thief who trusted no one trusted her. He was willing to unleash her into the world and rely upon her efforts. No one in her entire life had done that. A flush of excitement surged through her. Just two weeks earlier, she wouldn't have believed she'd care about the opinion of such a man.

"I won't let you down." Another thought slipped into her mind, though, and humor replaced surprise. "Though you don't strike me as the type to revel in physical labor."

He stiffened, looking like a fish in the market. A drop of juice rolled off the pear and traced a path down his finger and the back side of his hand.

"Judas!" Horror rounded his gaping mouth. "I hadn't considered that!"

CHAPTER ELEVEN

SARAH

THOUGH SARAH WAS an expert at the oud, all her practice in quiet Baghdadi gardens hadn't prepared her for the struggle of playing in a noisy tavern. A flare of apprehension surged with each burst of communal laughter and shouted argument. Twice, she was so distracted that she plucked the wrong chord.

But, while the crowd in the large *tapia* tavern was spirited, it didn't seem particularly dangerous. Fading sunlight filtered through the pair of small windows and blended with the light from a large hearth to define the basic layout of the tavern. Candles in the center of each uneven wooden table brightened the faces of the men clustered around them. Along the perimeter, others lounged on cushioned benches within chipped *tapia* booths.

She would have hesitated to be in their company alone, though, and was thankful for Yasin's presence. He leaned against a long counter in front of several barrels along the right wall, engaged with the rosy-cheeked Mozarab in an apron who had hired her. Despite what appeared to be a fairly intense conversation, he nonetheless glanced her way occasionally with expressions of doting concern.

Sarah played a bawdy, local favorite, at least according to the tavern's owner. Though the simple rhythm, which repeated the same cadence with minor variations, made it easy to sing along, the majority of patrons were too engrossed in their own conversations to join in.

The few who weren't ignoring her watched her with a naked desire that clearly had nothing to do with the quality of her performance. One repeatedly licked his lips as he stared. Not once did those eyes shift to her oud. He leered at her as if she existed only to titillate him, and his expression reflected desires whose nature she didn't care to imagine. The hunger in them reminded her of Gonzalo, standing in the frame of her doorway, but this time it was unsolicited and unwanted. All at once, she recalled the slanderous rumors about a *qiyan*'s training whispered in the library. It both unsettled her and drained of her usual enjoyment at playing for an audience.

She fell behind in the song's rhythm the faintest amount, distracted by the implications of those stares.

Stepping away from the counter, Yasin began to circulate. As he did, he offered her a reassuring smile.

The rest of the room faded from her concern. His was the reaction she wanted to evoke. Of all the men in this room, only Yasin seemed to understand the joy and bask in the irresistible pleasure of her music.

Resolve strengthening, she sped the next few notes to catch up again and ended the song crisply and cleanly. Resting the oud on her shoulder, she massaged some stiffness out of her fingers. She hadn't played this long in many years.

A ten-year-old serving boy tentatively approached with a goblet. He bit his lip as he extended it to her. "Would you like something to drink, miss."

Sarah accepted it with a smile. A sniff identified it as a small ale that was just alcoholic enough to render it safe to drink but not so potent as to dull her senses. "Thank you, good sir."

Blushing, the boy scurried away. Sarah smiled as she watched him go, touched by his embarrassment. After refreshing herself with a few sips, she set the goblet on a nearby table and began another song, this time a smooth pastoral ballad that steered clear of amorous topics. The tavern owner may have wanted a bawdy atmosphere, but stoking it made her uncomfortable.

Halfway through her song, the sudden movement of a man pushing back his stool and jumping to his feet drew her attention. Opposite him, Yasin stood with hands raised innocently. She couldn't hear his words, but his gestures suggested an apology.

Unfortunately, the other man wasn't buying what he was selling. At his sides, his hands balled into fists.

Halting her song mid-verse, Sarah quickly reset her fingering and pitched her voice higher to carry over the noise. "Here's one for all you loyal sons of Valencia."

She plunged into a quick, snappy tune celebrating the beauty of Valencia, from the wide fields and rolling hills to the lovely women who called it home. It drew attention, and after a few notes, the crowd began to clap along. Even the man who had squared off against Yasin halted to listen. Before she'd finished the first verse, he, too, was clapping in rhythm with his friends.

Yasin, having already backed away, migrated to the other side of the room. As he casually opened distance from his adversary, he offered Sarah an appreciative grin.

"Your song saved me," he explained later, after they'd returned home to eat. "Thank you."

Her thoughts returned to the hollow mix of indifference and lusty leering of her audience from earlier in the night. He'd saved her, in a way, too. Only his reassuring presence had enabled her to continue.

"I saw you were in trouble and thought I'd lend a hand." In truth, she had acted not by deliberate intention but an instinctive desire to spare him from harm. She'd had one weapon to defend him, and she'd done so without thinking about it.

Seated on the other side of her bed opposite their simple meal of bread and cheese, he suddenly seemed too close. His scent teased her nostrils and, the very fact that she found it pleasing troubled her after how easily she'd sprung to his defense. Unsettled by the implication, she instead nibbled on her cheese until its aroma overrode all else.

When she'd swallowed, she asked, "What was the cause of the argument?"

"A mistake." He sighed with a raw frustration. "I assumed they were Valencians, when they actually came from Burgos with El Cid. They didn't appreciate when I tried to commiserate about northern invaders."

"Oh, my…" She brought her hand up to her mouth. "I'm glad I chose the song I did, instead of one celebrating Valenica's independence as a *taifa*."

Eyes dancing, he released a light laugh buoyed by genuine delight. "Me too!"

Sobering, Sarah considered the near miss. "Do such things happen often?"

He shrugged. "I only have a few moments to make my target like me. Usually, I can guess their background from their tone, how they dress, or how they carry themselves, but sometimes I make mistakes."

"I do the same when choosing what music to play, though my mistakes only cause disinterest."

He tried to hide it by taking a bite of bread, but she caught the faint smile on his face that lingered through until he finished chewing. "I can't imagine anyone finding fault with your music."

She felt her cheeks warm at the compliment, but any satisfaction faded as she recalled the leering men from earlier. Perhaps the stakes of her own choices were equally high, after all. "It does happen."

"Well, I'm glad you were there." He chewed for a few moments. "The tavern owner keeps an ear open for anything of interest. He's exactly the kind of man I need, and a brawl could have alienated him."

"You were talking with him for some time."

Yasin nodded. "He's a slippery one. Was sizing me up as much as I was him."

"Can you trust him?"

His lip twisted into a smirk. "I don't trust anyone."

Except for her, it seemed. "Hopefully, something sweet will grow in that soil." Eyes widening, she gasped. "*Ya salaam*, I almost forgot!"

"What?"

Twisting, she fished a hand beneath the bed to retrieve her satchel. "I got something for you from the markets." Straightening, she presented a pair of plump oranges.

He raised an eyebrow. "Oranges?"

She bit at her lip. "In Toledo, you said you used to steal them from the emir. Now, you don't need to."

He took them gingerly, first with only his fingertips, cradling them as if they were made of glass. Turning over his hands, he then allowed them to slip into his palm. He continued to gaze down at the oranges, and she could not see his eyes. "I'm surprised you remembered."

How could she not remember the first time she'd seen beneath his bravado, the first indication that he was more than a greedy thief? She cleared her throat.

"Thank you, Sarah." When he finally raised his gaze, the veil concealing his thoughts had dropped, just as it had on the road. "Why?"

Something had changed within her when the landlady had drawn all the wrong conclusions about her pregnancy. Throughout the years of her training and the many more years of her servitude, she had cared only for herself. For a moment, she had contemplated a life that included a child, and now, she could not remain blind to the struggles of others, particularly a man who had trusted her with his fate.

Yasin had helped her during this journey, and she could no longer pretend he did so out of obligation. He had seen her struggles and had sought to alleviate them. How could she not do the same? He had opened up about his sacrifices, and she understood sacrifice all too well.

"You've been laboring hard these past few days, and before that, you carried the burden of bringing a stranger along on this mission."

"You're no burden."

She had been anticipating the delight of this evening ever since Yasin had arranged for her to play at the tavern. And the evening had delivered, though not in the way she'd expected. For, the chance to perform had brought her only lusty attention and cold indifference. It hadn't felt as it had on the plains of La Mancha, playing for doomed travelers and simple farmers. In the tavern, she'd felt like the prostitutes walking the streets, only she'd enticed her listeners' lust with her music rather than her body. She had done what she believed she'd been born to do, yet she felt empty.

She'd always desired the gifts and privileges of a celebrated *qiyan*. Yet, in this quiet room, a few moments with a man who thanked and appreciated her filled her with more joy than she'd experienced in years.

YASIN

Deception relied on believable detail, and Yasin had devoted himself to the art. He had spent many hours in the streets observing the fluid comfort of friendship, the bubbling frenzy of anger, and the looseness of ease. When he lied, he did so with his entire body and demeanor, not only his lips. Deception, Yasin had learned, required acting like everyone else. Even the most skilled of guards merely had an instinct for recognizing inconsistencies that screamed of subterfuge.

So, as Yasin carried the crate with the false bottom into the potter's workshop on his seventh day as a wagoner, he grunted as if it was as heavy as the other dozen crates he'd already delivered. His face never wavered from the worn-down weariness of aching labor, even as he inwardly admired his own performance. Even a trained eye wouldn't imagine this crate carried rare crystal goblets packed in straw from Iraq instead of raw clay from pits up the Spanish coast.

Setting it beside the others, Yasin approached the potter hovering just outside the door. The man clearly remembered his contraband would be in the final crate, but Yasin wished he wouldn't announce the fact by staring at it.

He was yet another man Yasin couldn't rely upon to breach the library.

"I set the *last* crate over there." He pointed.

"Ah, thank you, thank you." The potter's clay-stained fingers fidgeted at his belt. "I trust everything is there?"

Yasin forced a strained smile. "Exactly as Hisham promised." Even a novice guard would notice this man's agitation. "I'll return for the empty crates tomorrow."

Hisham really only cared to recover the precious false-bottomed one— replacing it would require a trustworthy craftsman, which would be expensive—but Yasin couldn't very well reclaim only one of them. An observer might form the silly notion that it was special.

The potter placed a hand behind Yasin's back to goad him onward, but Yasin walked past before he made contact. His *qamisa* may be wrinkled, but he had no desire to add dried clay to it.

He was only too happy to climb atop his wagon and spur its bay horse onward. Twitchy clients made him nervous, but Hisham claimed to have a long-standing relationship with that potter. Besides which, Yasin's cut for the delivery would help mitigate the cost of the new rooms Sarah had arranged.

He had one more stop to make today, his most important even though it would earn him nothing. Halfway down a side street so narrow that his wagon took up the entire middle, he came to a halt before the large *tapia* tavern where Sarah had played. The light of the setting sun cast long shadows across the entrance. Noise from carousing customers within overwhelmed the usual chatter and commotion of passing pedestrians and announced that, for most, the work day had already ended.

Yasin hobbled his horse with a length of rope, more to prevent it from wandering off than to avoid theft. The sail-shaped brand on its flank identified it as belonging to the port. Anyone who stole it had better eat it: no one would risk losing his stable by buying it.

Pushing aside the carved, half-open juniper door, he stepped inside. At first, the fire in the hearth dominated his vision, but as his eyes adjusted, he saw customers lounging on the cushioned benches. Most ate berries or slices of meat from communal wooden plates. A few short-haired Muslims and nearly every long-haired barbarian drank from goblets. From the way they nursed the liquid, Yasin doubted it was small ale, and it sloshed too freely to be fruit juice.

He picked his way through the tables toward the owner at the counter. Though his eyes focused on his destination, his ears drank in the tangle of conversation around him.

"—sister's husband drank unwatered wine and leered at my wife all night—"

"—since the night we saw the goat standing on the roof—"

"—fifteen real silver *dirhams*, not those copper ones—"

The last fragment tickled Yasin's ears, but his progress carried him away before he could hear more.

The owner wiped his hands on his apron and beamed when Yasin reached him. "Yasin the Almerian!" He pressed his fingers to his lips, then his forehead.

The greeting warmed Yasin's heart. He'd seen it far too infrequently these past years. "God bless you, Pedro."

"Long day?"

"Tiring." He offered no further detail. If Yasin revealed what he'd been delivering or to whom, this man would undoubtedly sell that information to someone. It was the same reason Yasin lingered here.

Pedro's grin exposed a missing tooth. "A drink'll fix that." He turned to fill a goblet from one of the barrels.

Yasin fished three copper coins out of his pouch and stacked them on the counter. "Any tips today?"

They disappeared before he could inhale. Voice low, Pedro muttered, "A bricklayer said they're out of material at a breach in the western wall, south of the weavers' district."

"How big?"

"Big enough for a person."

He doubted a hole that size would remain open for long. "Good to know." He drank from his goblet. The man had given him small ale, barely alcoholic and inexpensive. "Anything else?"

Pedro shrugged. "The patrol routes by the spice market shifted. They'll come two at a time now."

If he had still been staying at the inn, those new routes would have made his mission more difficult. He was glad Sarah had found a room by the port. "Hear anything about the courthouse? The library? The tax office?"

"You've asked about the tax office a couple times this week. Planning a burglary?"

"Not unless you tell me something very interesting." Yasin inwardly cheered that he'd managed to conceal his interest in the library. He needed information, but he needed to conceal his true intentions even more.

"Nothing today, I'm afraid." Pedro lowered his gaze to Yasin's pouch. "Perhaps tomorrow."

After a week of investigation, neither he nor Sarah had discovered anything to put the *Book of Healing* in his hands. Nor would he find another copy outside the library. If anyone in this city ever had one, it was buried deep down with the rest of the wealth they'd hidden from their Christian conqueror.

He needed something—a person, a rumor—to show progress. How long would Lord Gonzalo wait before suspecting betrayal? Yasin had warned that this heist might require time, but he'd never heard of a patient nobleman. Time was not his friend.

He finished his drink and set the goblet back on the table. "I'll see you tomorrow, then."

Yasin's muscles ached as he pushed away from the counter and headed for the door. Sarah had been right. He wasn't used to physical labor. His fingers had felt stiff before, after long hours bent over a workbench beveling or grooving an intricate design in a saddle or belt. He'd even felt tired after a night spent staking out a home, searching for the perfect moment to break in. But exhausted from physical labor? That was new, and he did not enjoy the sensation. Once he'd delivered this text and earned his payment, he resolved to never again experience it.

A dozen conversations swirled through the air as he continued toward the door.

"—imam admitted El Cid's solution was good—"

"—land in the north and quit the city entirely—"

"—the scribe who owes us all that coin from dice two days ago—"

Scribe.

Yasin strained his knee when he ground to a halt. He eyed the table that had produced that comment. A pair of men wearing crosses and linen *qamisas* ate from bowls filled with lumpy soup. The kohl around their eyes marked them as Mozarabs.

A scribe, particularly a scribe who had racked up gambling debts, could be his way into the library.

Fatigue and aching knee forgotten, Yasin approached them. "Excuse me," he greeted in Arabic. "Did you mention a scribe?"

After an awkward silence, the blue-eyed one to Yasin's right leaned forward. "Not to you."

Yasin withdrew a pair of silver coins from his pouch and placed them on the table. "Did you mention a scribe?"

The talkative one's eyes grew as wide as the coins themselves. "Aye. A clerk in El Cid's library." He plucked them up. "He owes me money."

The other voices and the clanging of goblets and plates on tables faded behind the hammering of his pulse in his throat. This was it! A scribe with a gambling problem: what a perfect opportunity! Sarah would be delighted.

"Where can I find him?"

The talkative one's stocky, long-haired companion laid a hand on his friend's wrist. "Why do you want to know?"

Time for a lie he could deliver with unwavering conviction. "I can't read or afford the scribes who work for the city. I need someone to write a letter for me. I figured this man might do it for a discount, if he needs money."

The blue-eyed Mozarab grunted. "Anything to get me my money faster." He jutted his chin toward the exit. "If he isn't hiding from his other debtors, he'll be in the tavern on the street between the silversmiths and jewelers. The sign has a pig on it."

"Name?"

"Orbanus Juanez."

A Christian, then, based on the patronymic. "How will I recognize him?"

"He's Aragonese, auburn hair styled like yours." The blue-eyed Mozarab curled his lips. "And I cut his left cheek two days ago when he didn't pay up."

Thanking the man for the description, Yasin ducked through the tavern door and untied his horse's legs. Leaping atop the wagon, he inhaled a deep breath of evening air.

His palms itched with anticipation. All his instincts, honed by years of slipping through the crannies between danger and opportunity, screamed that this was his way into the library. How the path would twist and turn, he couldn't say, but it would lead him to the *Book of Healing* and his pouch of gold.

Yasin smiled at the fingers of sunset painting the buildings in dark red and purple. It was a beautiful end to a true beauty of a day.

YASIN

In the tavern the Mozarab had indicated, the only tarnish was on the cuffs of the patrons' sleeves, the result of long days spent cleaning silver and other metals. The well-polished stone booths and finely sanded wooden tables bore none of the usual chips and nicks of hard use. The servants delivering food wore clean linen *qamisas* and thin lines of kohl encircling their eyes.

Yasin swallowed. Though he had changed into his finest clothes and trimmed his hair with copper scissors from the market, he had forgotten kohl. He had spent too much time among northerners in Toledo. Here among the Muslims and Mozarabs of Valencia, his unadorned eyes would mark him as an outsider.

He halted a passing man dressed in a plain *qamisa* like the other servants. "I'm looking for Orbanus Juanez."

The man shifted the jug of wine he bore to his other hand. "I'll not have trouble in my house. If you want him, wait outside like the rest, or I'll call the guards."

This was the owner? What a hard-working fellow.

"I seek a conversation, not a confrontation."

As the man studied Yasin's build, the tension drained from his posture. What had Esmeralda called him? Harmless. Yasin supposed it had its advantages.

"Seems you're not alone." He jutted his chin toward a corner booth. One man with short, auburn hair reclined on a thick cushion and dropped an apricot into his mouth. Two others had just arisen and were departing.

Yasin sidled up to the booth.

Momentary panic flashed within the pair of quick blue eyes that met him. This was definitely the man. The slash on his cheek hadn't yet started to heal or darken.

"Orbanus Juanez?" Yasin asked.

"You just missed him." The words carried the immediacy of truth, free of wavering or strain. Gesturing with a finger that moved with ease, he added between chews, "If you hurry, you can catch him."

Yasin had both observed and practiced deception for many years, yet the flawless delivery impressed him. If not for the scar and the fingers stained with ink, Yasin probably would have believed him. That was good. This man knew how to lie well and wouldn't wilt under scrutiny.

"I'm sorry to hear that." Yasin sighed. "I hoped I might hire him."

Orbanus betrayed his curiosity with a brief hesitation when

reaching for the bowl of apricots. "Oh?" The word contained no velocity, a casual response to an uninteresting comment. "For what?"

Lowering his chin, Yasin met and held his kohl-encircled eyes. "A sensitive matter for his ears only."

Heartbeats stretched into a long moment. The scribe's unmoving eyes reflected an internal debate about whether to reveal himself. Yasin had contemplated the same many times, although he reached conclusions faster.

"Orbanus Juanez?" Yasin repeated.

The auburn-haired man's lip twisted before he nodded.

Yasin gestured to the other bench. "May I sit?"

The man nodded again. As Yasin seated himself, Orbanus pushed himself upright. "I don't owe you money," he muttered, somewhere between a question and a statement.

Yasin shook his head. "I need the services of a scribe."

"Plenty of those in this city." An eyebrow shot up. "Why me?"

"I ran into the gentleman who gave you that." He gestured to Orbanus's cheek.

Orbanus's subsequent scowl made him wince, and he raised a hand to probe the wound. "Are you his friend or a fellow victim of his unbalanced dice?"

Poor gamblers always made excuses. "I understand you owe him a sizeable sum."

Orbanus leaned forward. "And you're here to collect?"

"On the contrary." To avoid frightening him, Yasin rested his hands on the table. "I thought I'd pay your debts."

The rasp of an indrawn breath sounded like thunder. "You taunt me."

"Not at all. I think we can help each other."

Though his eyes narrowed, he licked his lips. "Help each other?"

This man had the temperament and motivation, but Yasin still had to be sure he had the means before revealing more. He leaned forward. "You work as a scribe in the royal library, yes?"

"I do."

"So you're literate and familiar with famous works?"

He grunted and reached for another apricot. "Obviously."

The casual response reassured Yasin. "I'm looking for a very specific manuscript."

Orbanus raised an eyebrow. "Which one?"

Yasin hesitated for the span of a deep breath. Once he answered, this man would know his intentions. If Yasin was sloppy and the guards started searching for their thief, Orbanus could identify him. Yet, what choice did he have? He'd traversed Iberia for this chance. He had to take the risk.

"*The Book of Healing* by Ibn Sina. I need an accurate copy of the section on metaphysics in the original Arabic."

"Only the *Metaphysics*?"

Yasin nodded.

The man chewed the inside of his lip. "The only copy I've ever seen is in the emir's collection."

Reference to the emir suggested Orbanus was one of the original scribes from before El Cid had captured the city. He would know the library well.

"You've seen it?"

"Of course." He held his hands apart an arm's span to mark the height, then shifted and narrowed it slightly to mark the width. Yasin imprinted the measurements in his mind. "Several codices, bound in leather-wrapped wood."

Gonzalo's information was correct, then. God be praised, this trip hadn't been a waste.

"You know where to find this text?"

The man grunted. "I've worked there for fifteen years. Of course I know."

Excitement threatened to bubble up as a bark of laughter. Every exertion since leaving Toledo three weeks prior had built to this single moment of clarity. Anticipation coursed through his veins. He wouldn't even have to breach the walls or dodge patrols. Orbanus would handle everything!

"How large are your debts?" Yasin asked.

"Thirty silver coins."

"God's wounds!" Yasin clenched his *jubba*.

Orbanus shrugged. "My enjoyment of dice outpaces my skill, I'm afraid."

It was a steep price, but the siege had produced shortages the markets could not fulfill. Satisfying those demands would make up the difference, with some hard work. "And in exchange, you'll retrieve the codices I need?"

"Of course not."

Yasin stiffened, eyes flying to the corners of the room, searching for overlooked threats. "Excuse me?"

"I can't remove the original, but I don't need to. I'll make you a copy."

A copy. The word swirled in Yasin's mind like the fog of too much drink. Why hadn't he considered commissioning a copy? Perhaps all the smuggling and theft of the past three years had corroded his soul without him realizing it.

Orbanus started to chuckle. "What, did you think to slip past several dozen guards and steal from El Cid?" He barked a laugh and reached for another apricot. "Are you a madman?"

"How long will it take?"

The Aragonese scribe pursed his lips. "You want an exact duplication, yes?"

"Yes."

"And illustrations?"

Gonzalo hadn't mentioned illustrations, only the text. "Irrelevant."

"Good. Illumination takes the majority of the time." The man shrugged. "A few weeks."

Would Lord Gonzalo wait that long? "No faster?"

"I can only work in the library itself, after completing my normal work." The main raised his chin and smirked. "Fortunately, I'm a fast worker."

It was longer than he'd hoped, but it would obviate the dangerous prospect of burgling a hardened, vicious warrior like El Cid. A warlord who had executed dozens of Almoravids wouldn't hesitate to condemn a thief.

This would work.

Logistics. He needed to know everything. "They won't question you?"

"Why should they? I can work on the book at my copying table and return it by the end of the day. No one will notice."

"How will you get the copy past the guards?"

The scribe's broad grin twisted the scar on his cheek. "The same way edicts leave: through the official dispatch. It'll just be one more parcel."

Yasin barked a laugh at the thought of El Cid's men delivering a text their lord had already refused to surrender. The brazen simplicity was magnificent.

"Deliver a faithful copy and you'll have your thirty silver coins."

"Sixty."

Yasin glared. "You said thirty."

"I said I owed thirty." The scribe crossed his arms. "Looming debt isn't sufficient incentive to risk discovery."

He leaned back. That was the nature of these things. Yasin needed him, and Orbanus knew it. In truth, Yasin couldn't blame him; he'd done the same to Gonzalo. Besides which, Orbanus would work harder for profit than he would to erase a debt.

"Sixty it is."

SARAH

Sarah lifted the pot over the fire, which was already crawling up the split logs and throwing off considerable heat. With a grunt, she hefted the great handle over the trammel hook hanging off the lugpole embedded into the side walls, suspending the pot just above the flames. Only a little water splashed over the sides; thankfully, it struck the wooden floor beyond the stone hearth instead of extinguishing the coals.

Stepping back, she wiped the back of her hand across her forehead, only to find it damp. Not since her first owner had purchased her in Barcelona had she needed to boil water. She'd almost forgotten how much work cooking involved…and why the other women of the building arose so early to begin.

She'd resolved to prepare a nice meal for Yasin today. After all, he'd started his deliveries early this morning, and she had no performances tonight to prepare for. They were partners in this cause, and she would do her part.

The fire grew further and licked the bottom of the iron pot. Doubt nagged at her. It seemed to be too close to those flames, but it was probably already too hot to move. With a shrug, she decided to let it stay; Yasin would be home soon enough that she needed that water to boil sooner than later. One by one, in went the chopped carrots, lentils, beans, artichokes, and onions. She'd bought only a few of each, both to conserve their funds and in the hope that variety would enrich the flavor. Yasin hadn't tasted her cooking yet, and, as with all things, she intended to impress.

Sarah chewed at the inside of her lip. Without meat, the soup might still be too bland, but the butcher had already sold out of the day's stock by the time she'd decided on this meal. Spices would have to suffice.

With a twirl of her dress, she stepped outside, shut her door, and crossed the hallway leading to the landlady's private chamber. Clearing her throat once, she knocked on the door.

The woman's pinched eyebrows relaxed when she recognized Sarah. "Ah, hello, dear." She wiped her hands on her apron. "How is the baby?"

Sarah suppressed a pang of guilt at the lie. "Fine, thank you." Again, she cleared her throat. "I was wondering if you had a few pinches of spices I could use." She quickly added, "I'd gladly pay for them, of course."

"For a few pinches? Nonsense," the woman scoffed. "Not for a tenant who pays a full month in advance."

The remarkable generosity left Sarah suspicious that perhaps she'd overpaid for these rooms, but if so, it was too late to do anything about it.

"What kinds of spices?"

Perhaps she could give him a taste of home after all these years away. "Black pepper and salt, of course. Also, some turmeric, if you have any."

"Turmeric is very strong by itself." The landlady narrowed her eyes. "What are you making?"

"A soup."

"Which meat?"

Sarah sighed. "None."

"I recommend a pinch of turmeric, balanced with cumin and coriander."

The priest she'd cooked for had preferred plain dishes out of some vow of humility. "I'm thankful for the advice."

The woman retreated into her chamber. After some time, she returned with a clay cup. "Try this, dear."

Sarah accepted it and eyed the modest mixture of spices of different colors within. She'd have to trust that it was the right combination. "Thank you."

"Of course, dear." The woman offered a polite smile.

Turning as the woman closed the door, Sarah sniffed at the contents. The amount was smaller than Sarah expected, but the aroma was still powerful. She could, indeed, smell the turmeric, but it wasn't as strong as the great piles in the marketplace. The other spices layered atop it like a musical chord. Sarah had never considered the complexity of something as simple as preparing food.

As she approached her door, though, a smell other than the

turmeric began to dominate the air. Nostrils flaring at the tickle of smoke, Sarah rushed forward, spilling some of the spice as the cup bounced in her hand. Flinging open the door, Sarah confronted a wall of smoke.

*Ya salaam…*the fire!

Her panicked eyes searched the room for high flames licking the walls and biting into the wood, but she saw only a gray haze. Coughing on the choking air, she rushed to the window and threw open the shutters. The evening's fading sunlight brightened the procession of thick air escaping. Holding her sleeve over her mouth, she swept her other hand toward the window to clear the room.

The air thinned enough to ease her fears of fire, revealing a hearth waterlogged from the coals to the backlog. The pot, too close to the fire, had evidently boiled over and spilled onto the flames, extinguishing them.

Coughing again, she sunk onto the bed to slip beneath the layer of smoke drifting out the window. By the Prophet, this was a disaster! Not only that, but she'd rendered the hearth unusable until it dried. *Ornamental emptiness*, that *fuero* woman in La Mancha had said. *You can't appease starvation with a song.* At the time, Sarah had dismissed the insults as rudeness. But she could not deny the wet coals and waterlogged hearth before her.

"Sarah!" Yasin's voice penetrated from beyond the door even before he thrust it open. Finding her, he charged forward to kneel before her. "Sarah, are you alright?"

Elbows on her knees, Sarah leaned her cheek on a palm. "Yes, yes. It's more smoke than fire."

"What happened?"

Feeling her cheeks redden, she glanced away. "I tried to make us soup."

When he said nothing for some time, Sarah ventured a glance. He coughed in a vain attempt to conceal his grin.

"I'm glad you're amused," she grumbled. "We'll smell like smoke for weeks."

"It's not that." His grin returned, broader than before. "Well, it is funny." He pursed his lips to regain some semblance of control. "But that's not why I'm grinning."

"Why, then?" she demanded.

The muscles of his lips and cheeks drained of humor, shifting into a genuine smile. "You tried to cook for me. No one's done that for a long time."

The simple words of appreciation pierced her embarrassment and might have dispelled it entirely, if not for the sudden sizzle of water touching one of the still-warm coals. "For all the good it did. I couldn't even successfully boil water."

"Success…" Eyes brightening, he grasped her free hand. "I did it. I've found a way into the library!"

Excitement replaced exhaustion at the desperately needed good news. "You have it?"

His expression darkened. "Well, no."

"Oh, of course, of course." She rubbed her hands together. "I need to identify it."

Yasin grinned impishly, as if he'd hidden a rabbit in her bed. "No need."

A wave of relief washed over her as he reported his arrangement with the scribe. The most tenuous of salvations had preserved her from sharing the caravan's fate, and she was eager to avoid another risk.

"Now I understand what you meant about finding another way."

Shifting his weight onto his back foot, he grinned. "I'm a very good thief and smuggler. One of the finest around, you understand? That's why Lord Gonzalo needed my help."

His high opinion of himself was nothing new. Truth be told, he was probably right.

His smile faded. "But I'm no fool. Every theft and lie is a risk, and eventually, even I'll run out of luck." His gaze became more distant. "Those small risks add up to ruin."

She resisted the urge to glance at the still-smoldering coals of her own failure. That wasn't his meaning, in any case. "Esteban?"

Yasin's eyes narrowed, and he offered a curt nod. "I gave in to anger, and that mistake ruined everything I'd built in Toledo. That's why I agreed to this job." He met her gaze again. "With my payment, I can start my own workshop, control my own destiny."

His words touched the part of Sarah that longed for freedom. She had accomplished everything Emir Abdallah ibn Buluggin had expected when he'd sent her to Baghdad, but she'd lost it all to a pirate ship on the horizon. "Anything can be taken away."

Sympathy softened his eyes and pinched his eyebrows. "True. But at least working leather doesn't endanger my life."

"Why all the smuggling, then? Why do you take such risks?"

Like curtains drawn across windows, his bravado returned with a smile. "My tastes exceed the wages of an apprentice leatherworker."

A pang of regret accompanied the end of that moment of honesty. The depths of the soul lingering just behind those eyes intrigued her, but glimpses were all too brief. He refused to reveal them except on his terms, and all she could do was wait for the next one.

"I suppose you share those tastes with a certain Valencian scribe."

"Aragonese, actually." He folded his arms. "Strange. I don't think I've ever seen an Aragonese wearing kohl."

Sarah imagined Yasin's eyes ringed with the dark cosmetic. They already had a certain intoxicating appeal that had, if his boasts held even a grain of truth, ensnared many. Framed in a thin line of kohl, any woman would drown in those hazel irises…

Suddenly warm, she crossed to the table and poured herself some of the remaining water she'd drawn from the local well. That was a dangerous thought. "Do you endanger him by asking him to copy the text?"

"Better him than us." He shrugged. "The Christians call the man in charge of this city *the teacher of the battlefield.* The Muslims call him *the lord.* He earned neither title through forgiveness. This scholar knows I'm really paying him to assume the risk."

Was that how he justified his actions, by believing every man walked into his fate knowingly?

She hadn't written Lord Gonzalo for a week, but she suspected her next letter would delight him. Yasin had found both the text and the means of acquiring it.

"What was the price of his help?" Coughing, Sarah reached for a cup of water to banish the smoky taste from her mouth.

Yasin, however, hadn't answered by the time she'd finished drinking.

"What was the price?" she repeated, setting down the cup.

His lips twisted. "Sixty silver pieces."

"*Ya salaam!*" With that much money, she could establish herself in the South and need never return to Toledo. "I didn't realize we had so much."

He scratched at his temple, but the gesture didn't conceal his grimace. "We don't."

Sarah clenched at her skirt. "How close are we?"

His nervous shifting from one foot to the other prepared her for his response. "About half."

Half. And from that amount came their food, oils for their hair and skin, lodging in this inn for however long this scribe took to make his copy, and a dozen other expenses.

"Can we gather the rest?"

"Your playing will help, and this fine city holds plenty of opportunity for a man of my talents."

Her mistake had ruined a hearth for a day and wasted the ingredients. His could see him hanged. "You just said taking risks would catch up with you."

He nodded. "One cannot live a life without risk." He released a sigh. "Even a hundred little thefts wouldn't match the danger of stealing from El Cid."

Calculation. His mind was always calculating, weighing his options, assessing the next most advantageous action. What would he do, she wondered, when his luck finally ran out?

YASIN

Yasin waited until the flow of men unloading the trading vessel dwindled to a trickle before working his way up the gangplank. The ship was wider and shorter than he expected, shaped more like an egg than a narrowed eye. A pile of deck planks sat against the far railing, removed to expose the cargo beneath. Lowly seamen hauled themselves out of the mostly-empty hold beneath the orders of their officers, shouted in crude Arabic.

Yasin imagined all those wonderful crannies where a free trader could hide packages.

He ascended the stairs to the aftercastle at the ship's rear. The captain, a bald man with a bushy beard and a long nose that hinted at a whisper of true Arabic blood, stood at the top. He was the only man wearing a *jubba*, and a fine cotton one at that. Dried salt clinging to the cuffs and bottom edge suggested hard use at sea. It seemed a shame to waste the fine material on a sailor, but Yasin supposed the man had to distinguish himself from his crew somehow.

"You're in the wrong place, land rat." The captain's deep voice rolled like thunder. "No cargo up here."

Though he made no motion to leave, Yasin spared a glance to confirm they were alone. "That's a shame."

The man's beard twitched. "What's that?"

Yasin offered his most charming grin. "Look around you." He faced the port but restrained himself from gesturing. Doing so from this elevated perch would draw attention. "All those people are crying out for someone to provide basic necessities."

The captain narrowed his eyes. "Basic necessities, is it?"

"Indeed." Yasin faced him again. "The siege caused suffering. Too few can enjoy fine linens, Egyptian cotton, or silk. Iraqi crystal goblets. Porcelain from the far orient." He decided to take a risk, based on this man's attire and features. "Even an illuminated Quran from Baghdad or Alexandria."

The captain's eyes widened the faintest amount. So, he was dealing with a Muslim.

"All that seems available enough in the markets."

Quickly, he adjusted his pitch. "True, but not in the quantities desired, and not without those men from the north"—he jutted his head toward the officials in the port—"doubling the cost with their taxes."

The captain's eyebrows pinched together. "I run an honest ship. I'm not interested in smuggling." The stilted words couldn't quite mask a hint of excitement.

"Woah, now!" Cocking his head, Yasin gestured at waist level, low enough to avoid attracting attention. "Who said anything about smuggling?"

Yasin could appreciate the caution. He could have been an agent of El Cid seeking to entrap this captain and cost him his docking rights. Paying to transport cargo from another dock would ruin his profits.

"I merely point out the pain of the city's merchants. I was just telling my friend Hisham how grateful they'd be if someone alleviated it."

The captain's Adam's apple bobbed up and down. "You know Hisham?"

Yasin typically hesitated to rely on another man's reputation, but he needed money to pay the scribe. Hisham, Yasin had learned, had a good reputation for concealment. False bottoms, hidden pockets, hollow spokes…

He nodded once, meaningfully. "I do."

"Interesting." The captain stroked his beard. "And these merchants would show their appreciation for that relief?"

Having spoken to several of them during his deliveries, Yasin nodded. "I'm certain of it."

"What would that appreciation be worth?"

Yasin considered. He might save a few percentage points by haggling, but he ran the risk of the captain walking. Yasin didn't have time for that hassle. He needed money now.

"Add sixty-five percent to your expenses."

The captain sucked in a breath. "So much!"

Yasin clenched his hands behind his back to hide their shaking. He'd never offer such generous terms in Toledo, where he knew which routes to use, which men he could bribe, and whom he could trust. He knew none of that here, though. He needed to buy loyalty, at least for a little while. This captain was less likely to report to the city guards the man who lined his pockets with silver. In Toledo, he could always flee if the guards closed in around him. He couldn't do that here until he had that book. Sarah depended on him.

He had told her the truth: life was filled with risk, but the intelligent man minimized it where he could. He didn't need riches, only enough to cover his expenses.

"Just keep in mind what you're earning if cargo space runs short." Yasin couldn't afford to disappoint his customers with delays.

The captain grunted. "At that rate, I'll toss my crew ashore to fit your cargo."

Yasin extended a hand. "Then we have an accord?"

With a toothy grin, the captain clasped it. "*Inshallah*, we do."

Pumping the man's hand, Yasin inhaled a long breath. He now had a piece of Valencia's smuggling. Now, he only needed to avoid the attention of El Cid's guards long enough to pay the scribe. He'd been careful for three years in Toledo. Surely, he could do the same for a few weeks in Valencia.

CHAPTER TWELVE

Sarah

A YOUNG GIRL BEARING a jug of oil crossed the marble floor of the *hamam*. Each muted slap of her slippers on the damp floor echoed off the vaulted ceiling and mosaics inset into the walls. Though she struggled with the weight, she spilled nothing as she rose onto her tiptoes to refill the lamp hanging from the ceiling.

That was her third refilling circuit through the bathhouse, which meant Sarah had played long enough to fulfill her contract. Cutting her song short by two full stanzas, Sarah stilled the strings of her oud and rubbed the ache out of her fingers.

A quick glance confirmed that no one would mind her rushing the song. Despite the dimness of the hazy, humid air, eye-level lamps hanging in the corners illuminated the arched alcoves along the perimeter. Only one was occupied. A bare-chested, middle-aged northerner with rich, long brown hair that matted against her shoulders leaned against the wall with eyes closed. The only other remaining occupants were a dark-skinned woman lying face down on the star-shaped, heated stone platform in the center of the room and the fair-haired servant girl massaging oil into her skin. Neither had glanced in her direction for some time.

At first, Sarah had looked forward to the prospect of performing in a *hamam* near the palace as much as Yasin had regretted being unable to accompany her. She could barely wait the two days until the women's turn came. She hadn't set foot inside one since Granada, when she'd soaked and gossiped with the other servants, female relatives, and concubines.

She hadn't known how to play then, and evidently that made all the difference. Now, her instrument isolated her from the others cleaning themselves with scrapers, soap, and oil. She had heard some of the bathers tapping their feet to her music above the sound of water splashing into stone bathing basins along the perimeter. Regardless, Sarah had little opportunity to interact with them. She was being paid to play, not socialize. She felt more alone among a crowd of Valencia's finest ladies than among the priests in Toledo.

Hitting the right notes had become progressively harder as the strings of her oud swelled from humidity billowing from the nearby steam room. Her dress felt sticky and clung everywhere it touched her body. Everything felt slippery, and simply gripping her instrument proved more and more challenging. She would have preferred to play somewhere drier, but this corner was the only space large enough in the *hamam* to perform without obstructing the bathers.

She was done now, though, Allah be praised. She wiped at her precious instrument with the edge of her dress but succeeded only in leaving wet streaks. She would need to dry it completely before she left, else the wood would warp. They would have extra towels in the changing room near the entrance, and she could leave her oud there while she enjoyed her payment: a full cleansing treatment and massage to wash away the road, with its dirt, wind, and narrowly avoided death.

Her legs felt stiff as she rose from her stool. She should have negotiated a break.

"You play beautifully," said an echoing voice from across the room.

The woman who had been resting in the alcove was staring at her with eyes the color of sapphires on an emir's scepter. Her thin eyebrows pinched together the faintest amount, giving her an appearance somewhere between humor and hauteur. Sarah envied the smoothness of her chin and the skin around her eyes. She was quite beautiful. Despite wearing only a loincloth, the woman leaned back against the wall at complete ease. Stretched scars at her midsection indicated she had given birth some years ago.

Unable to leave without giving offense and unwilling to shout across the room, Sarah instead approached and bowed her head. Drying her oud and enjoying her well-earned soak would have to wait. "Thank you."

"Where did you learn to play?" Her Arabic held only the faintest inflection of Castilian around her vowels.

A whisper of caution warned that revealing her training would mark her as a slave, like all *qiyans*. Here in Valencia, she could be free, but only if no one knew her background. And yet, she had completed her training when so many others had failed. She had mastered music and dance, debate and recitation. Few in the world—men or women—could match her knowledge of history and art. Allah did not grant such gifts for her to deny them.

She raised her chin. "I am trained as a *qiyan* of Baghdad."

Eyes widening, the woman pushed herself upright. "Is that so?"

The reaction surprised Sarah. Most northerners familiar with the term believed wild rumors about sexual skills. Even Yasin had questioned the nature of her education. But Sarah sensed none of the outrage she would expect from a Christian.

"I wasn't aware we had a trained *qiyan* in the city."

Who was she, to claim familiarity with everyone who passed through Valencia? Sarah would believe her delusional in other circumstances. Yet her ease in her nakedness, her nearly flawless Arabic, even the way she held herself still… This woman was no commoner.

The woman continued, "You are trained in recitation and song, as well as music?"

"And dance and debate."

"What is your name?"

"Sarah al-Bayda."

Her eyes shifted slightly, as if searching Sarah's features. "A fitting name." She raised her chin. "I am hosting a feast in three days. My guests would greatly appreciate the playing of a trained *qiyan* from the East. Are you available for hire?"

This was it! By playing in this particular *hamam*, so close to the fine estates near the palace, she'd hoped to attract this kind of attention. In the *taifas*, such feasts were for men, but women often organized them in Christian lands.

Heart fluttering, she clutched her oud tighter. "I would be honored."

The woman nodded once. "Then I will have your name added to the guest list." She rose with the fluid grace of the most skilled *qiyan* and stood before Sarah with a straight-backed boldness she had never before observed in either a Christian or Muslim woman. "I assume you have an escort?"

A woman could never attend such an event alone. "Yes, my husband."

"Then I shall expect both of you. I look forward to your performance, Sarah al-Bayda."

She glided past, toward the exit.

"But we haven't discussed terms." Sarah nibbled her lip, mind racing. "I don't even know your name!"

Halting, the woman raised an eyebrow. "Truly, do you not?" She offered a single, soft chuckle. "How interesting."

Sarah resisted the urge to frown at the strange response.

"Terms are of little consequence. Perform as well at the palace as you did today and you'll earn whatever payment you wish."

Eyes widening, Sarah drew in a breath. "The palace?"

"Yes." The smile widened. "You will perform for my husband and our guests."

The hair on the back of her neck tingled. "Who are you?" Her voice was barely a whisper.

"Jimena Diaz."

Sarah clenched the hand supporting the weight of her oud. She'd hoped for a rich patron, but she hadn't dreamed to impress the wife of El Cid, one of the most powerful women on the peninsula.

The palace! She need never play for leering drunkards in a darkened room again. This was her chance to fulfill all her dreams of being a real *qiyan*, playing for a crowd of refined noblemen who would appreciate her talents and admire her. After all these long years of insignificance, all the hardship and suffering, finally she would justify her training. Finally, she could share the skills Allah had granted with an audience who might truly appreciate it.

But a chilling thought dampened her excitement after Dona Jimena had departed. She had come to this city to steal from the city's rulers, not attract their attention. Yasin's future, as well as her own, depended upon secrecy and anonymity. Was she endangering their purpose here?

What would Yasin say?

SARAH

"This is fantastic." Yasin rubbed his hands together. The surprise on his face melted into abject delight. "Oh, well done, Sarah!"

A wave of relief washed away all her carefully prepared arguments. "I thought you'd be upset."

"Upset?" His voice cracked at the word.

"I thought you'd prefer we remain unnoticed, keep to the shadows to avoid attention."

He laughed. "All the best opportunities are in the light with the people who don't go into the dark." His grin broadened until his eyes seemed to twinkle. "Oh, you were right, beautiful Sarah, when you said that instrument was worth bringing. I didn't see it, but you were right!"

SARAH

Sarah angled the palm mirror to re-check the lay of her blue dress. Every time she looked at her reflection, a new doubt nagged at her. The Almoravids would insist she veil herself, while Christians forgave nearly every vanity. Which way did the Valencian court lean? Every fingerspan of exposed hair risked condemnation. While no one had yet rebuked her fashion choices, her performances to date had merely been a prelude to this crowning achievement.

Palming the mirror, Sarah repositioned the shawl further back, risking a little more boldness. Jimena Diaz had seemed at ease in only a loincloth. Such a woman was unlikely to condemn a little exposed hair.

She would condemn tardiness, however, if Yasin didn't show soon. He knew how important this night was for her. He'd promised to return early from his day's work, but the sun had nearly fallen and he was nowhere to be found. Why did he have to ruin this for her?

She raised the mirror again and gazed hard into it, convinced she'd looked better a few moments ago. For all his supposed success with women, Yasin evidently hadn't learned that leaving one too long on her own led to fussing and second-guessing.

The door squeaked as it swung inward.

Finally.

"You look beautiful," Yasin said from behind.

Clenching her teeth, she turned to remind him how late he was, despite his promise. When she saw him, though, all she could muster was a whimper. His face glistened with a faint application of oil, and his skin looked supple as never before. The hair that had grown wild and been blown by the windy journey was now neatly trimmed and combed forward. He stood before her not in the wrinkled clothes from that morning but in his dark blue cotton *jubba* and his fresh *qamisa* peeking out at the neck. Neither they nor his *sirwal* pants bore any wrinkles.

His eyes, ringed with a thin layer of kohl, reached across the distance and grabbed hold of her as they hadn't done on the road. Those hazel irises drew her in and threatened to drown her. A hint of smoky ambergris tickled her nostrils, exactly the right amount to be noticed without overpowering her few precious drops of jasmine-scented oil. The aromas intertwined in a pleasing way.

Concerns about her performance, the *Healing*, and everything else fell away. He had changed. He stood straighter and bore himself with the virile confidence of *adab*. He more resembled her emir in Granada than the skulking thief in Toledo or the ragged traveler in La Mancha. This man before her would put the courtiers in Baghdad to shame.

He would play the role of her husband tonight. Even Sarah was starting to believe it.

Where had that thought come from?

"You're…" Her voice cracked, and she swallowed to wet her throat. "I didn't expect…" Once again, her eyes rose toward those kohl-encircled eyes, but she stopped herself. "I thought you'd forgotten." The comment seemed ridiculous given his obvious care with his appearance.

"I took longer at the *hamam* than I thought. I'm sorry."

Given the results, his time in the bathhouse had been well spent. Surprise fading, she considered his tunic and pants. "I thank you for the effort."

"It's the least I could do. What you do tonight is important."

Excitement danced in her chest. Her playing had awed him twice before, but to hear him admit the value of her abilities filled her with a surprising comfort. "It is?"

"Absolutely."

He crossed to her oud and picked it up, one hand cradling the neck and the other supporting the drum. As he did, she detected a hint of musk, probably from whatever oil he'd applied. He must have smoked his clothing with the ambergris. If he retained even a fraction of that intoxicating scent into the small hours of the morning, it would keep her up with unexpected thoughts.

He ran his hand over the neck of the instrument. "Beautiful playing, good wine, bounteous food…" He grinned. "The Almoravids would hate everything about it. How could I not appreciate this night?" His lips twisted. "Besides, if this goes well, you'll be in high demand. We'll earn more than enough to pay our scribe."

There was the Yasin she knew. Her fluttering breath and the warmth in her chest snuffed out as if they'd never existed. Now, those eyes were no different than on the road.

"We should go," she said.

While streetlamps still illuminated the Valencian streets, they were fewer and more widely spaced than in Toledo. As Sarah and Yasin made their way to the palace, they passed through large gaps of darkness interrupted by small islands of light. Her heart fluttered with each step, and she couldn't decide whether anticipation of their destination or fear of those dark corners was to blame.

The palace complex included a series of limestone buildings near the Great Mosque and the city's administrative buildings. The stout stone walls surrounding it bore an uneven, blotchy grain. Torches affixed at intervals along the battlements illuminated watchtowers built into the corners.

Sarah's breath quickened as they approached. Though this palace had a different layout than the one in Granada, the walls were the same. They were great arms, embracing and sheltering the softness and music and gardens found in every Andalusi palace.

They weren't protecting her this time, though. They were an obstacle to all her dreams.

"It's just as well you don't need to break into the library," she murmured. "Those walls look solid."

"There's always a way in," he chirped. "Though it seems the emirs of Valencia had more trouble with their citizens than their neighbors."

She frowned. "Why do you say that?"

He gestured to two spots that had been patched with a different type of stone than the rest. "The city walls show less damage than these ones."

They joined a stream of finely dressed Valencians that was converging on a pair of large wooden gates. A bald priest verified the guests while four armed guards watched from either side of the archway.

"This was a bad idea." Yasin tugged on her sleeve, slowing her. "They could recognize me from the port."

She doubted he meant his work as a wagoner. "That won't happen."

"How can you be certain?"

She dared only a brief glance at the kohl around his eyes and his supple skin. "Your own mother wouldn't recognize you."

The priest stood at the end of a tree-lined walkway of crushed shells that led to the emir's residence. He eyed Sarah's oud when she approached. "Name?"

"Sarah al-Bayda and my husband, Yasin ibn Faraj."

The priest ran his finger along the paper in his hands. As he reached the bottom, the top half curled over and Sarah recognized it as a list of names.

His finger halted at the bottom of the third column. Squinting, he ran his eyes over the page. "Ah, yes." He gestured to one of the guards.

Beside her, Yasin stilled.

"Escort them to Ibn Fanan. Report that the *qiyan* has arrived." The priest turned back to Sarah. "Lord Diaz's steward will provide instruction."

The guard led them down the pathway, each step on the tiny shells making a crunching sound. Following stiffly, Yasin eyed the guards behind them who had remained with the priest.

"What is it?" she whispered.

He frowned. "I'm not used to them knowing I've gotten inside."

Torches on high poles illuminated batches of apple, peach, plum, and orange trees arrayed in colorful patterns along the walkway. Guests strolled in small groups in between the rows of trees.

A pair of nightingales warbled to each other from somewhere out of sight. The simplicity of their song soothed her ears. Sarah hadn't appreciated the silence while traveling through the plateau of central

Iberia. After a week of chatter, stomping, and shouts, she found herself missing the quiet peace of nature. She missed the sounds of absence.

Yasin nearly collided with her when he tilted his head back to gape at the trees. Offering an apologetic smile, he gestured around them. "This reminds me of home."

Sarah recalled his story about the gardens. "They won't mind if you pick fruit tonight."

He reached for a nearby orange but stopped himself. "No, I think not."

Such restraint didn't seem in his nature. "They have plenty of food inside. What's one more?"

His narrowed eyes flashed toward their escort. "It's the kind of thing they'd forbid."

The emir's residence unfolded before them as they cleared the final tree. The bright limestone composing most of the structure shimmered in the light of torches affixed periodically along its length. Shadows danced within the arched colonnades of open corridors along the exterior of the second and third floors. Mosaic designs flowed up and around each window, door, and fixture, layering colorful patterns of tiny tiles over the white surface. Such artwork must have taken a great many craftsmen years to complete.

Yasin blew air between his lips. "Can you imagine living here?"

"The emir's palace in Granada was larger than this."

His eyes widened. "Truly?"

She nodded. "Granada was a major city during the Caliphate, but Valencia didn't grow into what you see here until the *taifas*."

His eyebrows knitted together. "Why would someone need a space so large?"

"It's not just for one man. It has workrooms, servants' chambers, stables, offices, greeting and feast halls, the treasury, record rooms, the harem—"

"Treasury *and* the harem?" He shook his head. "Why would anyone ever leave?"

She sighed. "Some emirs never did."

"At least, not until their subjects removed them," he supplied.

"I suppose."

"And you lived in a place like this?"

She smiled at the memory of the long, winding corridors, the painted walls and carved reliefs, the censers that filled the air with hints of spice, and the music…oh, the music that emanated from the private quarters to echo through the halls. "The less luxurious part, but yes."

The building's entrance sat atop a set of four marble steps flanked by thick columns. A Muslim in a blue silk *jubba* directed a swarm of servants who were taking cloaks and exchanging shoes and boots for slippers.

The guard halted before the silken man. "This is the *qiyan*." Duty completed, he turned on his heel and strode back to the gates.

Eyes widening, the steward pressed his hand to his lips and forehead as Yasin often did. His eyes carried a gloss of amazement. "It is a very great pleasure to meet you."

Yasin's indrawn breath matched her own surprise at the respectful greeting. These past five years, those who knew of her training had responded with derision or dismissal. And yet, this steward of one of the most powerful men on the peninsula had shown her deference.

A servant bent down to place a pair of slippers in front of her, then held her boot as she slipped her foot out. She had done this same task for translators when she'd first arrived in Toledo. She yearned to relieve the man of this demeaning task but restrained the urge. This was how things were done. She had waited to perform at such a gathering for a long time and wouldn't squander the opportunity by acting inappropriately now.

"You will perform after Dona Jimena greets the guests. I'm told she will announce you herself."

A swell of pride warmed her cheeks. To be introduced by the lady of the palace was a true honor. Not three weeks earlier, no one would have noticed her passage. Tonight, all attention would be on her.

"Until then, you are invited to explore the palace and enjoy the feast." As an afterthought, he gestured to Yasin. "And your husband, of course."

"Your mistress permits musicians to interact with her guests?" Yasin asked.

"Musicians wait in the antechamber." He smiled again at Sarah. "A *qiyan* may do as she wishes."

After pressing his hand to his chest and bowing, the steward turned to greet the next guest.

Yasin offered her his arm. "I am astounded."

She took it. The image of Abdallah ibn Buluggin's kind face formed in her memory. "Now you understand why an emir would pay for a young girl to learn their ways in Baghdad."

The muscles of his forearm stiffened beneath her hand. "Yes, I'm beginning to appreciate the value of a *qiyan*."

The uncertainty of his meaning evoked a tingle across her skin. Her fingers twitched where they touched his forearm. She once again noticed his delightful musk after having ignored it during the walk over.

She released his arm to open distance between them. It was just the oil and the kohl and his fine, new clothing. He was the same man as always.

They halted at the entrance to the feasting hall. Braziers along the walls illuminated the vaulted ceilings and offered a clear view of the sculpted designs on the pillars and arches. Bouquets of colorful flowers adorned the balustrade of a second-floor gallery. Rounded tables bearing food sat like motionless islands as guests fluttered around them amid swirls of silk, brocade and lace. Two dozen of El Cid's soldiers stood guard at a respectful distance.

Most of the guests were men, about half of whom wore thick beards and chortled like northerners. The remainder were Valencians, unmistakable in their richly colored Muslim *jubbas* and hair styled short like the southern courts. Or, rather, like the fashion of the courts before she'd left for Baghdad. They moved with the entitled ease and defiant undercurrent of Valencian lineage; this was their city, despite El Cid's conquest. A scant few—exclusively men—with clear Berber blood and unadorned, pale-colored *jubbas* had somehow escaped El Cid's execution of the Almoravids. They stood on the periphery glaring with naked disgust at the women who dared to mingle with the men.

Women. Though she'd expected their presence since Dona Jimena was hosting this feast, she still couldn't believe her eyes. Neither during her *qiyan* training in Baghdad nor in stolen glimpses at feasts in Granada had she witnessed respectable women attending such a gathering. And yet, here they were, a mix of pale northerners whose hair escaped their lacy shawls in curling tendrils and native Valencians with kohl-lined eyes and linen veils.

What a strange city!

Yasin released a contented sigh. "Well, I intend to enjoy myself." He offered a grin so wide that his eyes twinkled. "How often can I explore a palace?"

A surge of apprehension set her heart beating faster. "Yasin, if you're caught—"

He laid a hand on her arm. "I promise to use my eyes, not my hands. Did you notice the watchtowers? Four guards each, and more throughout the gardens." He shook his head. "I won't take any chances tonight."

She forced a steadying breath. He honored his promises. "Thank you, Yasin."

YASIN

Half an hour later, a servant arrived to prepare Sarah for her performance, leaving Yasin alone in a room of wealthy Valencians.

Golden rings and silver necklaces reflected the torchlight. Emeralds, rubies, and sapphires battled with rich silks and fine cottons for his attention. Some of those rings sat loosely on fat fingers and would slip off easily. Two strides away, a delicately braided silver necklace with a loose clasp hung from the neck of a woman with brazenly unbound hair. A single tug, easily covered by a stumble, would make it fall. A fold in clothing obviously hid a dagger, while another obscured a heavy pouch. He saw it all as clearly as if these people willingly presented their valuables for his inspection.

Servants bearing goblets circulated through the crowd. Even if Yasin stumbled or bumped someone too aggressively, they'd soon be too addled to notice. It was a pickpocket's paradise, but he could do nothing about it. Dozens of guards stood between him and escape, and he had only the drawstring of his waist to conceal plunder. The risk of it jangling or falling out was too great. Stealing under these circumstances was madness.

He clenched his fists until the tingling in his fingers departed with the temptation. Even if none of that were true, he'd given Sarah his word. He could still take advantage of this opportunity, though.

Quietly weaving through the crowd, Yasin caught fragments of conversation. Grumbling about northern priests imposing the Latin Rite suggested a healthy religious controversy, but stoking it wouldn't profit him, given the tiny Christian population. Occasional fragments confirmed a general deprivation following the siege, and a few exchanges about new regulations would have interested Yasin if he intended to remain in Valencia. The rest of the chatter mentioned invitations to dinner, eligible sons and daughters, and frustration about lazy servants. A group of drab Muslims clustered at the periphery muttered at the injustice of undermining their emir only to have a Christian replace him. Having spent too much time grooming himself to risk his head on treason, Yasin kept his distance.

Though he'd looked forward to the chance to learn the secrets of the city's elite, a simple stroll through the market would have yielded more useful information.

Guests were moving in and out of the feasting hall without the guards halting them, so he followed their example through one granite corridor after another. Rich tile mosaics and floral patterns adorned every wall and blended with the carvings on the thresholds and architraves of doorways.

Frequent clusters of loitering guests slowed his progress. They didn't keep to one side of the corridor, and opportunities to slip past were few. From their overheard chatter, Yasin gathered that the previous emir had kept his palace firmly sealed. Yasin suspected El Cid had opened it up to swell attendance by reluctant, yet curious, subjects.

After a quarter of an hour, he had grown comfortable enough to nod to those he passed. Concern that they would identify him as a commoner faded with each reciprocal greeting. In the peristyle garden with a canal-fed stream and canopies of fig trees overlooking rows of patterned flowers, a woman with bone-white skin even offered an elegant bow. The softness of her cleavage called to him, but he limited himself to a nod before escaping the narrow-eyed scrutiny of her male companion.

At the next intersection, he stumbled upon a guarded archway leading to an open-air colonnade. The short walkway led to a heavily stained *tapia* building of considerable dimension.

A guard straightened at his approach. "This area is closed to Lord Diaz's guests."

Yasin's fingers twitched at his side. Why should an ordinary building merit such protection when other rooms lacking even doors—let alone locks—contained Iraqi crystal, Egyptian glass, porcelain from the East, and a dozen other treasures?

He offered an easy smile. Revealing his interest would only raise suspicion. "I seem to have lost my way. Can you direct me to the feasting hall?"

Tension melted from the guard's stance. He pointed down the corridor. "Turn at the second right, then take an immediate left. You'll run into it."

Yasin pressed his fingers to his lips, then his forehead. "My thanks to you." He took a step before turning back and gesturing at the archway. "What's through there, anyways?"

He expected a gruff warning to mind his own business, but the guard simply lowered his eyes to Yasin's *jubba* and twitched his lips. Yasin had quite forgotten his kohl and fine clothing. He truly must look as if he belonged here, as Sarah claimed.

"Administrative buildings. Record storehouses. The library."

Yasin spared a single glance at the building that held his future before forcing a shrug. "Nothing of interest, then." With a flip of his hand, he headed down the hall, back toward the celebration.

Gaze fixed on the stone beneath his feet, he ignored the beautiful wall designs flashing past as he marched back toward the din of conversation. The library was so close! If he could just slip inside for a few moments, he could steal the text and wouldn't owe the clerk a single silver coin. Tonight could profit him more than all his efforts this past month.

No. He pressed his hands to his forehead to crush the thought. Finding a way around that guard would take too much time. Too many sets of eyes might notice him. A dozen more men probably waited in the courtyard surrounding the colonnade. Even if he did somehow lay hands on the *Healing*, he had no way past the walls. The entrances and watchtowers were well-guarded tonight. Nor could he do it without Sarah.

Ibn Sina's masterpiece might as well have been in his native Persia, for all that Yasin could access it.

Sudden silence made Yasin slow to a halt. Despite cupping his hands around his ears, he no longer heard the feast. Had he made a wrong turn? The corridor didn't look familiar, but he couldn't have gone so far as to leave earshot. A servant would have halted him.

The haunting chords of an oud rose out of the silence with the suddenness of the first lark singing in the morning. Yasin started to run, his feet carrying him through each intersection. The music grew louder with every turn.

Rounding another bend brought the archway leading to the feasting hall into view and clarified the music further. Now, he could distinguish the skillful transitions between notes that he'd enjoyed around the campfires of La Mancha. They had transported him to the marketplace of Almeria and wrapped him with comfort he hadn't felt for many years. He hastened through the archway.

Sarah sat alone on a stool on the raised dais at the far end of the room, plucking her oud with eyes closed. Her shawl hung low, letting her hair spill over her right shoulder in a flow of shimmering golden-brown. Her head swayed ever so slightly with the rise and fall of the melody, as if musician and instrument were fused into a single entity.

The song was a traditional one from hundreds of years ago. The lyrics that normally accompanied the melody recounted a heroic caliph who had liberated a village from a corrupt warlord. It was a difficult one to play, requiring frequent and intricate adjustments of her grip while still hitting quick notes. The market musicians had never attempted anything so complex. The risk of being jostled was too high, and other songs could impress equally without requiring such delicate and precise fingering.

Yasin had heard it only twice before. He had thought it a beautiful song then. As he listened now, the music enfolded him, conjuring visions of adoring villagers tossing flowers in the path of a conquering caliph. He stood helpless, enslaved by Sarah's magical fingers. Her performance tonight outshone all her playing during the journey here.

When she'd finished her final notes, Sarah opened her eyes. They sparkled with pride and delight in equal measure. Lowering the oud, she rose. For a moment, those green orbs owned the massive room.

"I should like to continue with a poem by Wallada bint al-Mustakfi." She bowed her head before straightening again.

She began to recite a sensuous poem about a woman and her lover, set during the Cordoban Caliphate some sixty years ago. Her expression shifted with each sentiment, infusing the words with the agony of loneliness, the wonder of the lovers' first meeting, and the anticipation of courtship.

Across the expanse between them, Sarah's eyes reached out to his, holding him with a feather touch. He held his breath, lest he break the fragile tether, as she began the next verse.

When the evening descends, await then my visit,
For the night is the best keeper of secrets.
I feel a love for you which, if the sun had felt a similar love,
She would not rise; and the moon, he would not appear;
And the stars, they would not undertake their nightly travel.

And then, she released him, turning to another within the crowd. A breath spilled from his lips, sending his heart racing. Sarah had once claimed her training involved seduction but not lovemaking. He hadn't understood the distinction then. Now, it aroused an intoxicating hunger to enfold himself within both her voice and her body, all at once.

She had become the nightingale her emir had desired, and her artistry put the songs of twilight to shame.

SARAH

Sarah sang a courtly song from Baghdad and recited one of Ziryab's poems before ending her performance with a Castilian ballad. It felt glorious. Every moment was a delight, and she sought to bask for as long as possible in their attention. She even added an extemporaneous verse at the end of her last song to draw out the sensation. There was precedent: the finest musicians added flourishes to established pieces to offer a memorable experience.

Yet, she could do only so much, and eventually her fingers and voice stilled.

The silence endured for a tense moment. Motionless eyes stared back at her. A giddy excitement coursed through her as she anticipated the torrent of frenzied applause that would follow. She had played well and could not recall a single mistake. After years of drudgery and suffering, she would finally bask in adulation of a crowd of noblemen!

She had done it. She had tugged at their hearts and silenced them with her arts. She had wielded Ziryab and Wallada bint al-Mustakfi as a Damascene mosaicist deployed tiles. Even her teachers, usually so dismissive of Andalusi sentiments, would have appreciated the acclaim of a *taifa* court. For, despite the rule of a northern warlord, that's what this collection of Valencian nobles, Christian administrators, and soldiers was. She had finally vindicated all the hopes of the *agha* and her emir. She wished she could tell them and perform for them, if even once.

Gradually, starting with pockets sprinkled throughout the room, the applause began. But while it spread, it didn't rise above the level of polite acknowledgement. No tears twinkled in the corners of eyes ringed with kohl or poking out from behind veils. No men lost their minds celebrating her subtle manipulations of courtly chords to match the stylistic preferences of al-Andalus.

The only exception was Yasin. While his cheering was no louder than that of the sea of faces surrounding him, his eyes shone with wonder and admiration like beacons in the darkness.

And then a great shout rose up, startling Sarah into pressing a hand against her chest. In less than the time it took her heart to beat again, the applause came in a torrent of frenzied excitement. Whispered chatter between companions charged the air as before a thunderstorm, overfilling a hall suddenly too small to contain it.

It had been a delay only, that was all! Sarah bowed her head, both to signal her appreciation for their reactions and to hide her swelling pride.

But as she did, she noticed movement behind her, a flurry of bright colors. Four young girls no older than sixteen bounded onto the dais wearing dresses far too sheer, flowing, and low-cut for their ages. One of them waved her hand at Sarah as if brushing her aside.

The burst of excitement hadn't been for her, after all.

Her outrage at being dismissed by a mere girl was short-lived, for the tumult around her only continued to grow. Neither Jimena Diaz, conversing with one of her guests at the perimeter, nor her steward acted to avenge her.

Her time was over, and she'd been replaced by four far younger entertainers.

Dumbly, Sarah stumbled away as the dancers began to sway to a heavy-handed drummer beating an amateurish rhythm. From the smiles on the faces of the men, even the Muslims who had stood apart until now, Sarah doubted they noticed the poor quality of the playing. They were all too busy enjoying the feast of legs, hips, breasts, and arms.

Sarah's elation evaporated, leaving only an aching hollowness in its place. For years, she had hungered to play for the finest nobles and courtiers. This chance was supposed to gain her esteem and wealth and importance. But in their minds, she would only ever be a performer, valued merely for the enjoyment they could extract from her. And always, there would be someone younger waiting to replace her.

"Allah has truly blessed you, my dear," came a deep voice from behind.

Startled, she turned. A dark-skinned man in a white cotton *jubba*—Sarah could not begin to fathom the cost of pure white clothing, let alone cotton—and a golden-hued *qamisa* smiled at her. The shape of his eyes and slope of his nose suggested nearly pure Arabic ancestry. Only the oldest and most noble families in al-Andalus could boast more than a drop of Arabic blood. This man must have descended from an august family, indeed.

Sarah lowered her eyes to hide her shattered pride. "I am pleased to have entertained, my lord."

A suggestive motion by the girls on stage drew his attention, but only for a moment. "Can I look forward to seeing you perform at Lord Diaz's next feast?"

The question only underscored how brief her moment of triumph had been. "Alas, I was hired for tonight only."

"That's a shame." He cocked his head. "Does that mean you're free to entertain other offers?"

Sarah held her breath. Perhaps she had made more of an impression than she'd thought. "Other offers?"

His lips curved into a smirk. "A permanent arrangement."

"Permanent?" She had hungered for a nobleman to elevate her as his wife many times in her tiny chamber in the translation school. Back then, it had seemed an impossible dream. The men who had listened in the marketplace lacked the means, and the nobles would have never sullied themselves with a slave. The image of herself holding her child, evoked by her landlady, formed once again. But this time, she imagined this Arabic lord as the father, standing over her as his wife.

He nodded once, slowly. "I want you to perform for my wife and I at all our celebrations. They'd be whispered about with excitement if people knew they would enjoy such fine entertainment." The man twisted a ring on his finger. "Enough to attract even El Cid and his wife."

All Sarah's life, people had spoken of *qiyans* with hushed reverence. They were the voices of the past, preserving and recounting the stories and hopes of a people. Even those in her village recounted tales of celebrated *qiyans* who had become wives of viziers and highest ranks of noblemen. Her teachers in Baghdad had spurred their novitiates to excel by emphasizing the fame their abilities could earn them, the rewards that were limited only by the extent of a girl's skill and hard work. Such thoughts had driven Sarah forward through even hard lessons on diction and intonation. She had been convinced that her fate laid entirely in her hands.

But this Arabic nobleman's casual comment, squeezed out with the twist of a ring, had exposed the truth. The noblemen who married such woman didn't care about musical or oratorical skill, only the influence they would gain.

Why hadn't anyone told her? That answer was easy. No one in Baghdad could conceive of a time without emirs, sultans, or caliphs.

There would always be powerful rulers to impress, rulers whose courts *qiyans* could adorn and magnify with their skill. For them, *qiyans* would always find honored marriages, because noblemen would always want to curry favor with their emirs by marrying an accomplished woman.

"And other needs I may have," the man continued. "I suspect you displayed only a fraction of your talents tonight, and I'd like to explore the rest personally." Desire thickened his voice, leaving no mystery as to his true meaning.

Once, she would have delighted in the prospect of a wealthy lover, like the great Wallada bint al-Mustakfi herself. But now, that dream seemed unsatisfying. Tonight had proven how quickly she would be forgotten. A younger woman would eventually attract his eye. Four dancers were doing that now, and it hadn't required years of *qiyan* training, only taut bodies shamefully displayed. Without marriage, where would she be when his interest faded?

She had already lost five of her best years. She could not settle for being a mistress. It might give her riches for a while, but marriage to a man who possessed *adab* and treated her with respect would give stability and security for a lifetime. She need never again worry about her safety. She could lay down the fear of losing all she valued that had tormented her.

And what of Yasin? He needed her to finish this job. His future depended on it. He might taunt or tease or argue with her, but he had always treated her with dignity. Despite knowing her status, he'd never dismissed her worth. He didn't deserve to have his trust repaid with treachery, especially not when it wouldn't even satisfy her desires.

"Your offer is generous, my lord. But I could not dishonor my husband in such a manner."

Jealousy flashed in his eyes, and Sarah slouched to spoil the view of her breasts and render the angles of her neck and shoulders less appealing. The last thing she needed was trouble for either herself or Yasin.

It had the desired effect. Regret, not hostility, weighed down the man's voice. "I hope your husband recognizes what a treasure you are."

Whoever that man might be, Sarah hoped he would, too.

YASIN

Yasin leaned against a column on the third-story arcade overlooking the palace grounds. Below him, the light of the quarter moon offered only a hint of definition to the darkened canopies of the trees. Beyond the garden, the uneven roofs of Valencia stretched out in all directions like used cups and goblets in the alehouse, gathered for rinsing after a long night of drinking. The silvery crescent of the Turia River cut through them, shimmering in the darkness. Beyond it all stretched lush fields, verdant vineyards, and a hint of moonlit greenery punctuated by veins of irrigated canals. He'd never seen so much greenery before.

"It's a beautiful kingdom."

Yasin turned to the speaker. A northerner, unmistakable with his bushy black-and-gray speckled beard and matching curly hair, stood in profile beside a column two arches further down the arcade. He wore a simple green cotton tunic with a strip of yellow and black brocade along the edges.

Yasin eyed to the verdant fields again. "I've seen little enough of it, but I know of nothing to surpass this view."

The man grinned to reveal a chipped incisor, albeit a clean, white one. At his age, that meant nobility, yet he wore no gold or jewels like the revelers two stories below. "I've been all over this peninsula, from Leon and Santiago de Compostela in the west, to Barcelona and Zaragoza in the east, and Seville to the south. Valencia is a prize."

His reference points suggested a distinctly Castilian perspective. "You are well-traveled."

The man grunted. "Not always according to my will."

Yasin couldn't help but chuckle. It seemed the madness spreading through al-Andalus had affected more than just himself. "It never is."

A long, straight scar ran along the side of this man's neck. The very thought of the injury that produced it made Yasin shudder. "You're a mercenary, then?"

Mirth shone out of his eyes for reasons Yasin didn't understand. "I was, yes."

The man sauntered a few steps forward. A worn leather sheath dangled from his hip. Its rich patina and signs of wear showed its age, but two different kinds of stitching suggested careful repairs. To waste resources repairing such a simple sheath meant he was either very poor or it was a cherished possession. Since it held a dagger with a jeweled hilt that Yasin could sell for hundreds of silver coins, Yasin suspected the latter.

"And now?"

The man leaned against the column beside Yasin's. "Now, I spend most of my time ruling this kingdom."

Yasin froze.

Rodrigo Diaz de Vivar. El Cid. El Campeador. The scourge of Allah. This man had killed and looted his way through the Spains and al-Andalus, not merely traversed it.

Yasin's pulse throbbed at his neck and filled his ears with thumping. Coming to Valencia had meant eventually confronting this man's soldiers and preparations, but Yasin hadn't expected to face the man himself.

Fingers shaking, Yasin reviewed every word of the last few moments. El Cid was a *taifa* lord, not a rich fool. A mistake here could see him hanged. He had to proceed carefully.

He dipped in a perfunctory bow. "Forgive me, my lord. I didn't realize who you were."

"Yes, I noticed." Rodrigo raised an eyebrow. "That's surprising, since I drew up the guest list."

"I'm new to the city."

"You move more like a local scout than a Valencian noble." Rodrigo jutted his chin forward. "Where do you come from?"

Yasin supposed the description suited him well enough. Both thieves and scouts wished to avoid being seen. Yet, the perceptive comment convinced Yasin to keep as close to the truth as possible until he could extricate himself from this conversation.

"I arrived from Toledo a little more than two weeks ago."

"Ah, Toledo." Rodrigo leaned against the column. "And what do you intend to steal from me?"

Yasin suppressed a twitch. Neither Hisham nor his smuggling contacts knew his true intentions in Valencia. Only the scribe could have betrayed him. Though, why would he when it would implicate him, as well?

He heard only the muted rustling of the other guests and the occasional chord of a *rebab* far below them. His peripheral vision caught no movement suggesting approaching guards. Perhaps El Cid believed he needed no assistance to capture a simple thief.

Merciful God...

His lips felt thick with dread. "Steal from you, my lord?" What would a man like El Cid do to a thief?

"Since I captured Valencia, no one comes from Toledo without another demand from Alfonso." Rodrigo snorted a laugh. "He's jealous of my glory. I took Valencia with my army, while he *negotiated* for Toledo." He sneered the word with a curl of his lip.

The tightness passed. El Cid had spoken from exasperation, not accusation.

"I've never met His Majesty, and have only rarely spent time in a nobleman's presence." His skin tingled with a wave of strangeness. These men decided the fates of kingdoms and peoples as casually as Yasin selected breakfast. He could hardly conceive of them as anything but their titles, yet El Cid spoke of his liege-lord with the same vitriol as Yasin ascribed to Esteban.

Rodrigo knitted his eyebrows together. "How have you come to be present at my feast?"

Yasin forced himself to answer more slowly than his ragged mind desired. "I accompanied my wife, whom Dona Jimena asked to perform."

Rodrigo gasped and pointed down the arcade. "The *qiyan*?" His eyes drained of suspicion. "I stand corrected. You are wealthier than every other man here."

"Excepting yourself." If not for Sarah, Dona Jimena would have been the most beautiful woman in the hall tonight.

God above… What had provoked that thought?

Rodrigo acknowledged the compliment with a tilt of his head. "You are courteous and polite, usual for a man from Toledo."

"In truth, I'm an Almerian Mozarab." He swallowed. "Or I was, until the Almoravids came."

"God protect us from fanatics of all faiths."

Yasin found himself immensely liking this warlord. He had an easy smile that made Yasin want to trust him. Perhaps that shouldn't have surprised him. After all, El Cid's men had followed him into exile and into the service of both Christians and Muslims, through impossible odds and outnumbered battles. A warlord would need charisma to maintain loyalty, just as a thief needed it to ease his mark and disappear in a crowd.

Rodrigo sighed and returned his attention to the vista before him. "Though, I have to admit the effectiveness of Almoravid tactics."

"I don't understand your meaning." The Almoravids had forced the women of his home to cover themselves, purged the markets, and pressured his fellow Christians to convert. How could this man, of all people, defend them?

El Cid leaned an elbow on the column. "I ended starvation, brutal taxation, smuggling, riots…but I've had nothing but problems since entering Valencia. They should be thanking me."

Yasin doubted any conquered people ever thanked their conqueror. Yet Yasin could appreciate the point. The feel in the marketplace reminded him of home before the Almoravids. The *hamams*, the fashions, the performers… In fact, Yasin now stood in the emir's palace because El Cid had preserved the *taifa* culture that revered music. Toledo had squandered Sarah on manual labor. In Almeria, she'd be constrained by lock and veil. Yet here, she—and the education, grace, and art she represented—might thrive.

The Almerians had traded everything they valued for the strength they believed they needed to defend against conquest. In truth, the *taifas* had already been dead, like the ruins of a burned hut. If the Almoravids hadn't knocked them over, the Castilians or Aragonese would have.

"It's no surprise the Almoravids are harsh. They understand what's required to maintain order." El Cid grunted. "Just today, my men discovered one of my trusted scribes was copying works from my library to sell to collectors."

Yasin drew in a breath, but the night air clung to him like a cold emptiness. The brilliance of his elegant solution for getting the *Healing* shattered like blown glass falling to a marble floor.

Rodrigo showed no signs of noticing Yasin's growing panic. "I could crush them like cicadas beneath my boot if I wished, yet they test me every day." The Castilian lord released a long sigh. "Perhaps I should cut off the hands of the man responsible, as the Almoravids would. It's crude, but effective."

Yasin paled. Those desert fanatics had silenced the music of the markets and repressed the wine, women, and wonder of Almeria. How could a man celebrated for his tolerance and wisdom praise such barbarism?

El Cid glanced at Yasin, and after a moment, his eyebrows knitted together. "Such things are necessary when ruling a kingdom. The squeamish have no business attempting it." He scowled. "Nor judging those who do."

Yasin wished he were back home, enjoying the quiet simplicity of working leather. "It's just as well that I never desired that vocation for myself."

He had lost his easy path to the *Healing*. That left him only one option, and it would put him beneath the sword of a man who admired the ruthless efficiency of Almoravid rule. That thought sent a chill down his spine.

SARAH

Sarah was conversing with a group of musicians from Zaragoza who had performed after those accursed dancers when Yasin tugged on her arm.

"Pardon me, gentlemen, but I must borrow my wife."

Her surprise at the sudden interruption faded when she noticed his expression, darkened like a thunderstorm rolling over the hills. "What has happened?" she asked as he guided her through the crowd.

He didn't speak until he reached the entrance. He gestured at one of the slaves hovering near the entrance to bring their boots. "Our scribe has been discovered."

Sarah drew in a breath. "How did you learn this?"

Yasin grunted. "From El Cid."

If the scribe had revealed who hired him… "Are we in danger?"

"Not now, but we may be by tomorrow night."

She frowned. "Why tomorrow night?"

"Because we have to steal the codex by then, before they move it or add more guards."

She swallowed. The thought of sneaking through these hallways and gardens seemed foolhardy. "I thought you wanted to avoid that."

"I tried my best." Regret oozed out with his long sigh. "But I failed, and we have no other choice."

CHAPTER THIRTEEN

YASIN

THE NEXT MORNING, Sarah waited outside while Yasin visited Orbanus's home. To his relief, the clerk still had both his hands.

"Diaz wouldn't dare mutilate me." Orbanus leaned back in his chair, threading his hands behind his head. "Not if he wants to rule here. If he abuses a fellow Christian, the Muslims would expect even worse treatment. The city would riot."

The warlord Yasin had met at the previous night's feast seemed a bit thin on patience and not particularly concerned with cooperation. Yasin also suspected this clerk overestimated his value.

"It's not as if I was stealing from him." Orbanus gnawed at his lip through a scowl. "Diaz doesn't own Ibn Sina's words, only the paper it's written on. If he punished everyone who profited from his position, he'll have to sweep his own stables and clean his own boots."

"What went wrong?" Yasin crossed his arms. "You said no one would notice."

"They wouldn't have, either." He lowered his arms to his lap. "I made a mistake. I was working late and fell asleep at my desk with my face in the middle of Ibn Sina. One of El Cid's northerners figured out what I was doing and dismissed me on the spot."

Some mistake. Yasin bit the inside of his cheek. "Do they know who you were working for?"

Orbanus snorted. "They didn't even ask."

Relief washed over him, but in its wake flowed Sarah's words. The clerk's gambling may have made him desperate, but Yasin had endangered his life and livelihood. "What will you do now that you've lost your position?"

Orbanus rubbed his hands together. "Many in this city look favorably on those El Cid mistrusts. Few appreciate his meddling."

Yasin released a breath. "I'm pleased to hear that." He leaned against the wall. "What did they do with the *Healing*?"

The clerk shrugged. "They put it back, of course."

Yasin scratched at his chin. "And where might that be?"

"You intend to steal it." Orbanus leaned forward, resting his elbows on his knees. "Do you truly desire it badly enough to risk such danger?"

The wax seal of the folded pardon within his *jubba* pressed against his chest. Until Yasin delivered his end of the arrangement, Gonzalo could withdraw it at any time. "If I did?"

Orbanus barked a laugh and bolted upright. "Then I'd draw you a map to it."

Good news deserved scrutiny. "Why would you do that?"

"My debts haven't vanished."

"There are safer ways to earn coin."

The scowl returned. "I served two Muslim emirs while retaining my faith. That was not easy. I earned my position. Now, a Castilian mercenary who stole his throne from the man he should have protected dares to turn me out?" The corner of his lip quivered. "I know nothing of war and cannot challenge him, but I can help those who would steal from him."

Revenge. Defiance. Yasin understood those urges well. And paying this clerk would prevent him from changing his mind and reporting what he knew to the city guards.

"You owe thirty silver coins, yes?"

The man nodded.

"If your map proves accurate, I'll cover your debts."

"Done." Orbanus grinned. "I'll even give you the copy I was working on."

Lord Gonzalo wanted the complete text, and Yasin could see little value in a fragment. Still, he never turned down a gift. "Gladly accepted."

Yasin emerged from Orbanus's home a quarter-hour later with a leather-bound codex containing the partial translation, a sheet with a hastily drawn map, and detailed descriptions of the embellishments on the codices of the *Book of Healing*.

Sarah approached from across the street when he emerged, and they fell into step. "How did it go?"

Yasin raised the small map. "Between Hisham's advice for getting past the walls and what I learned today, I have what I need."

She pulled her shawl tighter around her head. "Then we're really going to do this." Her voice quavered in stark contrast to its strength at the feast the night before.

"Are you nervous?"

"This is why we came." She drew in a long breath. "But now the moment has arrived, I'm…" She licked her lips. "I'm afraid of the repercussions if we should be caught."

Yasin took her shaking hand. "I am too."

She turned, eyes wide. "Truly?"

"Every time." He'd never admitted that before. Releasing that secret left him feeling lighter. In fact, he hadn't spoken so openly with anyone since his sister Amira, so many years earlier. He missed that candor.

"You don't look it."

He smiled. "That's a lifetime of keeping my thoughts from my face." He squeezed her hand. "Anything is frightening if you contemplate it all at once. Focus only on the next decision. One step at a time."

"I will try." She faced ahead, but the tension in her forehead didn't fade.

At the feast, he'd seen what Sarah's life should have been after leaving Baghdad, but for those pirates. She had lost all that time. He couldn't erase the past, but he could ease her worries for the next day.

He squeezed her hand again to draw her attention. "If we're caught, tell them I forced you to help me, and they'll let you go."

Her eyes filled with disbelief, and she began to bristle.

"I mean it." He halted and turned her to face him. "Your enslavement has caused you great pain, but it can protect you if the worst should happen."

Her mouth fell open a fraction. "We're partners. I won't abandon you to punishment."

Before him, he no longer saw the proud woman from Toledo, only the shining singer who had commanded the attention of so many the night before.

"Your task is to identify the right text. Mine is to see us in and out again with it. You should not suffer if I fail."

"Yasin—"

He raised a hand. "I can do my job better if I risk only myself. Promise me you will do as I ask."

She cocked her head to the side and studied him for the span of a deep breath. "If it eases your mind…" She swallowed and nodded. "As you wish."

A weight slipped from his shoulders, carrying with it his worry. Now, all that stood before him was a simple burglary, and he'd faced such danger before. A flame of excitement kindled.

"Then let's go rob a library."

YASIN

"That's your way in."

Hisham's outstretched hand pointed through the darkness toward a ramshackle warehouse along a side street off the waterfront. Splintered shutters and a wooden overhang suggested neglect, while refuse piled along the base of the walls indicated outright abandonment. It seemed utterly out of place compared to the fresh paint and carved wood architraves on the shipping offices on either end of it. Even Yasin had marked it as undeserving of attention.

"That doesn't look like an entrance to the palace." Sarah scratched at the woolen skullcap concealing her hair. Her delicate voice clashed with her men's tunic and black northern breeches. Admittedly, hers was a convincing disguise. She'd even bound her breasts so a casual glance would mark her as a male servant, and her clothes were far less likely than a dress to knock something over. Most importantly, they hadn't absorbed the usual oils Sarah anointed herself with, so they had no scent to attract the attention of passing guards.

"There's little point in a secret entrance if everyone knows what it is." Hisham turned back to Yasin. "Be quick. Dawn comes shortly. When you emerge, I'll signal if the way is clear."

Yasin adjusted the leather shoulder bag he'd purchased with Sarah's disguise and felt for the comforting outline of his toolkit. "You have my thanks."

"Gratitude is best expressed by introductions to your clients."

"You'll have them." Hisham deserved to inherit his customers for this help. By the morrow, Yasin would either be returning to Toledo or moldering in Valencia's dungeons. Either would render those contacts worthless.

"This passage should put you near the servants' quarters."

"Should?" Sarah asked.

The Arab snorted. "I've never been foolish enough to investigate." He glanced down the street. "I will stay as long as I can, but I won't risk being caught if you raise the alarm."

It was as much as Yasin would expect from anyone.

"May Allah preserve you both." Hisham pressed his fingers to his lips and his forehead before stepping back into the shadow of the alley.

Yasin glanced toward the sky. "Whatever name you prefer, I hope you heard that." He turned to Sarah. "Ready?"

Her eyes carried fear, but also resolve. "As I'm likely to be."

He hadn't yet witnessed her face mortal danger. Fear might paralyze her. "Stay alert. Focus on your next action. The rest will attend to itself."

She gave a curt nod.

"From this point, you must follow my every instruction. Understood?"

Her bright eyes were as wide as a pair of spinning silver coins. "I understand."

Their turnshoes produced no sound as they crossed the street. Periodic torches brightened the waterfront and the main avenue, but only the quarter moon illuminated these side streets. Even if anyone had been awake to witness their passage, they'd have struggled to identify Yasin and Sarah.

Though the planks nailed over the door to the building Hisham had indicated appeared to secure it tightly, as Yasin turned the handle and pushed, they opened inward with the door as a single solid piece shaped like the teeth of a great wooden gear. Sarah followed him inside. Enough moonlight poured through the open windows to expose the precision of the irregular angles of the door. When he closed it again, it fit snugly into the door frame.

Yasin grunted his appreciation at the skill required for such a design. A master carpenter had probably carved it on location in this room.

"What is it?" Sarah clutched his shoulder with fingers like daggers.

He gestured to the door. "Clever deception."

"Oh."

He squeezed her hand to reassure her. "We'll be fine. Come."

"Let's just finish this quickly."

Enough light filtered through the open windows for Yasin to pick his way over the scraps of fabric, piles of dirt, and more than a few bird droppings littering the room. A pile of cloth scraps lay in one corner, suggesting someone had previously sheltered here.

Set into the far wall was a solid oak door with a complicated integral lock. Despite weathering and a layer of dust, it appeared to be in good repair. That was good. Rust would make his job harder.

Yasin fished his toolkit out of his shoulder bag. He searched the floor for a relatively clean spot to unroll it. He was already wearing hideous clothing; the last thing he wanted was to set his precious tools in something sticky. He only hoped whomever had slept in this building had relieved themselves outside.

Raising its strap over his head, he handed the bag to Sarah. "Light the torch that's inside." She had gotten plenty of practice on campfires during their journey.

Freed of his burden, he selected his awl and needle and set to work on the lock. It was an antique, older than anything he'd ever worked on. His fingers itched at the chance to explore such an ancient device in more depth, but not when they were chasing the sunrise. Now, he needed speed.

He inserted the tools into the lock and felt around. With each movement, his tools struck unexpected metal. Nothing was where it should be.

Flickering light filled the room as Sarah ignited the torch with the flint and steel. "Is everything alright?"

His toolkit sat perilously close to a pool of some foul substance. Revulsion building, Yasin moved it away. As he did, he swapped the needle for a beveler. When he repositioned his tools, shadows covered the keyhole, leaving him as blind to what lay within as he'd been in the darkness.

He chewed on the inside of his lip, trying to recall the locks he'd picked over the years. He probed around until he felt a slight wobble on the other end of his beveler. Its positioning reminded him of a lock on the old garden gate back in Almeria.

A smile curled across his lips as he recalled the young woman who had lived there. More than once, he'd picked that lock in a hurry to avoid an irate father.

He pushed hard first to the left, then to the right with the awl as he applied pressure with the beveler—if he'd have continued to use the needle, it would have snapped—until the latch tripped, breaking the silence with a soft click.

That was one of the sweetest sounds in God's creation. "There we go." He released a contented sigh.

Stale air with a hint of mildew seeped into the room when Yasin pulled the door open. Wrinkling his nose, he studied the stone steps descending into the darkness. The first few, at least, were dry. That was good. He wanted to break into the palace complex, not break his neck slipping on wet stone.

Sarah handed him the bag, and he stuffed his re-rolled toolkit inside before slinging it over his shoulder. Accepting the torch from her as well, he began to descend.

The stairs were shallow, twice as wide as deep, and led perhaps a story below ground before leveling off and continuing down a long pathway. Fallen bricks and crumbled mortar littered the path. Periodic patches of dampness on the walls reflected the torchlight, and while they could probably travel abreast, Yasin kept in front to avoid accidentally brushing against the slimy surface.

"I don't see any rats." Sarah's voice reverberated off the narrow walls.

Yasin elected not to draw her attention to a spider crawling down the wall near the ceiling, and instead repressed a shudder.

They crept forward for some time. Though Yasin's legs itched to rush ahead, he clenched the torch and the strap of his bag to restrain the urge. He neither knew how far this corridor went nor what lay at the other end. Haste led to disaster.

Sarah followed a step behind, but other than the sound of her footsteps and the occasional gasp when he would stop suddenly, she moved silently. When this was all over, he'd have to compliment her knack for infiltration.

Imagining her reaction to that compliment made him smirk.

Gradually, their advancing torchlight illuminated a set of steps leading upward. He ascended until the light of his torch defined the outline of a door made of solid wood with the same kind of lock as on the other end. No grates or windows gave him a view of what lay beyond. A pair of empty sconces jutted out from the wall on either side.

He pressed his ear against the door. Common sense suggested a secret egress would connect with an out-of-the-way corridor to avoid attention. Hisham had claimed it would open into the servants' quarters, but that information could be decades or centuries old. Who knew if the palace's rooms were still used for their original purposes?

He tried the handle, but it didn't budge. Sighing, he handed Sarah the torch and retrieved his tools. Of course, it wouldn't be that easy.

The locking mechanism had the same configuration as the previous one, and this time it gave quickly. Again, he pressed his ear to the door, but still he heard nothing beyond.

Hand resting on the handle, he whispered to Sarah as softly as he could, "Go back down the stairs." He made a pushing motion back into the passageway. "As far as you can."

She nodded once and retraced their steps. The light of her torch receded until it faded to a dim reddening around the edge of the passageway.

Turning forward again, he put pressure on the handle. When it didn't move, he gritted his teeth and added a little more, hoping the ancient door didn't squeal. A flare of panic spread through his neck and throat. Had he mistaken the mechanism and only thought he'd unlocked it? That would be fine fortune, to travel from Toledo, dodge Almoravids, and reach this secret passageway only to fail at picking a lock!

When the handle finally turned, he jumped a little and immediately felt silly for it. He had warned Sarah not to think beyond the next decision, and here he was, working himself into a panic. He had done this a hundred times. Why should he worry now?

Of course, he knew the answer to that question. El Cid.

But his entire future hinged upon completing this job. God himself could be waiting beyond this door and Yasin would still have to step through.

He gave a little more pressure and the handle turned again, this time with a high-pitched squeak. He winced and pressed his ear against the door, listening for motion beyond.

Maddening silence.

Yet whether he was clear to proceed or the door was too thick to admit sound, he couldn't say. He hadn't yet moved the door to test its sturdiness, and knocking would pose the same risk as this damned handle.

He turned the handle again, and this time it moved until it came to a stop. Swallowing once, he opened the door a crack. The hinges groaned, and beyond the door the sound echoed off the walls—probably stone, based on the reverberation. A thin cascade of dust drifted down with the motion of the door. Sarah's torch was far enough away that its light wouldn't expose him, but that didn't matter if someone saw the door open.

He listened again but still heard nothing. The faintest amount of light entered through the opening. Moonlight, or perhaps a torch in the far distance? He opened the door the rest of the way and stepped through.

Dim light spilled into the corridor from either end of the hallway, illuminating blind arcade arches of limestone running down both sides of the walls. Wooden doors sat nestled beneath each archway. Though the moonlight limited detail, each door looked the same. He counted off from the far end to remember which one led to this passageway.

Dirt collected in the corners and cobwebs hung from the ceiling. The spaces above the empty sconces bore no ashy stains. Yasin doubted anyone visited this part of the palace. Hopefully, that wouldn't change in the next few minutes.

Still… This passage clearly didn't open into the servants' quarters.

As best as Yasin could tell, this was a forgotten storage area. Hisham's information was outdated.

He needed to orient himself. No matter how careful he was, he'd eventually stumble upon someone if he wandered around aimlessly.

Stepping back through the door, he hissed down the passageway, "Sarah!"

The torchlight wobbled back and forth, rising in illumination as she approached. He averted his eyes from the sudden brightness, only to jerk away when he noticed a freshly lit spider crawling along one of the sconces near his forehead.

Sarah drew in a breath at his sudden motion. "Guards?"

"No, worse." He pressed his hand to his chest to soothe his thumping heart. "Spiders."

The lines of tension on Sarah's forehead faded as she began to smirk.

Embarrassment for his overreaction gave way to relief at the break in tension. "Follow me." He gestured to the torch. "And leave that here."

He stepped through and glanced back down either end of the corridor, listening carefully. Behind him, the scraping of Sarah sliding the torch into the fixture on the wall echoed in the empty hallway. He winced.

After she had passed through, he closed the door but did not latch it. Once again, he counted doors, just in case a breeze closed it fully before they returned. "Fifth door," he whispered to Sarah.

She gave a curt nod.

To the right, the corridor ended in a T-junction. The hallway beyond was free of dirt and cobwebs, and soot formed dark cones above the sconces. A burning torch rested in one of them, partway down the corridor to the left. These walls bore no mosaics or carved designs like near the feasting hall. Across from the intersection sat an open portal with no door. The ink and parchment stacked on the desk and the shelves lining the wall of the room beyond suggested this was an administrative work area.

This was better than emerging into the servants' quarters. No one should be passing through this corridor for some hours yet. God be praised, their luck was holding.

"Which way?" Sarah whispered.

He scratched his chin. They were clearly inside one of the ancillary structures at the rear of the palace complex. If this was an administrative building, then the library should be…to the left, eventually, assuming the corridors ran as straight as they did near the feasting hall.

"This way."

He headed toward a door in the distance at the end of the hallway. Every few steps, he looked backward, both to check for witnesses and to imprint the return route in his mind. Belatedly, he halted. "Try to remember our route, just in case."

"In case of what?" she hissed.

He swallowed. In case he forgot. In case something happened to him. In case someone blocked their path and they had to find an alternate route back. He could think of a dozen possible scenarios, all of which set his belly twisting. Seeing no benefit to burdening her with more worry, he continued down the corridor.

An intersection stood between them and the end of the corridor. Indistinct sounds spilled out from the hallway to his left.

Grasping Sarah's arm, he pressed her against the wall. To his relief, she allowed him to move her.

The sounds refined into a pair of men's voices. Fingers shaking, Yasin dug them into the indentations in the corner column and leaned forward, intending to peek around the corner.

He froze once he realized the voices were growing louder and headed in his direction.

Steadying himself with a silent breath, he forced himself to focus. What could he do?

"—not the last…someone insulted—"

"—used to being—"

The few words recognizable at this distance were in Castilian, not Arabic, and were spoken in the deep bass of burly men. El Cid's soldiers.

He considered backtracking toward the last open archway, but they'd never reach it in time. The voices were rising too quickly. These men were close enough that they'd hear his and Sarah's hurried turn-shoes slapping against the stone floor.

"Let's get some wine before he drinks it all," one said.

"Cut a left. We'll do one last pass through the courtyard then head back."

The words filled Yasin with excitement. They would turn away from him. He had a chance.

God, be merciful in these next few moments.

Turning to Sarah, he pressed his finger to his lips and waved his flattened palm toward the wall. She glared at him in horror and glanced back toward the nearest archway, several dozen strides away.

The voices were almost upon them.

He touched her upper arm. *Trust me*, he mouthed. The Corinthian column at the corner extended out the length of his forearm and would provide some protection. He crowded closer to the column to cut down on the angle should the guards glance to their right as they passed.

It was a risk, but they had no other option.

They were laughing about something, but Yasin could hear only the hammering of his pulse in his ears.

A swinging arm came into view first. As it did, Yasin lowered his hand to the ring knife hidden in his belt. It was a paltry weapon, but perhaps, if he was quick…

It all happened in the span of a heartbeat. Amid a cloud of body odor, two armed guards strode into the intersection and curled to the left, toward the same door Yasin had been approaching. Their boots thumped on the stone with a rhythmic clopping that echoed off the smooth stone walls of the corridor.

As the guards continued past toward the door, Yasin waved Sarah forward. With the faintest of glances to verify the intersecting hallway was now empty, he tiptoed around the column and slipped down in the direction the guards had come, pressing his back against the far wall out of their sight. Sarah did the same as the door latch lifted.

They hadn't so much as glanced in his direction.

The door did not squeak as it opened. Only the brief mix of nightingales and footsteps seeped in before it closed again with a thud.

He released a long breath and slumped forward to rest his hands on his knees. Both were shaking.

"Allah be praised," Sarah exhaled beside him. "That was too close."

Yasin heartily agreed, and they still had further to go. He turned the corner to follow the guards.

Sarah pulled on his sleeve. "What are you doing? They just went though there!"

"Yes, and another patrol won't be coming for some time. This is our chance."

Crossing to the door, he pressed his ear against it and listened. Only the faint warble of nightingales penetrated the wood. He turned the handle and pushed it open enough to peek through.

Structures dotted the landscape around him. Off to the left sat the looming palace, looking much as it had the night before. The great serpent of the palace walls surrounded it all in the distance. After his eyes adjusted, he recognized the dark blotches of the fruit groves by their bushy canopies rising above the sharp profile of the battlements.

From the orientation of the landmarks, the colonnade directly before him must have been the one he'd seen through the archway during the feast. That meant the weathered *tapia* structure far to the right was the library.

He took a deep breath.

The two guards had already passed the colonnade and were bobbing in and out of view behind the trees flanking the pathway. Yasin searched the battlements, but the only guards, standing in the tower halfway between himself and the library, faced the city, not the palace.

After all, who would expect danger from within El Cid's palace?

"There's a guard tower to our right," he whispered to Sarah. "If I tell you, hide behind something. Are you ready?"

"No, I'm not." She rubbed her shoulders.

This was a lot for anyone to handle. He placed a hand on her cheek and caught her gaze. "Remember what I said. Focus on the moment."

"We were nearly caught."

"I know," he soothed. "But we weren't. We've slipped past the gates and through the corridor. We just have to avoid a few guards, then we're in."

"And we get to do it all again to get out," she stammered.

"Yes, but by then, we won't need to do anything we haven't already done once."

Though she frowned, doubt tugged at the corners of her lips. Releasing her, he grasped the handle. "Keep close. Don't run. Natural movement will fool a casual observer into thinking we're servants."

She gave a strained nod but held her breath.

He opened the door just enough for them to slip out before easing it closed—again, without latching it. When he extended his hand behind him, Sarah took it and they began to cross the courtyard.

He eyed the battlements, the carefully manicured gardens, each pillar of the colonnade up ahead, and the doorways of the other out-buildings, anywhere someone might be hiding. He had no intention of making the same mistake he hoped any observers might.

Up ahead, the guards in the tower continued to survey the city, their backs turned to the scampering thieves beneath them.

Yasin grinned with growing excitement. They were actually doing this.

The motion of a servant crossing the second-story arcade toward the front of the palace drew his attention. Before Yasin could even react, the man had passed through the archway and back inside again.

He forced himself to loosen his tight grip on Sarah's hand. Just like that, it could have all come crashing down.

They were almost upon the colonnade leading to the library. A pair of oil lamps hanging near the entrance to the palace dusted the stone pillars in an orange glow. With no guests this evening, no one protected that portal.

Clenching Sarah's hand, he rushed the last few strides to the library. The edifice consumed his view until it blocked the tower out entirely. He prayed no one had noticed their hurried movements.

He tried the door more out of habit than hope. To his surprise, it opened, albeit with an ear-twisting groan. Panic rising, he pushed Sarah inside and squeezed through before closing it behind him.

He pressed his back to the door and held his breath, offering a silent prayer that no one knocked on it. Only after several tense heartbeats did he allow himself to breathe again.

El Cid needed to assign someone to tend to these squeaky doors. "*Mashallah*, we've done it."

He opened his eyes. Beyond a small entryway, high windows admitted enough moonlight to reveal the silvery outlines of endless shelves surrounding a series of tables and benches in the center of the chamber. Scrolls piled in haphazard stacks filled some, while wooden- or leather-bound codices sat both upright and stacked on others.

Sarah had advanced into the chamber and was turning in a small circle, surveying the dusty tomes. Her eyes had shed their fear in favor of wonder. Yasin had quite forgotten that, despite working in the translation school, she hadn't been allowed to touch the texts. Standing here must have been intoxicating for a *qiyan*.

But all he could think was that it would take forever to find the right one.

He shook the oil lamps on a nearby table until he found one with enough fuel for their work here tonight. Reaching into his bag, he grabbed his flint and steel and scraped a few sparks onto the wick. After a few tries, it ignited and cast a dull red glow that only extended an arm's length or so beyond him. He doubted it would reach the high windows to reveal their presence, but even if it did, he had little choice. She couldn't read in pitch darkness.

"Please be careful." Sarah watched the lamp. "Everything here is flammable."

Yasin offered a curt nod. Starting a pyre would get them caught. Stowing the flint, he retrieved Orbanus's map. "Now, it's your turn." He handed her the map and lamp.

Accepting them, she studied the map for a few moments, then gestured deeper into the library. "This way."

Sarah's sure footsteps led him past four rows of shelves before she ducked into one aisle and followed it to its end. Yasin trailed after, his hand pressed to his nose to guard against the dust and smell of mold.

"I don't understand the appeal. Just keeping these texts dry would be difficult." Water always seeped between roof tiles, through cracks in the floor, and even through windows during a stiff breeze. "Why would anyone waste their time fighting the inevitable?"

"I could ask you the same, struggling against the Almoravids."

"That's different. I want to preserve something precious."

She chuckled. "Exactly."

Before he could respond, she halted before an angled pedestal against the outer wall. Atop it sat a square, leather-bound codex as wide as his elbow to the tips of his hand and as thick as two fingers.

"Is that it?" Yasin studied the tome. "I don't see the embellishments Orbanus described."

"According to the map, that's it." She frowned as she stepped closer.

"You don't sound confident."

She sniffed the air. "It…smells wrong. Parchment doesn't smell, nor does any ink I've ever worked with, not once it's dry." She sniffed again. "But that smell… I know it from somewhere."

He stepped closer. "Probably just mold."

Sarah glanced back to the scribe's map before returning her gaze to the codex. "This is the spot, but this codex is too small. Each volume should be hundreds of pages. And where are the sections on mathematics, logic, and physics?"

Yasin rubbed his palms. Now wasn't the time to debate smell and manuscript materials. "Only one way to be certain." He lifted the codex with both hands. It was lighter than he expected.

He leafed through the pages. The first few were blank, but as he continued flipping he realized that wasn't an aberration. "Even you would struggle to find meaning in these pages." She leaned forward as he thumbed through a few more. The light of her lamp illuminated something damp on his hands. "And it's wet!"

Sniffing once more, she gasped. "Hemlock! Wipe it off, now!"

Yasin dropped the book to lie in a heap and searched for something to clean his hands. Using his tunic or breeches would risk further contamination, and hemlock could be absorbed by touch. Reaching back, he wiped the deadly liquid on the outside of his leather bag. Though his hands felt dry, they were also rough. Some had already sunk in.

His heart beat in his throat. Poison.

"El Cid set a trap for whoever commissioned the copy." If he hadn't absorbed a fatal dose, they had to escape before he started to feel the effects. If he had… "We need to get out now."

"But the book—"

"It's not here," he said. "El Cid never put it back. We've failed."

He yanked the door open and stepped through without checking that the courtyard was clear. Even if it wasn't, he didn't have the time. The hemlock would be in his blood now. Already his hands were tingling.

After all these years, all the risks, he never imagined meeting his end by poison.

Ignoring his advice from earlier, he ran down the path toward the rear of the complex. The large wooden door was still open a crack, as he had left it.

His vision began to blur. Two steps before he reached the door, he stumbled over his foot but caught himself before falling.

His fingers felt thick as he pawed at the door. He couldn't open it with one hand and instead had to wedge his fingers into the opening and pull.

"Qu…quickly," he stammered as Sarah slipped inside. He was

breathing heavily now, heavier than he should. The effects were coming quickly now.

They passed beyond the first intersection and headed for the dirty hallway that led to the hidden passageway. With each step, his legs felt heavier. The hallway rocked back and forth as he ran, and he braced against the wall to stay upright.

"Yasin?"

"Followed?" He forced the word out.

A pause. "I don't see anyone."

That was good. "Keep going."

They turned the corner into an endless row of doors that wobbled rapidly. His vision must be blurring. Surely there hadn't been that many before. "Which?"

She led him to one in the middle that looked like all the others. As she swung the door open, he clung to the wall to stay upright. That simple exertion made him pant. He rubbed his forehead with the back of his hand. It came back moist. He was sweating.

"Watch the steps." Sarah's arms were beneath him, helping him descend.

The rough wall of the passageway felt like needles against his hand. His feet dragged on the edge of each step until it sunk to the next. Twice, he nearly fell, but Sarah's arms were under him, holding him up. His heart was beating its way out of his chest.

"I…don't understand." She pushed him forward. "Hemlock paralyzes, but it shouldn't make you feel clammy or stammer." Of course, she would know about poison; a *qiyan* trained to live at a royal court would have to.

Sarah. At least she hadn't absorbed any. But, if she was holding him upright, she might brush up against the bag he had wiped his hands on.

"Bag…"

His numb tongue tangled between his teeth. Try as he might to warn her, he could only manage a few additional guttural sounds.

She shifted around him. As she did, he collapsed, and the floor rushed up to meet him much faster than it should have if he were still on the steps. They were at the bottom. A whimper sounded from somewhere. It must have been his, but his ears felt as if they floated apart from his body.

"I'm here." He felt arms around him, but how could they be Sarah's when her voice came from across the passage?

They were moving again, but he didn't remember standing. The passageway twisted and roiled so badly that he had to close his eyes to avoid vomiting. He could no longer hear anything. He was only dimly aware of Sarah's arms supporting him.

He stubbed his toe on something hard. The other set of steps? Had they truly reached it already? They were out of the palace, then. At least she would be safe. He prayed she remembered her promise and fled before they captured her. He could no longer speak. If he could, he'd have told her to run.

Steps. If they were at the steps, he'd have to climb. One at a time, he raised his feet as high as he could. The world rocked around him. The hard wall, Sarah's arms, the pressure of his feet on the stone… He barely felt any of them. He couldn't even tell whether he was making progress.

He'd never see his mother or sister or brother again. He'd never have the chance to reconcile with his father. He would die in this dank passageway with no one to remember or mourn him.

He felt himself twist as he fell out of Sarah's grasp. His back landed on something flat and long. He must have still been at the bottom of the steps.

Before his vision faded entirely, he saw Sarah looking down at him, her forehead strained and eyes filled with terror. Sarah, the beautiful woman who had unlocked his long-lost joy when she'd played her oud. Sarah, the fiery woman with that quick wit whose smile and company had brightened these past weeks. Sarah, who represented everything he sought to preserve from the world he loved.

As he slipped into unconsciousness, he held onto that image to accompany him into the next life.

SARAH

"Yasin!" Sarah pounded her shaking fists into his chest, but he didn't flinch. Every muscle ached from helping him up those final steps, only for him to collapse at the top with his feet dangling over the side.

She grabbed his arms and hauled him far enough inside the abandoned warehouse that she could latch the door. She fiddled with the lock, but without either a key or knowledge of lockpicking, she could do little else. Someone might have seen their sloppy escape. Hopefully the darkness of the passageway would dissuade pursuit.

They had failed. Someone would find the upturned codex when the sun rose and search for the thieves. They'd find Yasin's body. One of the guests at the feast would recognize him as her "husband" and they'd come for her.

She clenched her hands together to still their shaking, but it didn't settle the vibrations in her stomach. She glanced beyond the open windows. The faintest hint of dawn light tinted the night's darkness.

Yasin had told her to save herself if the worst should happen. That thought had outraged her. Now, she understood the sense of it. She could tell El Cid she hadn't known of his plans, that she was innocent.

No, she couldn't risk her life on the chance that he'd believe her. Even if he did, it would only leave her disgraced and alone. Nor would Dona Jimena likely be in a forgiving mood after inviting a criminal into her home.

Oh, why had she agreed to come here? She had believed herself so abused and insulted in Toledo, but at least she'd been safe. Why had she risked her very life on such a foolish quest? Allah was punishing her ingratitude.

She had to get away before they locked down the city. She could escape to the South, to cities untainted by northerners who viewed her as a prize to be displayed. She didn't need the writ of emancipation from Lord Gonzalo if she never came north again. She could take the coins from her playing and from Yasin selling the caravan salvage. It was less than she'd hoped, and she'd need to work a little longer to earn the rest, but would be enough to establish herself. Surely Lord Gonzalo wouldn't follow her into Almoravid lands, and Yasin would have no need of the money.

Yasin. He twitched on the filthy floor.

He wasn't the arrogant rogue she'd believed him to be. She'd seen the longing in his eyes as she'd played her oud. He'd protected her and trusted her.

And she trusted him.

That admission surprised her. In fact, she felt more comfortable around him than anyone else, including her father, the eunuchs of the emir's palace in Granada, and her teachers in Baghdad. He had shown her true kindness, that of the soul and not of sentiment or artifice. Yasin had accepted her as she was and had asked nothing of her. Even the instrument maker in Toledo only viewed her as a means of profit.

What they had shared had forged a bond as real and tangible as the iron bands he had removed from her wrists. The more she sought to define it, the more confused she became.

Sarah pressed her hand against his clammy cheeks. His twitching settled at her touch.

His employer and landlord had abandoned him. His father had abandoned him. He had lost his home and belonged to no one, to nowhere. Just like her.

She wouldn't abandon him too.

Her sense of unease grew as she studied his symptoms. Something was amiss here. Long-ignored lessons about common poisons raced through her mind. The odor of hemlock definitely emanated from the oil on his shoulder bag, but hemlock paralyzed without affecting the mind. Pure hemlock should have rendered him unable to cross the passageway or ascend the stairs.

She lowered her head to his chest. His heartbeat drummed inconsistently.

Very few poisons could kill through contact with the skin. One was wolfsbane. It had no smell and produced all the effects she had observed: his clammy skin, his labored breathing, his struggles to form words. But why would someone mix it with pungent hemlock?

She sucked in a breath as it came to her. El Cid had mixed poisons to ensure that Orbanus's employer didn't escape with his prize. Wolfsbane was odorless, but it had a cure. Hemlock had an odor an eager thief might mistake for old parchment or mold, but it would seal his fate even if he treated the wolfsbane.

Unless that thief had a *qiyan* familiar with poisons who warned him quickly enough to wipe most of it off.

Yasin might still have a chance.

She thrust the door hard enough to slam it against the front wall. Hopefully, Hisham hadn't abandoned them.

"We need you!"

Across the street, Hisham emerged from the shadows.

"Help me." The words carried all her desperation. "Please."

He dashed across the street at a run.

She guided him inside. Enough of the dawn's light seeped through the windows that she could differentiate Yasin from the shadows in the back of the warehouse. "It was a trap. He's been poisoned."

"Poison!" Hisham turned from Yasin to the now-closed door to the passageway. "You'll lead them here." He took a step back, toward the door.

Sarah raised her hands. "No one saw, but we have to get him out of here. If they find him, they'll ask questions, and it'll lead them to us."

"To you, perhaps."

He really was planning on leaving them. "To both of us. Surely men have seen you together in the port."

His face twisted beneath a scowl. He clenched and unclenched his hands at his sides as he paced like a trapped animal. "Here or elsewhere, a dead man drags us down with him."

"I can save him." She prayed to Allah it was so. If it was wolfsbane and Yasin had wiped most of it off, she had a chance. "If you have somewhere nearby we can go."

He scowled again. "Fine." Crouching down, he put his hands beneath the unconscious thief.

Sarah felt a pang of irritation as Hisham lifted him without apparent difficulty. Her muscles still throbbed from dragging Yasin up the steps.

"Stay close," Hisham instructed. "If anyone asks, your husband was drinking deep into the night."

Yasin would no doubt appreciate that story.

When Hisham passed her, Sarah reached out and squeezed Yasin's dangling arm. It still felt warm. A good sign.

They stepped out of the warehouse and into the breaking dawn. Sarah whispered a prayer to Allah—such a plea required more than a silent wish—that he lived through the day.

CHAPTER FOURTEEN

SARAH

SARAH MARCHED FORWARD, heedless of whether the slap of her turn-shoes echoed off the buildings lining the avenue or disappeared within the clamor of shopkeepers opening their storefronts for the day's business. Though she had changed into her blue dress when she'd stopped by their room to pillage Yasin's coin pouch, she had forgotten to swap the thin leather turnshoes for her usual boots. Her feet throbbed with every errant stone in her path. Each stab of pain reminded her of Yasin, fighting for his life on the upper floor of a sympathetic netmaker's shop in the port. Even a moment could mean the difference between Yasin recovering and…

Like the spiders clinging to the walls of that dank passageway, the city's residents emerged from doorways and alleys to crawl across the streets. Reason shouted that they took no notice of her, but she couldn't shake the sense that they all knew what she'd been doing half an hour earlier. Sarah pulled her shawl closer.

Whereas the exotic goods for sale in the market had tempted her before, now they taunted her. The exotic odors of the spice market reminded her of pungent hemlock in a dusty library. The fine fabrics and silks stacked on tables evoked Yasin's search for somewhere to clean his tainted hands. Any of those lengths of cloth might have lessened his sweat-caked shivering.

A pair of guards entered from a side street and surveyed the crowd. When one glanced her way, she sucked in a breath and froze. She hadn't thought to memorize the faces of the soldiers framed in shadow and torchlight on the battlement. What if one of these men recognized her?

But the guard continued down the avenue with his partner. Sarah released a breath and uncoiled her fingers from the edge of her shawl.

The city's apothecaries occupied a side street some distance from the market. Excepting a few pedestrians, it offered blessed relief from the morning crowds. Surely one of these peddlers had musk and birthwort to counter the toxins in Yasin's body, if she could get him to drink it. She headed toward the closest shop, a well-weathered one with a sign bearing a mortar and pestle.

Movement to her left caught her attention. A man in a long brown cloak straightened from leaning against the wall of an intersecting alley. As he did, the morning sunlight reflected off something metallic at his hip.

The hilt of a sword. Only El Cid's men carried swords.

Stumbling, she regained her footing and deliberately passed the shop. Her mind reeled. By now, the scribes would have noticed the book lying on the library floor. Not finding the body of the thief nearby, of course the guards would watch the apothecaries for anyone seeking treatment. By Allah, they moved fast!

Up ahead, another burly man sat on the stone steps leading to a nearby building, picking at the top of his boots. On the opposite side, a Muslim leaned against a wall, nibbling at a drumstick. For all she knew, his bulging *jubba* concealed a sword too.

However, the presence of these guards also confirmed that she'd diagnosed Yasin's symptoms correctly, despite the many years since her studies. Hemlock and wolfsbane. She could do without musk, but birthwort was the only reliable treatment for poison.

It undoubtedly lay in one of those shops, yet it might as well have been in Granada for all the closer she could get.

She passed one apothecary shop after another. Without Yasin's skills, she could never sneak past these men. Even if she knew someone who might purchase it for her, they would likely face interrogation before being allowed to purchase it, and that would lead back to her.

Her breath came in shallow puffs as she reached the other end of the street. The sun was starting to creep out from behind the buildings. She had already been gone too long.

A pair of women strolled down the other side of the street. Both wore beautiful long cotton dresses in the northern style with lace shawls covering their heads and shoulders. One cupped her belly while the other chatted in her ear.

An idea blossomed. Apothecaries weren't the only sellers of birthwort.

She approached the women and interrupted the talkative one mid-sentence. "Forgive me, but where might I find a midwife?" It had worked for her landlord; why not now?

The pregnant woman arched an eyebrow as she ran her gaze over Sarah's figure. "You are with child?"

"Yes." The lie slipped from her lips unsettlingly easily. Yasin had taunted that she would become like him. At the time, the thought had revolted her, but a lie was a small price for his life.

Sarah followed the woman's directions to a door beneath a sign bearing the outline of a swaddled baby. She paused at the threshold to steady her shaking hands. As she did, she reviewed her prepared arguments. Birthwort could be deadly if abused, and while it was legal, a midwife might hesitate to sell it to a woman who wasn't noticeably pregnant. Sarah would claim it was for a sister.

What if this woman refused? Would she try another midwife? Each door she visited wasted precious time and shrunk her chances of counteracting the wolfsbane. Time was her enemy, as much as the guards lying in wait outside the row of apothecary shops.

Yasin's life depended on her. She would have to force her way inside. With luck, no one would hear the commotion. Hopefully, she could still identify the right herb by sight. It was a risk, but as Yasin said, no one could live wholly without risk. Some were worth the taking.

She prayed Allah would forgive her. If he did not, she would bear her sin gladly to save Yasin's life.

Satisfied at her preparations, she knocked.

An ebony-skinned woman with graying hair coiled into a bun answered. She wiped her hands on her apron. "Yes?"

"Good day." Sarah bowed. "I hoped I might purchase a supply of birthwort."

The midwife glanced up and down the street, but her only response was a curt, "Do you have the coin?"

Her ragged anxiety fell away along with all her now-unnecessary explanations. Finally, something had gone right for them. *Inshallah,* she had a chance to save Yasin. She only hoped she wasn't too late.

YASIN

Yasin expected to awaken in heaven, but the dull ache in every corner of his body convinced him he was still alive. Though he tried to flex his muscles, they felt sluggish and heavy.

The indistinct rise and fall of a muffled sound came into focus as the muttered cadence of a woman's voice.

"*...God is therefore one in its entirety and one in number. Rather, it is a meaning, the explication of whose term belongs only to it, and its existence is not shared by any other...*"

Silence swallowed up the voice again, broken only by the occasional hum or murmur.

Was that the voice of an angel? Perhaps he teetered between life and death.

He fluttered his eyes tentatively. A wash of light blinded him at first, but after several attempts he recognized Sarah sitting nearby with her legs tucked beneath her.

His body, at least, had chosen to live.

He must be lying on the floor, probably at the bottom of those steps in the passageway. But this light was too bright for torchlight. Dawn? How long had he been here?

"Yasin?" She gasped. "Allah be praised!"

After a nearby thump, her hands pressed against his forehead. Her fingers felt soothingly cool, yet slick as she moved them. He must be sweating. That wasn't a good sign.

"I wasn't sure I got to you in time," she continued.

The comment made little sense. She'd been beside him all the way down the passageway. Or had he imagined her face? The implications of that possibility raised even more questions. "Wh…what…"

"You fell unconscious as you reached the top of the steps in the warehouse."

He'd made it after all. Satisfaction filled him with vigor.

"Have to get out…" He slid his hand beneath his body and pushed, but he couldn't raise himself.

"Easy." She pressed him back down with surprising strength. "Hisham helped us to safety. We're in a room above a storefront in the port."

Forcing himself to keep his eyes open, he studied the unfamiliar surroundings. A single splintering window interrupting wooden walls. A rickety table with a spoon sticking out of a bowl. An old hole in the ceiling hastily patched with a different kind of wood. This clearly wasn't the warehouse, and he saw no sign of the great door leading to the passageway. He'd been unconscious for some time.

"How long?"

"Six hours."

Yasin gasped, convinced he'd closed his eyes a moment ago. Yet as he rubbed his fingers together, he felt neither the moisture of the slimy walls of the passageway nor the stickiness of poison. That he had been helpless for so long unsettled him.

"The poison was both hemlock and wolfsbane," she continued. "The market had the ingredients to treat the wolfsbane, but I didn't know if you'd absorbed too much hemlock to recover."

"You went to the market?" She had taken a terrible risk. "I told you to leave me." He swallowed, and his mouth began to feel normal again. "I wanted you to be safe."

"I know." Her gaze shifted, filling with pain. "But knowing that, how could I leave you?" Agony warped her voice, bending it to ever so slightly toward a wail.

His heart beat faster. He could almost imagine the invisible threads connecting them, woven by their experiences over this past month. Such a short length of time for so many to form!

"You saved my life." His muscles released their heaviness. He managed to lift himself onto his elbows, but no further. He wanted to be closer to her, to slip deeper into those threads binding them together. "Thank you."

He had made so many decisions, dared many dangers since escaping the Almoravids. He'd told himself he was living as he wished, refusing to allow the Almoravids to take his future when they'd taken his home. He'd concocted so many schemes and frauds. He'd thought himself so wise, but that had been before he'd known the real consequences, the final accounting. Now, he understood that all those decisions had led him to delirium and death in a urine-stained warehouse in the dankest quarter of a strange city.

His choices, his way of living had very nearly destroyed him. He had failed.

He hadn't chosen to travel with Sarah, but she had saved him. Their days and nights alone on the road, the unintentional kindnesses and deliberate taunts... He hadn't planned any of it. God had brought them together. And Sarah, despite having witnessed his many sins, had seen something within him worth saving.

His thoughts rushed ahead in a tangle he couldn't comprehend. The implications of that revelation would have to wait until he recovered.

He lowered himself back to the floor. "What were you saying a moment ago?"

She picked at the folds of her dress. "Saying?"

"You were mumbling something."

"Oh, I was reading the *Metaphysics*."

Yasin bolted upright. "The poison!"

Face awash with surprise, Sarah rested her hands on his shoulders. "No, no. It's in the library where you dropped it." His pulse thumped in his throat. "I was reading the unfinished copy from your scribe."

Rising too quickly had made him dizzy. He closed his eyes until he recovered. "I can't believe a few words about God are worth fifty gold pieces and a woman's freedom."

"It's much more than that." She retrieved the codex beside her and opened it. Her lips curled into the trace of a smile. "Nature, the heavens, the soul, existence… Ibn Sina gathered all the finest knowledge in his *Metaphysics*." She lightly set a hand on the codex, as if too much pressure would shatter it. "*The Healing* contains everything worth knowing in *Dar al-Islam*." She shook her head slowly. "Did you know he dictated much of it from horseback?"

Yasin believed it; even the little he'd heard seemed to ramble. Still, if Sarah believed it held value, it must be so. Her learned judgment surely outweighed his skepticism.

He slid his legs beneath him to sit upright. The world wasn't spinning anymore. "Perhaps Lord Gonzalo will be satisfied with what Orbanus managed to copy."

Without a word, she rose and approached the room's small window, leaving the codex beside him.

He listened for something that might have drawn her attention but heard nothing. Perhaps the effects of the poison still dulled his senses.

"Sarah?"

When she turned, she was biting her lip. Eyes fixed on the floor, she picked at her right sleeve. "A fragment won't benefit him." Her voice dripped with certainty.

A moment earlier, he had felt connected to her as if they'd been the only people in this city. Now, she stood apart.

"Sarah, what is it?"

She inhaled a long breath and released it just as slowly. Only then did she raise her eyes. They carried a concerning amount of apprehension for one who had so recently risked her life to save his.

"Your suspicions in Toledo were correct. Lord Gonzalo instructed me to update him on our progress and your plans." She lowered her eyes again. "I was told to report any indication you intended to betray him."

"*Ya salaam!*" All this time, he had misjudged her. She was far more cunning than he'd believed.

"I couldn't pass on the chance to reclaim my life."

He blew a breath between his lips. "I don't suppose you could." After Lord Gonzalo's warning of retribution, of course he'd want to stay informed about their movements. Sarah could hardly refuse his demands with her future at stake.

"I hoped it wouldn't matter, that we'd steal the *Metaphysics* and you'd need never know." She lowered her hands and began to pick at her nails. "I'm sorry I kept this from you. At first, I didn't trust you." She released a shaky sigh. "Once I realized I'd been wrong about you, the idea of telling you became harder and harder."

He had no right to judge her for protecting herself in the company of a known criminal. "I understand why you didn't." He cracked a smile. "What bothers me is that I didn't realize you were hiding something."

After three years, he'd gotten sloppy. He'd surrendered to temptation by stealing Esteban's money pouch. He'd sorely misjudged the loyalty of both his employer and his landlord. Just the previous night, he'd ignored his senses and grabbed a poisoned codex. Now, he'd missed deception right under his nose. He wasn't as good of a thief as he believed.

Each decision brought risk, but his inattention and laziness had worsened it. That had to stop, or he'd find himself in another prison cell. Next time, he might not claw his way out again.

"*Qiyan* training emphasizes subtlety. We're taught to avoid drawing attention to ourselves, except when we wish to."

Sarah had evidently mastered that skill. How had she sent her messages? He hadn't noticed her stealing from him, but she had to have paid someone to risk a hazardous journey back to Toledo. And she'd done it several times, all in complete secrecy. He needn't have fretted about bringing her along on this heist. She had the skills for subterfuge.

"What does Lord Gonzalo know?"

Her fingers stopped their motion as she folded them together. "Assuming he received my letters, he knows we've reached Valencia and about your agreement with the scribe."

"Did you express any suspicion that I would betray him?" He raised an eyebrow.

"No."

"Not even when I hesitated to resort to theft?"

She pressed her lips together. "I kept that concern to myself until I was confident you would do what was necessary."

He inhaled a reassuring breath. "I thank you for your discretion."

"I need to write him again, but what can I say? He needs the entire *Metaphysics* and won't react well if we can't deliver it."

"Why does he need it so badly?" Yasin crossed his arms. "It must be more than just expanding the translation school's collection."

She sat, tucking her legs beneath her. "His father suffered some kind of disgrace. He believes presenting King Alfonso with the last volume of the *Healing* will restore him to favor."

If that was true, returning to Toledo without the *Metaphysics* of the *Healing* would see Yasin back in prison. If he fled, Gonzalo would hunt him down. Thwarting a nobleman's pride was dangerous.

"We need to fulfill our obligations," Yasin muttered. "We need that volume."

She drew an audible breath. "How? Do you dare to try again?"

He closed his fists, recalling the slickness of the decoy codex. El Cid had lived up to his legendary cunning, and the thought of making another attempt against that man terrified him. "I lack the skill to out-smart El Cid." Despite the stab of humiliation, Yasin couldn't delude himself with so much at stake. "Regardless of whether he believes I'm dead, he'll move the codex. Without Orbanus to show us where it is, we'll never find it again."

"Then, how?"

God protect him, he had only one choice. Reaching into his *jubba*, he rubbed the scrap of his old satchel. "I know where to find a copy." The prospect twisted his stomach into an aching knot. "Write to Lord Gonzalo about what happened. Tell him I still intend to honor our agreement but need more time."

"I'll need to give an explanation."

He sighed. "Tell him we'll be returning with his text through the Martyr's Pass in the Sierra Luenga Mountains."

"That's the gateway from Toledo to the South." She narrowed her eyes. "Where are we going?"

When he'd headed north three years earlier, he'd sworn never to return to the desert fanatics who'd swept away the life he loved, to the city streets scrubbed clean of beauty and music and laughter, to his father who had disowned him. Only by never returning might he preserve his memories against the cold reality of decay.

He had tried to get away, but his future—and Sarah's freedom—had other plans.

"To Almeria."

After three years, he was going home.

SARAH

Sarah stood by the water's edge, staring at the gangplank leading to the looming round ship. Long cracks blistered the top layer of wood. The seams peeled back enough to catch the moonlight and create tiny, broken streaks along the length. Touching it would assuredly litter her hand with splinters. It reminded her too much of the ancient warehouse where all their plans had nearly disintegrated, much like this very wood.

She eyed the darkened city. Within those ridiculously straight streets were markets filled with treasures from across the Mediterranean and *hamams* with warm water and hard marble floors. Moonlight frosted the tops of the trees sprinkled throughout the city. After a little searching, she identified the dense collection within the palace walls. She had achieved her dream within those walls, yet it had left her unfulfilled. If not before such a crowd, where would she find the contentment she sought?

"Sarah?" Yasin extended his hand from atop the gangplank. His skin remained pale even though he'd rested throughout the day. He staggered beneath the weight of his own sack, containing those possessions Sarah hadn't sold this afternoon, just before delivering Orbanus's payment. "It's time."

She adjusted her grip on the sack slung over her shoulder. The sailors were untying the ropes tethering the ship to the shore. She remembered another gangplank like this from years earlier. It had flexed when the slavemaster dragged her down it.

No. That was the past. Those chains lay behind her.

She took one step at first, and then more when the gangplank held her weight. The wood may have been damaged, but it had survived to serve its function. She would, too.

She scampered the rest of the way to stand beside Yasin. The dockworkers withdrew the gangplank and the vessel shoved off.

Her fingers were clenching the railing so tightly that they ached. When he rested his hand on hers, she relaxed her grip.

"I'm sorry we have to leave." His voice carried only sympathy.

"That was a certainty, no matter what happened in the library."

He squeezed her hand. "But you have opportunity here. So much to leave behind. And I feel the same."

She studied him for a time. "You do?"

He gazed across the buildings. "If I ignore the lush fields around the city, I can pretend it's Almeria, back before the Almoravids."

His eyes softened, just as when he'd watched her playing her oud. Now, she could name the emotion in them: longing. He had lost part of himself when he'd fled home, leaving a hole that had remained unfilled. She understood that feeling all too well.

She inhaled a long, cleansing breath. Hope filled her veins. From the deck of the ship, Sarah could see much farther now, beyond the northern walls to the great fields, filled with life.

Valencia had endured conquest by a Christian warlord. If this city could survive a heathen, surely the Almoravids hadn't ruined the other *taifas*. Almeria couldn't be as unwelcoming and hollow as Yasin feared.

V

ALMERIA

AD 1094

CHAPTER FIFTEEN

YASIN

THE PALE SKY and rich blues of the Mediterranean water framed the rocky shore and rolling hills of the eastern coast of Iberia as if God had painted them with great strokes of his finger. Only the occasional flock of seagulls interrupted the endlessness of the vast ocean of sky. Tufts of white breakers flashed as the waves crashed into the shore before subsiding again into the turquoise shallows.

Yasin braced himself against the ship's rocking and watched the coast roll by. Despite living by the water for most of his life, he'd never witnessed its beauty from so far out to sea. While these lush, green hills so near to Valencia bore little resemblance to the barren vistas of Almeria, the sea air, thick and wet, was the same.

A line of camels laden with goods followed the contours of the jagged coastline, crawling southward. It was the second caravan he'd seen this morning, in addition to smaller groups of travelers along the roads hugging the shore.

Beside him, Sarah shielded her eyes with her hand and searched the eastern horizon in a slow turn. Her free hand shook at her side.

He couldn't blame her for searching for sails. He had spent the day prior to their departure either unconscious or resting in their hideaway, but Sarah had ventured out twice, first risking capture to heal him and again to pay their debts and sell their goods. And now, she faced a sea voyage. That had to bring back unpleasant memories.

He rested a hand on her upper arm. "We'll be fine." He eyed the shore again. "Pirates used to prey on the borders of the *taifas*, but the Almoravids cleared them all out. They patrol frequently, now that they own everything on both sides of the sea."

Sarah's fist loosened and the fabric of her dress slipped free. "That's the first positive thing I've heard you say about them."

His gaze fell to the misting wake of the ship as it skipped over the rocking waves. Not two days prior, El Cid had spoken admiringly about the veiled ones, and now he was doing the same. What had changed, and was wisdom or desperation responsible?

"Well, I'm delighted to be heading south again." The breeze caught Sarah's hair and blew it behind her, exposing the soft, smooth skin and graceful slope of her neck.

"Are you?" South took them ever closer to all he'd lost and the people who'd stolen it from him.

"Oh, yes." She nearly purred the words. "Al-Andalus is beauty and wisdom and holiness. Whatever future I have, it begins anew in the cities of the South."

She hadn't yet experienced how their home had changed. She still believed in the dream.

"Yasin?"

"Yes?"

She continued to stare across the water. "I will keep my promise to help you, but when we're done, I'll be staying in Almeria, beyond Lord Gonzalo's power. I've earned enough from the palace to make a fresh start now that I don't have to pay for passage south. I risk too much by going back."

He had imagined starting his own workshop somewhere in the north once he delivered this text. He hadn't thought beyond that dream. But Sarah had dreams of her own, and she'd naturally want to enjoy her well-earned freedom.

"I see."

The day of their success would be the last day he'd ever see her. That thought filled him with an unexpected sorrow. He had spent three years by himself; why should it trouble him now?

Long after Sarah left, he remained at the railing, trying to understand his jumbled feelings. All he could say with certainty was that, once again, Almeria would leave him alone.

SARAH

Three days after departing Valencia, the trading vessel docked at Cartagena to replenish its supplies and drinking water.

Sarah skipped down the gangplank the instant the sailors positioned it. For her first few steps on solid ground, the world still seemed to rock. Allah be praised, keeping her eyes fixed on the horizon had helped to settle her nausea, and she hadn't voided her stomach yet. Then again, the constant dread of seeing another sail might have caused that nausea in the first place.

Yet Yasin's predictions about maritime safety under the Almoravids had proven true, at least so far.

"Sarah, wait!" Yasin was still adjusting his *jubba* when he bounded after her. Her white shawl fluttered in the breeze as it lay across his arm.

"After three days on that monstrosity"—she pointed toward the ship—"I need good food and solid ground."

"I won't deny it to you." He released the breath of a whimper as he reached a finger beneath his coat to fish out his tunic's bunched sleeve. "But this is Almoravid land."

"Yes, I know—"

"If you knew, you wouldn't have forgotten this." He presented her the shawl.

She laid it over her head, just above her hairline, and wrapped the ends to cover her nose and mouth as her teachers had taught her in Baghdad.

"No, it must cover all your hair." He reached up to reposition it.

She shooed his hands away. "It's one thing to fuss about your own appearance, but I know how to dress myself."

He raised an eyebrow. "Only men in the Maghreb wear the veil across their faces. If you—an Andalusi woman—did the same, the Almoravids would consider it an insult worthy of flogging." Fear tinged the wild anger that usually filled his eyes at mention of the Almoravids.

Visions of the burnt caravan sprung back to mind. Swallowing, she adjusted the positioning.

He nodded. "It'll work until we can buy you a thicker one."

"This worries you that much?" She slapped his hand as he fidgeted with his *jubba* and finished adjusting it herself.

"You didn't see them throw the emir's harem onto the street with only the clothes on their backs."

His gaze slipped to study something behind her, and she turned to follow it.

A pair of guards in indigo *tagelmust* veils that concealed all but their eyes marched through the port. The crowd parted before them, and most of the pedestrians lowered their eyes until the desert nomads passed.

Sarah watched with growing admiration. Only the emir and the most powerful members of his court in Granada merited such respect. These Almoravids had managed to make themselves revered in only a few short years.

"Come." Sarah tugged on Yasin's sleeve. "I'm hungry."

Yasin followed but kept his eyes on the backs of the departing Almoravids. "We'll get you something on the way."

"Just not fish." She'd eaten enough recently to last a lifetime. "To the market for a new shawl, then?"

"A whole new set of clothing."

She clenched a fold of her dress, salvaged from the caravan so many weeks ago. She had already sacrificed so much when they left Valencia. "Is that necessary?"

"You can't go to Almeria in a Castilian dress…or wearing blue."

She hadn't worn proper, Islamic clothing in many years, not since the slavers had stripped her *qiyan* attire to sell in the Barcelonan markets. The priests in the translation school had insisted she dress like a Christian, probably in the foolish hope of converting her. As if anything in Christendom could match the beauty or sophistication of *Dar al-Islam*!

She saw little indication of that beauty on the main avenue leading from the docks. Everywhere, her eyes fell only on pale-colored wool and linen. Other than the ubiquitous Almoravids in their unmistakable rich indigo, only the occasional *jubba* bore the deep color of a long soaking in the dye tubs. Embroidery was limited to thin lines of geometric designs on hems, sleeves, and necklines. Where was the brocade, cotton, and silk so common in Valencia?

She doubted it was a matter of poverty, for prosperity surrounded her. The weaves on some of the shawls and coats was so fine that Sarah couldn't identify individual threads. Turnshoes and boots bore no holes or split seams. The nearby buildings were well-tended and smoothly sanded, a mark of remarkable care against the constant assault of salty air.

Finding food that didn't come from the sea proved more difficult than Sarah had expected. Peddler after peddler sold fish, shrimp, or octopus with various sauces and seasonings. Though it took half an hour, they eventually found one selling vegetable soup on a dingy side street. Despite her skepticism about its quality, it had a good flavor. A haunch of bread settled her nausea.

"Do you hear it?" Yasin muttered once they'd re-emerged onto the main avenue.

Sarah listened carefully. A few peddlers called out above the quiet din of the crowd. Feet shuffled. Clothing scratched as layers brushed against each other. Coin pouches jangled with each step. "I only hear people moving around."

He nodded. "No music, no laughter, no excitement." His voice shook with obvious unease. "It sets my ears twitching. If I turned down this street looking to lift a coin pouch, I'd keep walking."

Perhaps his experience in the library had affected him. Sarah rested a hand on his forearm. "Fortunately, we don't intend to lift any pouches."

"I know, I just…" He shook his head. "Let's go before we give the veiled ones a reason to notice us."

They stopped at a shop off the main avenue with a sign above the door bearing a spool of thread and the word 'dressmaker' in Arabic. Inside, lengths of thick cotton dyed a deep burgundy covered a series of tables along the perimeter. Atop the rich coverings sat rolled bolts of linen and wool in the same drab colors as worn by the pedestrians outside.

Sarah cocked her head at the bizarre scene; that fine cotton was worth more than all the bolts sitting atop them. It was such a profligate waste. Linen would suffice to protect against ruinous splinters. And where was the rest of the quality fabric?

The shopkeeper explained that most of his customers sewed their own clothing, but not every woman had the skill for it. Likewise, Sarah and Yasin had neither the time nor the tools to do so. After flashing a few silver coins, Yasin convinced the man to bring out a few dresses he'd completed but hadn't yet delivered.

"Fashions have changed in recent years." The pug-nosed, balding shopkeeper felt the fabric of each of three sets of garments he'd draped over one of the tables. "The Almoravids have reminded us of the value of humility and modesty."

What this man called humility, Sarah called simplicity. The three *qamisas* before her were cut long and plainly fashioned, featuring high necklines and straight sleeves. Yet despite the uniform plainness, they bore signs of quality. The linen weave was incredibly fine, and stitches ran even and straight, an impressive feat. Each came with *sirwal* pants and either a veil or shawl.

Sarah brushed her hand over the first set, a pale yellow *qamisa* draped over maroon *sirwal* pants. The fabric soothed her fingers, but the garish combination made her shudder. An occasional glance down would horrify her.

The second set was made for a more voluptuous woman, but the third set looked about right for her dimensions. A pair of tan *sirwal* pants in linen complemented the dark green of the *qamisa*. Though the pants were a little too long, the matching tan shawl bore embroidered brown trees that extended an arm's length from the edge. It didn't offer the comfort or luxury of cotton, but at least it had some adornment.

Beside her, Yasin said to the shopkeeper, "I've been away for many years, but I hear many things about the Almoravids. How do you find them?"

The shopkeeper's sudden stillness seemed unnatural after his fluttering. "The Almoravids swept away crime and corruption. They ended the brutal taxes that supported the emir's vices and debauchery." His stiff monotone resembled a novice *qiyan*'s recitation and lacked the ring of truth. "The Almoravids deserve praise for purging the decadence of the *taifas* and restoring holiness and modesty."

"Priests and scholars repeated that complaint my whole life. Telling others how to live comes naturally to them," Yasin muttered.

Sarah shifted. If his tongue ran away with him as it had the first night of the caravan, it would buy them trouble, and they already had more than their share.

Yasin rubbed his chin. When he spoke again, he'd restored his control. "Then you are entirely pleased with their rule of your city?"

The shopkeeper squirmed, rubbing the edge of his *qamisa* between his fingers. Abruptly, he circled to the other side of the table and glanced at the door. "Such questions are dangerous."

Yasin stepped closer. "On the tide, I'm returning home to Almeria." His soft voice carried a bristling energy. "I must know what I'll face."

The shopkeeper locked eyes with his customer. Sarah grew steadily more uncomfortable as time progressed. Yasin was pushing this man too hard. She gathered up the green and tan outfit in her arms. They should just finish this transaction and return to the ship.

The man eyed the doorway once more before approaching Yasin. "Surely, you've heard the rumors."

Yasin leaned closer. "Rumors?"

The shopkeeper chewed on his lip. "Brutal punishments. Trials of heresy. Poems once praised in the streets now cost men their tongues. Honest mistakes, misinterpreted as thievery, cost men their hands."

"Here, in Cartagena?" Yasin pressed.

"Well, no." The man rolled his tongue over his lips. "But I trust the men who bring the tales."

Sarah listened to the litany of horrors with skepticism. Christians accused the *taifa* kings of such things; why wouldn't they do the same to the Almoravids?

And yet, the conviction in this shopkeeper's voice suggested he believed these rumors.

"Does no one speak out?" Yasin pressed.

"Those who do disappear, and their families later learn they were executed for treason." The shopkeeper straightened. "It is no matter. Who can deny that the veiled ones brought strength? No city has fallen to a Christian army since Toledo."

"No, they've fallen to the Almoravids." Yasin scowled. "We've traded freedom for the illusion of safety."

The man chewed his lip. "That choice sits more uneasily now than three years ago."

Sarah eyed the cotton draped across the tables with new understanding. Such rich fabric signaled pride and wealth, a defiance against the enforced modesty the Almoravids demanded.

Yasin pressed his fingers to his lips and then his forehead. He offered one of his charming smiles. "My wife and I thank you for your honesty."

After paying nearly double what such garments would cost in Toledo, they departed with their purchases. Yasin pushed his way through the crowd, drawing more than a few glares as he shoved men aside. She struggled to keep up with his quick march.

When the crowd had thinned enough that she could speak without being overheard, she tugged on his arm. "It was dangerous to press him."

He allowed her to slow him and offered a strained smile. "I know, but I had to. I've heard precious little about Almeria."

He had so often spoken with certainty about the evil Almoravids that hearing him confess his fragmentary knowledge of his home unsettled her. He must be worried to abandon his bravado. "And what did you hear?"

"It confirmed every fear that drove me away." He released a long, weary sigh. "If anything, the price was higher than I imagined."

Sarah walked beside him in silence. She'd believed Yasin had succumbed to the tendency of all men to believe the worst about their enemies. A part of her had even wondered whether the prospect of renewed Muslim vigor terrified him as much as it had the Toledan priests.

But the shopkeeper's comments sounded alarmingly like Yasin's previous comments, and Sarah couldn't ascribe the same motivations to a member of the faithful. If fashions could shift so strikingly, what else might have changed?

The muscles of her neck tightened until her head began to throb. The South was her salvation. She needed these rumors to be false.

Yasin stirred. "We should remain aboard the ship until it departs."

Sarah thought back to the shopkeeper's discomfort. She didn't want to be caught in the city if he decided to report his disgruntled customers to a passing Almoravid guard, even if it meant the ship's rocking would twist her stomach.

"That may be wise." They were already hitching their fates to a great gamble and couldn't risk additional unnecessary ones.

YASIN

Almeria glittered in the setting sun like a woman's silver necklace nestled in the valley between the Sierra de Enix and Sierra Alhamilla mountains at the edge of the Mediterranean. The deep oranges and reds of sunset erupted over the western mountains to touch the tops of the palm and almond trees surrounding the city, but they didn't quite reach the valley below. Only the flickering torches and steady light of the streetlamps illuminated the sparkling city.

Yasin had always enjoyed the dance of color as the long sunset swirling overhead faded from firelight to shadowy hues of purple and blue. The long Toledan evenings were a comparatively dull affair, evoking only the fading memory of a beauty he'd thought forever lost.

But once again, he stood beneath that colorful sky in the magical hour between sunset and dusk, clinging to the railing near the bow of a ship surging toward the mighty stone piers of home. Watching the advancing city expand before him, he could almost pretend nothing had changed.

But it had. Now, beneath that painted sky crawled indigo-veiled devils.

A rocking wave forced him to tighten his grip to remain standing. When he glanced back, his eyes fell on the Mozarab district that contained his family home and his father, with his judgment and disappointment. They had quarreled the last two nights Yasin had spent in this city, all those years ago. They would probably do so again.

The ship had come close enough to the dock that Yasin could dimly hear the *muezzin* calling the city's Muslims to prayer. He listened for some time, but no Jewish horn or Christian bell followed the cry. The silence screamed in the darkness, more damning than any noise.

Almeria. He would rather never again set eyes on its beauty than witness the hollow ruin it must assuredly have become. He shouldn't have returned. He wouldn't have if his own future and Sarah's hadn't depended upon it.

At least, God willing, he would have the pleasure of stealing back a little of the culture the Almoravids had taken from his people.

Sarah emerged from below deck while the ship sidled up to the pier. She wore the loose qamisa and baggy pants they'd purchased in Cartagena, with a sack bearing her oud—and probably her beloved blue dress—slung over her shoulder. The sight of her shapeless garments inspired a fresh curse. Of all the Almoravids' crimes, forbidding the graceful sway of a woman's hips beneath the shapely cut of a beautiful dress numbered among their greatest.

And yet, they could not wholly succeed in burying her beauty, for Sarah moved with a grace that teased the outline of her curves. She would mock Almoravid impotence to their faces in a way all his vices the previous three years could not. Yasin accompanied her down the gangplank with true pleasure.

Reaching the solid stone pier, he swept his gaze across the other piers, the crates piled along the water's edge, the warehouses, the shipping offices, the netmakers, and the boatswains working on beached hulls. He had run through this port many times as a boy, getting into mischief with Salim and making deliveries for his father.

Home.

"Yasin?" Sarah's expression carried no hint of worry, only a question.

He offered a quick smile. "I'm fine."

An Almoravid strode down the pier toward them. A strip of cloth, dyed indigo like the rest of his loose robes, held the sheath of a curved knife at his waist.

He'd have to confront these devils before even having a chance to appreciate being home again.

Yasin sucked in a breath, realizing what he'd forgotten. Turning to use his body as a shield, he drew the ring knife from his belt and quickly cut the string holding his cross at his neck. "Here." He thrust it into her hand. "Hide it."

"If they catch me with—"

"Just do it!" he hissed.

He turned back as the Almoravid came to a halt.

"Peace be upon you," the guard mumbled from beneath his veil. Those desert eyes didn't convey the same sentiment or offer welcome.

Studying the complicated way the man's *tagelmust* wrapped around his head, neck, and shoulders, Yasin realized how inaccurately he'd wound the garment during his final job in Toledo.

He pressed his fingers to his lips, then his forehead. "And upon you, be peace." The comforting gesture, made on familiar ground, settled his nerves.

"What brings you to the righteous city of Almeria?"

The phrasing struck Yasin like a slap, reminding him all at once that this was not his Almeria. "I've been trading in Christian lands for many years. I'm returning home to introduce my family to my new wife."

A single, thick eyebrow shot upward. "You trade with Christians?"

Yasin hadn't anticipated that accusation. Were these Almoravids so conservative that they forbade even commerce with Christians? He adjusted his approach. "In the hopes that Allah will open their eyes to the truth through the wonders the faithful create in his name."

"What was your last port?"

Yasin raised his chin. "Cartagena."

"And before that?"

He saw little point in lying. The Almoravid could find out from any of the ship's crew. "Valencia."

The man grunted and took a step forward. "You will submit to a search."

If the man found his hidden knife, it would raise uncomfortable questions. Yet, Yasin could only force a smile and answer, "Of course."

The Almoravid leaned in so close that Yasin could smell body odor beneath the musk meant to mask it. He patted Yasin carefully, testing each gap and space within Yasin's clothing.

"What is this?"

He glanced down, but the Almoravid wasn't studying the tiny

knife. Instead, he held open the flap of Yasin's *jubba* and pointed to the straps inside.

Yasin dared not release a relieved breath, not with this Almoravid so close. "It serves as a hidden pouch."

The Almoravid fell back a step, opening up space between Yasin and the sheath at his waist. "You are a smuggler."

"Certainly not!" Slowly, Yasin reached up and withdrew his toolkit, the folded pardon, and the scrap of fabric. Using one hand as a platform, he unrolled the toolkit. "It protects my precious tools against thieves. My trade is leathercraft."

The Almoravid thumbed through the tools, one at a time. Awls, bevelers, creasers, groovers, needles... He even felt the fabric of the leather roll for hidden compartments. Once he had studied each, he moved on to the scrap of cotton. "What is this?"

Other than his *jubba*, it was the last piece of Almeria Yasin had left.

"A sample of fabric I considered purchasing." A thrill tickled his skin as the lie slipped from his lips. He had never before had the opportunity to lie to the men who had forced him into exile.

The Almoravid turned the pardon over lazily before shrugging and handing it and the fabric back to Yasin. "It's past dusk. You've missed the Maghrib prayer."

Yasin halted in repositioning his toolkit to meet the man's gaze. "We will perform it the moment we reach my family home."

The Almoravid nodded slowly. "Then do not let me delay you, brother." He stepped aside and waved Yasin forward. "Allah protect you."

Swallowing, Yasin began to pass.

"Wait."

He halted mid-stride but lowered his foot when he realized it was shaking. Slowly, he turned.

The Almoravid gestured to Sarah without looking at her. "Your wife should not carry such a burden."

Yasin needed a moment to realize he meant the sack over her

shoulder. With another smile, he reached over and took it from her. "Thank you for reminding me."

Without another word, the veiled guard turned his attention to the sailors descending the gangplank.

Yasin forced his shoulders to relax and took a fortifying breath. Rumors indicated various gruesome punishments for crimes in Almoravid lands, but they all agreed that a Christian impersonating a Muslim was unforgivable. Though he had merely claimed to sell goods created by Muslims, Yasin doubted that nuance would have mattered.

He'd passed his first test. He suspected the next one would be even harder.

Once they reached the end of the pier, Sarah whispered, "You knew he would search you."

"I did."

"He could have done the same to me."

"Never. That's why I had you hold Orbanus's fragment." Yasin adjusted his grip on the heavy sack containing the partial translation. They'd accumulated a surprising number of goods in their journey.

"How could you be sure?"

"A woman is too delicate to be a smuggler." He grunted. "Almoravids are predictable in their fanaticism. They'd never harass another man's wife nor grant a woman the authority to conduct searches."

Her eyes twinkled. "You exploited their prejudices."

Yasin grinned. "If they insist upon having them, I'll put them to good use."

Yasin led Sarah down a side street that would eventually lead to the family's workshop and second-story home. The Almoravid hadn't mentioned a curfew, yet the streets were surprisingly empty. The few people he passed scuttled by as if chased by demons. Normally, families would be visiting friends for supper, young men would frequent the alehouses, or groups of women would gather in the parks for recitations or performances.

Normally. He couldn't assume any similarity between this city and the Almeria he knew, nor trust his memories. Perhaps not even his old friends. Everything could be different now. He had to remember that.

A rush of memory consumed him. He had gotten into his first fight down that alley, an embarrassing endeavor consisting of a single shove and his foot catching on the gap of a missing cobble. He could still remember how his stomach dropped as he tripped. The other boy, Yousef, had stood over him, laughing helplessly until his friends pulled him away.

A girl with whom he'd fallen desperately in love as a boy of fifteen used to lay her shawl over the ledge of that terrace garden to signal he could visit. The neighbors would always leave out barrels that he could climb on. A puddle would form near their wall after every rain, but he'd always forget and splash in it.

No shawl dangled over the edge now. That girl had probably married long ago.

Yet he noticed subtle differences from his memories. The walls of homes that used to bear careful mosaics were now smoothed and painted over. The damp lengths of cloth hung across second-floor windows to cool the breeze entering them used to be of richly colored silk or airy cotton, but now they were almost exclusively pale, thin linen.

Even the smell was more earthy and visceral. Bronze censors visible within first-story windows, framed by candlelight and cooking fires, pumped out musk, with no hints of the richer frankincense or more expensive agarwood. Flower beds and terrace gardens once lined these streets with bright roses, orange blossoms, purple irises, and vivid red tulips and filled the air with a delightful combination of floral scents. Few gardens colored the streets now, and most contained only green herbs and spices.

As they walked, Yasin increasingly felt as if someone had duplicated the neighborhoods of his memory but had hurried the details. Reason said this was his home, but his heart hung suspended between sentimentality and discomfort, familiarity and foreignness.

Yet, he still knew the way to his family's home, a simple two-story structure. No light peeked through the slits in the shuttered windows of the ground-level workshop, but a few candles flickered from a second-floor window. His family used to take their meals in that room.

After three years, he had come hundreds of miles, yet his heavy feet hesitated to go the final ten strides. Beyond that door awaited his father's angry disapproval. Faraj wasn't the kind of man to forget an insult nor forgive the manner of his son's departure.

Sarah slid up beside him and threaded her fingers through his. "This is it, isn't it?"

Though his feet would not move, he nodded easily enough.

She squeezed his hand. "I'm right here."

Her grip was an anchor, tethering him. He squeezed Sarah's hand, and her fingers tightened in response. She escorted him those last few steps. Her presence enveloped him like a thick cloak on a cold evening. Strength flowed from her through his arm, his chest, and into his other hand as he raised it without trembling and knocked on the door.

He had never knocked on this door before. He'd simply walked in. The sensation deepened his discomfort.

The latch squeaked as it always had. More than once, its squeal had exposed him. He'd always hated that latch, but the second story windows sat too high for him to use when returning from late-night troublemaking.

The door swung open slowly, revealing the short entryway and the set of stairs leading to the family rooms. It looked exactly as he remembered, except for a pair of sandals lying in a heap just clear of the door.

However, he did not recognize the broad-shouldered man who answered.

"Peace be upon you." The man studied Yasin and Sarah with narrowed eyes. "The shop is closed for the day."

Had Faraj taken on a new apprentice after disowning his son? Or could this man be Amira's husband? While any man worthy of his sister should have his own home, the Almoravids may have rendered that option impossible.

Sarah squeezed his hand, replacing his surprise with confidence.

"And upon you, be peace." He raised his chin. "I am Yasin ibn Faraj." The name produced no reaction. He clenched his free hand around a fold in his *jubba*. "I should like to speak to Faraj ibn Ramiro."

The man again ran his eyes over Yasin's frame. "I'm afraid you have the wrong house." He stepped back and began to close the door.

"Wait!" Releasing Sarah's hand, Yasin thrust his palm forward to halt the door. "My family has lived here for decades. I grew up in this house. I handled leather"—he pointed toward the workshop door further down the outer wall—"right there for many years."

The man straightened, raising his shoulders until he blocked the remaining opening. "You have the wrong house." His voice rose in volume. "This is my home, and that is my carpentry workshop."

Dread crawled down the back of Yasin's neck. What had happened to his family? He stared at the interior wall of the entryway. It still bore the chip in the *tapia* from when he and his brother had thrown chairs at each other during a particularly visceral fight.

Sarah tightened her grip around Yasin's arm and turned to the man. "How long have you lived here?"

"Two years."

"From whom did you buy it?" she continued.

"A man named Salim sold me this building." His eyes widened. "In fact, I believe he was a leatherworker."

"That's my brother." Why would he sell the family home? And why would his father trust Salim with such an important task? Anger swirled behind his eyes. It seemed Faraj had rewarded the son who had committed apostasy while disowning the other for remaining true to his faith. "Do you know where they live now?"

The man rubbed his chin. "No, but if he's a leatherworker, he'll likely be with the others near the great market."

The concern slipped away all at once. Of course. Once Faraj

converted, remaining near other Mozarabs would have only raised questions about the sincerity of his faith. Joining the other Muslim leatherworkers would earn him more business.

The carpenter closed the door so quickly that Yasin could barely stammer a quick, "Thank you."

He'd made deliveries to the leatherworking district several times over the years. Occasionally, a Muslim craftsman would receive too many orders and pass work to a Mozarab eager to raise his reputation among the Muslim elites.

Yasin had no trouble navigating the twisting streets now. While the pattern of missing adornments and scrubbed walls endured even this far into the city, the structures and their positions hadn't changed in his lifetime and would probably endure for centuries afterward.

At the second door on which they knocked, the mention of Salim's name produced instructions to a large *tapia* structure occupying an entire block. Rows of blind archways, one atop another, adorned the front of the top floor. Juniper double doors marked the entrance to the extensive workshop. For perhaps two-thirds of its length, the first-floor wall was inset from the overhanging second story. That shadowed space would allow workers to load wagons even in the rain. This workshop was far larger than the single, cramped room where Yasin had learned his craft. Faraj had clearly profited from betraying his faith.

They stopped before the entrance to the private house, an oak door with diagonal patterns carved into the edges. Though more beautiful than their old door, the cracks and grooves held no meaning for Yasin.

"Do you want me to knock?" Sarah asked.

Yasin steadied himself with a breath. "It's just a door." He brought his fist down on it three times.

The solid, even footsteps of a confident stride sounded from within.

Yasin rubbed his hands against his *jubba*. He had been wearing this same coat when his father had disowned him. What would he say now? Should he acknowledge the argument, or simply greet Faraj anew after all this time?

The door opened to reveal a young man with thick black eyebrows that matched the hair poking out from beneath his knitted cap. "Peace be upon…" Eyes widening, he huffed in surprise and braced himself on the door frame.

"Salim!" Relief washed over Yasin at the friendly face. He rushed forward and embraced his brother. "God be praised, it's good to see you!"

Beneath his grasp, Salim remained stiff. Yasin couldn't help but laugh at his brother's surprise.

"Yasin!" Pulling back, Salim studied his brother with wide eyes. "What are you doing here?"

"Did you say *Yasin*?" came a call from within.

Tears welled in Yasin's eyes. That voice had lulled him to sleep and soothed his pains all his life.

"Mother?"

She circled Salim and gazed up at her son, tears welling. "Yasin… Oh, my son." Three years of added cares had barely affected Elvira Vermudez's beauty. The bright softness of those eyes, lined with a thin treatment of kohl, remained undiminished. No blemishes marred her pale Castilian features, even if a few more age lines than Yasin remembered creased her eyes and lips.

He embraced her gently. Soft sobs sounded from where her face pressed against his *jubba*. Fearing father might discover his intentions to leave, he hadn't said goodbye to her. He had regretted that. He should have spared a few words to soothe her worries. But now, finally, he could reassure her. He was alive. He was safe.

For the chance to experience this joy, he would confront a hundred hostile fathers.

Elvira stepped back, and his sister—with hair of so dark a brown that it was nearly black—approached from behind her with a smile large enough to envelop his heart. But most delightful of all to Yasin, his sister wore not a *qamisa* and *sirwal* pants, but a long, beaded dress. He could not mistake the meaning of that defiance, that stubborn adherence to the old fashion of their people, of the Almeria he loved.

Almeria and Cartagena may have submitted to the Almoravids, but his glorious sister had not.

"Amira…"

She rushed forward and took Yasin's face in her hands. Pulling him down, she pressed his forehead against hers as when they were children. "Welcome home, brother."

He was smiling when he released her. "A fine dress you have there."

Amira darted a triumphant smirk at Salim.

Movement from further within the house drew Yasin's attention. A young, amber-eyed woman in a plain, floor-length linen *qamisa* peeked out from a doorway with a pensive expression. A pregnant young woman.

"Salim?" she ventured.

His brother gestured to soothe her. "It's fine, beloved. Only my brother, Yasin, back from the north."

Her gaze shifted to the darkness outside for a moment, but relief quickly washed over her face. "If they've been traveling, they must be thirsty. I'll prepare something." With a quick bow of her head, she withdrew deeper into the house.

Eyes widening, Yasin gasped. "You're married!"

Brow still knitted, Salim nodded. "Aishah. She carries our first child."

He'd be an uncle! "Congratulations, brother." His lips softened into a smile.

Still, his brother's glare hadn't lessened. "Why have you come home after all this time?"

His mother waved her elder son off. "Whatever the reason, I'm glad he's here. You must stay with us, of course."

Amira gestured to Sarah. "I bet it has something to do with the lovely woman beside him."

Yasin grasped Sarah's trembling hand. Only a moment ago, her touch had given him strength. Now, he could return the favor.

"Mother, Amira, Salim…" He hesitated to lie to his family, but he had come for a reason. More than just his future depended upon it. "This is my wife, Sarah al-Bayda."

Cries of surprise gave way to eager embraces and quick chatter that left Sarah frozen in surprise. Yasin grinned with genuine pleasure.

"You married a Muslim?" Salim asked.

"So I did."

"Then you converted, after all." The triumph on his brother's face carried a baffling hint of hostility.

"No."

The ensuing flare of passion might have suited a devout Muslim, but Salim had never been such a man. Yasin hadn't thought his brother capable of mustering such outrage at a Christian marrying a Muslim woman. How easily his new religion rested upon him!

Regardless, he was too happy at seeing his mother and sister again to quarrel with his brother. "I went by the old house. No one there knew of Father."

Salim's eyes widened for a moment before he relaxed them. Yasin suspected he'd been expecting an argument. "Most of the Mozarab craftsmen converted to avoid the *jizya*. We needed a larger space, and moving here brought even more clients."

"A fitting reward," Yasin muttered.

Voice drawn tight, Salim continued, "Once we did, our profits tripled. I had to add more workers because of the extra work."

His brother's boasting couldn't hide the added fact that moving would also distance them from their Mozarab taint. They had abandoned their heritage as easily as the rest of al-Andalus.

His sister laughed at a comment of Sarah's. He smiled again at her dress. At least she still defied these desert devils.

"Where is Father?"

The question silenced them all. Amira lowered her gaze. The mirth dropped from his mother's eyes, replaced with a hint of pain among a flood of pity. Her lip quivered.

"He never forgave you for leaving." Salim's words punctured the air as sharply as the awl in Yasin's toolkit pierced leather.

Dread swirled over him. Yasin could not bear the sympathy in his mother's expression. "Salim, where's Father?"

His brother's face had gone blank, emptied of outrage, triumph, and hostility. Foretelling doom settled in Yasin's heart even before his brother spoke.

"He died two years ago."

CHAPTER SIXTEEN

YASIN

DEAD.

The word echoed in Yasin's ears as his family described the stroke. He listened to the details mutely: the pitiable drooping of the right side of Faraj's face, the surrender in his eyes that had reminded his sister of a snuffed candle, the look of peace when he'd finally succumbed to another stroke a month later. Their explanations resembled the hollow recitation of a poet across a crowded square, describing someone else, not a man he'd known all his life.

At some point, they'd stopped talking and guided him toward a spare room where he and Sarah could stay.

A spare room…their old family home had no such luxury.

Fragments of the familiar sat amid a sea of foreignness. He passed the table where he'd practiced stitching leather with the oversized needles unique to his father's craft. The cooking pot his mother would use for her baharat lamb stew sat beside an unfamiliar hearth.

Dead.

Sarah had asked if he wanted her to stay. At the time, her offer had seemed strange, unmerited. Why should he need help? He didn't understand until his mother drew Sarah off to help her and Aishah prepare supper, leaving Yasin alone in the unadorned room. Only then did the implications of their words strike him and make him wish she hadn't left.

His father—the man who had shared his knowledge of leather, who had patiently endured all his sons' quarrels, who had disowned his youngest son for refusing his command to abandon his faith—was dead. In Toledo, he hadn't spared a thought for reconciliation. Too many pleasures begged to be enjoyed before some tyrant stole them away. Only on the week-long voyage from Valencia had he contemplated the looming reunion.

In the end, it hadn't mattered. That chance had been gone long before he'd left Toledo, even before his impulsive mistake of stealing Esteban's pouch.

Yasin took a breath. His chest felt light, as if a belt had loosened and fallen away from around it. He had wasted too much time on anger and resentment. They'd dragged him down. It was time to lay them aside. They couldn't change anything now.

A quick set of knocks interrupted his thoughts. Before he could stand, the door swung open and his sister poked her head inside.

"It's no good, you sitting in here by yourself." She perched on the edge of the unfamiliar bed. Her lips curled into a wry grin balanced between humor and sympathy.

For a moment, he imagined he hadn't left, that the previous three years hadn't happened. She offered something familiar in this almost unrecognizable city. "Sarah offered to stay."

"She seems nice." Amira removed her shawl and straightened her hair where it clung to the fabric. "You've changed in the last three years."

"Oh?"

A smirk tugged at the corner of her lips. "The Yasin I remember wouldn't have settled for just one woman."

Her words rekindled enough spirit to let him grin. "I suppose not."

He suspected the man he'd been in Toledo wouldn't have, either. Much had changed in a single month. "You never married?"

She waved a hand casually, but a tightening of her jaw suggested the topic bothered her. "A few inquired, but then Father fell ill. Nothing came of it since."

The absence of his father loomed like a dark hole in the center of the room.

Dead.

After a long silence, her voice came as a soft caress to his ears. "I'm sorry you learned of it this way."

Stirring, he raised a hand to straighten his hair. "I'm fine."

She lowered her chin a fraction. "I know you aren't."

"Why should it bother me?" He swallowed. "He disowned me."

"You still loved him."

The comment shocked him, and he spent the first few moments struggling to organize his outrage. But as he formed one argument after another, he unhappily admitted the truth of her words. "I'm sorry I wasn't here when it happened."

She rolled her eyes. "No, you aren't."

He arched an eyebrow. "Excuse me?"

She shrugged. "To have been here, you'd have had to convert as Father demanded. The part of you that made you my favorite brother would have died." She frowned. "I'm glad you weren't."

The events of those final few nights rushed back. Regardless of how his heist went, he couldn't remain in Almeria, not because of pride or pain but from fear of Almoravid retribution. He wouldn't have another chance to ask certain questions.

"Which of you told him where I was?"

Amira rubbed her shoulders. For a moment, her eyes widened. "He kept saying he was protecting the family. He reminded us of everything he'd sacrificed for us. He made us both feel so ungrateful." She swallowed. "I was half a heartbeat away from telling him."

It had been Salim, then. "So that's how he convinced you." He'd imagined that conversation many times over the years.

She bit her lip and picked at a loose thread on the blanket lying on the bed. "He told me all the terrible things that could happen to an unmarried woman in the north."

He recalled Sarah's hopelessness as she recounted the fate of a woman on her own. "I don't blame you for staying."

"I shouldn't have." Her forehead wrinkled. "Father saw the opportunity in converting, and he made the most of it. But he wasn't a woman. The Almoravids are more restrictive than even the raving preachers in the market. I'm not allowed to show my hair or my figure."

"Surely your friends remain," he began.

"Spread out across the city. But I have to reach them, and I can't travel alone. I have to sit in here, just…just waiting."

Yasin lowered his eyes, uncertain what to say. Amira had always loved the markets, gardens, and waterfront. He'd lost Almeria when he'd fled north, but Almeria taunted Amira every day, visible yet out of reach without the most exhausting of preparations. Though Sarah had been a slave in Toledo, even she could walk freely.

"What's the north like?" she asked.

The change in subject felt like a hand releasing his throat. He rubbed his thighs while he considered how to summarize everything he'd seen. "They still play in the streets. Beautiful songs. Simple ones from the northern mountains accompanied by a single flute, complex ones from the Arabian courts, and even some new ones, sung by French musicians in the style of the South. I listen to them all. They remind me of why I left."

"It's been so long since I've heard such music." Sorrow clung to Amira's eyes. They begged him for more details.

"The church bells ring out boldly, every day. You can find priests everywhere. And new churches seem to spring up every week."

"We were right." She watched him with wide eyes. "Toledo did keep its *taifa* heart."

The memory of Esteban's smirk came unsummoned. *Why should I trust a Mozarab tainted by heathens?* She deserved the truth. "Not exactly. No matter how hard I work or what I achieve, I'll always be a Mozarab, suspected because I willingly lived under Muslims."

Amira sat with her gaze lowered for a time. "But women can walk in the open." The words wept from her lips with a longing that threatened to break his heart.

"They can."

A deep breath restored her strength and the clarity in her eyes. "You're not staying, are you?"

A part of him wanted to tell her the truth, but he'd shared his plans with her once before only for her to reveal them. He had to be careful now. He'd already failed in Valencia so badly that he'd have died if not for Sarah. He only had one more chance. He could trust only Sarah now.

"My life is in Toledo."

She frowned. "And you won't be coming back."

He eyed the walls of this unfamiliar room, in an unfamiliar house, in a city he didn't recognize anymore, owned by Almoravids who had outlawed everything he treasured. Too much had changed for him to ever think of this city as home again.

"No, I won't."

YASIN

The comfort of a solid bed after seven days at sea let Yasin sleep uninterrupted until morning. He awoke to the smell of fresh bread and the sounds movement throughout the house. Rubbing his eyes, he searched for Sarah but found only her shawl on the floor. She had to be here somewhere, then; the Almoravids would tear out their hair in unbridled desire if they witnessed her free-flowing locks.

He shuffled down the unfamiliar hallway while straightening hair that had matted over while he'd slept. Surely he could find a dab of oil somewhere.

Voices rose and fell from the pantry, along with the shuffling of several pairs of feet from different directions. He didn't understand the cause of so much traffic until an unfamiliar woman carrying a jar of oil emerged from one door and ambled through another. Servants! Faraj hadn't been prosperous enough to afford servants when Yasin had lived under his roof. The sound of scrubbing near the entrance, probably cleaning up the mess from their late-night arrival, suggested Salim employed several.

Only a sliver of the pantry was visible from the hallway, but he recognized Aishah standing near the threshold. He was about to ask her for some oil to tame his hair when his brother's voice silenced him.

"Are the boots I made helping with your feet?" Salim asked from somewhere out of view deeper within the pantry.

"They feel much better. Thank you, darling," came Aishah's reply.

"I can add another layer of padding."

She offered a gentle smile. "Salim, I'm fine. Truly. Please don't worry about me."

His brother's hand came into view near her head, only to curl around her ear and tuck a tendril of her hair behind it. "How could I not worry about you, beloved?"

Even from a distance, Yasin could appreciate the beauty of the smile she offered her husband. He hadn't noticed quite how attractive she was last night.

"Are the herbs I bought helping with the sickness? The apothecary insisted they would."

Her hands pressed against her belly. "They are, thank you."

"He also recommended something for the aches."

She shook her head. "I'd rather not, darling."

"But if you're in pain—"

Her hand extended out of view into the pantry at head-level, probably to touch his cheek. "*Mashallah*, God has granted me this gift, and it seems ungrateful to dull my wits with concoctions."

"If it should grow worse, I will insist." His voice more resembled a plea than the command his words alone would have suggested. Much had happened these past three years to turn his brawling brother into a doting husband.

"Should that happen, I will take them, if only to soothe your worries."

Yasin jumped at the movement of a fluffy gray and white cat trotting cheerfully down the hall. The interruption stirred him and prompted a wave of embarrassment at his eavesdropping on the tender moment. Thankfully, he doubted the cat would tattle on him.

As he backed away, an intermittent thumping grew louder, a sound that wasn't intimate but which he knew intimately. It had awoken him every day for the first two decades of his life. Forgetting the voices in the pantry, Yasin passed through the plain door connecting the family rooms to the workshop.

He stepped into the slaps of leather on worktables, bursts of conversation, and even louder tapping of wooden mallets on the backs of tools. The workshop was massive, far larger than when Yasin had left and comfortably accommodating ten tables, twelve workers, and dozens of racks and shelves for both raw and finished goods. A small room, carved out by integral *tapia* walls, sat in the corner.

"Yasin!" A dark-eyed man crossed from the rear of the workshop in a quick series of great strides to wrap his thick arms around Yasin. "Merciful God, you've come home!"

"Lope!" Yasin gasped for air when the man released him. A few more heads Yasin recognized had risen. He offered them each a cheerful wave. "I didn't expect so many of Father's old workers."

"Who are you calling old?" Lope demanded with an undiminished smile. "We'd be fools to leave. Not many Muslims hire Christians."

Yasin gritted his teeth beneath his easy smile at the inequity of it all as one man after another greeted him. Faraj had allowed his workers to keep their religion while demanding his son surrender his.

"Alright, alright, we've all seen Yasin before." Salim approached from the private chambers with his hands on his hips, as Father always had. "We have customers waiting for these orders." A flash of some hostile emotion washed across Salim's face before he turned to instruct one of his men.

Master Sanchez used to give that same look when struggling with a large order. Yasin had evidently returned at a busy time. Perhaps Salim would look a little less sour if he offered his help.

He strolled through the workshop, studying the work around him. Lope led a group working on a massive wall covering near the back. They'd pushed two worktables together to accommodate the sheer size. Others labored over pouches, harnesses, belts, turnshoes, and a dozen other items. A wealth of full-grain leather sat on those tables, more than he'd ever seen in either his father's or Master Sanchez's workshops.

He stopped beside an unfamiliar worker—a Muslim, based on his skullcap and the crescent pendant laying atop his *qamisa*—carving patterns into the embellished strap of a satchel. Yasin caught a strong whiff of musk when he hunched down for a closer look. The man had already finished intricate trees with detailed leaves and was adding a nightingale on a branch. The apprentice was beveling the lines of his design, but all his cuts were of the same depth, creating an overall flat appearance.

Yasin touched him on the shoulder. "You have a steady hand. Yet, instead of cutting, if you impress the feathers here"—he pointed to the body of the bird, then to the tree's trunk—"and the texture of the bark here, you'll add depth."

"Impressing?" Salim abandoned his student to approach. "Beveling shows more skill and crisper lines than pressing the leather in."

Yasin shrugged. "True, but impressing works for this kind of embellishment and would vary the appearance. We do this in Toledo all the time."

"Continue with your beveling," Salim commanded. Meeting Yasin's gaze, his lip twitched, desperate to curl. "In Almeria, our refined techniques stand on their own without the taint of heathen habits."

Heathen! Yasin ground his teeth together. "I see Islam sits so heavily that you forget where you came from."

Salim's eyes widened briefly before narrowing again. His chest heaved, and the tiny muscles around his eyes twitched with nascent rage.

Yasin recognized his mistake when the worker looked to Salim. In one sentence, he had reminded him of Salim's recent conversion and the Christian faith of his brother. Once again, he'd acted without thinking. From this one worker could spring the suspicions of false conversion that his father had so desperately feared. The whole family might suffer.

In a low voice, Salim growled, "If you cannot restrain yourself from misguiding my workers, then you may leave my workshop," before storming toward the room in the back.

Yasin followed behind, struggling to keep up with his brother's trudge. Salim slammed the door behind him, but Yasin caught it before it closed.

Within was a chest, a stool, and a central table with a stack of papers upon it. Yasin eyed those papers with envy. It seemed Salim had learned to read in his absence.

"Get out."

"Salim, I'm sorry." Yasin extended a hand. "I shouldn't have said that in front of your people."

Salim brushed him further inside and closed the door. "Why did you come back? Do you expect me to split this workshop with you?"

Yasin gaped. "That's what you think?"

"I'm the older brother. I have the better claim, even if Father hadn't disowned you." Salim balled his fists as the anger tinted his scowl and the slope of his eyebrows. "The magistrates would never favor a Christian over a Muslim."

Yasin had always suspected Salim had capitulated for a greater share of Father's inheritance. "I don't want anything from you."

"How can you even come back here after what you've done?"

Yasin frowned. He couldn't possibly know about Valencia or Esteban or any of his crimes in Toledo. "What have I done?"

"You killed Father." The wail echoed off the walls to strike his ears twice.

Yasin gasped. "I wasn't even here."

"He never forgave you. Every night, he would mutter about his treacherous son." Salim stabbed at Yasin with his finger. "Your betrayal, your abandonment gnawed at him and left him weak to the stroke that killed him."

He fell back a step. "You believe that?"

"It's the truth. He cursed you with his last breath." Salim's intention to inflict pain sat on his curled lip as smug triumph.

Yasin stumbled backward until he pressed against the wall of the small room. Regret at losing the chance at reconciliation evaporated. Three years or thirty, it wouldn't have mattered. Faraj hadn't regretted disowning and rejecting his son. Right until the end, he hadn't shown even a whisper of remorse for forcing his family to sacrifice their faith.

Straightening, he stepped forward. "If our quarrel killed him, then he had only himself to blame," he began slowly. "A tyrant has no right to outrage when others resist his commands."

"He was the head of our family. It was our duty to obey him."

"In temporal matters, perhaps. But my soul was never his to convert." Perhaps he could still make his brother understand. "You recognized that once. Both you and Amira wanted to come with me."

"I was a fool," Salim muttered. "Convinced by your twisting words. Muslim, Christian, and Jew all worship the same creator. The only difference is in ritual."

"If it matters so little, why did he demand it?"

"Because not everyone is as enlightened."

Yasin scoffed. Enlightened? His brother was a coward and a simpleton who had let himself be led like a puppy.

"You always were too stubborn to understand what we'd gain." Salim spread his arms. "All this is mine. A workshop with a dozen men. Esteem and respect among the elites of the city. Freedom from the *jizya*."

"You're a fool if you believe you have freedom under Almoravid rule."

"Oh, I have freedom. Freedom to expand my workshop without prejudice. Freedom to provide for my workers and servants. Because of my choices, they live good, prosperous lives."

"But the culture…" Yasin swept his arms wide. "We've lost the musicians and poets who stirred us to pride and reminded us how to live."

"We've lost worthless men whose vocation earned so little that they couldn't attract wives or maintain families," Salim countered. "Wanton women who lead men to sin by dancing with the barest of clothing. Beggars demanding our coin for their playing. Troublemakers who would spend their nights drinking, brawling, and robbing. The worst were the court performers, funded by the emir's ever-increasing taxes. He clothed them in silks with money taken from the pockets of our people." He raised his chin. "The Almoravids put an end to that waste."

"Not for Christians."

"They ended piracy and crime—"

"By executing any who protest," Yasin said, recalling the shop-keeper's tales in Cartagena.

"Troublemakers," Salim retorted. "Traitors and apologists who take advantage of discord for their own profit. No Christian invasions threaten our safety anymore. Food is plentiful."

"But not instruments, perfumes, books, silks—"

"You can't eat instruments or silks," Salim interrupted. "I'd happily trade a few musicians and fabrics for protection and prosperity."

"Man cannot live on bread alone," Yasin maintained.

"Yes, but man still needs bread to live."

Yasin glared at his brother. "The taint of heresy outweighs any advantages."

Salim scoffed. "Tell that to the Christians I employ. How many of their jobs would you sacrifice to appease your soul? Will you deny their children food so you feel better about how you worship Allah? Is the peace of your soul more important than the lives of their wives and children?"

"I doubt you had them in mind when you converted," Yasin charged.

The response came immediately. "No, but Father did. Now that I carry his burdens, I admire his decision."

He drew in a breath to respond, but that brief hesitation allowed his brother's words to sink in. He could not deny Salim's success, from the size of this workshop to the servants working within the house. And his brother's employees seemed more content than those of Master Iustez or Master Sanchez in Toledo. Converting had allowed Faraj to protect all those people.

And yet, they weren't his family. "What of Amira?" He nodded toward the house. "Did you think about her?"

"When have you?" Salim retorted. "When you were caring only for yourself in Toledo?"

"She's treated worse than a slave," Yasin pressed. "She's forced to cover herself and forbidden to roam the streets. You haven't even bothered to find her a husband."

Salim straightened. When it came, his voice had a new control. "Amira is protected from abuse and assault, from the scorching sun and brutal labors. That's not slavery. That's safety."

For years, Yasin had hated the Almoravids for robbing his beloved Almeria of the pleasures that made life enjoyable. All that time, he had misunderstood his own outrage. The routing of the performers, the purging of the markets, and the closing of the taverns had all been symptoms of a far, far worse problem. The real horror of the Almoravids wasn't their beliefs but the fact that they compelled everyone to follow them. They had chosen for everyone, just as Faraj had chosen conversion for his whole family.

Yasin was staring into the eyes of a man who cared nothing for the delights Yasin admired, but the city was filled with men like him, men who continued to acquiescence to that compulsion. And that made them no better than the Almoravids.

"Even if everything you say is true, Amira should still be allowed the choice." Yasin shook his head. "But Father forced conversion upon her."

His brother scowled. "He didn't force her. Persuaded her, pressured her, yes. But in the end, she chose for herself."

He scoffed. "What other choice did she have? Father believed that even one relative remaining a Christian would ruin the family. Was she supposed to refuse and be thrown onto the streets? Or harassed and insulted for the rest of her life? The Almoravids you praise gave her no means to fend for herself, no option but to submit."

Salim crossed his arms. "We're all better for it."

Even a few moments earlier, he might have reacted instinctively, but the recklessness of his tongue on the workroom floor was still fresh. Instead, he simply gave up. He'd had this same conversation in an alley three years earlier, and he doubted he'd fare better now. Faraj hadn't understood the distinction, and neither did Salim.

He felt sick even standing in this building. The happy memories of his childhood may have soaked into the old family home, but this building smelled of tyranny and capitulation. He hated it.

"I promise to never again set foot inside your workshop." He pushed past his brother toward the door. "You are Father's heir in every way, Salim. I suspect that makes you proud."

He stepped through and kept going past the workshop without looking back.

SARAH

For the first time since seeing that pirate sail on the horizon so many years ago, Sarah prayed openly among others of her faith. As she worked her way through the noon prayer in the family's common room, the motion of Yasin's mother and Aishah in her peripheral vision kept distracting her from contemplating the meaning of the silent words. Twice, she lost her place.

Amira did not join them. Sarah supposed Yasin's sister was experiencing her *haidh* and could not pray until she purified herself after her bleeding. It was the only possible explanation for her absence.

Her prayers often left her feeling renewed, but now, she felt the full embrace of Allah standing over her, sheltering her and all his children. She had finally reached the warm embrace of her own people. The suspicions from Cartagena melted away. This was where she belonged.

When they'd finished, Elvira squeezed Sarah's hand and offered a grateful smile that roused her curiosity. Sarah hadn't done anything any woman in this city couldn't do. But, before she could inquire further, Yasin's mother departed.

Sarah smiled at Aishah. "Thank you for allowing me to pray with you."

As Aishah bowed her head, a tendril of nearly black hair slipped free of her shawl, but she quickly stuffed it back inside. Her eyes never left Sarah's own hair, flowing free within the safety of a family home. "We should welcome all who wish to glorify Allah."

"It means a great deal that you opened your home to us." Sarah hesitated before deciding to venture into potentially dangerous territory. She couldn't ignore the discomfort of Yasin's argument with Salim and still maintain the pretense of their marriage. "Particularly given the tension our arrival caused."

Aishah's smile was quick but unmistakable. "Such things happen between brothers. I'm certain they'll resolve whatever matters lay between them." Head still bowed, her eyes rose toward Sarah's hair again. "Nothing is more important than family."

She was right, of course. No anger burned forever. But Sarah doubted they'd be here long enough for the brothers to work out their disagreements.

"Your hair is beautiful." Aishah bit her lip. "And you wear it so freely."

"Thank you." Appreciative of the compliment, Sarah absently ran her fingers through her hair, and they snagged on every crack in the dry strands after days at sea. "Perhaps later you can show me the markets, and I'll buy us some scented oil to comb into our hair. It's the least I can do to repay your kindness."

A flash of panic shone in Aishah's eyes before the woman lowered her gaze. "Oh, I didn't mean…" She picked at the edge of her dress. "I'd never hazard the markets for a frivolous luxury."

Sarah offered a reassuring grin. "Beauty is never frivolous. I'm sure our men would agree."

Aishah glanced down, but Sarah caught the start of a blush. "I'm sure one of our husbands would fetch it for us later."

Sarah could understand not wanting to be alone among these Almoravids. "Why don't we go together, now?"

Her eyes widened. "We cannot do that."

The rumors came flooding back. "Are you truly not permitted to leave your home?"

Aishah's expression softened. "No, of course not. Naturally, women are allowed to travel during the day with escorts."

Allowed. The word grated at Sarah. She had endured the limits of *allowed* for five years. Only this past month had she reveled in freedom from it. "You mean keepers."

Aishah arched an eyebrow, and only then did Sarah realize her response contained a little too much hostility. "I mean protectors. Seas of men jostle and push in the markets. They take liberties that a pious woman should not have to endure. And each one that goes unpunished encourages another. I can't count how often I was groped or swatted away an unwelcome hand before the Almoravids came."

"Why don't the Almoravids punish them, then?"

The woman's tone didn't change. Only an arched eyebrow indicated her growing disquiet. "Who can prove whether an unwelcome hand violated a woman through intention or accident?" She wrung her hands together. "The *taifas* punished the perpetrators when they could, but that didn't prevent such abuses. Only a proper escort can protect those who are most precious to Allah."

Sarah frowned at the response. "This goes beyond protection. This is restriction."

"I can see how someone used to the sinful North might think so," Aishah conceded with unmistakable judgment. "But, in three years, not once have I suffered such an indignity." She pressed her hands together. "That safety is worth a delay in acquiring a frivolous bauble."

"At the cost of walking the streets alone, or at night?" Sarah pressed.

"As a married woman, where would you wish to go without your husband's knowledge?" Accusation filled the words. "And knowing of your wishes, why wouldn't Yasin indulge them?" Her eyebrows pinched. "Only shameful women with sinful intent would trawl the streets at night."

Sarah hesitated, both because she'd clearly roused Aishah's suspicions about her morals and because Aishah had a point about sinful intent: all her and Yasin's crimes on this journey had come at night, and they would commit yet more. But she'd also run afoul of jealous, bitter men often enough in the library that she could only imagine the consequences to a wife if a husband didn't act as honorably as Aishah posited.

"As you say, the ways in the North are different. How do women work under such rules?"

Aishah frowned. "Why would she want to? Organizing a household and managing the servants already requires more time than in a day." She rubbed her fingers at the joints. "Besides, a man's labor is grueling, brutal work. Every day, my husband returns with aching hands and a stiff back from bending over his leather. And his craft is a skilled one. I couldn't imagine the damage caused by a lifetime of lifting or digging or hauling under the burning sun." She shivered. "I'm thankful for Salim's sacrifice in bearing that burden."

Sarah had endured both the aches of daily labor Aishah described and the restrictions men like the Almoravids had imposed, and she would gladly endure the former to preserve herself against the latter.

"But you need not worry about such things." Aishah's crisp tone carried a finality that suggested she'd reached the end of her patience. "You are fortunate to have Yasin. He clearly loves you and would not deny you whatever oils you wish."

So unexpected was that observation that Sarah simply froze. Aishah believed Yasin loved her? They hadn't arranged any particular demonstrations of affection for the sake of his family, yet this woman believed their supposed marriage.

After a curt nod, Aishah swept past Sarah and into the hall with surprising speed for a pregnant woman. Sarah followed her progress as the woman passed Yasin, who was leaning against the door frame.

Sarah met his gaze. Yes, she supposed she was fortunate. "How much did you hear?"

He smirked. "Enough."

She gestured to where Aishah had been standing. "What *was* that?"

"A good Almoravid wife, I suspect."

Even in Toledo, her movements hadn't been as restricted as Aishah had described. Yet, thinking about that Christian city reminded her of her own difficulties: the exploratory hands when she would pass through crowds, the lusty advances of the guards near the library, even the boldness that allowed a man like Lord Gonzalo to enter her room without an invitation. Could she blame a wife who neither needed to attract a husband nor labor to feed herself from wishing to be spared such treatment?

But those same restrictions would leave no space for a *qiyan* without a patron to support her now that the emirs were gone.

Yasin cleared his throat. "Should the need ever arise, please know I'd be delighted to rub oil into any part of your body you wish." His grin brightened his entire face.

Despite lacking kohl, his eyes caught and held her, snuffing her breath. The taut slope of his chin and the suppleness of his smirking lips banished all thought of humility and prayer. Was Aishah right? Had she missed something in his smirks and bravado that was obvious to others?

Struggling to reclaim her poise, she tugged at a fold of her dark green *qamisa* where it had bunched during her prostrations. The gesture recalled her purpose in this room. "Men aren't permitted to watch women pray."

He gestured down the hallway. "I came when I saw my mother leave." He raised a bemused eyebrow. "Though, I don't understand that prohibition. Aren't Muslims taught to admire the beauty of Allah's creations?"

The tingling of her cheeks signaled the beginnings of a blush, and she looked away. Did women here ever have occasion to receive such compliments, or had those opportunities been banished along with unwelcome advances? "If the Almoravids hear that, they'll hang you for sacrilege."

"Fortunately for me, they evoke strikingly different sentiments." He pushed himself upright with an elbow. "Grab your shawl. Let's visit this library and see if we've wasted our time coming here."

When she'd returned, Yasin had changed into a plain brown cloak that hung too limply to be concealing his *jubba* and its hidden compartment.

"You aren't bringing your tools?"

He shook his head. "We're only exploring today."

"What if an opportunity presents itself?"

His eyes brightened. "You do listen to me!"

She smirked. "You occasionally share a worthwhile thought."

Pride stirred when, this time, he blushed and glanced away. "Even if it did, we can't exploit it during the day. Too many eyes." He set his hand on the door handle.

"Where did you get that cloak?"

"It's my brother's." He swung the door open.

"Will he mind that you're using it?"

"Hopefully." He stepped onto the street.

They worked their way through the city, past workshops hugging the streets that twisted with the contours of the uneven terrain.

Hammering, shouted commands, and the sounds of labor spilled out of one shop after another. Almeria's leatherworkers seemed busy this morning.

Scaffolds with workers crawling over them, repairing chips and damaged facades, clung to the sides of several buildings. The sunlight reflecting off the *tapia* structures cast Almeria in bright yellows and tans that stung Sarah's eyes. She pulled her shawl down further to shield them, much preferring the look of the city at twilight.

"We'll head through the market."

Sarah hadn't realized how accustomed she'd grown to Valencia's straight streets. The parade of Almeria's ancient and frustratingly similar buildings pressed in on her. Without Yasin to guide her, she'd get hopelessly lost.

They emerged into the Great Market. A swirling tumult of haggling and chatter blended with the bleating of caravan camels and the usual clamor of moving bodies. Fish, lamb stew, and fresh bread hung on the air. Yet, the tableau was a pale shadow of Valencia, or even Toledo. Clothing, awnings, and even blankets beneath the saddles of camels and horses looked washed out. Only the flowers and fruit for sale—and the bold indigo cloaks of the Almoravids—provided color.

Pulling her shawl tighter, she searched for something familiar. No poets, dancers, or jugglers delighted the crowd, and no musicians performed with oud, rebab, or naqqara. Where were the women? Sarah perched up on the tips of her toes for a better look, but only a few heads bore shawls, and none had unbound hair.

Aishah's discomfort at the thought of traveling through these streets came rushing back. No longer could Sarah pretend such a reaction was unique, not considering the scene before her.

She had put all her faith in returning to al-Andalus. She'd thought the rumors about the Almoravids had to have been exaggerated, embellished to demonize proud Muslims capable of resisting Christian conquest. Aishah's impassioned defense and this strikingly masculine crowd suggested otherwise.

"Sarah?" Yasin touched her shoulder.

She focused on him, the only familiar thing on this street. "I'm fine."

He nodded, but the concern didn't fall away. "Something to eat might help."

They halted a peddler strolling through the crowd. Yasin bought some cheese bread while Sarah waited nearby.

The muffled voices of a pair of men rose up above the noise of the crowd.

"—imprisoned him for fornication and stoned the woman he was with."

"Didn't you say they were betrothed?" the other replied.

Another peddler's shout masked the first part of the reply. "—wasn't good enough for the veiled ones."

Yasin handed her a haunch of bread. She accepted it with shaking hands, but her mind lingered on the brief exchange. Even the strictest of imams didn't punish a betrothed couple so severely, even though fornication was forbidden. She could understand prayer and atonement, but stoning?

Shouting and the noise of a nearby struggle drew her attention. The crowd parted, leaving her and Yasin standing on the edge of a circle surrounding the shattered remains of a stall. A peddler was shouting about a thief and jabbing a finger at a man in a stained *qamisa* being restrained by a pair of indigo Almoravids. After a few words too soft for Sarah to hear, a third guard drew a curved sword and raised it while one of the others extended the man's arm.

Sarah gasped as she realized what they were about to do, right in the middle of the street.

"We don't need to watch this." Yasin pushed his way back into the crowd, pulling her behind him with enough strength that she had to follow.

Bodies flowed into her vacated space, hiding the scene as the sword came down. At the scream and the collective gasp from the crowd, she slammed her free hand to her mouth. She imagined the severed hand oozing blood into the cobbles and the man writhing in agony.

The Almoravids were Muslims, not Christian heathens who shed blood as casually as they emptied a chamber pot.

"In the name of Allah, the merciful, the compassionate…" She whispered the words so they might wrap Allah's protection around her.

Yasin continued to pull her forward. Sarah searched the faces of the crowd for some reflection of her outrage, but she saw only dull acceptance. How could they tolerate this casual violence? The terrible possibilities made her shiver. Almoravids may have doled out the punishment, but the people of Almeria had acquiesced to it.

Yasin finally came to a halt and leaned against the side of a building two blocks away. Closing his eyes, he pressed his hand to his chest. "Is this what you wanted, Father?"

Sarah frowned. "Pardon?"

His eyes opened, exposing a momentary alarm. "It doesn't matter." He straightened his *jubba*. "The library is just ahead."

They traveled down two more streets with increasingly thickening crowds. Every time they passed an Almoravid in his indigo *tagelmust*, Sarah pulled her shawl down further over her eyes.

Yasin halted beside a quaint, *tapia* structure that seemed no larger than his family's old home. It couldn't possibly hold more than a few dozen volumes, let alone the multiple codices of a complete copy of the *Book of Healing*.

"This is it?"

He jutted his head toward an ornate limestone complex with external arcades and rows of blind arches across the street. Deep scoring and a few lingering tiles suggested mosaics roughly chipped away. A tall stone wall with towers at each corner ringed the structure except for a gap guarded by a pair of Almoravids. Beyond that entryway, olive trees bloomed along the palace perimeter. Though carefully positioned, they were overgrown and misshapen, much like the weeds reaching up from between the cobbles of the pathway leading from the street.

"*Ya salaam!*" One of the Almoravids glanced in her direction. Regretting her outburst, she turned her back to him. "That's a palace."

"It was." His lips barely moved. He kept his gaze on the ground, clearly trying to avoid drawing attention. "It's been abandoned for years."

"It's guarded," she reminded him.

A smile tugged at his lips. "That didn't stop us last time."

"It very nearly did." She had to look away when she remembered his eyes rolling back in that dingy Valencian warehouse. "And we had a secret entrance."

"Follow me." He led her further down the avenue and into an alley abutting the palace walls. Several of the adjacent buildings had second-story overhangs. She felt as if she were descending into that hidden passageway again. Terror fired in her belly, and she pressed her hands against it in a vain attempt to steady herself.

Halfway down, Yasin gestured to a semicircular opening along the base of the palace wall large enough for them to fit through if they crouched. "It's an old Roman sewer, long since dried up," he explained as he passed. "That's our way in."

The opening looked no dirtier than any other part of the street. "I can't believe they left it open."

He led Sarah further down the alley. "Guards used to patrol when I was a boy. The towers had a direct view of this opening. As I grew, so did the trees inside the walls. They're so overgrown, they hide the opening from the towers."

She craned her neck to search the nearest guard tower and noticed the flutter of an Almoravid's *tagelmust* within. "I'm amazed the emir didn't fix that."

"If he'd worried about things like that, he wouldn't have lost his kingdom to the Almoravids." He grunted. "And I'm sure the Almoravids already removed everything they value."

They were emerging onto another large avenue and continued around the walls toward another opening. "But not the books?"

"The library of a contemptible ruler, led into decadence by scholars, poets, and heathens?" He grunted. "I'm surprised they didn't burn it."

Sarah had dreamed of being among members of her faith, but the reality opened a hollowness in her chest. Where had the culture and sophistication gone? A desert wind had blown through the city streets, stripping them of ornamentation and vigor. Almeria was a city of anxious and joyless shuffling and summary punishment, a city of men whose women were kept out of sight, and a quiet city bereft of the vibrations of oud or the vibrancy of dazzling color and intoxicating scent. Fear of Christians had caused them to abandon everything that made them glorious.

These streets felt empty after only three years of Almoravid rule. What if every city in al-Andalus was the same? Why should any of them, even her Granada, be different? What place did any of them have for a *qiyan*?

She nearly collided with Yasin when he stopped suddenly. His face was carved in marble, agonized and severe, as he stared at the overgrown garden on the other side of the arched opening.

He had spoken with reverence about a garden in this city when they'd left Toledo. His musical words had had a poetic cadence.

At a single look at his despondent face, she knew he had been speaking about this garden.

But the scent of pine and the mouth-watering sweetness of fruit didn't hang on the air now. No colorful flowers brightened the sea of green, and no starlings or nightingales sang. Dried irrigation ditches contained only isolated pools of stagnant water overgrown with algae, and whole sections of vegetation lay withered from the lack of nourishment. But for the surrounding city, Sarah would have mistaken this garden for an overgrown forest path.

Yasin slumped to his knees. "What have they done?"

The agonized wail broke her heart. She knelt and wrapped her arms around him, desperate to hold together the fragile pieces of this man before her. She supposed the Almoravids would object to a woman embracing a man in the street, even a man who was supposed to be her husband. She no longer cared. One by one, the memories of his past had been taken from him. First his father, then his home, and now, even the immutable beauty of Allah's creations had slipped away, leaving him with nothing.

"Oh, Yasin, I'm sorry."

He leaned his head against her shoulder. "I wish you could have seen it." His voice sounded hollow like an empty waterskin. "I think you would have liked it."

He was Ibn Hazm, mourning the glories of his lost home. The walls of charm and confidence were gone, leaving him with only the longing of despair.

He had come back, but he could never go home again. The places of his childhood had become unrecognizable. Even his most cherished memories had been tainted by the cruel taunt of the reality before him. She could imagine no worse suffering than the death of hope.

She knelt beside him and wept, not for the remains of the once beautiful garden left to wither, but for a world that no longer offered a place for either of them.

CHAPTER SEVENTEEN

YASIN

DRAINED BY THEIR exploration, Yasin felt little urge to make that night's dinner a pleasant affair. While his mother and sister kept attempting conversation, they eventually acquiesced to uncomfortable silence. Even good-quality and well-spiced lamb stew and ripe, sliced fruit couldn't improve his spirits. The sounds of the servants buzzing around them, refilling water goblets and removing dirty dishes, echoed loudly in his ears.

He excused himself as soon as possible and retreated to his and Sarah's chamber. At least there, he could surround himself with his blue *jubba* and the fragment of his sack, the final relics of the Almeria he had loved.

The mosaics, the beautiful flowers, the rich fabrics, musicians, dancers, and poets… They had lived only in his memory for many years now. The Mozarab district was gone, too. The Almoravids had swept his people away as the desert winds erased footprints in the sand. They had done it all at the request of its people, who now had no choice but to live as their conquerors dictated, even if they regretted their saviors. And if Salim was the norm, they likely did not.

Sarah had once said he compensated for his loss with his vices. Yet, they had achieved nothing. They couldn't bring back his Almeria any more than they could reconcile him with his father. Worse, in the end, they'd left him with nothing but a small pouch of silver and a few scraps of fabric. Salim had sacrificed his faith and had gained a family and a thriving business. Heresy, it seemed, paid well.

Twilight had begun to fade when Sarah's oud broke the silence. Eyes widening, Yasin followed the sound through the door and down the hall. The music conjured memories of those long nights under a dome of stars and the quiet repose of those travelers and settlers who'd had the good fortune to hear her play.

Sarah was sitting on the same bench as at dinner, plucking the strings with eyes closed. The slow, stirring melody recounted the first emir of Almeria's break from Cordoba. It was the most revered composition among his people, a tale of glorious defiance against tyrants who demanded obedience.

Yasin closed his eyes and basked in the riveting ballad. Each chord stirred the Almerian within. The pain of the ruined garden, the scoured mosaics, and the silent musicians faded away. His people hadn't always been as they were now. Once, they had stood on their own, long before the Almoravids and the fracturing of Yasin's family.

"Stop!" Salim charged through the doorway.

Knocked off balance, Yasin clasped the frame to avoid falling over. By the time he looked back, his brother had snatched the instrument out of Sarah's hands. His mother and sister jumped to their feet in surprise.

Salim's eyes burned with wild panic. "Do not play the music of the *taifas*."

"Give it back!" Sarah's desperate fingers reached for the instrument.

His brother was clenching both the neck and strings. Sarah had often warned about the damage that kind of hold could cause.

"Give it back, Salim," Yasin instructed.

Salim continued to glare at her. "Not if she plays that song."

Her eyebrows knitted together. "Whyever not?"

"Do you know what will happen to me if someone hears that coming from my house?" Salim's voice came in a furtive hiss. "Such songs corrupted our people during the *taifas*. They encouraged disobedience and made us lose our way."

Yasin clenched the door frame until his fingers throbbed. Was nowhere safe from these desert devils? Did they have to dictate what happened inside private homes, too?

Sarah gasped. "That's absurd!"

"Perhaps so." Salim clenched the instrument tighter. "But I'll not have you call Almoravid anger down on my family."

"Give it back to her!" Yasin's voice erupted from his mouth with the sharpness of a good leather knife.

Salim's head snapped around to face Yasin. His grip slackened enough that the strings ran straight again. Seizing the opportunity, Sarah snatched it out of his hands and returned to the bench. She studied the neck and tested the strings before releasing a relieved sigh.

The instrument was a work of art, a magnificent, fragile creation with sleek lines and gentle curves. His brother's eagerness to abase himself to fanatics had nearly destroyed a masterpiece.

He pinned Salim with a glare. "I won't let you force your ways upon her the way Father did to me."

Salim scoffed. "You have no right to question him."

Yasin drew in a breath. He was one of the few in Almeria who still had that right. He'd lost his home because he'd refused to submit to tyrants, because he refused to watch his city fall into mediocrity. He wasn't about to submit now.

"Salim, this is no—" their mother began.

"Father called it a small sacrifice, but I knew it was just the first of many," Yasin interrupted. His voice trembled with growing anger, but he managed not to shout. "Worst of all, you don't even realize what you're doing." The neglected garden, overgrown and half-dead, intruded on his thoughts. "Our history, songs, and our very essence are gone. All we have left is terrified obedience."

"And more wealth than Father ever dreamed." Salim's smirk curled the corner of his lip.

"What good is that if we've lost everything else?"

"What good is everything else if you don't have a roof over your head and food in your belly?" Salim grunted. "I'd gladly sacrifice music for basic necessities."

"Then you're a fool. Worse, you're forcing that sacrifice on everyone else, just like the Almoravids did." He pointed at Sarah. "The work of her fingers gives meaning to all our labors. She's more precious than all the profit you'll ever earn. How dare you tell her to hide that?"

"I have a family to protect." Salim's words came out in a jumble. "And I'll sacrifice anything I must—or force sacrifices upon those living under my roof—to safeguard them."

Fear shone in Salim's eyes, wild and uncontrolled. It had sped his words, and it had driven his choices. He was afraid, afraid of bringing harm down upon those he loved. Yasin supposed he couldn't blame him for that.

Salim raised his chin to glare at his brother. "What in your life do you value equally to make such sacrifices for?"

Sarah's hair hung freely over her shoulder, flowing and graceful like every part of her, as she gazed back at him with wide, rounded eyes. It was there, right there before him. The world he admired still lived within this cultured, willful, beautiful, irritating woman. They had faced danger and adventure together. They had triumphed and suffered. Yet, he hadn't really understood how precious those moments had all been until now.

Sarah was the dream he had sought in vain for so long. He'd been a fool to seek it in a place or in empty pleasures when he should have opened his eyes to the woman beside him.

SARAH

Sarah opened the door just enough to slip inside.

Yasin, sitting on the bed with his elbows on his knees, looked up, startled. "Sarah…"

The breathless way he spoke her name tickled her like the finest silk. He had removed his *jubba*, and his thin cotton *qamisa* hung open to expose his chest. Her eyes focused on that patch of forbidden skin.

She silently closed the door and slide the latch into place. Her fingers trembled on the handle. They had spent many nights pretending to be husband and wife. She had never before felt nervous to be alone with him.

His words after dinner had changed everything.

She clasped her hands to steady their shaking. "Thank you…" Her voice cracked. She cleared her throat, embarrassed at her own awkwardness. "Thank you for defending me."

His Adam's apple bobbed up and down. "I couldn't let him decide for you."

"Did you mean what you said?" She had intended to work up to that question gradually, but the words would not wait.

Panic shone in his eyes for an instant before his features softened. He had come to some silent decision. Whatever followed would be the truth.

"Every word."

Her heart hammered in her chest, frightening her with its intensity.

His gaze never slipped. It clung to her as if she alone could nourish him. "Your playing is precious." His lip quivered. "Nearly as lovely as you are."

Prior to his impassioned defense of her earlier that night, she would have not believed those words. But now… Her breath caught in her throat.

His lips formed a faint smile, wistful and charming rather than his usual sardonic smirk. "I understand now that everything that's happened had a purpose."

"Purpose?" The word came as a whisper.

"Almeria, Toledo, Esteban, Valencia… All these years, I was so focused on what I'd lost that I hadn't bothered to build a life." He swallowed. "The pleasures of the world are empty without someone to share it with. I kept trying to satisfy myself with more, to fill this void. But I was searching for the wrong thing."

His eyes swallowed her up in their depths. His passion for a lost world swirled around her, wrapping her in the substance of his heart. She could feel his longing and pain as if it were her own.

"But now, I'm thankful for all those wasted years, because they brought me to you." His expression softened into a gentle smile. The veil in his eyes fell, leaving nothing but that hidden depth she had glimpsed only a handful of times before. "I wouldn't change any of it."

She hungered only to reach out to him, to embrace him. If that was sin or sacrilege, she no longer cared.

It seemed so long ago when she'd accused him of lacking *adab*. She had believed only men who lived in palaces, surrounded by glories and righteous causes, could possess it. But it was easy to be bold when one had everything. Yasin had risked everything to hold onto his heart and soul, to wrap his arms around an idea and never let go.

A fire burned within him that his father, the Almoravids, and the ruin of the world could not extinguish. Within him lay everything she had ever valued in her poems. She hadn't found it in the court of Valencia or the people of Toledo, and certainly not among the Muslims of this defeated city. He alone had understood the song that beat in her heart. Yet he was flesh before her, living and vibrant, not the echo of a poetic figure shrouded in legend.

Despite all her training and poise, she felt clumsy and awkward as she approached him. Her hands shook as she raised them to his cheeks. His skin felt soft and smooth, as if he had shaved only this morning.

The outside of her legs rubbed against his knees. The warmth where they touched evoked ripples of excitement. She lowered her head to press her lips against his, softly at first, but with more pressure as his parted in response. A shock of delight spread across her cheeks, down her neck, over her stomach, between her thighs…

His arms came up to cradle her, and she nestled into his caress. He pulled on her *qamisa*, tugging it upwards until it drew taut. She shifted to free the edge from between their legs and he pulled it up and away. Her hair lifted up with the fabric before falling back down over her naked shoulders in a thrilling trickle.

She eyed her *qamisa* in his hands. "Thief."

He didn't smile at her jest, though. His soft eyes, filled with awe and an uncharacteristic humility, continued to watch her while he ran a hand over her forehead, down along the line of her hair, and to her cheek.

"My nightingale." He kissed her neck just beneath her chin.

A burst of pleasure pulled a gasp from her lips, and not for the last time that night. She was a nightingale again—his nightingale—and in that dwindling candlelight, she soared.

SARAH

Most nights in Toledo, Sarah would awaken every time she shifted and a limb struck a cold spot on her cot. The other servants' muted conversations and the drifting sounds of carts making nighttime deliveries always kept her on the edge of sleep.

Sleeping beside Yasin was different. She awoke to warmth. Like fingers reaching for a fire on a winter's night, she wrapped her arms and legs around the source and released a contented murmur. They pressed against something supple that slid over her, sending a tingle across her skin. For the first time she could recall, the act of waking filled her with pleasure.

It took her a few moments to remember the reason. She ran a hand over the flesh beneath her, grazing the hair of Yasin's chest. Back came the burning intensity of her need to be close to him. The sensations of last night came flooding back. The tingling spread to her thighs as she squeezed him tighter, desperate to hold onto that feeling.

He released a murmur, a precursor to his own waking. She held her breath as her mind raced with the implications of what they'd done. She had sinned, not just with a man who wasn't her husband, but with a Christian.

Her training had included ways to influence and persuade. She had the skill to dismiss the entire affair as a casual comfort without wounding his pride. But, did she want that? He had once promised he would not touch her until she wished it, and by Allah she had wished it last night. She had pounced on him like a kitten on a mouse. Even now, she quivered with the desire to do it again. Her muscles froze, refusing to separate from him even to adjust the lay of her hair to be more pleasing before he awoke fully.

"Good morning." The eagerness in his voice set her heart beating faster. He rubbed his leg against hers and tightened his embrace.

Delight at his reaction shattered her still-forming responses. "Good morning."

He shifted, and whether by intention or coincidence, his chin settled against her head, nestling her closer. She melted into his embrace. Here, she felt safe and comfortable as never before, even in Baghdad.

But things needed to be said now, before courtesy or obligation set in, so she propped herself onto an elbow. "What happened last night…" She cleared her throat to purge the hesitation in her voice. "I don't want you to pretend it meant something deeper to spare my feelings."

"But it did mean something." The sincerity of his expression left her speechless. "More than anything else in my life. Enough that all I can think about is leaving everything and running away with you."

She twisted to face him. "Do you mean that?"

"I do." He gave the same soft smile as last night, tender and welcoming. "Last night, my brother asked what I valued enough to make sacrifices for. For a long time, I thought that was the culture of the *taifas*, but I never really sacrificed anything for that. My father took my family away from me with his demands, and the Almoravids took my home away with their rules. I didn't choose to give them up." He swallowed. "But I'd sacrifice everything for you and the way I feel when I'm with you."

Her thoughts raced as she recalled their every interaction over the previous month. "When did you realize this?"

"Little by little, but it wasn't until last night that I realized how dear you are to me." A smile crept onto his lips, and his eyebrows lifted. "Despite all his failings, Salim dotes on Aishah. He'd do anything for her. And that's how I feel about you. All the things I wanted to preserve by leaving Almeria pale in comparison to the contentment I feel right now." He shook his head. "I hadn't experienced that before, and it took me a long time to put a name to it. Love." He offered a dry chuckle. "I want to hold onto it forever."

Stomach quivering with excitement, she settled back against him so he wouldn't read the eagerness on her face. With her ear resting on his chest, his breath sounded like a soothing breeze through an open window, rhythmic and natural. Like home should feel. Safe, free of burdens. As if the last five years hadn't happened.

She could imagine them returning to Valencia or working their way East—but not by sea—side by side. Plenty of cities had both Muslim and Christian populations, and they both had skills to build a life upon. Such a journey would be dangerous, but they now knew those risks and could avoid them. They'd have each other. For the first time, that seemed like enough.

Yasin released a sigh. "But I know that's impossible."

"Impossible?" she asked more sharply than she intended. "Why?"

His muscles shifted, and though she couldn't see his eyes, he must have been looking at her. "Your reasons for staying in the South are the same ones that made me leave Almeria. I refuse to tempt you into abandoning them as my father did to me."

Yes, she had dreamed of returning to Granada to reclaim her old life. That hope had sustained her through her captivity in Barcelona, those long years in Toledo, and that disappointing night in Valencia when she'd finally achieved her lifelong desire. Yet, Almeria and Cartagena were as hollow as the shattered cart on the road to Valencia. She'd dreamed of bright color, laughter, and rhetoric, of song, wit, and *adab*. Instead, she'd found severed arms and terrifying men in indigo veils.

Yasin had confronted his old life only to find it utterly changed. That discovery had reduced him to tears. She dared not imagine returning to Granada only to find it had fallen into the same ruin. A dream could sustain her. Facing the reality of its loss might destroy her.

He twisted and opened some distance to look at her. "Breaking into the library is the biggest risk we've faced yet." She recalled his warning in Valencia. Eventually, luck ran out. "I understand if you'd prefer to stay behind. Draw the symbols, and I'll use them as best as I can to find the right text."

Only her presence had saved him the last time he'd tried to steal the *Book of Healing*. In his eyes, that truth reflected back at her. He would do it. He would risk himself to spare her.

She placed her hand on his cheek. "I gave you my word."

"I can't guarantee we can do this cleanly." He bit his lip. "If someone identifies you, it would cost you the chance to stay here."

Since her father had sold her to the palace, all the beautiful, magnificent things she had desired had been out of reach. Baghdad had dangled them before her, an endless line of promises that were no longer possible. There were no emirs anymore, no one who might reward her skills. Salim's terror that her playing might offend the Almoravids only confirmed that there was no place for her here.

"I've decided not to stay."

His eyes rounded in surprise. She couldn't help but laugh. Of all his many expressions, those that escaped by accident were the most delightful.

Right now, she held the thing she desired most, and she would not let it go. "I'm going back. With you."

He pressed his lips against hers, simply but firmly. He lingered there with eyes closed for a moment. His only movement was a faint twitch of his eye. "Why?" he asked after he pulled back.

She shook her head. "Your sister-in-law may find comfort here, but there's no place for a woman like me. I came searching for a dream, but like Ibn Hazm, I don't recognize it in these streets." She raised her other hand to his cheek. "But I do feel it when we're together."

He swallowed. "You do?"

She leaned forward and brushed her lips over his. "I do. Souls ignite one another, and I burn when I'm with you."

His lips broke into a gentle smile. "That's beautiful."

"It isn't mine," she admitted. "But it's what my heart tells me." She took a long breath. "Though Lord Gonzalo doesn't care about my heart." The Castilian lord's feral glower had terrified her. At the time, it had only made her more eager to escape the clutches of such men. "He's not a man to forgive or forget failure."

Yasin released a weary sigh whose duration proved his stamina as much as his performance last night had. "It always comes back to what others want, doesn't it?"

"Such is the nature of the world. Rarely can we control what happens to us."

He wrapped his arms around her, and she nuzzled into his embrace. "But we can control how we react." Now, his familiar smirk returned, mixed with something feral and wild that set her heart thumping. "So, let's finish this and leave." He kissed her again. "Together."

CHAPTER EIGHTEEN

Yasin

Yasin rummaged through the chests in his family's pantry. Though he'd needed a torch in the unfamiliar passageway in Valencia, its brightness would only expose them in the unoccupied palace. Familiar with Almeria's streets, he'd need only the faintest illumination for this infiltration.

Pushing aside one of the humble clay plates predating his family's newfound prosperity, he found a pair of bronze oil lamps no larger than his palm. A little oil sloshed from within when he shook them. They would serve the needs of larceny well enough.

When he turned, his brother was standing in the doorway.

"When we were young, Mother would check on us with those lamps before she went to bed," Salim said.

Yasin hadn't been able to fall asleep until she had. "I remember."

"I wonder if Aishah will do the same with my children." Though his stare became distant, it maintained an intensity that matched that of their arguments.

Memories of that unexpected, tender moment between his brother and his wife returned. "She loves you."

Salim smiled, albeit faintly. "And I love her. There's nothing I wouldn't do for her."

"I know. It's good that you realize it."

His brother's lips drew tight. "I've worked hard to prove that I've embraced the faith. It hasn't been easy."

"I believe that." These Almoravids hardly seemed like the trusting sort.

"That I continue to employ the Christians who worked for Father, even though they refuse to convert, already casts suspicion on me."

"It's kind of you to take care of his old workers," Yasin offered, hoping to avoid another quarrel.

Salim's next words destroyed that hope. "I know you intend to steal from the old emir's library."

Yasin halted in mid-breath. He forced calm into his voice to stem the rising panic. "Why do you say that?"

"I heard you and Sarah talking this morning."

"You were eavesdropping?" Thank God he hadn't said which text he intended to steal. "Why would you do that?" Even among family, it was a blatant violation of hospitality.

Salim remained damnably calm. "I had to know why you investigated the old palace yesterday."

Yet another thing his brother should not know. "Who says I was investigating anything?"

"I followed you."

Yasin had been so concerned with the Almoravids that he hadn't noticed his brother trailing him. "Then you witnessed me showing Almeria to my wife."

"I've seen you stroll the city and I've seen you stake out a target. I can tell the difference."

Swallowing, he forced himself to mask his growing apprehension. "Why?"

"Did you consider what would happen to us if you were caught?

This is our home. My workshop and customers are here. My wife's family is here."

He grunted. "I thought the Almoravids believed every man was responsible for his own actions."

Salim's head did not move except to blink. "I welcomed you into my home. That alone would implicate me."

Yasin thought of Aishah, laboring in the mornings despite her growing belly. Of his mother, who wore weariness a little more heavily and moved a little more slowly than he remembered. Both of them, and the baby, and their servants, all were in danger. Danger he'd put them in.

"Salim, I'm sorry. I didn't think about that."

The expected anger did not shine in his brother's eyes. Instead, they simply rounded with evident weariness. They warned Yasin well before his brother spoke that Salim had hefted another burden, this time because of him.

"If I thought it would stop you, I would warn the Almoravids to guard against thieves." Salim spoke calmly, with an unexpected maturity. "But we both know you'd only view it as a challenge."

Yasin had squeezed the lamp in his right hand until it threatened to puncture his skin. Salim was probably right; at least he had enough wisdom to realize it and hadn't done anything truly foolish.

"You will leave this house," Salim declared. "Now. I'll make known to my servants, employees, and neighbors that I'll have nothing more to do with you. I won't let you drag us down with your actions."

Swallowing, Yasin loosened his grip. Only the night before, he'd confronted his brother for Sarah's sake. He was willing to confront those veiled devils to buy them a future together, despite the very real memory of a slicing chop in the marketplace that demonstrated Almoravid punishments. How could he now blame Salim for protecting his beloved from the same fate?

"Very well."

He would have to commit their heist tonight, before he needed to find alternative accommodations. Presenting himself as a stranger to a landlord would raise questions and attract attention. His countrymen had lived under Almoravid rule far too long for him to trust them. Every set of eyes could belong to collaborators willing to inform on their neighbors.

Success in theft relied on predictability and the reduction of risk, two things he now lacked. Without the time to learn the guards' patterns, he'd need to rely on luck, and luck eventually ran out.

Sarah. She had insisted *adab* lay within him. For the first time, he could feel it blooming within his chest, filling him with an unfamiliar strength.

He was done running. He would test whether this *adab* of Sarah's poems existed. Too many futures depended on finding that dusty tome lying somewhere within a dilapidated palace for him to quit now.

SARAH

Yasin's dented bronze oil lamp bobbed up and down far too slowly for Sarah's tastes as he guided her through the streets of Almeria. The dull halo of light announced their presence to the hidden eyes Sarah was certain lurked within the darkness beyond. She hadn't felt this exposed since her teachers tested her mastery all those years ago. She hadn't enjoyed their scrutiny then, and she hated it now.

"We have no secret tunnel here, so we have to act naturally," he had explained as he stowed Sarah's empty satchel beneath his *jubba* before leaving Salim's home. "Stay calm and relaxed, and people won't notice us, even if they see us."

Yasin moved as casually as when they'd walked through the fields of La Mancha, but such forced ease didn't come as easily to her. Her legs itched to speed ahead, and she kept crowding too close to him before willing herself to slow.

The black-on-shadow outline of a face flashed in the uncovered window above a storefront, but when Sarah blinked, it vanished. The brief glimpse set her heart hammering. They had to succeed tonight. She could not do this a third time.

They had been walking some time, through streets she didn't recognize. "Where are we?" She clutched Yasin's arm tighter.

"We're approaching the old palace from the other end of the avenue so we needn't pass the gate."

If this burglary ended with Yasin unconscious again, she'd never find her way back to Salim's house. Nor did she have Hisham to carry him. "What about the tower guards?"

He grinned. "Trust me."

A shuffling rasp echoed off the buildings. She whirled, expecting an approaching Almoravid patrol but seeing nothing in the shadowed crannies and nooks between buildings.

She jumped at a hand on her wrist.

Yasin held her from recoiling with both hands on her shoulders. "It's okay." He nodded over her shoulder. "Look."

A shaggy dog trotted down the street carrying something in its mouth.

She tried to keep her hand from shaking as she patted Yasin's wrist. "I'm fine."

He lifted the lamp higher so he could meet her eyes. "Once we turn the bend, the tower guards will see us. They must judge us unworthy of their attention."

"I understand." She couldn't afford to jump at a strange sound, not in the protective presence of her supposed husband. "I won't let you down."

He raised his free hand to cup her cheek. "That was never a question." His voice carried a quiet sincerity. "But that's not what I meant." He pulled her shawl forward to drape over her forehead, then tucked a stray lock of her hair beneath it. His fingers trembled as they touched her skin.

He was frightened, too.

"He needs to believe you're ordinary. One look at your beauty and he'll never forget you."

A blush warmed her cheeks. Men had complimented her in the past, but the tenderness of Yasin's voice., stirred her as never before. The words themselves didn't even matter. In fact, she delighted in his spontaneous comment more than the most romantic of Baghdadi poems. "Yasin…"

His eyes brightened. He looked lovely when he smiled. "I've wanted to say that for a long time."

"And you choose now to do it?"

His eyes danced. "No better time." He offered her his arm.

She grasped it but resisted when he started to pull away. "When you saw the palace gardens…" She had no desire to make him regret revealing his feelings, yet neither could she ignore her concerns. "Can you control your reaction?"

Though he did not meet her eyes, when he smiled, his face contained neither injury nor regret. "I was unprepared last time." Though he continued to stare ahead seemingly without moving, strength flowed into the angles of his face. The transformation mesmerized her. "Much has changed. I'm stronger now."

If the memory troubled him, it didn't make his voice waver or the lamp shake in his hand. Fears dispelling, she squeezed his arm, and he led her onto the wide avenue.

The torches set along the palace walls punctured the darkness like lighthouses, reaching all the way to the *tapia* buildings across the avenue. The streets were empty except for two guards in *tagelmusts* and bundled cloaks, standing in the torchlight by the archway in the walls.

Yasin led her across the avenue and toward the closest tower. Shifting shadows atop it resolved into the shape of a man.

"Easy," Yasin muttered as they continued walking.

Realizing she was clenching his arm, she forced herself to relax.

Three buildings away, Sarah peeked out from beneath the edge of her shawl at the figure in the tower. He had turned and was looking in their direction. She lowered her head, letting the shawl drape over her vision to conceal her face. She could only see her feet and the space immediately before her.

This was it. This guard studied people all day long. He would see past their feigned ease and recognize her and Yasin's true intentions.

Two buildings away from the wall, she peeked again to find the guard still studying them. As she lowered her head, her hair shifted beneath her shawl and began to slide forward.

She sucked in a breath. "It's falling," she whispered as softly as she could. Another building slipped by. They were getting close.

Instead of a reply, Yasin swapped the lamp to his other hand, away from her. Her hair fell free a moment later. It grazed the side of her chin, tickling her skin, but the light of the lamp didn't illuminate it. Yasin's body now obstructed its light and concealed her in shadow.

Clever man!

"He's turning," Yasin murmured.

She risked a look. The tower guard had turned away, and the torches near the archway below illuminated the deep indigo of his *tagelmust*. The presence of that complicated head covering delighted her; all those folds would blind him to anything to the side. Allah bless the pride that induced those nomads to wear such heavy garments so far from desert storms!

The sidewalk gave way to the lowered cobbles of the alley running along the palace walls. Yasin leaned into her, driving her to the right. A few steps into the alley, he pressed her against the outside of the palace wall beneath the tower. With a quick puff, he extinguished the lamp, leaving them in a darkness broken only by the crescent moon.

Yasin studied the top of the tower for several long moments, but no head poked out to search for them. Turning back to her, he pointed toward the sewer opening.

Sarah grasped a fistful of his *jubba* and crept behind him. In the darkness, she couldn't tell a safe footfall from the hole of a cracked cobble. Gritting her teeth, she picked her way one tentative step at a time. Turning her ankle would provoke a cry or a stagger. Both could expose them.

Yasin stopped abruptly at a scraping sound ahead. His *jubba* slackened, and Sarah halted in mid-stride with surprising responsiveness. A flush of pride warmed her cheeks at her self-control in not gasping. She could do this!

She listened, motionless, for some time. Howling dogs and chirping insects blended into an indistinct drone. The scraping, though, didn't repeat, and the *jubba* before her began to advance again.

Swallowing, she reassessed her opinions about burglary. In Valencia, she had feared the guards, but their true enemy was noise.

They reached the opening to the ancient Roman sewer several heartbeats later. The apex of the arch reached Yasin's waist. Sarah bent down to peer through the semi-circular tube that traveled through the wall into the palace courtyard.

Beside her, Yasin sighed and rolled up his *jubba*, bunching it at his waist. She frowned. "Yasin, your clothes…"

He glanced down. After a moment, a faint smile crawled across his face. "There are more important things than wrinkles."

Her mouth fell open in the darkness. He truly had changed.

With a quick nod, he crouched. His boot ground sediment into the cobbles with a sound like thunder. She drew in a breath.

He met her eyes and offered a tight grimace before entering the aperture. Despite its having been a sewer in the past, Sarah smelled only mustiness and decay, but it was strong enough that she bundled fistfuls of her *qamisa* to prevent it from dragging in the filth. Absorbing such an odor would render it impossible to hide from any guards within the walls.

After a few steps, her shawl caught on something hanging from the ceiling and pulled free. When she turned to retrieve it, her hair snagged on something, too. Biting back a cry, she worked it free while trying not to imagine what oozing or crawling things might now be in it.

Shawl draped awkwardly, she forced herself to keep moving. *Allah, be merciful.* She had seen enough dank tunnels, moldy passageways, and dark nights for a lifetime.

It was over quickly, though, and they reached the courtyard. She ran her hand through her hair, checking for debris but finding none. Exhaling, she shook out her shawl and looked around.

Shaggy olive and fruit trees clawed haphazardly toward the sky. Thin shafts of faint moonlight pierced the uneven canopies, dotting the ground like the first drops of a spring shower. Leaves littered the ground, and weeds sprung up within the crushed shell path encircling the interior of the walls. Rotten fruit sat in brown, gooey piles throughout the garden. With no emir to demand delicacies, no one had harvested it.

That overgrown path filled her with sorrow. In Granada, whole teams of servants would curate such walkways. Sarah had considered their work demeaning until the *agha* explained that they honored Allah with their labors. The servants here had probably thought the same. She prayed they weren't aware of its sad state now.

So many things had fallen into neglect these last few years.

Sarah searched for the towers, but overgrowth obscured her view. If she couldn't see the tower guards, silhouetted in the moonlight, they assuredly wouldn't see her and Yasin scampering beneath these shadowed trees.

"You were right," she whispered.

Yasin pressed a finger to his lips and stared ahead.

Chastened, Sarah fell silent. Patrols could be anywhere. Yet, she neither saw nor heard any Almoravids. In fact, they had confronted only fears, not dangers, thus far. Perhaps Yasin was right and no one in this city cared about a Persian's musings. *Inshallah*, the *Book of Healing* might be entirely unguarded.

He stirred after a few moments of silent listening. "Let's go. Stay off the shells if you can."

Yasin guided her down one row of trees and up another, halting at intersections only long enough to verify the next corner was empty. The certainty of his movement proved he had, indeed, explored these gardens as a boy.

Wild growth and ruined lines marred the orderly design that

would have dazzled Yasin in his youth. The gardens of paradise, it was said, ran straight, symmetrical and obedient to the creator's will. Hints of that order remained in this expanse. A skilled hand had evenly spaced each tree so their branches formed an unbroken canopy when fully grown. With a little pruning, the shrubs framing each expanse of grass and separate grove would run straight. She imagined the trickle of fresh water filling the dried irrigation channels running like a lattice along the pathways. Once, it must have been a breathtaking display of greenery, white-shelled paths, and clear water, variegated by bursts of colorful flowers and swirling with the scents of ripe fruit. It would have been an Eden on earth and a stolen wonder to the son of a Christian leatherworker.

No wonder the sight of its current state had moved him so deeply. She reached for his hand.

He turned with wide eyes. "Did you hear something?"

Of course, he had faced all these thoughts the day before. Tonight, he was a thief, focused on the moment and the dangers lurking behind every corner.

"No. Let's keep moving."

The palace stood in the center of the garden, rising above a row of pomegranate trees that obscured its base. Its blind arches, external arcades, and ornate columns resembled the palace in Valencia. She supposed that made sense; the same architects would have constructed them during the Caliphate. This palace, however, had no mosaics, banners, or topiaries.

Crossing behind a hedge row taller than Yasin, they crept toward light pouring into the path from the nearest intersection, one step at a time to muffle their footsteps on the crushed shells. At the end of the row, Yasin brushed aside the branches of the hedge to peer through. As Sarah did the same, they tangled on the sleeves of her *qamisa* and dragged over her hands and wrists.

Four men in indigo *tagelmusts* and cloaks stood before the large limestone columns flanking the entrance.

Sarah pulled back too quickly and scraped her wrist on a branch. She rubbed at the shallow wound. "What do we do?" She more mouthed the words than whispered them.

He withdrew his hands and stared at the shell path. "I didn't expect four," he breathed. "Two, I could lure away by throwing a rock or setting a fire."

She bit her lip. "How do we sneak past?"

Yasin's narrowed eyes searched up and down the path. His chest rose and fell with quick breaths. In all their time together, he'd never shown such reserve. The change frightened her.

All at once, the tension drained from his face. Even his breathing returned to normal. "We can't."

"We can't give up." After all they'd gone through, there had to be a way.

"We aren't." The eyes that met hers shone with certainty. "We're going to walk up to them and ask for what we want."

She searched for some indication he'd gone mad in the past few moments. Perhaps his mind had unraveled while traveling though this garden if simply seeing it had brought tears to his eyes. "Why would they give it to us?"

"Because while burglary has gotten us into trouble, deception has served us both well."

She drew in a shaking breath and reflected on all their lies these past weeks. They had been practicing for this moment without knowing it. "You'll pretend you're one of them."

He nodded.

The possibility tantalized her, both for its audacity and its danger. "It's a risk."

"Every choice is a risk. Without the *Healing*, I'm bound for prison and you to servitude. I'd rather risk capture now than live as a fugitive the rest of my days."

Adab. It blazed like the flames of a campfire within his eyes. Such bold decisions sounded glorious in her poems, when she knew how they turned out. Now, facing the vast uncertainty of the future terrified her.

She rubbed her shoulders. "I'm afraid."

He squeezed her hands. "As am I. But God brought us together and prepared us for this chance."

His was an unconventional theology. "That's not how Allah works."

He shrugged. "In a world that shatters the *taifas* and allows good people to die, perhaps lies are legitimate weapons of the righteous." He pulled her hand toward him and kissed the back of her palm. "Will you take this risk with me?"

She remembered the open sky, the sweet flowers, and the fresh breeze of La Mancha. The excitement of exploring Valencia without anyone objecting. Every moment of her time with Yasin…not just their lovemaking but all the conversations and peeks into his heart. If she returned to Toledo empty-handed, she would never again experience any of it. Lord Gonzalo's offer was her only chance.

"I'm with you."

They stepped out onto the crushed shell walkway. Yasin led her between the tall torches with an even, confident stride and his head held high, so unlike their creeping passage through the garden.

The Almoravids noticed them immediately. One who had been sitting on a step rose, while another approached with his hand on the sword hilt at his hip.

Yasin pressed his fingers to his lips, then his forehead. "Peace be upon you," he began in flawless Andalusi Arabic.

Sarah clasped her hands before her so tightly that her knuckles ached.

Eyes narrow, the closest guard halted two strides from him. "And upon you, be peace." He spoke with the heavy inflection of the desert. When he shifted his attention to Sarah, she lowered her head in a show of humility. "Turn around and leave. You have no business here."

"In fact, I do," Yasin countered. "We've received a warning about thieves targeting this palace. I have instructions to secure certain codices from the collection against theft."

Sarah raised her gaze again. He was holding his chin up, staring down the weathered eyes poking out of the blue garment.

The Almoravid shifted his weight. "Why the middle of the night?"

"Others will remove the rest tomorrow, but certain items are too important to risk delay."

"Too important?" Another guard approached. "Why now, after all these years?"

Sarah's gaze settled on the blade of the guard's sword, glinting in the torchlight. Those men could do more than sever hands with those weapons.

Yasin shrugged. "I merely obey the instructions of my betters."

With a satisfied grunt, the newcomer returned to his seat.

The first Almoravid relaxed but still gripped his hilt. "Why would the governor trust an *Andalusi*?" He sneered the word as if he'd meant to add *dog* after it.

Yasin bowed at the neck. "I served in the library prior to our city's liberation and can identify the proper text."

"And this one?" He pointed at Sarah.

He was asking too many questions. Skepticism dripped from his words. If they had to flee, she would run for the sewer grate and hope her shorter stature let her pass more quickly while they struggled to crouch.

Yasin flipped a hand in casual dismissal. "A slave to carry the texts."

He spoke the words with a sincerity she would have believed were she not still moved by his vulnerability the night before. Not only were those words designed to please the hated Almoravids, but he spoke them with conviction. He, who had fled this city rather than submit, sounded like the most loyal of collaborators. And now, he had dismissed his feelings with a casual wave. She couldn't begin to imagine the pain his performance was causing him.

The Almoravid extended a hand. "Show me your orders."

The two remaining guards rose and advanced. One circled to the side. If he continued on that course, he'd cut off her escape.

She fell utterly still, restraining her bubbling terror. This desert guard had seen through their ruse. Allah had led them to the slaughter.

"Certainly." Opening his *jubba*, Yasin withdrew and presented a folded piece of paper. The seal on the outside identified it as his precious pardon.

He had gone mad. Did he expect the Almoravid not to look at it? He would see the language of the script, recognize the seal as belonging to King Alfonso, or simply read the contents. Their blood would mix with the rotting fruit to nourish the weeds sprouting amid the crushed shells.

The Almoravid carefully unfolded the document, one flap at a time, as if it were the Quran itself. Once open, he shifted a step closer to the torch and angled it to catch the light. The man's eyes, peeking out from beneath his indigo veil, raced over the sheet, first from the right to the left, then in the other direction.

She held her breath.

Hands folded before him, Yasin released a slow sigh and let his gaze wander with a natural ease that made her want to scream. How could he lounge at the threshold of doom?

All at once, she understood. He was no addled fool. He simply behaved as if he had every right in *Dar al-Islam* to be here, demanding access to a library so he might plunder it. He played his role with such devotion that he'd fooled even her.

The Almoravid thrust the pardon back toward Yasin quickly enough that it flapped in the breeze of the gesture. Yasin accepted it as the guard waved one of his companions over. "My man here will help."

It had worked!

Yasin shook his head. "No. Your men must ensure that this thief doesn't succeed."

The Almoravid snorted. "Who cares if he does? There's nothing valuable here."

"True, but it all belongs to the Empire."

The man tilted his head to indicate his companions. "Three men are enough to prevent that."

"I'm sure they are." Yasin raised his chin. "But if not, I'd lose my head for pulling them off their watch, and I won't risk that."

Scowling, the man waved a hand. "Be damned, then. Do your business and get out."

Yasin glanced over his shoulder. "Come, girl." He refolded and stowed the pardon within his *jubba* and strode forward.

None of the Almoravids followed to help with the entrance, so Yasin pulled on the heavy wooden doors until they swung open. Stepping inside, he struck a flint to light his lamp. Once the glow had grown enough, he closed the doors again.

Sarah drew in a ragged, shaking breath, but Yasin pressed his finger to his lips and beckoned her forward. Their footsteps echoed off the stone walls of the abandoned corridors. Sarah jogged to keep up. Giddiness swirled as each step took her further from the Almoravids beyond that door.

Only when they had entered the library and closed the door behind them did he release a long sigh. "I was masterful." He broke into an all-encompassing grin.

She couldn't deny that assessment. "When you handed him your pardon, I thought they would kill us right there."

"Fortune favors the bold."

"How did you know he couldn't read?"

Yasin's hand shook as he ran it through his hair. He had been afraid. Had he felt such fear during every lie and theft?

"The Almoravid at the port couldn't. Very few in this world have your education, my darling. If I, a master leatherworker, never learned, why should a desert warrior?"

"But you didn't know. You took a chance."

He nodded. "Every decision in life—"

"—involves risk," she finished.

He leaned forward to kiss the top of her head. "Thank you."

It banished the knot in the pit of her stomach. "For what?"

"For convincing me I had *adab*. I couldn't have done what I did back there without your reassurance."

"Yasin…"

"But we're only half-done." He lowered his hands and looked past her. "Can you find the *Book of Healing* in this mess?"

Hundreds of years of binding techniques sat side-by-side on bookshelves in the center of the room. A Persian wooden-bound text sat against a smaller, dark brown leather codex, followed by another with gold leaf inlaid in the grooves in its supple leather spine. Dozens of even older scrolls stuck out of wide, glazed clay pots at the end of each bookshelf. Scroll racks with slotted rows lined the walls. Some slots simply contained curled paper, while other texts had wooden or cork cores that extended beyond the parchment and vellum. A scant few even had silver or bronze handles extending outward. Nearly every slot was filled.

She pressed a hand to her mouth. A hundred years wouldn't be enough to read everything. The garden surrounding this palace may have been a paradise to a young Yasin, but this library was hers.

Her senses disagreed, though. The back of her throat felt dry from the dust hanging on the air. A substantial layer clung to the tops of each scroll and codex. Already, discoloration and curling indicated degradation from inattention. The moisture and unmistakable taint of mold clung to the insides of her nostrils. A water stain oozing down the wall from the far corner nearly broke Sarah's heart.

Wonder yielded to outrage. How could these Almoravids allow such treasures to disintegrate? Even the Christians in Toledo valued such compositions enough that they risked the condemnation of heresy rather than let these ideas be lost.

"The guards will expect us to return quickly."

She nodded absently. She now appreciated Yasin's pain. She couldn't save everything endangered by the fall of the *taifas*. She had a task to finish.

Her footsteps kicked up tufts of dust as she shuffled from the first bookshelf of exclusively religious texts to the next containing studies on magic, botany, and medicine. Their organization—first by format, then by topic—offered no help. The *Healing* discussed every possible topic and could be in any of these collections.

But, it would be large. Shifting tactics, she stopped reading each title and instead searched for several codices with the same binding. No work was as large as the *Healing*.

She took the oil lamp from Yasin and worked her way up one row and down another, taking in huge swaths of shelves at once. Yet each bookshelf she searched, she found no more than one or two adjacent texts with the same appearance.

Not until she began searching along the perimeter did she discover the wide pedestal along the back wall, positioned between two scroll racks. On it sat nearly two dozen codices arrayed in a neat row, varying only in thickness. Each bore the same glossy, dark brown leather cover with lines of inlaid gold filigree crisscrossing the spines. Each bore Ibn Sina's name and its title, *Kitāb al-Shifā*, in Arabic. *The Book of Healing*.

She drew in a shaky breath. "That's it." Her voice came out as a whisper.

It had taken months of journeying by land and sea. They had dodged death more than once, while others hadn't been as fortunate. All the maddening waiting, struggle, and turmoil had finally paid off. Allah be praised, they were finally here, standing before the object of all their toils.

She reached a shaking hand out for the closest codex.

"Wait!" Yasin shot his hand out to catch hers. "Check for poison."

Her pulse thumped in her neck. He was right, of course. Though the fine detail and weathering of the spines suggested these texts were authentic, she suspected the Almoravids wouldn't hesitate to ruin such a treasure to kill thieves.

Lifting the hem of her *qamisa*, she rubbed it along the spine.

Though it left a smear of dust, it remained dry. Relief flowed through her. "It's safe."

Sarah wiped her sweating fingers on her *qamisa* before lifting the first codex. The textured leather felt smooth beneath her fingers. She struggled to withdraw it from the stack and pulled harder. A grinding sound like sand beneath a boot made her wince. She'd probably damaged this volume and one beside it.

When it came free, she nearly dropped it, for it was surprisingly heavy. The inlaid filigree on the spine extended onto the cover, forming trees at the corners, all connected with the same gold leaf. For a moment, she simply held it and rested her other hand on the cover.

Yasin ran his fingers along the spine. "Mmm. Full-grain, and very high quality. This would have cost a fortune."

"It's a treasure." She traced the filigree. Still tight and secure, it showed no flaking. "All the finest ideas of the ancient world, distilled into a single great compendium of knowledge." She released a nervous chuckle.

"It's a wonder."

"Do you think so?"

"It must be, to move you so deeply." With a loud inhalation, he reached into his *jubba* and withdrew the satchel. "Let's steal it."

The codex she'd chosen was part of Ibn Sina's *Mathematics*. Setting it on the edge of the pedestal, she searched through the various volumes on physics, philosophy, and logic before finally finding one on metaphysics and stuffing it into her satchel. She searched the other codices until she found the remaining three that composed the *Metaphysics*.

Yasin pulled the sides of the satchel up over their plunder, but Sarah lingered on the remaining volumes. "I wish we could take them all."

Yasin rested a hand on her shoulder. "This satchel already carries two lives, and we have a long way to go before we can claim them."

"I know." With a sigh, she tore herself away. "How do we get out?"

"The same way we came in." Hoisting the satchel over his shoulder, he gestured for her to lead with the lamp.

Sarah strode between the nearest two bookshelves toward the door. After passing the second stack, she glimpsed *Elements of Geometry* written on a thin suede cover unworthy to house Euclid's fine treatise. Beside it sat a hard leather-bound copy of Ptolemy's *Almagest*. The last time she'd seen that text, two translators had been grieving over its incompleteness.

She came to a halt so quickly that Yasin collided with her.

"Sarah!"

She fumbled with the lamp before grasping it tightly again. "I'm sorry," she said between inhalations to ease the surge of blood through her veins. She pointed to the *Almagest*. "The translation school only has a partial copy of that book."

"They'll pay for it?"

"Certainly."

Yasin grinned and turned. "If they're not too heavy, stuff a few inside. Better we take them than let them molder."

She scoured the codices, selecting a few of the lighter ones and adding them to the satchel. "So many… It's hard to choose."

"The lament of every thief."

"It appears you were right after all."

"That's true in so many ways." He adjusted the distribution of weight in the satchel. "To which were you referring?"

She placed a kiss on his cheek. "You did turn me into a proper criminal."

CHAPTER NINETEEN

Yasin

Yasin returned for Sarah at first light after spending a restless night in the familiar alleys of his old neighborhood. He would have preferred a few hours of sleep before the impending journey, but he'd needed to keep moving to evade Almoravid patrols.

Mollifying Salim's servants with a pledge to depart after retrieving the rest of his possessions, he went to Sarah's room. She was kneeling on the floor, stroking a volume from the *Metaphysics*, when he entered. She glanced up, reddening with embarrassment. The circles beneath her eyes suggested she'd had a long night, too.

"I can't believe it." She shook her head. "We actually did it."

His smile came easily. It felt good to smile after a fitful night spent listening for approaching guards. "It took both of us."

"Then you're glad you brought me along?" Her teasing smile brightened her eyes.

"For many reasons." She had helped him heal from all he'd lost, helped him to look beyond the resentment and anger that had kept him from moving forward. In her, he had found both the pleasures he'd wanted to preserve and a reason to sacrifice them all.

"You're just saying that because I slept with you."

"Sarah!"

She laughed, a sweet sound that floated high and delighted his ears. He held onto the sound until the final echo had faded. He would never grow tired of that laugh, but only if they finished this commission. They still had to escape with their plunder.

"Are we ready?"

Sobering, she gave a curt nod.

Once more, Yasin check the contents of his *jubba*: the pardon, the toolkit, and the remnant of the satchel he'd brought from Almeria the first time. He rubbed that scrap between his fingers. It felt as soft as ever, but the fraying threads now dangled freely, catching on his toolkit.

He set the scrap on the bed. He'd clung to the echo of a lost life for so long. For the first time, he could see a future filled with joy and contentment. This scrap was his past, not his future. It belonged here.

Sarah followed him into the hall. Though he tried to move quietly, he struggled under the weight of his baggage. Once they reached the common room, Yasin set the sack down to adjust the satchel.

His mother emerged from the pantry, wiping her hands on her apron, and halted when she noticed him.

At least he could say a proper goodbye this time.

Her eyebrows pinched together as she studied their bags. "You're leaving."

"Mother—"

She crossed the distance and clutched his forearms. "Don't let an argument with your brother drive you away again."

He maneuvered a hand around her grip and laid it against her cheek. "It isn't Salim, Mother."

"What other explanation is there? You only just came back, and now you're off again."

She deserved an answer, but the truth would only endanger her if the Almoravids started asking questions.

"There's no place for me here. Salim and Father may be content with what Almeria has become, but everywhere I look, I see what we've lost." Almeria ceased to be his home when he'd knelt on the cobbles before the ruin of that garden. He stepped forward. "Why not come with me? What kept you here is gone."

She shook her head. "I still have important work here with Aishah and the baby. They'll need my experience." Her lips curled into a sad smile. "Faraj may be gone, but I still support the future he wanted."

"How can you say that?" He shook his head. "He took your faith from you as much as me."

"Oh, Yasin, Faraj never took anything from me." Her eyes softened as her lips bent into a sad frown. "Do you imagine he would make such a decision without consulting his wife?"

Beside him, Sarah drew in a breath.

He swallowed a lump the size of a peach pit. All these years, he had regretted abandoning his poor mother to his father's tyranny. "You both agreed."

"You had the luxury of leaving. You could ply your skills anywhere. But we had family, friends, and a reputation built over years. Starting over would have been too difficult at your father's age." She folded her hands before her. "You feared for the future of our city. I worried about our family's future. You weren't thinking about marriage yet, but Salim was. Leaving would have ruined those prospects. I wanted prosperous lives for you all." She stretched her neck and straightened. "If you wish to judge me for that, then so be it."

Sarah sidled up to him and took his hand in her hers. Strength and stability flowed into him.

Years ago, his mother and pleaded with Yasin to consider Faraj's arguments, but those arguments had been hers, too. She had simply respected her husband enough to let him voice them. She'd chosen to serve the interests of her husband and her family. At least she had chosen freely. That was more courtesy than his father had accorded him.

He had dwelled in anger and resentment long after they'd ceased to be useful. Faraj was dead and Yasin had resisted the tyranny that had demanded his conversion. Indulging further in his loss would only weigh him down. It was time to lay it aside.

Crossing to her, he pressed his lips against the top of her head. "Thank you for everything you've done for me."

Elvira leaned her head against her son's chest and began to sob. The gentle whimper of her tears squeezed his heart. He could only imagine how difficult losing a son for a second time must be for her, but he had no choice.

When she stood apart again, she wore a forced smile. Pulling him down with hands on his cheeks, she rose on her tiptoes and kissed his forehead.

This was the better way to say goodbye.

Elvira looked past him, toward Sarah. "Keep him safe. He gets into the worst sort of trouble."

Sarah bowed her head. "I will."

The solemnity of those two words and the sincerity in her eyes wrapped Yasin in warm comfort. They were a pledge, not an empty response to ease his mother's mind. Honoring it would require that they remain together. What need did he have of home or country with Sarah at his side?

Elvira drew a long breath. "Then I wish you a safe journey."

"You're leaving Almeria, then?" Salim had arrived and was leaning against the door frame, watching them with a pinched expression.

Releasing his mother, Yasin crossed to the doorway. As he did, Salim straightened, as if expecting trouble.

But Yasin merely extended his hand. "I wish you and your young family continued fortune."

Frowning, Salim eyed the hand for a moment before clasping Yasin's forearm. "Thank you."

"I'd tell you to keep Mother safe, but you've been doing that for three years."

Salim broke the contact. "As she said, safe journeys."

Before his mouth could ruin this tranquil parting, Yasin retrieved the bags and slung them over his shoulder.

Sarah offered a reassuring smile.

Amira emerged from the corridor, wearing a traveling cloak and a maroon shawl over her head. The strap of a satchel ran diagonally across her chest. That attire could have only one purpose.

His sister raised her chin and cleared her throat. "I'm going with them."

Silence descended for a few long breaths, during which Yasin's heart hammered in his chest. Now, he understood why she'd asked about Toledo.

"Amira, why?" The cry tore from his mother's throat as she closed the distance and clasped her daughter's hands. "This is your home."

"Haven't I kept you safe all these years?" Salim's words resembled an accusation.

"You have. And I thank you for that." She sighed. "But this life isn't what I want."

"What do you think you'll find out there?" Salim stabbed a finger toward Yasin. "What can he offer you that I can't?"

Amira raised her chin. "The life we all wanted when we talked about leaving. Perhaps conversion improved your future, Salim, but not mine. At least under the *taifas*, we could live as *dhimmis* and keep our ways. But now, if I try, I'll be flogged or killed. I'm wasting away in this house."

Elvira shook her head. "This decision is too important to make rashly."

"It's hardly rash. I let Father talk me out of it three years ago and regretted it ever since. Now, I have a chance to break free." She squared to Salim and leveled a stare. "Will you deny me my right to choose how I live my life?"

"Yasin, you cannot take her from me," his mother begged.

He shifted his gaze from his mother to his sister. Both sets of eyes contained silent pleas.

"I command no one but myself. If she understands the risk, I'll honor her decision."

"I forbid it!" Salim thundered.

"Now, I hear Father again." Yasin no longer cared about a pleasant parting, not if it meant acquiescing to another tyrant. "You sound like an Almoravid, dictating how everyone else should live."

"This was your intention all along." Salim glared at him. "You came to steal our sister away in order to spite me."

"This has nothing to do with you. It's her choice, not mine and not yours."

"I'm the head of this family!"

"You are head of this family, Salim. You've inherited both Father's spirit and all his worldly goods." Amira took a step toward him. "But my soul is not yours to command. In my heart, I know I should have left three years ago."

"I won't let this happen." Salim stormed over and reached for her sack.

Yasin charged forward. Clamping down on Salim's wrist, he slammed his shoulder into his brother's, knocking him to the ground. Salim flung a hand down to avoid falling but succeeded only in pushing himself further away and colliding with the hard *tapia* wall.

Amira used the distraction to cross to Sarah, who stepped protectively between her and her brother.

Salim raised a hand to his head where he'd struck the wall. Thankfully, it came back free of blood. Yasin hadn't meant harm, only to free Amira.

His brother's glare suggested the distinction mattered little. "You'll regret this, Yasin!"

Seeing his mother's fresh tears, he already did. Yasin crossed to her and kissed her cheek. He didn't doubt it was the last kiss he'd ever give her or the last time he'd lay eyes upon her. Despite what she'd revealed today, he still loved her. He wiped his eyes so he could etch every slope and curve of her face into his memory without the distortion of his tears.

Hand in hand with Sarah and beside his sister, he departed, leaving behind all the burdens and struggles that had clouded the previous three years.

YASIN

Yasin, Sarah, and Amira rode north over the gentle foothills of the Montes de Toledo at a conservative pace. He'd purchased discount horses at the outskirts of Almeria, and he didn't want to exhaust them in the wilderness. He doubted he'd stumble upon another horse as on the road to Valencia. Nor did he wish to: that would indicate nearby raiders.

Though Amira and Sarah both pleaded to sleep in nearby settlements, Yasin hesitated to leave witnesses to their passage. He instead chose a nestled valley between the many gentle hills for their camp that first night. It provided little comfort, but it had water and concealed them from passing travelers. Though al-Andalus had no *fuero* militias to torment travelers, both Almoravids and Christian horsemen prowled these hills for easy victims. His experience since leaving Toledo had taught him caution.

Amira and Sarah didn't grumble, but they wore sour expressions while erecting the tent. Only when he saw them massaging their thighs did he realize they were sore from riding, like him. None of them had much experience with horses.

They spoke little and slept well that first night. In the morning, the horses seemed cheerful and ate heartily, so Yasin risked a longer ride. The Almoravid guards would have assuredly reported their late-night visitors, and he wanted to put as much distance between their superiors' anger and his party of criminals as possible.

Spirits seemed to improve throughout the day. Yasin recounted his activities over the past three years to his sister, and she listened as eagerly as when they'd been children. He spared no detail. She took news of their thieving intentions in Almeria well. After all, they had succeeded and the danger was past. If she raised an eyebrow at his brief stint in prison, she recovered and hung on Sarah's every word about El Cid and Jimena Diaz. Only news of his poisoning disturbed her. Too late, he remembered that despite his youthful indiscretions, he'd never suffered more than a sore bottom. Prisons and poisons were entirely different matters.

On the second day out of Almeria, they camped in a valley with a good, fast stream. Though the mountains on either side were shallow, bushy trees growing along the water shielded them from unfriendly eyes.

After erecting the tent and distributing some food, Yasin retreated further downstream to attend to certain necessities. Sarah and Amira were huddling around one of their stolen texts when he returned.

"*In our immersion in this world and our vices,*" Sarah read from the codex in her hands, "*we do not sense the higher pleasure of wisdom unless, by God's grace, we have cast off the noose of appetite, anger, and their sister vices.*"

Those words, penned a century earlier by a Persian, echoed his argument with Salim. He had needed both the refinements that enriched life and the necessities that sustained it. Yasin had lost a reason to drive onward, something worth striving to build and nurture. Only now, freed from his resentment, could he appreciate that.

"Why did he call his work *The Book of Healing*?" Amira asked. "It doesn't say much about curing wounds."

Yasin settled across from them, hands clasped around his knees. How wrong she was!

Sarah rested the codex in her lap. "Ibn Sina believed knowledge could cure the world's ills, that if mankind simply studied the wonder of Allah's creation long enough, we could rise above our weaknesses and sin."

Amira picked at a piece of grass. "Do you think that's true?"

Sarah brushed her fingers over the cover. "For a long time, I believed I could find everything worth knowing in scrolls and codices. I used to believe pure knowledge was enough."

"And now?" Yasin prompted.

She met his gaze. "Knowledge is a start, but the world is more complex than I thought." She bit at her lip. "I wouldn't have learned that without this journey."

She had taught him what lay within, and he had shown her a world beyond her texts. The symmetry proved the hand of the divine.

"I've dreamed of leaving Almeria for so long, but now that I'm here in the wilderness…" Amira bit her lip. "I'm afraid."

"I won't let anything happen to you," Yasin assured.

"He made me the same promise," Sarah agreed, "and he kept it. He even safeguarded me at the risk of his own life."

Yasin swallowed. He remembered little about their escape from the palace in Valencia, but he did remember telling her to leave him.

Sarah squeezed Amira's hand. "There are dangers beyond the city walls, but also beautiful sunsets of every color over seas of grass and truths about the world hidden far from the strict order of the great cities." She rested her gaze on Yasin again and formed an easy grin. "Some things that at first appeared wicked are, in fact, quite beautiful."

His breath caught. She wasn't speaking about La Mancha or Valencia. If Amira had not been present, he would have taken her in his arms and made love to her. He hungered for the soft tenderness of her skin against his, for the tickling cascade of her hair on his flesh. If he lost himself in her embrace for eternity, he would deem it a worthy fate.

She had touched his heart, healed it of his pain, and chosen to hold it close to her own. Any joy that didn't include Sarah would be hollow. Any pleasure she didn't share would leave him unsatisfied.

"What will you do with them now?" Amira gestured to the volume in Sarah's hands.

Cheeks reddening, Sarah stirred and clenched the codex. "We'll deliver to the man in Toledo who hired us. Lord Gonzalo Martinez."

"And we'll get our reward," Yasin added. "Within the week, we'll reach Martyr's Pass and enter the old *taifa* of Toledo."

Amira winced. "An unsettling name."

"During the Caliphate, Muslim soldiers would use that pass to join the army in Cordoba," Sarah explained. "Some never returned."

"And after that?" Amira asked. "When it's all done, what will you do?"

"*Inshallah*, I'll be free." Sarah shifted, and the codex settled into a depression in her dress.

"I'll be at your side," Yasin assured.

"Celebrating a lost world like Ibn Hazm?" Sarah asked with a smile.

Yasin, though, shook his head. "Celebrating a world regained."

Sarah's expression softened into a smile. "I like that."

Amira turned to Yasin. "And you, brother? What will you do, other than keep Sarah company?" Her lips dimpled into a grin.

He leaned back, resting his palms on the ground behind him. "I'll open my own workshop and show these Castilians how a Mozarab without a master works leather."

Amira smiled. "You're Father's son too, you know."

He had spent days at his father's hip, watching him bevel a piece of leather or shave rich depth into a design. Only coming home had allowed him to finally remember those days with tenderness. "As he was. As he should have always been."

A breath straightened Amira's back. "I don't imagine a master leatherworker could succeed with a reputation for smuggling and theft."

He'd committed many sins over the years. At the time, he'd thought he was reclaiming the life the Almoravids and his father had taken from him. But he'd lost his way, and his choices had nearly destroyed him. It was time to make better ones.

Yasin shook his head and pointed to the codex in Sarah's lap. "The *Healing* is my final heist," he assured. "Such a life isn't compatible with what I truly treasure."

Sarah pressed her lips together and gave a satisfied nod before turning to Amira. "And what do you hope to find in Toledo?"

His sister released a long sigh filled with anguish and weariness, and perhaps even a little relief. "The chance to walk down the streets unaccompanied by a father or brother."

The answer tugged at Yasin's heart. Returning home had been worthwhile if only to help his sister escape.

"And, perhaps…" Amira shifted to sit on her legs. "Perhaps learn to read."

Carefully balancing their stolen codex on her knees, Sarah shuffled closer to Amira. "We need not wait to satisfy that desire."

As Sarah pointed out the words to Amira, Yasin swelled with a satisfaction so complete that he had to blink away nascent tears. He hadn't thought to ever see his sister again, let alone accompanying the woman he loved.

God, Allah, or simple fortune had kept him safe these past forty days. If that protection would endure just a few more weeks, he would reach the Castilian nobleman who would fulfill his dreams.

YASIN

Six days later, Yasin awoke to morning sunlight stabbing him in the eye. He raised his head out of its path and peered toward its source. The tent flap fluttered in the morning breeze and exposed a wider shaft that blinded him again.

Sarah or Amira must have risen during the night and forgotten to seal the tent. He glanced down at them, still sleeping beside him. Sarah had curled around him in a way that made Yasin regret the close proximity of his sister. Amira lay on Sarah's other side, wearing a frown that proved she'd never make a good traveler.

Freeing his arm from beneath Sarah, he shimmied out of the tent without knocking over the supporting poles with his foot. He tried his best to seal the flap to spare the women from the same irritating awakening he'd had.

The cool morning felt good on his bones and sore muscles. Stretching the stiffness out of his back and joints, Yasin shuffled toward the edge of the shelf upon which they'd camped until he could survey the wide vista of the valley below. The sun had only just vaulted the wide mountain on the eastern horizon, exposing the rich greens and yellows of the trees and grasses of the foothills below. Mist clung to the bottoms of some valleys, muting the colors with a subtlety beyond even the most skilled artist.

They'd slowly worked their way up the shallow slopes of the Sierra Luenga Mountains. At this pace, they'd reach the Martyr's Pass by evening and Toledo in six days.

A grunt and shuffling sounded from within the tent. They were waking.

The mist was already dissipating below, revealing one valley at a time. Eventually, only one patch remained, clinging to the shallowed valley through which they'd passed the previous day. Instead of fading, though, it grew larger and crawled north toward the mountains.

Frowning, he considered the possibilities. More travelers? A herd of animals?

Returning to the tent, Yasin opened the flap. Sarah was only beginning to stir, but his sister was sitting upright, rubbing her face.

"Come look at something."

Amira released a grunt, much like the one from earlier. "It's too early."

"You have the best eyes of anyone I know."

"Is that so?" Sarah's teasing voice made him jump. He had thought her mostly asleep.

"Best vision, then," he corrected.

When she joined him at the edge, he pointed into the distance. "Past the stream and that large hill, east of the olive grove. What is that?"

She craned her neck forward. "Horses with riders, three of them."

He still saw only blurry dots moving against the green and brown backdrop. "Pilgrims?"

She continued studying them. The dots broke free from a shadow and into the full light of the sun.

She gasped. "Almoravids!"

Sarah scrambled out of the tent. "Where?"

Yasin stiffened. "Are you certain?" His voice sounded so tight he feared it would snap.

"I see their indigo."

Sarah stared to the south. "Do we try to outpace them or hide until they pass?"

Yasin doubted they could hide. If these Almoravids had tracked them from Almeria and weren't just a random patrol, they'd assuredly notice if they lost the trail, and then Yasin would have to sneak past them to reach Toledo.

They might reach one of the Castilian watchtowers before being overtaken. "We ride." He rushed for the tent and tore off the cover. They couldn't afford to leave it behind. "Sarah, gather your things. Amira, unhobble the horses."

"Maybe I can hide our fire pit." Sarah secured the sack containing her oud atop her horse. "So they won't know how close we are."

It was a good idea, but Yasin shook his head as he lashed the packed tent to the back of his horse. "No time." The Almoravids were perhaps an hour behind, a paltry lead that would disappear quickly over six more days of travel.

"How did they find us?" Amira unknotted the rope around one of the horses' hooves. "Did Salim report us?"

His brother had warned of retribution, but sending the Almoravids after him would endanger Amira, too. Was his sister following Yasin a sufficient betrayal to justify Salim putting her at these desert devils' mercy? Yasin considered that unlikely, not when it would cast suspicion on himself and his wife. The guards had seen Yasin's face and could describe him. It probably wouldn't have taken long to learn he'd bought horses and was last seen heading north.

"It doesn't matter how." He helped Sarah atop her horse. Mounting his own, he spared one more glance south before pulling his horse's head around. "The Martyr's Pass is half a day away. We ride hard and don't stop."

They surged up the shallow path toward Toledo. Yasin's hands shook as he rode. He felt the presence of those pursuers like demons at his back. They probably rode the finest of the emir's mounts, while his group were novice riders atop whatever animals had been available at the northernmost stable. He hadn't paid very much for them, either.

He inhaled a steadying breath, but the cool air left him shivering. The pass. A watchtower lay a short distance beyond it. They just had to reach it before being overtaken.

If they didn't, they'd die in possession of their prize.

SARAH

The horse's hooves slammed into the soft earth in a quick four-thud rhythm. Sarah bounced atop its back, dimly recognizing but unable to focus on the dirt path rushing past. Her eyes swirled with the memory of the downward stroke of an Almoravid sword and the bloodstain it had left in the marketplace. Having stolen far more than that thief, she doubted her pursuers would satisfy themselves with removing only her hands.

Her horse shifted suddenly to avoid a divot. The motion kicked her to the side, and she pulled a muscle as she tightened her abdomen to remain upright. Riding required an entirely different set of muscles than singing or playing the oud. Her sides ached so badly that she could no longer twist backward to check whether the Almoravids had closed the distance.

So far, they hadn't, but that fact provided little comfort. The mountain path had risen so steeply and twisted so often that she wouldn't see them until they were upon her.

Two strides ahead, Yasin's head bobbed up and down so quickly that she couldn't distinguish his features. "Just a little further."

He'd been saying that for two hours. They'd alternatively galloped, ambled, and trotted, but always the pass was just a little further.

At a scrambling from behind, Sarah twisted to look despite the pain. The wind of the horse's passage threw her hair into her face, and she swept it aside. She expected to see the rhythmic bobbing of an indigo rider, but the path was still clear. Through the cloud of dust thrown up by their passage, a collection of rocks slid down the eastern slope. A brief flash of movement revealed a small animal scampering out of sight.

She faced forward again, but neither the pain in her sides nor the hammering of her chest lessened.

"There it is!" Yasin panted, pointing.

They rounded a bend, and the slope of the western mountain receded, revealing the pass between the hills on either side. Beyond a long stretch of level ground, the path dipped over the horizon, marking the start of the northern descent. Open sky peeked out from between the hills, welcoming them to the old boundaries of the *taifa* of Toledo.

Martyr's Pass. The pain in Sarah's muscles diminished.

But they weren't alone. Interposed along their route were three riders atop fine Spanish stallions. Allah be praised, none of them wore indigo. The two on either side wore domed iron helmets, and she recognized the central rider, one hand holding the reins and another resting on his thigh.

She gasped. "Lord Gonzalo!"

He looked more magnificent than the night he'd watched her play her oud. A giddy euphoria enveloped her. The man who had promised to secure her freedom had come to her rescue. Her blood wouldn't water these grasses after all!

Mouth hanging open, Yasin reared to a halt, and Amira and Sarah did the same. All three animals' nostrils were flaring.

"You received my messages," Sarah cried.

His eyes darted to Yasin as if he expected a reaction. After a short pause, he said to Sarah, "Thank you for writing so frequently."

"But…" Yasin sucked in a deep breath as he surveyed the riders. "How did you know we'd be coming today?"

"We camped at the watchtower just beyond the pass." Gonzalo gestured northward. "My scout recognized at least one woman in your party and retrieved us." He swallowed. "Do you have what I asked for?"

Yasin shook his head. "We don't have time." He twisted and started to point behind.

"Tell me!" Gonzalo shouted with the same dangerous edge as when he'd warned Sarah to obey him in the translation school.

Yasin fell silent. Except for the tiny adjustments to his posture as his horse stamped the ground beneath him, he did not move. He wasn't breathing either, despite the hard ride.

"We do." Yasin clipped his words.

Thin slit of a grin forming, Gonzalo twisted the reins in his grasp. His horse shifted, but he controlled it with a skill Sarah could have used these past few hours. "Give it to me."

Yasin's mare shifted again, sidling closer to Sarah's. He made no attempt to prevent it. "And our reward?"

The Almoravids could be right behind them. They didn't have time to quibble over their payment.

"It's awaiting you in Toledo, as I promised," Gonzalo assured. "Give me the *Healing*."

After her experiences on the road these past weeks, she couldn't blame Lord Gonzalo for keeping his gold inside Toledo. Only a fool would risk losing it to brigands or *fuero* settlers.

She guided her horse forward.

Yasin reached out and stopped her. His eyes burned with a silent warning. Something was bothering him, and it wasn't the trio of Almoravids following them. Not even in the palaces of Valencia or Almeria had he looked so unsettled.

He raised his chin at Lord Gonzalo. "I think I'll keep it for now."

"Brother…" Amira warned.

"If he wants it, give it to him," Sarah hissed. "We don't have time for this with the—"

"There is no payment." Yasin stared at Gonzalo. "He played us for fools."

"What are you talking about?" He couldn't speak to a Castilian lord like that, nor should he treat the man who freed him from prison with such disrespect. He was jeopardizing all their futures by offending Lord Gonzalo.

But instead of outrage or anger, the Castilian's eyes contained only smug triumph. His lips pulled back into a grin so wide that it exposed his teeth. "Did you really think I'd pay fifty gold pieces for a codex?"

Ya salaam.

Her eyes welled with tears. Gonzalo had admired her playing. He had sympathized with the burden of her servitude. He'd offered her a way to end it and reclaim the life she most desired. She'd risked her life more than once to deliver her end of the agreement. Yasin had nearly died.

It had all been for nothing. Every word had been a lie.

Yasin released a long sigh. "I thought you were buying the restoration of your family's position."

"Why would I pay for something I can get for free?"

Slumping, Sarah planted a hand on her horse's neck to keep from falling. Dozens of scholars in the library could identify the *Book of Healing*, but only a slave could be discarded afterward. He could betray her as easily as an imprisoned thief. The Sarah who had labored for her Christian masters hadn't understood that, but she'd spent so much time with Yasin that Gonzalo's scheme seemed obvious now.

"You said you'd free me," she pleaded.

He shook his head. "I'm afraid not, my dear. After what you two did, I can't let you reveal how I acquired *The Book of Healing*. As far as the library knows, you're already dead."

She wrapped her arms around herself to steady her shaking.

"What do you mean, after what we did?" Yasin asked.

Gonzalo swept his hands wide. "You infiltrated Almoravid lands and stole secret knowledge from one of their libraries. An impressive thing." His eyes narrowed. "So impressive that if anyone learned about it, *you'd* receive *my* acclaim."

"This is about fame?" Amira scoffed.

Gonzalo glared at her. "I've sworn to restore my family's position. I won't let anything threaten that, certainly not a thief, a slave, and a whore." He jabbed a finger at Yasin. "You'll give me that codex, then you'll go back to prison."

A rhythmic thumping pulled Sarah out of her anguish. It started quietly at first, but it grew in strength until it drummed in her ears. It definitely wasn't her beating heart.

It was coming from behind.

"Yasin—"

"I hear them," he whispered. Jaw tightening, Yasin leaned toward the satchel dangling from Sarah's saddle and rummaged through their plundered texts. After retrieving a codex, he flung it forward. It struck the dirt and slid to a halt several strides shy of Lord Gonzalo.

"There's the prize that cost you your honor," Yasin grumbled.

She watched the codex sitting there amid a cloud of dust that obscured the gold leaf on the cover. The tiny rocks would have scraped the leather binding. At least Yasin's throw had only damaged one volume.

Desire flashing in Gonzalo's eyes, he dismounted. One of his men grabbed his horse's reins.

The drumming grew louder, faster than the Baghdad musicians' liveliest rhythm.

"Get ready to ride," Yasin whispered. She couldn't tell if the Castilians heard him.

Amira obviously had, for she adjusted her grip on the reins from his other side. Leaning forward, Sarah did the same.

"Wise decision." The Castilian lord halted at the codex. "You certainly made me wait for this." He angled the hilt of his sword down to make the tip rise behind him as he crouched.

He never made it. A trio of indigo riders swung around the bend, having finally caught their quarry. As they halted to assess the scene before them, their horses whinnied and sniffed the air.

Before they could react, Yasin shouted in Arabic, "There lies your property!" He pointed at Gonzalo, standing over the codex several strides from his horse. "And there are the men who stole it!"

Gonzalo glared in blistering rage but did not move. Showing more presence of mind, his men cried out and rushed forward to protect him.

"God is most great!" the lead rider cried with the same obedience as the heroes of the great poems. The indigo warriors rushed forward amid the hiss of drawing swords.

"Now!" Yasin ordered.

Sarah jabbed her horse in the ribs, and it bolted forward. She guided it in a wide arc to the left of the Castilians while Yasin and Amira flowed around the right.

One of the Christians glared at her, but he made no move to pursue. Drawing his sword, he instead surged forward to guard his master. Sarah admired his loyalty.

"Faster!" Yasin pulled a little further ahead and was rushing through the pass toward Toledo.

She leaned forward, urging her horse onward. Metal clanged against metal behind her. She shuddered with each strike. They sounded much too close.

The ground sloped downward as she reached the pass. A scream preceded a sickening gurgle. Weight shifting with the descent, she spared a glance backward. A Castilian tumbled from his horse within a swirl of indigo before her horse carried her down the mountainside and out of view.

Heart hammering in her chest, she faced forward and drove as fast after Yasin and Amira as she could, desperate to distance herself from any survivors of the struggle behind.

SARAH

By the time they reached the Castilian watchtower defending the southern road, their horses were near collapse and could go no further without several hours of rest. The guards were happy to provide water, food, and a room, but they laughed at the suggestion of trading their fine war stallions for exhausted nags.

Amira ate heartily, but Sarah and Yasin stood by the room's lone window, watching the path leading to the pass. She was certain a vengeful Lord Gonzalo would come riding up at any moment.

After an hour, Yasin finally concluded, "I don't think anyone's coming."

Sarah peeked back down the road, still empty. "Lord Gonzalo and his men are probably dead."

"I sincerely hope so."

Once, Sarah would have never prayed for anyone's death, but she did so now. Lord Gonzalo would exact a terrible retribution if he'd survived. "Will the Almoravids follow?"

He bit at his lip. "I doubt they'd risk crossing a Castilian patrol, particularly if they took injuries. There were only three of them."

She thought of the codex Yasin had thrown on the ground being damaged or shredded by a horse's hooves or a sword slash. "I only wish we hadn't sacrificed one of the *Healing's* codices to escape." They could hardly risk retrieving it when they'd barely escaped with their lives.

Yasin started to chuckle. "Who said we did?" Leaning forward, he opened the satchel. All four of the gold-inlaid books of the *Metaphysics* were still inside.

She bolted upright. "Then, what did you—"

"I gave them the partial copy Orbanus made." He grinned until his teeth showed.

"You wily liar." Filled with a sudden euphoria, she released a trilling giggle. She'd thought the dust had hidden the gold filigree, but her eyes hadn't betrayed her after all.

"Yes, well…" He chuckled. "It seemed a shame to dirty something so beautiful." He rubbed his chin where the stubble was growing again. "Our client is dead, but at least you're free."

"Oh, my…" She gasped. "That's true!" The library wouldn't be looking for her if Lord Gonzalo told them she was dead. "All the same, I won't risk them learning I'm alive by returning to Toledo."

"I can't say I blame you." He shrugged. "There's no need to return, anyway, since there's no one left to reward us."

"Not necessarily." She drummed a finger on the cover. "We have a satchel of precious texts. The translators would pay well for them."

He barked a laugh. "I told you you'd be a proper criminal."

Threading her fingers through his, she curled her lips into a mischievous grin. She supposed she was. "You sell them, and Amira and I will wait at one of the taverns on the outskirts. They'll surely pay enough for passage to Valencia and a workshop."

"Valencia?"

"Our rooms are still paid up through the end of the month." Valencia could always benefit from another skilled leatherworker, and Sarah had her oud. Now that she had Yasin, she could simply enjoy the playing without worrying about her status.

"Valencia." He took her hand and offered a light squeeze. "Where no one will complain too loudly if a Christian marries a Muslim."

She met his gaze. Gone was the veil that had closed him off from the rest of the world. Now, he exuded only confidence and honesty and *adab*. There it was, on display without reservation. The true Yasin finally shone through.

Chest fluttering with excitement, she returned his squeeze. She no longer cared whether it was forbidden or not. They'd pretended to be married for weeks now, and she didn't want to pretend anymore. "That sounds perfect."

VI

VALENCIA

DECEMBER, AD 1094

EPILOGUE

YASIN

Yasin ducked his head through the door. "Are you two ready?"

Sarah was sitting at her dressing table, staring into the polished copper mirror and applying a thin line of kohl to her eyes. His sister was dabbing her cheeks with powder to add a little color. Both, at least, had fully dressed, except for the shawls that lay draped over a nearby chair. "The feast starts in half an hour."

"Nearly." Sarah leaned in for a closer look at the mirror. She was evidently as satisfied with her appearance as he was, for she set down the kohl and instead began adjusting her dress.

She looked magnificent, from the gentle sweep of her hair to the dab of oil glistening her neck. Yasin loved the way that part of her shimmered when the light caught it in just the right way.

The other leatherworkers had bristled at the arrival of more competition, but her playing tonight would end the grumbling, if only because embracing him also meant welcoming the incredibly talented *qiyan* who accompanied him.

A lock of her hair had slipped free and dangled in front of her ear. Shifting the two bundles he carried—one sizeable and the other fairly small—to his left arm, he approached and knelt beside her. Reaching up, he tucked it back. "My darling wife… I'll never grow tired of being able to do that."

Sarah gave him one of those gentle, content smiles that made him want to kiss every part of her. He leaned toward her.

Amira's hopeful voice halted him. "Are those presents?"

He would have a lifetime to kiss his wife. With a grunt, he rose. "One for each of you." Crossing to his sister, he offered her the larger one. "This one's yours."

She unfolded the rough wool wrapping to reveal a fine linen shawl within.

"Oh, Yasin!" She held it up.

The pale blue fabric was thin enough that the light from the candle behind her showed through even the full weave. A line of lacework two fingerspans wide along the edge that would hang over her hair made swirling flower patterns.

"It's beautiful, Yasin." Amira's face brightened. "I love it. Thank you."

"I'm sure Vermudo will too, once he sees it tonight."

Widened eyes preceded a blush that reddened her cheeks despite the powder she'd applied. "Vermudo?" Lowering the shawl, she tugged at the neckline of her dress. "I don't even know if he's coming."

Yasin grinned. Amira had happened to visit his workshop at the same time the young soldier arrived with several crates of military equipment—leather belts, scabbards, and boots—for Yasin to repair. They had immediately taken to each other. "He seemed pretty certain when I saw him today."

"He did?" She cleared her throat. "You saw him?"

"He collected the order for the army," Yasin supplied. "He made a point of asking if you'd attend." Again, he grinned. "And there's only one reason a soldier would feast with leatherworkers."

She glanced away, but the distinct curve of her lips warmed Yasin's heart. Now that he'd ceased his illegal activity, befriending soldiers had yielded many advantages.

He turned back to his wife. "And this one is for you."

She had twisted to face him, feet pumping up and down with excitement. He supposed she hadn't received many gifts over the course of her life. He'd make up for that.

She accepted the small parcel, rolled in a piece of leather from his workshop down the street. Carefully, she turned it end-over-end until she revealed the ivory comb within. Carvings of tree branches extended from the handle up the spine to the very top of the comb. Perched atop some of the branches were tiny nightingales.

The comb she'd been forced to use when they'd first met had been damaged, missing far too many teeth to be worthy of her.

She swallowed as she ran her fingertips over the intricate carvings. Her eyes were glistening when she raised them. That reaction filled him with more delight and contentment than any words, even her magnificent words delivered with the music of her voice, could produce.

Her hand came up to her mouth, but it couldn't conceal the smile stretching beyond either side of her fingers. "It's magnificent." She swallowed. "Can we afford it?"

He'd put in many extra hours over the past few weeks, first to scrape together additional commissions and then to complete them. He'd never really worked hard at his craft before, but then he'd never before had a cause worth working for. She had given him that.

"I can always afford a little luxury for my wife."

She smiled again, bringing the sun back into this candlelit room. "I have something for you, too." She retrieved a parcel, wrapped in undyed wool and tied with a red ribbon, from beside her table and presented it.

It was soft and flexible, so he pushed aside the ribbon until he could slip it off. Whatever it was, it was soft, probably clothing. A new *qamisa*, perhaps?

Unfolding the wool wrapping revealed a flash of deep green. The expense of the rich dye surprised him. But as he opened one flap after another, he saw that size mitigated the cost. Whatever it was, it was small.

Freeing the last flap of the wrapping, he let it fall away. The contents were undoubtedly clothing, but he couldn't initially identify the item. Only when he unfolded it and held it up did he recognize it.

Green was the color of fertility.

His heartbeat hammered. It was a tiny gown, too small for him to wear but perfect for a baby.

His mouth fell open. "Is this…" He gawked at Sarah. "Are you…?"

Behind him, Amira gasped.

Smiling, Sarah gave him a quick nod.

"*Ya salaam!*" Draping the gown over his wrist, he reached out to cradle her cheeks with both hands. He found her lips but, remembering the miracle she now carried, he kissed her gently, softly. He dared not risk harm to either her or the baby.

"You are pleased?" The soft words contained a tender vulnerability.

"Pleased?" He kissed her again, and when their lips parted, he leaned his forehead against hers, desperate to maintain the contact. He had found a greater happiness than he'd thought possible. "Within these hands is everything I need."

He wrapped his arms around her, and she nestled into his embrace. They fitted together like the two halves of Yasin's leather pouch, though between them lay something far more precious than coin. She had altered the course of his life. She had finally, completely healed the wounds he'd carried all these years. She'd given him back a future.

He had found his home.

MAJOR CHARACTERS

Almeria

Yasin ibn Faraj, Mozarabic smuggler and leatherworker
Faraj ibn Ramiro, Yasin's father, a leatherworker
Elvira Vermudez, Yasin's mother
Salim ibn Faraj, Yasin's brother, who remained in Almeria
Aishah, Salim's wife
Amira bint Faraj, Yasin's sister

Al-Andalus

Sarah al-Bayda, a Muslim woman who trained as a qiyan in
    Baghdad before being enslaved by pirates
Hisham al-Hasan, Valencian dockworker and smuggler

Toledo

Gonzalo Martinez, a scholar, courtier and son of a Castilian count
Esteban Pelayez, an apprentice leatherworker in Toledo
Esmeralda, Castilian *fuero* settler in La Mancha

Valencia

Rodrigo Diaz de Vivar, El Cid, famed warrior and lord of Valencia
Jimena Diaz, Castilian noblewoman and wife of El Cid
Orbanus Juanez, Aragonese scholar at the library of Valencia

GLOSSARY

adab – idealistic virtue encompassing manliness, culture, righteousness, and especially boldness of action

al-Andalus – the name for Islamic Iberia

Cordoban caliphate – "golden age" empire that controlled most of Iberia from 712 to 1031

dhimmis – second-class yet protected status for Christians and Jews

fuero – a Castilian town chartered to settle re-conquered territory

hamam – bathhouse with steam rooms and running water

Inshallah – hopeful Arabic phrase meaning, "If Allah wills it"

jizya – tax paid by Christians and Jews to allow them to worship

jubba – an Arabic outer garment; as used in the novel, a heavier coat

Maghreb – desert in northern Africa, original home of Almoravids

Mashallah – phrase meaning, "Allah has willed it"

Mozarab – Christians living in the Islamic cities of al-Andalus

qamisa – a knee-length tunic worn by both men and women

qiyan – female slave entertainers trained in *adab*, dancing, music, history, debate, calligraphy, literature, and other refined skills

rebab – three-stringed bowed instrument

salat – Islamic prayer, one of the five pillars of Islam.

sirwal – baggy pants for both men and women

tagelmust – a long strip of cloth formed into a hat and veil common to the desert tribes of North Africa, usually dyed a rich blue indigo

taifa – series of breakaway kingdoms after the Cordoban Caliphate whose rivalries created a silver age of art, poetry, and culture

tapia – a style of building constructed from packed mud or clay

Ya salaam! – expression of surprise, "Oh, my God!"

From 712 to 1013 AD, the Caliphate of Cordoba dominated al-Andalus, the Islamic name for the Iberian peninsula, consisting of modern-day Spain and Portugal. The vast majority of people spoke Arabic, wore Muslim clothing, and looked to Baghdad as a cultural center. Islam was the dominant religion. Muslim cities were connected to the wider Mediterranean world by great trade networks. Many had planned layouts that had grown out of Roman colonia. Perhaps surprising to a modern reader, they had running water from aqueducts and covered canals, paved roads with raised sidewalks, designed gardens, and streetlamps. In many ways, they were sophisticated, innovative, and prosperous.

Much of Andalusi culture came from one man, Abu l-Hasan 'Ali Ibn Nafi', known to history as Ziryab. Originally from Persia, Ziryab was the Leonardo da Vinci of the Islamic world. He was a composer, poet, musician, and singer, and he had knowledge of astronomy, geography, meteorology, botany, cosmetics, culinary arts, and fashion. Trained in Baghdad, he moved to Cordoba and immediately took al-Andalus by storm, setting the fashion for clothing, grooming, hairstyles, music, poetry, and etiquette. He single-handedly transformed Andalusi society.

One of the concepts Ziryab introduced to Andalusis was *adab*, the collection of characteristics that every nobleman should exhibit. It blended several virtues, including good morals, appreciation of good taste, adherence to the established order, decorum, and—critically—a sense of boldness and the aggressive pursuit of nobility and excellence. Poets and musicians sang about it, and emirs in their palaces fretted over whether they were sufficiently demonstrating it. Failing to exude *adab* was a weakness that could cost a man his throne.

Another contribution of Ziryab was the appreciation for *qiyans*. These women, often slaves, were trained as entertainers and cultured conversationalists in great schools in the Middle East. They were skilled in poetry, music, shadow-puppetry, history, philosophy, and a functional knowledge of the scientific disciplines. Emirs and caliphs coveted accomplished qiyans to imbue their courts with sophistication. Many eventually converted to Islam, and after successful careers, *qiyans* quite frequently joined the upper class by marrying high-ranking courtiers. Offering sexual services wasn't an implicit part of a *qiyan*'s role, but such was often demanded of female slaves in the Muslim world. Of course, like Sarah, some also employed their sexuality as a tool to achieve their own goals.

A few Christian enclaves remained unconquered in the north, clustered in Medieval villages and a few towns with rickety buildings, dirt roads, and no sanitation. Conquering them would have required too many resources, so Cordoba was content to extract regular tribute in exchange for independence. That changed when the caliphate fragmented into dozens of *taifa* kingdoms (named from the Arabic word for "party", in our political sense) in the 11th century. These weakened kingdoms began quarreling with each other just as the Christian kingdoms of Aragon and Barcelona grew in strength and Castile absorbed Galicia, Asturias, Leon, and Portugal under its banner. The balance of power shifted, and tribute began flowing from the south to the north.

Yet even as their power was waning, *taifa* culture blossomed. Like the princedoms and despots of Medieval Italy, the emirs of the Muslim *taifas* competed against each other not only for territory but also for cultural dominance. Each emir wished to outdo the others by attracting the greatest thinkers, inventors, poets, musicians, and craftsmen to their realms. Culture, learning, and innovation exploded. Uniquely, they also fostered tolerance of *dhimmis*, Christians and Jews. Religious restrictions on intermarriage, fraternization, and elevation of *dhimmis* over Muslims were quietly ignored in favor of excellence, achievement, and ability. Both Jews and Christians were permitted to govern themselves and appeal to judges of their own religion.

The fall of Toledo in 1085 changed all that. Though Castile acquired it by settlement rather than conquest, the residents of al-Andalus—both

Christian and Muslim—viewed it as a catastrophe and responded appropriately. Their emphasis on cultural development left them soft and militarily weak, so the remaining *taifas* invited fanatical Muslim Almoravids from northern Africa to halt the Christian advance. Though they succeeded, they ultimately destroyed the tolerant *taifa* culture more completely than Christians would have. Disgusted by the lax morals and loose interpretation of Islam, the Almoravids swept through al-Andalus, conquering each *taifa* in turn.

Out went the decadent pursuits that fueled the taifa courts. The Almoravids forced Jews and Christians back to the bottom of the social ladder where they belonged. Punishments became draconian, not just for crimes like sodomy or heresy, but also for marriage between Muslims and non-Muslims, theft, and dissension. Jewish and Christian officials were exiled or killed. Fanned on by Almoravid fervor, mobs pillaged and murdered their way through *dhimmi* quarters. All subjects had to follow Islamic law. The tolerance that had marked Islamic rule in Iberia was forever destroyed.

One of the groups that keenly felt this loss was Mozarabs, Christians who had lived under Muslim rule, spoke Arabic, dressed in Muslim fashions, and enjoyed the benefits of the Muslim world. They didn't want to give up the safety, public services, and running water of the Muslim cities to live like the Christians of the north. The Almoravids pressured men like Yasin, Faraj, and Salim to either convert or emigrate through oppression, persecution, and taxation. Those who fled to Christian lands found little sympathy. They were mistrusted because they'd willingly lived under Muslim rule. The very term *Mozarab* means "wannabe Arabs". Many migrated to the two *taifa* cities that had avoided Almoravid rule, Toledo and Valencia.

King Alfonso of Castile undertook great pains to preserve the *taifa* traditions that had made Toledo so wealthy and influential. One of the institutions Alfonso inherited from the previous emir was the Library of Toledo and its vast collection. Most Greek and Roman texts were unknown to European scholars, while the Muslim texts included commentaries and new publications on a wide range of sciences and disciplines. The Castilian crown put this knowledge to good use, commissioning a translation school at the library that copied these texts from Arabic or Greek into Latin and Castilian before distributing it across Europe. Over the next hundred and fifty years, the Translation School of Toledo reintroduced ancient knowledge to Europe. Thus, the Reconquista laid the groundwork for the Renaissance.

Valencia was the only other *taifa* that initially remained free of Almoravid influence, due entirely to the efforts of El Cid. Rodrigo Díaz de Vivar was a Castilian nobleman and a skilled warrior. After quarreling with and being exiled by King Alfonso, Diaz became a mercenary and proceeded to trounce every army he confronted, including those of Aragon and several *taifa* kingdoms. The Muslims called him El Cid, "The Lord", while the Christians called him El Campeador, the "Teacher of the Battlefield", for how he schooled everyone he fought. In 1094, he captured Valencia from rebels who had overthrown their emir, establishing the city as a Christian *taifa*, the only one to successfully resist Almoravid conquest. He balanced Christian and Muslim interests, creating a hybrid culture that preserved the best of each for a time.

In Christian Europe, women often managed household estates and family businesses. Women could walk the streets, attend feasts, and travel. In *taifa*-era al-Andalus, women enjoyed some of this freedom, excepting the feasts that men—and *qiyans*—exclusively attended. Veils that preserved modesty were common, though they varied from thin, see-through gauze to thick wrappings that concealed all but the eyes, based on personal preference.

Upon their arrival, the Almoravids severely curtailed women's freedom to work and travel alone outside the home, ostensibly to protect them from a brutal world. After all, as Aishah says in the novel, there were no easy jobs, only back-breaking labor that strained fingers, left muscles sore, and usually involved heavy lifting or repetitive work. The sun would beat down on and age anyone laboring outdoors, and sun protection was rudimentary. Some viewed this sheltering as a kindness. While these restrictions oppressed women like Sarah, outrage wasn't universal, and Aishah's perspective was more common than not. Of course, it also effectively made wives, daughters, and sisters dependent on the men in their lives, something that could be catastrophic if those men happened to be drunks, invalids, or brutes. A woman like Sarah who relied upon her own skills had few options.

Ultimately, the arrival of the Almoravids marked the end of a way of life, one mourned by those who witnessed its passing. Not until modern times would a place exist where the Peoples of the Book could live together in relative harmony, albeit a harmony that was never universal, equal, or complete.

For a deeper exploration of the culture and history of al-Andalus, I recommend *Kingdoms of Faith* by Brian Catlos and *Ornament of the World* by Maria Rosa Menocal, which offer different interpretations of daily life and culture at this time.

I hope you enjoyed reading *The Thief and the Nightingale* as much as I enjoyed writing it!

ABOUT THE AUTHOR

K.M. Butler studied literature at Carnegie Mellon University and has always had an avid interest in history. His writing influences are *The Lions of al-Rassan* by Guy Gavriel Kay and Colleen McCullough's *Masters of Rome* series.

He lives in Philadelphia with his wife and two daughters. His wife is his first and harshest editor, while his daughters always want his stories to feature more blood and talking animals, but never at the same time.

Contact K.M. Butler at kmbutlerauthor@yahoo.com or on Twitter at @kmbutlerauthor.

Enjoyed the novel? Please remember to leave a review on Goodreads and Amazon!